Estabr-   Estabrook, Barry
ook
          Bahama heat

DUE DATE

BAHAMA HEAT

BAHAMA HEAT

Barry Estabrook

A THOMAS DUNNE BOOK

St. Martin's Press ● New York

To Suzanne

This is a work of fiction and all names, characters, and incidents are entirely imaginary, and any resemblance to actual events, or to persons living or dead, is coincidental.

Production Editor: David Stanford Burr

Library of Congress Cataloging-in-Publication Data

Estabrook, Barry.
      Bahama heat / Barry Estabrook.
          p.   cm.
      "A Thomas Dunne book."
      ISBN 0-312-06297-4
      I. Title.
  PS3555.S7B3 1991
  813' .54—dc20   91-21568
                                                CIP

First Edition: October 1991

10 9 8 7 6 5 4 3 2 1

BAHAMA HEAT

Chapter 1

Bingo Martin figured that if one of the two was going to kill him that night, it was going to be the pock-faced young black guy, the silent one. He had the look of someone who killed frequently and with neither morals nor scruples, who took life with about the same compunction and regret as someone snuffing out his thirty-third cigarette of a too-long day. The other one, the fifty-four-year-old mulatto everyone called Fat Boy, he was capable of killing, no doubt about that. What would hold him back would not be shame or sympathy—certainly not fear of getting caught—but a deep and abiding laziness.

These musings occupied the few scattered synapses in Bingo's brain not given over to cannabis shortly before midnight on November 29, which fell on a Tuesday. He was one-half mile directly offshore from the village of Fresh Creek on Andros Island in the Bahamas.

As arranged, Bingo had anchored the *Roach,* his fifty-four-foot, cement-hulled, staysail schooner, just where the fringe reef gave way to the six-thousand-foot-deep water of the Tongue of the Ocean. And he waited, looking at the handful of house lights onshore that were the only beacons against the island's profound blackness. Occasionally, he ran a hand through the tight, natural perm of his blond hair. Once every minute, he sucked on a joint rolled from some Santa Marta, part of his cut from a load he had brought across just before hurricane season. Bingo, who wore only a T-shirt advertising the Bahamas

Goombay Festival and a pair of hacked-off Wranglers, hunched his bony sunbaked shoulders against the cool breeze that blew from shore, bringing a cadaverous stink of mangrove and tidal flats.

Bingo was alone, unless you counted the packages—bales, really, wrapped in heavy green plastic—that occupied most of the floor space in the *Roach*'s cockpit. One was filled with cocaine, worth, even on the Bahamas side of the DEA's pond, nearly a million dollars.

The other contained one hundred pounds of icing sugar. Bingo had bought the sugar himself for fifty dollars two weeks earlier in Grand Turk, just before setting out on a charter with a dentist from Lowell, Indiana, his wife, and two kids. The dentist paid Bingo two thousand dollars for ten days sailing from the Turks and Caicos Islands, to Crooked Island, Long Island, the Exumas, then Nassau. A fellow could do worse than having an Indiana dentist and family as cover for the real purpose of the voyage, for which Bingo was to receive fifty thousand bucks.

At midnight, precisely, Bingo heard the slap of the flat bottom of Fat Boy's little boat and the whine of its struggling 6-horsepower outboard. He inhaled one more scalp-tickling haul from the joint and threw it overboard. It hit the water with a hiss. He then limbered his arms, which were long and apelike. Straining every muscle on his 138-pound, five-eight frame, he wrestled the nearest parcel, the one with the cocaine, onto the gunwale and gave it a heave toward the same spot where the joint had hit. It bobbed on the surface for a moment, then, aided by ten downrigger weights, disappeared slowly into the black water. The switch was a stupid trick, probably the oldest in the book, and certainly familiar to anyone who had copped a school-yard joint. But sometimes old tricks worked. Besides, Fat Boy didn't have the look of someone who purchased joints as a schoolboy. Still, for luck, Bingo reached into his jeans pocket and withdrew a worn 1974 Kennedy half-dollar his woman had given him for luck. He rubbed it, made one wish, then threw it after the bale.

Fat Boy came aboard first. He scrambled up from his boat, which looked no more seaworthy than a worn penny loafer. The scrawny, pock-faced guy came next. He breathed fast with hissing sounds through his teeth and carried an ugly-looking sawed-off Winchester Model 12—the type police forces once favored for riot control.

It took a full minute before Fat Boy said anything. During the silence, he half-leaned, half-stood against the cockpit rail until his own breathing slowed. In the faint light, Bingo could see that beneath a huge orange Mae West life vest, Fat Boy wore the same clothes he had on the first and only other time Bingo had met him: sandals with heavy socks, brown polyester slacks, a multipocketed safari jacket, fawn-colored, square-cut at the bottom, pleated up the front. His head was shaved bald. Even at ten feet with a stiff, pungent night breeze, he smelled of sweat and oily skin. "Good as your word, Bingo," he finally said, with the British inflections of a cultured Bahamian education.

"And you, too, Fat Boy?" Bingo was uncomfortable calling him that, but everyone, probably even his own mother, called him Fat Boy and nothing else, as far as Bingo knew.

Fat Boy waddled over to the remaining plastic-wrapped parcel without answering. "What have we here?" he said to no one in particular, and bent over casually, turning his ample backside toward Bingo. The skinny guy jumped beside his boss and made a jerky motion with the Winchester, but he said nothing. Might have been a deaf-mute, the perfect accomplice for Fat Boy, who shoved the stubby fingers of his right hand into one of his polyester pockets. They came out holding a two-blade Swiss army knife, which he opened, picking with his fingernails and having some difficulty. When a blade finally did come out, Fat Boy stabbed the green plastic, opening a two-inch-long white wound, clearly visible in the darkness.

The moment of truth had come. Bingo kept an eye on the ancient shotgun, whose muzzle wobbled in lopsided orbits that would have put its load, depending on when in the cycle Pock-face pulled the trigger, somewhere between Bingo's solar plexus and balls.

Fat Boy sniffed hesitantly at the pile of icing sugar he had shoveled onto the blade. Bingo had guessed right. It was an amateur's sniff, certainly not the great-vacuum cleaner snort a user would have employed in the face of a line of Colombia's finest—and uncut at that. Fat Boy pinched the wound in the plastic closed and struggled upright, one side at a time, like a circus elephant. "Good as your word," he said again, wiping the Swiss army knife on his pant leg.

Bingo allowed himself one of his famous lopsided smiles. He smiled because he really intended to be as good as his word—once they paid him. As soon as they got back in their boat, he would have told them about the real coke—provided his body and soul remained intact.

"There's a little matter of fifty thousand?" Bingo said.

Fat Boy chuckled through his nose, shaking his bald dome slowly so that the faint shore lights gleamed off it.

Bingo immediately knew he was in shit—deep shit.

"You know who I am. Surely you see that I cannot . . ." Fat Boy let his voice trail off, adding after some time a whispered "Impossible."

The shore lights blinked off Fat Boy's dome—once—as he nodded toward Pock-face, who, with neither word nor expression, pulled the trigger.

Bingo's third-to-last real fully conscious thought was that, Christ, they were all wrong, you do hear the one that got you. He felt no pain, but his ears rang with the roar of the old shotgun; his eyes lit with the burst of orange flame that gave way to the softer yellow light of death. To give him credit, Bingo took death in stride, much as he had its counterpart. He went down wearing that lopsided grin, just a little stoned on good pot and amused by two final ideas that played themselves out in his fading consciousness.

The first was what would happen to poor Fat Boy when he delivered a load of icing sugar to the hard boys stateside.

The second was of the woman Bingo loved, a randy, brawling woman named Stormy Lake who even then was probably on her fifth or sixth rum at the Turk's Head Inn. God and the Bahamas postal authorities willing, in a few days she would be getting Bingo's last will and testament, a crude but, all things considered, reasonably accurate treasure map that would lead her to the precise spot where the *Roach* lay anchored.

As Bingo's body began to shut down the circuitry that had kept it rambling and grinning through most of four decades, he clung to Stormy's image. It was no white-robed St. Peter who took his hand and led him up toward that final light but, rather, a tall, athletic angel, whose head was topped by a tangle of chocolate-brown curls, snarls and waves, and whose eyes were too brown, too big, and always looked out upon the world as if their owner was ever so slightly crazed.

Except Stormy wasn't crazy. If there was anybody sane enough to know just what to do with a million bucks' worth of uncut cocaine, it was Stormy Lake, Bingo thought, then died.

Chapter 2

Reverend Miles Farnsworth was one of three people at the December 7 emergency meeting of the Savior Network's management committee.

The meeting was held in a steaming Jacuzzi on the patio of The Manse, a Spanish-style beachfront mansion that once belonged to some insignificant branch of the du Pont family. Situated just south of the City Dock along Naples, Florida's gold coast, the mansion was now the official residence of Miles's big brother, and boss, Ira, pastor of the Savior Network. The meeting had been scheduled to begin at 7:30 A.M., but it started late because Miles overslept. Yet neither Ira nor the other man in the Jacuzzi seemed surprised when Miles slipped into the water at eight minutes after eight. Miles nodded sheepishly at Ira and at the other man, Drake Nettleship. Compact, fashionably slender, and still a year or two under thirty-five, Nettleship was the network's VP and controller, though Miles thought a more apt job title might have been Corporate Bearer of Bad News, a job Nettleship performed admirably, with relish, and at every possible opportunity.

As soon as he settled into the tub, Miles realized he had forgotten one crucial thing—to pee. A nagging little tickle played about his bladder. He thought about excusing himself, but the serious faces of Ira and Nettleship made that seem out of the question.

So Miles tried to concentrate on the meeting, a most unpleasant task. The task was made even less pleasant because he had to wage it through the haze of a full-blown rum hangover, a hangover he had sworn he would avoid—this time—when he had cracked the seal on the bottle of Appleton's a mere twelve hours earlier in his room at the Holiday Inn. Even in his weakened state, the Reverend Miles Farnsworth, evangelist, teacher, and, at least in some circles, beloved missionary, knew his big brother had some evil surprise to unveil, that morning and in that hot tub.

For the how and why, Miles simply would have to wait. Nettleship always approached the task of delivering bad news obliquely, darting here and there, nibbling at small corners of what was really on his mind, or going on at great length about totally unrelated subjects. That morning, it had been the Blue Mountain coffee he and Miles were sipping between nibbles from fresh croissants. Ira had a mug of hot distilled water with a crescent of lemon. He chewed absently on a dry rusk.

"Procured it myself, right at Mavis Bank," Nettleship said of the coffee. "Directly from an eccentric English chap who owns the plantation. Really the only way to get it, now. The Japs, you know, have been buying it all up—blending it for flavor in instant coffee—abomination . . ."

Miles stopped listening. Through the chlorine-smelling steam of the tub, he watched as a lone pelican took off from a wooden post beside a jetty in front of The Manse. It flapped over the calm gray Gulf, finally achieving the slow, goofy pelican flight rhythm that seemed to belong to the geological era when reptiles still ran the world—and did not a half-bad job of it, as far as Miles could tell.

". . . have to get it direct, really. Can't even trust the gourmet shops not to blend it with Costa Rican . . ." Nettleship droned on. He had both arms spread over the edge of the Jacuzzi, and even though he wore nothing other than a G-string bathing suit, he looked, as always, fresh and crisp and businesslike, with his hair, the same steely color as the Gulf's water, trimmed weekly to a uniform half-inch, neatly parted and held in place by mousse.

Miles, keeping an eye on the pelican, drank his own coffee. He marveled how it cut through the haze of last night's rum. A masterful example of God's handiwork: the same Edenic island that grew the cane that made the demon also produced the only antidote. A sermon in that? No, a little off-color. Nonetheless, he smiled, just as the pelican crumpled in midair, as if shot, and fell toward the water. At the last instant, it shaped itself into something lethal, aerodynamic, and as much a part of the late twentieth century as an F-15, and thrust downward with its neck. An instant later, the bird bobbed to the surface with the tail of a minnow sticking out of one side of its pouched beak.

"Miles?" Nettleship was asking, looking not at Miles but over to Ira with an "I told you so" superiority.

A small gull had come over and engaged the pelican in a tug-of-war over the protruding tail. Miles wanted to watch to see how the drama unfolded. "Pardon me," he said.

The little bird managed to get the fish, and, holding on to it by the tail fin, tried to take off.

"Really, Miles, if you'd rather do this another time . . ." Ira said, letting his voice trail off in an unspoken but clearly understood "when you're not so darned hung over."

"No, sorry. I was just thinking about something," said Miles. What he was thinking about, in addition to the pelican/sea gull drama, was his bursting bladder.

Ira let out a frustrated groan. He reached behind him for a small plastic pill case and plucked a handful of vitamins: 5,000 mg of C for general wellness, 250 mcg of B^{12} for stress, 400 IU E to ward off cancer, and 1,200 mg lecithin to lower his cholesterol.

Miles watched his brother swallow the pills. Even with the help of the vitamins, Ira did not look good. His skin had taken on an invalid's pallor. He was only four years older than

Miles—which made him forty-five—but he had the body of someone in his late fifties. True, Ira still had the same six-foot-three frame as Miles, the same sandy hair. But gone from Ira's face were the innocent good looks that made Miles a million-dollar success in the TV pulpit. Where Miles had a neatly squared jaw—bisected by a dimple and offset by a nose that been broken during a high school basketball game, leaving it an appealingly vulnerable quarter-inch off center—Ira sported a set of loose jowls and a snout that hung straight and too low over his lips. Miles's belly was still as flat as a seventeen-year-old's, despite the rum. Ira the health nut supported a paunch that had grown markedly in the three months since Miles had seen him last.

Miles realized they were waiting for him to say something. "And, anyway, I just thought you two were discussing the merits of the coffee, which is very good, by the way, Drake."

Nettleship opened his mouth, but before he could defend himself, Ira spoke in the cultured southern drawl he reserved for the most serious occasions. "We have called this meeting, Miles, because the entire future of the Savior Network is at stake." Ira nodded to Nettleship, then settled lower in the tub, allowing the bubbling water to come up around his double chin, another recent acquisition.

"Very well," said Nettleship in the soft, almost effeminate voice he affected for when he wanted to sound important. Miles had trouble hearing him over the bubbling of the tub, so he leaned closer, even though he knew it was just what Nettleship wanted. Nettleship went on. "I'd like to begin, if I may, by quickly reviewing The Vale's financials."

"I hardly think The Vale's financials are going to determine the entire future of the network," Miles said. He was irritated by the pain in his bladder. That and the coffee were beginning to make him feel punchy.

Nettleship shot a glance at Ira, who dipped his chins slowly into the tub—a sign to go on. Nettleship took his cue. "Miles,

I think you'll understand once you have the entire picture. If I may begin?"

Miles raised his hands above the surface in mock resignation. "It's Ira's hot tub, if Ira wants to start the day with a catalog of my grievous fiscal sins, who am I, a mere guest, to argue?"

The controller paused long enough to see whether Ira would come to his defense. When no help was forthcoming, he reached for a piece of Savior Network letterhead that had been on the redwood deck surrounding the Jacuzzi. He frowned at the paper, replaced it, and looked hard at Miles. "Salaries," he said at last. "Thirty-seven thousand four hundred and twenty-seven dollars." When no one seemed impressed by the bare number, he added, "That represents a budget overrun of thirty-nine point seven percent, for the fiscal year."

He glared a "so there" glare at Miles, who began to ease himself out of the tub. With his ancient boxer-style bathing trunks dripping water on the redwood and Nettleship's papers, Miles padded over to a beach chair hung with towels. He took one and rubbed it over his thick straw-colored hair.

"Where the hell are you going?" Ira said.

"Unlike you two, I don't do my best thinking in a hot tub, and this strikes me as pretty high-level stuff. So, if you two don't mind, I'll field questions from high ground—after I pee." He wrapped the big towel around his shoulders and disappeared behind a well-trimmed gardenia. When he returned, he smiled a smile of the purest, sweetest relief and settled into a deck chair facing his brother.

Nettleship had to turn forty-five degrees to address Miles. But in that position, his back was toward Ira, so he, too, got out of the tub and, not bothering with a towel, selected a chair that put him directly between the two brothers. Again, he consulted his paper. "We were talking about your salary overruns," he said to Miles.

Miles caught himself scratching the back of his neck, a nervous tic he was trying to control. He brought his hand down and used it to pick up his abandoned cup. "Maybe we should talk about your salary, Drake. The money we paid out in salaries at The Vale, overruns and all, wouldn't keep your BMW in tires—"

"Miles!" It was Ira.

Nettleship nodded in agreement. "The real issue here is not the total amount. Nobody will argue with that. It's the question of budgetary overruns. Ever since I came here—my Lord, it's been eighteen months now—I've tried to institute a system of strict fiscal controls without which the church, which, face it, has really become a multimillion-dollar business, would crumble."

"And I'm talking about thirty Bahamian kids who might not be getting a proper Christian education if I hadn't hired Prue. Thirty kids, Drake. You know what that means? We nearly doubled the size of the enrollment at The Vale's school. I'm sorry if she demanded twelve thousand bucks a year as living expenses. I'm doubly sorry I didn't plan at the beginning of your almighty fiscal year that a highly qualified person would just happen to be vacationing on Andros and would happen to become so inspired as to offer her services. She made four times that much in her last position. You guys should be praising me for driving such a great bargain."

"But we agreed . . . and you were at the meeting . . . to restrict salary increments to five percent," said Drake. "I," he added, gesturing meekly to his own chest with an open hand, "only took a four percent raise."

"So maybe I should fire Prue. Then go on the air and explain to our congregation how because of a twelve-thousand-dollar overrun we've had to kick thirty kids out of the school they built?"

Nettleship threw out his little hairless chest. "Come on, Miles. Let's call a spade a spade. We all know that the real issue here is that Prue is your girlfriend. Now, I'm sure many of our employees—myself included—would love to have girlfriends on the pay—"

"Fiancée. She's my fiancée, not my girlfriend. But before that, she was still a thoroughly qualified teaching missionary with—"

"Stop being so damn difficult, Miles." It was Ira, who had his head back against the padding on the edge of the Jacuzzi. Even though his voice had an edge of anger to it, he neither lifted his head nor bothered to open his eyes.

"Sorry if I'm being difficult. You guys called this get-together. I was quite happy over there on Andros running The Vale."

Before Ira could respond, a glass door leading from the terrace to the mansion's great room slid open. Three Yorkshire terriers, each wearing a red bow on the top of its head, bounded through the slit. They cantered across the terrace. Once on the thick, trim Florida grass, they squatted in unison and began to urinate.

A pretty blond woman, barefooted and in a pink teddy—nothing else—appeared after them in the doorway. Eight months earlier, at nineteen, she was second runner-up in the Miss Florida pageant. For the past six weeks, she had been Mrs. Ira Farnsworth—the fourth woman to hold that title. "Sugar," she called. "The driver is here."

"Thank you, dear," said Ira. He rose from the tub. "Can we move this along?"

"Very well," said Nettleship, shooting a glance at his paper. "Ten thousand unbudgeted dollars for epoxy resin. Two thousand for band saws. What, pray tell, does that mean?"

Miles brightened. "A brainstorm. Thought of it myself. Have you ever looked closely at the wood of a coconut palm. It's fibrous, you know. Beautiful really—but no good for construction. Too weak. Well I got the idea of coating it—soaking it, actually—in clear epoxy. You get the beauty of the wood with the strength of the resin. A new, unique product that uses a material indigenous to Andros. And we now employ three people in the shop—full-time," he added for emphasis.

"Are you proposing to sell this . . . this substance?" asked Drake.

"Exactly. Permanent jobs."

"Have you conducted market research?"

"Yes. Well, in a way. We made the parquet flooring and the desktops for the new classroom out of it. You should see them. Beautiful. Looks like mahogany."

Nettleship shook his head sadly at Ira. It was obvious no more needed to be said about *that*. "One other item here. Something called the *Come to Jesus Cruiser* appears on your capital budget. It represents another eight thousand dollars."

"Terrific buy. It was a run-down old thirty-six-foot Chris. Real wreck. So I bought it and had the boys and girls restore it as a shop project—woodwork, motor, interior upholstery, the works. Incredible what they learned. It's over in Nassau for a little tuning up at the moment, but normally I use it as a floating pulpit. Take it up and down the coast to little settlements, while Prue—did I tell you she was an ordained minister?—handles services at The Vale. Only way I can reach a lot of those people, especially since I broke the frame on that old LTD wagon. Lost it in a pothole. You know how the roads on Andros are."

"Fine, fine. You got yourself a new boat. I suppose it didn't dawn on you to inform me. Just so I could account for it? After all, we pay your bills," said Nettleship.

Miles had had too much rum, too much coffee. His temper snapped. "This is total garbage," he said to his brother, who had put on a terry-cloth robe and was crab-walking behind one of the Yorkies, balancing awkwardly with a garden trowel in one hand and a child's plastic beach pail in the other. The dog reached a border of wood chips beneath a trimmed hibiscus and began to defecate. Ira deftly slipped his trowel under the dog's rear end and caught the hard twiglike dung before it hit the chips.

14

"Go on. I'm listening," Ira said, moving over to where another dog had begun to sniff the base of a royal palm.

The first Yorkie to complete his morning's business trotted over to Miles and hopped on his lap, settling in a manner that suggested here was where he intended to stay for the rest of the day. Miles said, "Nice pooch," and began to stroke it under the chin as he addressed Ira.

"You and I agreed when I left to start The Vale that I would return to preach four times a year. In exchange for that, the network would fund my activities on Andros. Maybe we should have started this discussion by revealing how much came into the collection after my four sermons? You didn't happen to bring along the pledge reports." The last part, he directed at Nettleship.

"Really, Miles. You're confusing the issue. Anything that comes in through telephone pledges flows through general revenues. There's no way way to break it out, in accounting terms."

"Drake, it's you who is confusing the issue. The issue is that The Vale, which is about the only truly charitable work this church does nowadays, takes up less than a quarter of a million dollars a year. That leaves you guys with about five million to spend on fancy studios, big houses, and expensive cars."

"Enough!" said Ira. He stood, jabbing the trowel at Miles. His face had gone an ugly red and his jaw was quivering. "Don't you get so self-righteous with me, little brother. While you sit over on your island in the Bahamas, half-stewed most of the time, I, with the help of Drake, spread the word of our Lord to millions of good, deserving Americans, not just a handful of niggers on some Bahamas backwater. And, little brother, it takes millions of dollars to reach millions of people. Sorry, but that is a fact of life."

While he spoke, the Yorkie at his feet crapped on the grass.

Ira looked as if the world as he knew it had just collapsed. He made a threatening gesture—could have been at Miles, could have been at the offending Yorkie. Taking that as his cue, the third dog, which had been patrolling the hedge at the far edge of the property, stopped, moved its hind legs up into position one by one, and hunched its back. Ira, looking like a big-league outfielder, made the dash across the yard, and managed a circus catch just before that turd touched the ground. He tapped the side of the pail with the trowel and stood back up, regaining his composure. "Get on with it, Drake. I do have to leave soon," he said.

Nettleship took his time sorting the papers at his feet. He finally found the right one. "The long and short of it," he began, in a near whisper, which meant he was about to utter something truly important, "is I am concerned about your cost overruns because the Savior Network in general has experienced serious revenue shortfalls."

"If Bakker and Swaggart had only been able to keep their pants on . . ." added Ira. He put the pail down in a corner of the patio and rejoined them.

Nettleship picked up on Ira's comment. "He's right. Since the unfortunate scandals, all television ministries have suffered—even the innocent." It was obvious he included himself in the latter category.

"You trying to use the excuse that we're broke?" said Miles. "I don't buy that for a minute. Get a short-term note from the bank. The boys at First Union should be amenable."

Ira and Nettleship cast "you go first" looks at each other. Nettleship broke the silence. "Knowing your distaste for business matters related to the ministry, there is a project we had not intended to bring up until it was a little further along, but . . ."

". . . ah, so now we come to the real explanation."

"Miles, that was unnecessary," said Ira.

Drake continued, "Your brother and I have been planning a major new development for the network—revolutionary, really. There has been nothing like it before anywhere, and it will provide the financial underpinnings for a brilliant future—after some short-term—and I stress short-term—pain."

"I'm all ears."

Nettleship fished among his papers and handed Miles a folder bearing the title "Celestial City: A Prospectus" and under it in smaller type, "Confidential."

"It's all explained there," said Nettleship. "We're going to build a major planned community just east of town. Two eighteen-hole golf courses, lakes, recreation center, shopping facilities, a new production center for the Savior Network—the works. As you well know, a large percentage of our customers—congregation, rather—are of retirement age. We will offer them a place to live in Florida, in a religious community of twenty thousand like-minded people. We will not only benefit financially from the sale and development of the land but will get long-term revenue through a special property-tax levy."

"I see. Sort of a halfway housing development between here and the hereafter," Miles said, then added, "and the best part is you rake in a healthy profit in the process."

"Miles, I'm not afraid of the word *profit*. Not if we use it to further the Lord's work," said Nettleship.

Miles rolled his eyes at Nettleship but addressed his brother. "Congratulations, you've become a real estate developer. Strikes me as a far cry from what Father envisioned when he started this ministry. But go ahead. Do what you like. I just don't see how this should affect me and The Vale."

Nettleship answered. "Circumstances were such that we were forced to purchase the land earlier than we had anticipated—before our partners could come up with the financing. We borrowed heavily from the bank, at the same time that revenue fell. We are now several payments behind, and the bank is insisting we get something substantial to them by January third. I'm sure I don't have to remind you that's less than a month away."

17

"So where do I come in? I don't happen to have a 'substantial' sum of money on me."

"The Vale," said Nettleship.

"What about it?"

"A buyer has come forward. We have been offered four hundred eighty-nine thousand dollars for the land. Cash deal. But the purchaser insists we close by month's end. That money will carry us until the rest of our financing comes in."

Miles stood up, settled the Yorkie on the chair, and took two slow steps toward his brother. "You dirty . . ." he said.

"Now, Miles."

"Don't now Miles me. We had a deal. You gave your word. If I left you alone here to run the network's affairs as you wanted, I could operate The Vale without interference."

"This is a chance of a lifetime, don't you see? The Savior Network could become big . . . as big as any of them. We'd be able to do anything. Fund a hundred Vales, if we wanted . . ."

"Fine, fine. So unload this place." Miles swept his hand toward the sprawling mansion. "Must be worth ten times what you've been offered for The Vale."

"It's already been mortgaged for the down payment on the land for Celestial City," Ira said, averting his eyes.

Miles thought for a moment. He walked across the grass, which was as clean and trim as expensive broadloom. He stopped at the cement retaining wall that delineated lawn from beach. The sun was now fully up and walkers had begun to appear.

"No deal," he finally said, turning back to his brother and Nettleship.

Ira slowly nodded at Nettleship.

"I'm afraid you have no choice," said Nettleship.

"Since when do I take orders from you? I have plenty of choice. I wonder what our congregation will say when I go on the air and explain all this to them."

"You won't be doing that," said Ira. "I forbid it."

"Well then, maybe I'll just have to go public through the news media. They'd love another TV evangelist scandal."

"Really, Miles, you're being rather melodramatic. Go to the reporters if you like. The cold hard fact of the matter is that unless we come up with a half-million dollars by the bank's deadline, the Savior Network is bust—kaput. We—none of us—have the luxury of a choice."

Miles realized he had overplayed his hand. Ira was right. They were immune to his threats—thanks in no small part to their own stupidity. Nice irony there. Miles covered his eyes with his palms and dropped his chin to his chest, not even sure himself whether he was praying or merely putting his thoughts in order. Time passed, with nothing to disturb the quiet of the morning in this rich neighborhood other than the gurgling of the Jacuzzi and the jingle of the dog tags of a Yorkie scratching its ribs.

"Perhaps there is a way we could all get what we want," Miles said finally.

Drake jumped in. "I think we've looked at every . . ."

"What if I gave you the half-million?"

"Miles, you don't have two bits to rub together," said Ira.

"I was just asking a simple question: What if I gave you a half-million dollars by the end of the month? And further agreed not to go public? Would you then give me a written promise not to interfere with The Vale?"

"Don't talk nonsense," said Ira.

"One simple question. Yes. Or no."

"Well, if you gave us the half-million—provided you did not raise it by using the network, I suppose we would certainly agree. But . . ."

"No buts, big brother. That's all I need to know. I'll see you by the end of the month. The thirtieth. At the office, if you two can find it in yourselves to struggle out of this hot tub. I'll have the money."

Not waiting for a reply, Miles turned and walked toward the

guest wing of the mansion, where he had left his sandals, under-pants, fawn summer-weight Sears suit, and clerical collar.

Nettleship waited until the door slid closed behind Miles. "He won't . . . have the money," he said. "My people have already called the roster of major donors. Gotten every cent available."

Ira shed his dressing robe and began doing side-straddle hops. "Who cares. Miles finds the money. Miles doesn't. Just so long as we get paid. At least this way he's not going to be bothering us."

"Somehow I doubt that. . . . Ira, would you stop jumping around. It makes it hard to concentrate."

"I'll be done in a minute. Twenty-two. Twenty-three. Twenty-four, twenty-five." Ira exhaled once, loudly, then fell forward onto his hands and began doing push-ups. "You should really exercise more. You're skinny, but you lack muscle tone. Never do anything for your heart."

"Running the finances of this place gives my heart enough of a workout, thanks. We really need him on air," said Nettle-ship.

Ira answered, still doing his push-ups. "He has the gift. Fa-ther always used to say that. Right from when Miles was a kid, he had the gift for making people want to open their wallets. I think it's his face. Looks like a cherub that someone's boxed once or twice on the nose."

"Do you think he'll come back once The Vale's gone?"

"Oh, he'll be pissed off for awhile, but in the long run, he really doesn't have much choice. He'll come back to the fold. And so what if he doesn't come back? We'll have Celestial City by then. That's got to be worth a dozen Miles Farnsworths."

Ira rolled over, wrapped his hands behind his head, and started his sit-ups.

In his room back at the Holiday Inn, Miles finished most of his packing by nine that morning. The last item to go in his scuffed fake-leather Samsonite was the heel of Appleton's. But there didn't seem much sense in carrying the nearly empty bottle, so he took it into the bathroom and upended its contents into the previous night's dirty tumbler. He swallowed the rum in three great gulps, shuddered once, and sighed long and loud as the warmth spread out from his throat to the rest of his body.

Then, right there in the motel bathroom, the Reverend Miles Farnsworth fell to his knees and with his elbows propped on the sink's countertop, he prayed, asking that the Lord provide him with the means to continue the work at The Vale. A soothing peace came over him.

Could have been God. Could have been the rum. Miles had no way of being certain.

Chapter 3

Stormy Lake would have never fought back if she had imagined for a second that it was a .45 automatic the pock-faced guy had shoved into the base of her spine.

Blame the date—December 7—the eve of Stormy's third annual twenty-ninth birthday, an occasion she had marked by downing six rum and tonics in succession. Blame the paranoia induced by the two joints; or the sadness and uncertainty she felt because she was well and truly alone; or that she was bone tired and simply wanted to sleep. Blame Grand Turk itself, a Caribbean backwater if there still is one, adrift far beyond civilization's ragged edge, a place where damn near anything could, and would, happen to an unescorted woman at midnight on the street outside the Turk's Head Inn.

Whatever the reasons, for one critical fraction of a second, just long enough for her animal instincts to click into the "on" position, Stormy really imagined some joker had come up from behind, pulled his erection out, and shoved it into the small of her back.

Stormy knew a half a dozen guys—buddies of hers—who would have thought it a swell birthday prank; another five or six who would have done it with clear sexual intentions. Assuming it to be one of the latter, she kicked up and backward, slamming and twisting as hard as she could. The guy let out a grunt. His kneecap issued a muffled, moist popping sound. Something, a ligament Stormy hoped, gave way. At the same

23

instant, she wheeled. One hand shot, fingernails first, toward his eyes. They were startled and wide with pain above the pock-marked cheekbones. The other hand, Stormy clenched in a tight fist aimed at his groin. With any luck, he'd end the night crippled, blind, and impotent. And that was just fine with Stormy.

She knew she had goofed, badly, probably fatally, when the second hand hit—not flesh but metal. Stormy cried out, startled in pain from where the automatic's front site gouged a three-quarter-inch furrow across the top of her middle two knuckles.

The impact of her blow sent the gun into the gutter separating the street from a low seawall and the beach beyond. It skidded to halt, for an instant just another piece of rubbish in a clutter of discarded beer cans, broken bottles, and old cigarette packs. Not having a clue what else a person should do in situations like this, she dove for it.

He got there first. Stormy skidded past on her belly, then trying to recover, rolled, in time to see his hand raise the .45. She let the roll carry her over the low seawall. Not waiting for the gun to fire, she jumped to her feet and, struggling to gain momentum in the soft sand, dashed toward the water's edge—and darkness.

The pock-faced guy's feet made a thudding sound in the sand three paces behind her. To prevent him from taking aim, she ducked to the left, and to the right—which was a bad mistake. A discarded length of anchor line caught her ankle and brought her down hard and face-first into the sand. The wind left her with a *whoosh*. She lay in the dark, stunned, struggling to refill her lungs. The guy crab-walked in her direction, one hand holding the gun, the other gripping his knee, as he searched for her in the dark.

Two Turk's Head patrons had come outside. They stayed close to the door, and the streetlight. Stormy thought of calling out. But it was too late. The guy was close now, near enough for a good shot, and if she yelled, he'd see her for sure.

Stormy blinked to clear her eyes of sand. It didn't do much good. She could see clearly only for a few seconds after each blink. But during the good moments, she made out an old wooden sailboat, the kind the Haitians used to bring over fruit and vegetables. It lay on its side about twenty yards ahead.

She struggled with the conflicting desires to lie facedown on the warm beach, peaceful, resigned, and wait for the guy to do whatever he inevitably would do, or to stand and make a brazen run for it, to go down fighting—or fleeing, at the very least. Stormy bellied her way across the sand. The sailboat was almost close enough to touch. She got control of herself. Once on the other side, with its bulk between her and the pock-faced guy, she would run for it again—perhaps all the way to where the lights from the Hotel Kittina's waterfront rooms still shone.

The boat cast a heavy black shadow. To Stormy, it represented safety, a temporary refuge. She allowed herself a minute or two to lie in the dark sanctuary, breathing deeply, almost gulping, to fill her lungs with the air they would need for the sprint ahead.

Stormy stood, using the sailboat's rough hand-hewn keel as a support. She rubbed her eyes to take a final bearing on the hotel lights, maybe a half mile away, then launched herself onto the beach with one giant stride. It took her smack into the open arms of the fat mulatto.

He wrapped her in a soft bear hug that smelled of oily skin and days-old sweat. At first, Stormy was relieved. Someone had come to her rescue. But as the chubby forearms constricted around her chest, holding her immobile and crushing the air from her, cold terror supplanted hope. She went limp as the pock-faced guy hobbled around the stern of the overturned boat. He came directly up to her and jammed the barrel of the .45 beneath Stormy's right ear. Stormy let out a cry, then closed her eyes and waited for the explosion.

It didn't come. The fat fellow's arms loosened. He gave her

25

a gentle shove backward against the skinny guy. He and Stormy did an awkward dancing step until the skinny guy leaned against the boat. He wrapped an arm around her. His breaths came in short rasps and in increasing frequency. Something hard and round pressed against Stormy's buttock. This time, she was sure it wasn't a handgun.

The fat guy brushed his hands together, as if to cleanse them. He smoothed the front of his light-colored safari jacket. "Miss Lake," he said, in polished tones. "So considerate of you to run in this direction. If you had chosen the other way, you might have escaped. Or at the very least, I would have had to run down the beach to catch you. You'll excuse me, but I hate to run. My size and all. It would have put me in a very foul mood."

Stormy only half-listened to what he was saying. The other half of her mind took stock of the situation. One good thing. If they had wanted her dead, her corpse already would have been shark fodder. "You the boss?" she asked the fat guy.

"Indeed," he said.

Stormy let a three-count go by before going on. "Then tell this little fucker to stop dry-humping my ass."

"Raul!" the fat guy said loudly, then he, too, waited a three-count. The pressure of the pock-faced fellow's pelvis left; his hand dropped from Stormy's breast to a more chaste position just below her ribs. Stormy savored a moment of small victory. "Raul," the fat guy went on, quietly this time. "Later." He let the word linger as Stormy's confidence dissolved, then added, "Unless, of course, you choose to cooperate, Miss Lake."

"Stormy. That's my name. Stormy."

"Stormy, then. They all call me Fat Boy." He huffed out a mighty sigh. "So now that we know each other, I have a simple business proposition to put forward. Please come with us."

Stormy stayed where she was. "Suppose it would be a stupid question asking whether or not I have any choice."

Fat Boy said nothing. But she could see his white smile in the dark.

*　　*　　*

They had taken one of the Columbus Inn's ten ramshackle $19.95-a-night rooms. The only sign that anyone occupied the shabby room was one small plastic Bahamasair overnight bag, the type some travel agents give away as free promotions. It sat between two particularly large cigarette burns on the bedspread of one of the room's sagging double beds. Other than that, the place was devoid of possessions, so unlived in–looking, it might have been empty: no books, no magazines, no shoes on the floor, no articles of clothing over chairs, no used glasses, no booze bottles. Fat Boy signaled to one of two plastic upholstered chairs beside a fake wood–topped table whose plastic veneer had begun to lift from its particle-board heart. Stormy sat in the chair, blinking and trying to pick sand shards from the corners of her eyes. The pock-faced guy leaned against the dresser, one of whose three drawers was missing, and kept the automatic pointed at Stormy.

"Miss Lake, I have a little something here I would like you to sample. I need your opinion. You *are* familiar with cocaine?" Fat Boy spoke while he bent over the travel bag. His backside, in shiny brown polyester pants, looked innocent and vulnerable. It got Stormy thinking.

"I don't see how that's really your business. What are you getting at?" she said.

Fat Boy rose and turned toward her.

Stormy gasped. It was her first good look at him. His face, or what was left of it, was puffy and lumpy. One eye had swollen shut beneath an irregular smear of deep purple skin that had spread over the entire right side. A neat zipper of black stitches ran downward from his forehead, bisected the right eyebrow, sliced through both lids, and then connected to the corner of his mouth. The teeth below the lip, which quivered in a half-smile, half-sneer, were jagged and broken. A single thread of scab, black against his leather-colored skin, ran from one earlobe, across the fat under his chin, to the other earlobe, giving the mutilated face a permanent silly smile.

"Please. . . . Please be my guest." Fat Boy proffered a foil pack.

Stormy was just about to tell him to shove it when the pock-faced kid gave the smallest wiggle of the automatic's barrel. Besides, a little toot certainly would have gone a long way to straightening her out. She opened the pack. "You wouldn't have a small piece of paper or something," she said.

Fat Boy opened the top dresser drawer. While he pawed through its contents, back to the room, Pock-face stared at her with sullen, dead eyes.

"Here," said Fat Boy, handing Stormy a subscription card from *Newsweek* magazine. He stood back like an indulgent host fishing for a big compliment. She prepared two neat white lines on the tabletop. "Hope you find it enjoyable. Imported from Colombia. Cost nearly one hundred thousand dollars."

Stormy bent over the table and blocked one nostril while she shoved the rolled subscription card into the other. She smiled despite herself in anticipation of the prickly rush, then inhaled.

The rush never came. Her nostril filled with a dry, sweet powder. Stormy gagged, spat to clear the back of her throat, then sneezed, scattering the remaining white line over the table. "You been screwed," she said.

He smiled. "Precisely. That is why I called you to this little meeting. You see, I had a considerable quantity of pure uncut Colombian flown to South Caicos two weeks ago. I hired a guy with a boat to bring it up to Andros. Somewhere between Caicos and Andros, my cocaine turned into icing sugar. You might know the person who was providing transport. His name is Bingo Martin. You're his woman, no?"

"I'm no one's woman, Fat Boy."

"Pardon me. Maybe I should have said you have a part interest in a staysail schooner called the *Roach,* and your only permanent residence is the captain's cabin, where, from time to time, you share a berth with a man named Bingo Martin."

"Look, you mind if I have a drink of water—or something?"

Fat Boy went to the bathroom and returned with a glass of water. "In any case, I think you understand the point of our little chat."

"Why not come right out with it. I'm tired, frightened, half-cut, and it's supposed to be my goddamn birthday. Not really in any shape for clever games."

"You have good reason to wish this was a game. But let me assure you, I'm serious. Deadly serious. You know the where-abouts of my cocaine. I want it. Now." He came up close so Stormy could get a good look at his face.

"I haven't the foggiest idea what happened to your shit. Ask Bingo. You dealt with him, not me. If you really want to know what I think, it's that I'm amazed anyone would still fall for that stupid switch." She took a long drink. The water felt good washing the sugar from her throat, and the heft of the glass in her hand gave her an idea—not a great one, but better than anything else that had come to her since Pock-face had shoved the gun in her back.

Fat Boy went on. "Mr. Martin has disappeared. Took the money and disappeared. He double-crossed me. And I think you know where he and the cocaine are."

"Wish I did. Look, Fat Boy, this might come as a surprise, but we're on the same side. I could give a sweet damn about your merchandise, but if what you say is true, bastard's got my boat, plus a small fortune. Probably took off with some bimbo."

"I think she's lying to us," Fat Boy said, and tipped his bald dome once in the direction of his accomplice. Raul handed him the .45, took two shambling steps toward Stormy, and, putting on as close to a beatific smile as his pocked, snaggletoothed mug could form, he slapped her across the mouth.

The blow wrenched Stormy's head sideways. She tasted

blood, and with her tongue could feel where her incisors had punctured the inside of her lip. "Asshole," she muttered.

"Allow me to reiterate," Fat Boy went on. "Bingo Martin double-crossed me. Switched my cocaine for sugar and ran with both the money I paid him for delivery and the real drug. I should let you know, Miss Lake, that I was to receive one million dollars for handling that cocaine. That is a fortune to me. A life-and-death quantity of money, if you comprehend. Then there's the other matter . . ."

Fat Boy tried to grin at her. All he could muster was a slight quiver in the corner of his mouth to the left of where it had been sliced through. "See my face?"

He shoved it close to her, so close she could smell his oily aroma mingled with some food odor—garlic mixed with a bit of ginger perhaps. Stormy averted her eyes.

"Not pretty, is it?"

When she didn't answer, he drew even closer. "*Is it?*" he demanded, giving her a full waft of stir-fry.

"Pretty fucking ugly."

He stepped back, nodding his bald head. "Pretty ugly is right. It's all your Bingo's fault, you know."

"Didn't know the skinny little bastard had such a mean streak. Maybe it's just as well he took off with—"

"Raul!"

In a quick motion, too fast to see, Stormy smashed the glass on the edge of the table and brandished it at the pock-faced guy. "Shoot if you want, but if this asshole slaps me again, he'll be able to sing with the Vienna Boy's Choir."

Raul looked at his boss for instructions, eyes protruding with a dumb hatred. "Later, Raul," Fat Boy said, then turned to Stormy. "Miss Lake, it's time we brought this interview to an end. What I've been trying to talk about are promises and commitments. I had promised a certain individual in Florida to deliver the cocaine. He, in turn, has commitments. He is a very ruthless man, Miss Lake. The marks you see on my face were punishment for failing to keep my promise. But I am told I was lucky. He is also lenient. He has given me until the end of the year to fulfill my promise. Three weeks. If I don't, he will kill me. So you see, I have everything to lose. Now I'm offering you the same deal. Where is it, Miss Lake?"

"Don't have a clue."

Fat Boy spread his palms in resignation and shook his head sadly. "If that is true, Miss Lake, I apologize. Unfortunately, that means you are of no further use to me. Raul, she's all yours."

Raul hitched his trousers and turned to Stormy, his eyes bright, almost gleeful and puppyish with anticipation. His mouth opened to reveal brown teeth. His breathing came in short rasps.

"One step closer, asshole, and you lose 'em." Stormy threatened him with the glass."

He kept coming.

"I mean it."

She hadn't figured on his foot. In a fluid, fast motion, he raised it to hip level, then shot it out expertly. The glass flew from her hand and smashed against the wall. He was panting now. Stormy took a step away from him, and felt the plywood paneling on her back. He grabbed both her hands and pinned them against the wall above her head. She raised a knee to jam it against the bulge in his pants, but he blocked her blow with a quick quarter twist that left only the muscle of his thigh exposed. He opened his mouth as if to laugh, but no noise came out, just a series of exhaled croaking sounds.

"Fat Boy, maybe we can cut a deal."

Fat Boy said nothing at first. Pock-face lowered his mug toward Stormy. "Raul. Stop," said Fat Boy.

He came no closer, but didn't back off, either. Just kept her pinned. He panted, half-smiling.

"If this asshole does anything more to me, then I give you my sworn guarantee that I will never—*never*—do anything to assist you to find that merchandise. Got that, Fat Boy. You know anything about me, you'd know I'm just stubborn enough to keep my word."

Fat Boy sighed. "True. But you see, Miss Lake, you have left me in a position where I have nothing to lose. What can you offer me in return for your life? For your—chastity?" He laughed at that last line, but laughing must have hurt. He stopped and put a hand to the wound on the side of his face.

Pock-face looked back at his boss in disappointment, as if to say, You're not going to back down now. At that instant, Stormy brought her knee up again. This time, she landed a good solid blow. He bent ninety degrees, held that impossible position for but a few seconds, then flopped over on his side, his throat and mouth working in silent agony as he began to rock back and forth.

"Very well," Fat Boy said sadly. "Let's deal."

"I get you the stuff by year's end. You pay me the fifty thou you were going to give Bingo."

"One problem. The fifty thousand has already been paid. I pay only once per family, and I count you and Mr. Martin as a family. It's up to you to deliver. But if you do get me the cocaine by month's end, I'll give you something worth more than fifty thousand—your life."

"Where do I deliver?"

"Andros. Place called Fresh Creek. You can reach me there."

Stormy smirked. "So is this the part in your script where I get to leave?"

"Very funny, Miss Lake. But no. Not immediately. There is one other piece of information I want to impart. There is a preacher on Andros. Runs a mission school—"

"Thanks for the tip, Fat Boy, but preachers and I—there's no chemistry there, if you catch my drift."

"As I was saying, he runs a mission school. If you are telling the truth to me—which I doubt very sincerely—but if by chance you really don't know where my cocaine is, my own observers say you might do well to search his mission."

"A preacher involved in this sort of thing—for shame. What's the world—"

"Oh, he wouldn't know he had it."

Stormy looked at him, perplexed.

"There's a remote chance that someone who works for him has hidden it there. But that really doesn't change the terms of our little agreement, does it?"

"Whatever you say."

"What I say is that this preacher is booked on the afternoon flight from Miami to Nassau on Friday."

Stormy took a shortcut through the sandy yards of two shacks. Home, temporarily, was an air mattress on the floor of the room belonging to the cook at the Kittina. It was a place to sleep when *Roach* was out of port. The cook was clean and didn't snore any worse than Bingo. And for ten bucks a week, Stormy couldn't complain.

She stopped once. A rooster scuttled across the path—a starved black creature, half-wild, and looking like the result of an illicit coupling between a Cuban fighting cock and a buzzard. Because of some genetic malfunction, it insisted on crowing all night, every night. Stormy had declared war on the bird eight months earlier, but it was as clever as it was bothersome, and always dashed to the safety of the rusting wreck of a Morris Major whenever Stormy went after it. That night, it stopped, a few feet away from Stormy, and stood there, politely observing her as she stooped and picked up a discarded length of plastic pipe. She hefted the pipe, sized up the nemesis of her sleeping hours. One flick of the wrist was all it would have taken. But Stormy couldn't bring herself to make that flick.

When she finally tossed the pipe aside, Stormy discovered, to her anger and surprise, that she was crying. She attempted to stifle the sobs, looking from side to side as if there actually might be someone other than that damn rooster outside at that hour to catch Stormy Lake in a moment of weakness.

Trying to stop the sobs made them worse. She eventually found herself crying fully and unashamedly. She cried because of fucking Fat Boy and the pock-faced animal he kept at his side and what they had just put her through; she cried because she was thirty-one and living on Grand Turk—alone; but most of all, she cried because that morning she had gotten the letter from Bingo. The letter, which came with a crude treasure map, had begun, "Shit, Storms, guess I'm dead now. Wild, eh?"

Bingo. Not much of a man really. Skinny. Smoked far too much dope. Always wrecking a car or running a boat aground. Stormy had bailed him out of half the slammers in the Antilles. But he was harmless. He viewed life as some practical joke that he was the butt of. And for that, Stormy Lake had loved him, and some part of her probably wanted revenge on the bastards who had done him in.

By the time Stormy's tears had stopped, she had begun thinking about her situation. First of all, she knew damn well that the minute she handed the coke over to Fat Boy, she was dead—just like Bingo. Fact number two: She knew she would be equally as dead if Fat Boy got hold of it himself. Conclusion: If she had the coke, she could keep it away from Fat Boy and stay alive. There was a mellow taste of irony in that. And if she could keep it out of his hands until the end of the year, then Fat Boy would be dead, and she would be safe.

Alone, in the middle of the night, on an island like Grand Turk, when a person is eyeball-to-eyeball with a genetically cross-wired rooster, that sort of reasoning can make sense.

And besides, Stormy could think of a hell of a lot of uses for a million bucks' worth of cocaine.

Chapter 4

Miles first noticed her eyes. Round, a little kooky, and protruding just enough to be sexy, they looked on the world eagerly, with the sort innocence and amazement that most people lose at age ten. Not that there was anything exciting about the customs and immigration hall of Nassau's Windsor Field. It was 4:45 P.M., December 9—a Friday. Three jumbo jets had just landed and disgorged packaged tourists. They jostled and poked one another in lineups behind the baggage inspectors.

Even from twenty feet, Miles could tell she was not one of the tourists. For one thing, she didn't dress like someone who had just left Cleveland for seven days/six nights at Cable Beach. She wore a simple cotton pullover dress, white, without pleats or pattern, and running straight from shoulders to mid-calf. Her footwear consisted of a pair of foam-rubber thongs that looked as if they could well have been picked up at a used-clothing shop. As hand baggage, she carried only an airline-ticket folder. A battered haversack hung from a strap over one shoulder.

She seemed to spot him, too, as a fellow nontourist. Her lips, which might have been one size too large for the rest of her face, spread into a cheek-to-cheek smile. She slid over to him. Nodded conspiratorially. Rolled those big eyes. Tossed the chocolate-brown jungle of waves and curls atop her head in the direction of the crowd. He returned the smile, feeling a little awkward. Preachers shouldn't flirt.

Miles shuffled forward in the line. But he almost could feel her over his shoulder, and twice he looked back. Those big beaming eyes took in his gaze without flinching.

The customs inspector had opened all six bags belonging to a fat middle-aged man in pink trousers and a green golf shirt. The official burrowed through the belongings, tossing articles out until a crumbled mound of clothing had formed on the countertop. At last, he nodded. He stood back, arms crossed, and looked impatient while the guy tried to stuff his possessions back in the suitcase.

The official broke into a smile when Miles stepped forward. "Preacher. Welcome back. Anything to declare?"

"Just a bottle of rum—medicinal." Miles winked at the official.

"Yes, Reverend. Keep off the chill these cool nights. You can pass right through."

Miles was about to when the brown-haired woman looped both her arms around his left one and nuzzled his shoulder. She shot her one-size-too-big smile at the customs man and wrinkled her nose. "Come on, dear. He said we could go. People are waiting." Her knee came up behind Miles and she gave the smallest of shoves, just enough to cause him to take a stumbling step forward. The customs agent looked confused, but when Miles said nothing, the agent grinned again—broader this time.

Once beyond the counter, Miles turned to demand an explanation.

The woman dropped his arm. Without a word, she vanished into the crowd. Miles checked his wallet. To his relief, it was still there. But he had to admit, her little trick had been smooth—whatever it was.

If anything, the crowd was even thicker and more confused at the taxi stand than it had been in the customs area. Miles waited for fifteen minutes and made no discernible progress. Finally, he thought, somewhat guiltily, that he might use the line-cutting clout clerical attire always carried. After the meeting with his brother and Nettleship and then a miserable twenty-four hours in Miami trying unsuccessfully to raise a half-million, and coming back with pledges totaling $14,900, all Miles wanted to do was to get to his boat, have a drink or two to calm down, and sleep. He tugged at his collar to make sure it was visible.

But his conscience got the better of him. So he ended up waiting another thirty minutes before he stood beside the dispatcher. The dispatcher looked at him almost angrily, but softened as soon as he saw who Miles was. "One minute, Reverend," he said, planting two fingers in his mouth and whistling.

While Miles waited, he felt a gentle tapping on his right ankle. He looked down. The beggar with the dark glasses and white cane sat on the sidewalk in the spot he always occupied—strategically situated so anyone getting into a cab had to trip over him precisely at the point when he or she was most likely to have a wallet out to tip a porter. Miles was suspect of the beggar's blindness. When occasion demanded, he had an uncanny ability to dodge dropped suitcases. Still, Miles always slipped him two dollars—just in case. He surrendered the same sum to the dispatcher, and to the porter who had insisted on carrying his single fake-leather Samsonite bag, even though Miles had volunteered to carry it himself.

An immense ship of a Cadillac—mid-seventies vintage—nosed up to the curb. Embarrassed by the size of the car, Miles eased himself in through the opened door. The uniformed chauffeur closed the door with a solid thunk. But instead of going to his own door, he walked behind the car and opened the other rear door.

The dirty haversack came in first, tossed so it skidded across the floor and landed at Miles's feet. The woman with the big eyes followed.

Not saying a word, she retrieved her sack, rummaged in it,

37

and brought out a pint bottle of Cockspur rum. "Goddamn bastards," she muttered, and upended the bottle. Her Adams apple bobbed four times. She lowered the bottle and handed it to Miles. "You indulge, Rev?"

"Thank you," he said, and for some reason immediately wished he had uttered something slightly more appropriate.

"Bastards," she muttered again. Her voice had a husky, softened twang.

The limo crept into the traffic. Apparently, she was just going to go ahead and vent her rage, whether he liked it or not. "Never, never, never again am I going to willingly fly Bahamasair. You got a Bible on you, Rev, I'll swear. I mean, I had a confirmed reservation on this afternoon's flight to Andros. And the jerks bump me. Me! Say I should have been at the check-in counter an hour before flight time. Well, an hour before flight time, I was in the air on their own damn flight from Miami—an hour and forty-five minutes late. Did that make much of an impression? Fat chance, Rev. Then they tell me I'll have to wait two days—*two days*—for the next available seat. So what am I supposed to do in Nassau for two days. . . . Hey, you mind?"

She put out her hand for the bottle.

"My apologies," said Miles.

For some reason, what he said seemed to upset her. She took a drink and looked out her window at the fringes of Lake Killarney, which was blue and inviting under the clear sky. She was apparently content to let all further conversation drop.

Miles decided that something—anything—was better than the silence, which looked as if it was fast heading into the uncomfortable range. "That was a very, should I say interesting, stunt you pulled at customs," he said.

She opened her mouth and let out a single peal of laughter. "Did you like that? Hope I didn't piss you off or anything. It's just . . ." She paused and swigged. "Let's just say me and customs agents don't get along too well as a rule, and that guy looked like a ripe prick." She handed him the bottle. "Plus, I thought you were kind of interesting-looking—for a preacher."

He cleared his throat and straightened his back.

"Just joking. I mean, for God's sake—excuse the pun, Rev—" She tossed her brown curls and laughed, a loud, open-mouthed cackle. But whatever she had begun to say was obviously going to remain unspoken. "Well anyways, nice to meet you, Rev. Name's Stormy. Stormy Lake." She stuck out a hand.

He went to shake it. She tapped his fingers away. "The bottle, please. I wanted you to pass me the bottle."

Twenty-five minutes later, the Caddy stopped at the narrow lane leading under Paradise Island Bridge to Potter's Cay. Miles steeled himself, tightening his neck muscles and setting his jaw in stern preparation for the colorful commercial gauntlet that separated him from the *Come to Jesus Cruiser.* He withdrew his wallet and pulled out just enough to pay off the cabbie and get Stormy to some downtown budget hotel. The wallet went back into his hip pocket, which Miles buttoned and patted to make sure all was secure.

It was always a tough run for an inveterate buyer like Miles. From the sterns of sloops moored to the dock, fishermen hawked their gleaming silver-sided wares: kingfish, grouper, dolphin, mackerel. Women in makeshift stalls onshore bawled at each other and at passersby over piles of pumpkin, yams, finger bananas, miniature Eleutheran pineapples, mangoes, sugar apples, and papayas.

And there were even a few noncommercial sideshows to slow a determined person's progress. At that moment, a rickety crane hoisted a Dodge van over the rear deck of an Out Island mail boat. The van listed toward the rear and twisted from side to side, looking as if it was doomed to plunge into the water or come crashing down on the three crates of live chickens that shared the boat with a dozen passengers.

"I get off here. Been . . . let's say interesting," said Miles.

Stormy didn't hear him. She looked at the crane crew, eight guys with no obvious leader, each pointing and gesturing in different directions, all shouting.

"Pardon," she said.

"I said I get off here."

She became animated. "Look, we both got an evening to kill. I was thinking I've been kind of an imposition on you. So, what about dinner at some restaurant around here. I'll even pay." She paused. "For my share."

Miles considered her offer. Part of him wanted to say yes. Stormy amused him. He found her refreshing after his dreary stint in Naples and Miami. But another part knew it was all wrong. He was dead tired. And there was the matter of Prue. "Thanks. But I'm exhausted."

"Sure, Rev." He thought he detected a clear, sweet note of relief. "No big deal."

With a thud, the van dropped onto the boat's deck, allowing a few inches on either side for chicken crates and the knees of two elderly women passengers. The crane men looked at their handiwork, the only people on the wharf who displayed any amazement that the vehicle had landed safely and on target.

Miles took his suitcase from the driver and threw himself into the throngs on the dock, keeping his eyes on an empty patch of blue midway up the sky, dead ahead of him, and trying his best not to hear the huckster calls. And he did pretty well—a lot better than usual, in fact. But when the little girl, hair done in at least three dozen two-inch braids, whimpered "Mister, Mister," he looked down, made eye contact, and was doomed. A minute later, he straightened up, squared his jaw, found that same empty place in the sky—three dollars poorer and possessor of a hand of green bananas. Four paces later, an old woman coaxed him into buying a two-dollar papaw, moderately over-ripe and of which he had no need. The young man with the carvings asked twenty dollars for a sculpture of a woman's face, and seemed hurt when Miles didn't even bother to try to talk him down. But it was the guy selling white T-shirts emblazoned with the face of Michael Jackson who would long remember it as a banner afternoon: the afternoon the preacher with the bent nose came out of nowhere and, muttering something about senior students loving them, bought out his entire stock—three dozen assorted sizes. Paid for them in cash—$324.

So juggling his suitcase, a hand of bananas, one overripe papaw, a sculpture, and a box containing three dozen Michael Jackson T-shirts, Miles finally reached *Come to Jesus Cruiser*. It was moored between two fishermen's boats, and looked inviting with its long, low, old-fashioned lines, bright white hull and mahogany topsides. Miles glanced back, half-expecting he'd see the woman who called herself Stormy coming toward him. But she wasn't.

Once aboard, Miles shed his Sears suit coat, which was wet and stained with sweat. The breeze cooled his back. He kicked off his sandals, removed his socks in two deft strokes, and loosened his clerical collar. Comfortable for the first time in two days, he padded barefoot across the teak deck, tending to the routine of opening up: jiggling the padlock on the cabin door, unscrewing the porthole latches and throwing them wide to drive out the heavy smells of new varnish, diesel, and mildew. He tossed his suitcase and discarded garments onto one of the V berths in the bow, fished out the quart of duty-free Appleton's, and took it and a reasonably clean-looking plastic tumbler topsides, where he dropped into a chaise longue and let the setting sun warm his face.

No more than five minutes later, the first real drink of the day (Miles didn't count the nips he had taken from Stormy's bottle) began to work its own warm magic. He relaxed. Each heartbeat pumped soothing waves through his body and to every extremity. That little nagging headache vanished. Miles poured himself another three fingers.

It had, after all, been a heck of a two days. First, the session with Ira and Nettleship—in a hot tub, of all places. Next, the frustrating day in Miami, visiting and calling big donors to the Savior Network. Turned down nearly every time. In most cases because Nettleship had been there first trying to raise money for Celestial City. Business bad. Short of funds. Can't do anything now; see me in the New Year. Sounds great, but I have to discuss it with my associates. Miles had called every rich person he knew, and in return received a verbal bouquet containing every hackneyed excuse there was.

The realities of the previous day gave way to musings about The Vale: the boys, in the fading afternoon sun, playing ball on the diamond, Miles at bat, knocking a ball into the sky, farther and farther. . . .

A sudden lurch startled Miles. The *Come to Jesus Cruiser* dipped as someone stepped onto the gunwale. Miles snapped his head up and put his hands on the deck for support. One hit the bottle of Appleton's. It toppled and shattered against the brass latch on the engine-compartment lid.

Miles waffled between the twin problems of retrieving what might or might not have been left of the rum and identifying the person who had just come aboard. Self-preservation finally dictated that he squint into the sunlight and deal with the intruder.

"Hiya, Rev. Not a bad-looking stinkpot you got here. You going to sit there batting your eyes, or you going to help a lady with these groceries?" asked the woman who called herself Stormy Lake.

Ninety minutes later, Miles and Stormy sat in the cruiser's stern, both in folding deck chairs, bare feet propped against the gunwale, watching the lights of cars crossing Paradise Island Bridge.

"You got any booze aboard?" asked Stormy, breaking the silence that had begun the moment they'd both started to wolf the hasty meal she had stirred up in the galley: filets of grouper, well peppered, buttered, and browned with onion slices; fried plantain; a heap of fresh green beans; steamed carrots.

"A heel of overproof rum do? I keep an emergency stash way up in the bow under the V berth. Port side. You'll find it under the life jackets and lines."

"Well, Rev, if it's the only bottle you have, that makes this pretty much an emergency situation by definition, I'd say." Stormy took the dirty plates down to the galley. Miles enjoyed the way her white dress showed her long, tanned legs.

For five minutes, Stormy sent out a cacophony of clatters, clinks, tingles, and clunks.

"You dismantling my galley?" Miles called.

"Please! I'm concentrating."

When she emerged, wearing Miles's suit coat over her dress, Stormy brandished a frosted pitcher. "Take the juice of one grapefruit, ten oranges, four key limes, and one lemon, combine with equal measures of cane-sugar syrup and overproof rum, and pour over crushed ice. A genuine Stormy's Caribbean Cooler. Not for the faint of heart. And for dessert, a plate of Peek Freans Fruit Cremes—only marginally stale."

She put the plate and pitcher on the gunwale and poured two glasses. "Mud in your eye," she said.

They ticked plastic tumblers and drank. The concoction went down easily, then hit Miles like a punch to the head. "Lethal stuff," he said.

"Old family recipe."

"And an excellent meal. I'm surprised."

She snorted. "Surprised I can cook? Look, Rev, do me a favor and don't tell anyone. I happen to like cooking, okay? My single character flaw. Aside from that, I'm a total reprobate, I swear. Anyway, I was forced to learn to cook. I'm part owner of a sailboat. Take charters from time to time. You get these jokers who survive all year long on wifey's microwaved TV dinners cooked up in vast suburban kitchens and they expect me to be a goddamn seagoing Alice Waters in a galley about the size of a phone booth."

"That what you do for a living—charter?"

"Only when we run out of dough. Rest of the time, I like to lie around. Read mediocre novels. Drink rum. Get stoned. Sunbathe nude. All the stuff the preachers warned me against. Here, have a cookie."

He took one and held out his glass for a refill.

"Go easy on this, Rev, or you'll end up doing something you'll regret." She shot him a quick, kooky "just joking" smile.

The gesture was unnecessary. Rum punches or not, he was prepared to monitor his behavior carefully. He didn't find Stormy beautiful, or even what he'd call pretty, not in a conventional way. Eyes were too big; smile too wide. But there was something undeniably sensual about her, something he had trouble pinning down. He settled for lusty and yet incredibly innocent.

Miles drained most of his second glass. "I've been thinking about this afternoon. At customs. I mean you weren't . . . You haven't . . ." He shook his head and brought his hands forward in a motion that made it look as if he was trying to sweep gnats away from in front of his eyes. "Sorry. Forget it. None of my business. We should talk about something else."

"You afraid I was carrying a little contraband across? Afraid the DEA storm troopers will come aboard at any moment and seize this boat—along with your good name?"

"I've lived in the Bahamas long enough to know that someone like yourself isn't exactly on a pleasure trip. And then when you said that part about how you didn't get along with customs agents—"

"Well, it isn't what you think. I mean, I might have had a teensy little smidgen on me—strictly for personal use—but I wasn't carrying commercial quantities. Hell, I'm not that dumb. Give a girl some credit."

"No need to get upset. Like I said, I shouldn't have brought

44

it up. I just thought that seeing as how you slid through customs on my arm, jumped in my taxi, and then cooked dinner for me—well, can you blame me for being a bit curious?"

Stormy twisted her lips into a smirk. "I dunno. Can I?" She snorted. "Anyhow, let's just leave it that I don't like it when people get all self-righteous. We can all point fingers. Even me. Who are you? Bet there's a story there."

Miles didn't say anything.

"I didn't mean that last bit."

Miles exhaled one long breath and shook his head. "Oh there's a story, all right," he said, and even though he didn't mean to—frankly had no desire to—the overproof rum started talking, and by the time it had finished thirty-eight minutes later, Miles had gone and told her the whole damn, sorry thing.

"You mind if I smoke?" Stormy asked after he finished describing his fruitless day in Miami. "I promise to throw it overboard if any of the local narcs toddle by."

Without waiting for Miles to reply, Stormy extracted a neat white joint from behind her ear and lit it. She inhaled deeply and the air around the cockpit became heavy with sweet smoke.

Miles, who had been rendered melodramatic by his own sad tale—that and the rum—said, "I think I honestly love The Vale. That's what I call my mission school on Andros. Love the work. Love the simplicity. Love the kids, especially. There isn't anything I wouldn't do for those little devils. And maybe I've even done some good."

Stormy inhaled again and, holding her breath, gestured toward Miles with the joint. He took it and examined it doubtfully, looked at his rum glass and the pitcher—both nearly empty—and put the joint to his mouth. Stormy's lips had left the end wet. He inhaled.

It felt as if someone had poured a burning liquid into his lungs. He staggered to his feet, half bent over and coughing. He coughed until he saw red and thought he never again would be able to draw a full breath. Stormy threw an arm over his shoulder and rapped him on the back with her free hand.

The coughing subsided to the occasional rattle. Miles grabbed the pitcher and refilled his tumbler with the ice-water dregs. "Better stick with this," he said, panting.

Stormy took her arm from his shoulder and reached down for the joint, still clenched between his fingers. She calmly sucked down a lungful of smoke. "Sounds like you might live. So go on. Why all the doubt, Rev? Seems to me you help one single goddamn Bahamian kid get a better life, you done more good than ninety-nine point nine percent of the rest of us—even if you *are* the type of guy who slobbers all over someone else's joint."

Miles gulped air and sat on the gunwale beside her. "You ever heard of the Savior Network?"

"That the outfit where the guy got caught in the sack with his secretary?"

"No. Not so large as that one. But the same idea. Television evangelism. I used to preach there. Reached millions of viewers—"

"So what happened? Caught diddling a choirboy?"

"No. More mundane than all that. Just got tired of the commercial side of the whole thing: millions of dollars' worth of equipment, state-of-the-art studios, executive offices and bureaucrats to fill them, enough BMWs to start a dealership. It's going to sound corny to you, but it seemed we had gotten so far from the original purpose . . . You just have to look at Christ and the disciples. You do remember who they are? Or even my father, who started the ministry from a patched-up old circus tent. Look how they spread the word. So one day about seven years ago, some old guy died and left us his fishing lodge on Andros. I went over with a real estate man, intending to evaluate the place and unload it. Got there. Fell in love with the island, the people. And stayed."

"I can sympathize with that. You're looking at a girl who

came down here on a two-week vacation. That was eleven years ago. I mean, I haven't saved many souls, may have even led the odd one astray. But it's sort of the same thing—liking the people and all. Besides, where else in the world can a Utah girl sit on the back of an old Chris drinking rum and blowing dope with a preacher—a not-too-bad-looking one?"

She reached out and pinched the tip of his nose. "It's the snout that does it. Who busted it? Old lover?"

He tweaked her nose, which was small and slightly upturned. "Now look who's asking someone to tell dark tales of the past," he said, smiling.

"Why the dirty rotten pricks," Stormy said with traces of a slur in her husky voice. It was well into the night, with a full complement of southern constellations overhead and a crescent moon that looked almost fake hanging midair over the bridge to Paradise Island. "I can't believe you're just gonna sit around and let the bastards sell The Vale out from under you."

"There's not a thing I can do. My brother has all the power."

"Still no reason just to sit back and take it. I mean, even I know that the damn Bible says that the Lord helps those that help themselves. You even told me earlier you'd do anything for those kids. So get your butt in gear and do something."

Miles picked up the pitcher for the fifth time in as many minutes. As it had been the previous four times, it was dry. He shook his head sadly. "The Bible doesn't say that. It was Ben Franklin, and he probably stole it from Aesop. The Bible tells us to put our trust in God. And in this case, there's not much else to do. Meanwhile, looks like we've even run out of booze."

"Fear not, Rev, a little hoo-ha is just what a person needs at a moment like this. I'll even give you lessons on how to smoke it without coughing your guts out. Imagine. Me teaching a preacher how to blow dope." She put her hands to her cheekbones and giggled.

"Really, I don't—"

"Come on Rev. It'll bust you out of this goddamn depression. Any port in a storm. Bible say that?"

Forty minutes—and two joints of Santa Marta—later, Stormy tipped her head skyward and let out a whoop of laughter. "Prue? Her name's Prue? You gotta be shitting me, Rev. They don't really name people Prue anymore, do they?"

"Quiet, Stormy. You'll wake up the whole dock." He drew down smoke and passed joint number three back to Stormy. After he exhaled, he broke out in giggles. "Her folks were missionaries in Japan after the war. Had four daughters. Ready for the other names? Faith, Hope, Charity."

Stormy whooped again, louder this time. A Bahamian voice grunted a few complaining syllables from the cabin of a nearby mail boat. She stifled her laughs, but her sides still rose and fell. "Faith, Hope, and Charity—and just your luck to get stuck with Prudence. Tell me, is she wild in the sack?"

Laughter overcame her and she leaned her head against Miles's chest for support.

"Ooops. Shouldn't have asked that. Personal. Sorry, Rev." She burrowed her face in his chest to stifle another series of giggles.

The giggles wouldn't stop. She kept her face burrowed, occasionally coming up for air, and every time being overcome by another series of giggles. For his own part, Miles became very aware of his right arm. He couldn't recall being so aware of an extremity since his early dating experiences in the backseat of a 1964 Olds. The arm hung dead and useless, sandwiched between them. More to get it out of the way than anything else—he told himself—Miles raised it until his fingers touched her shoulder.

That stopped the giggling. "Hey, Rev, better watch it. I should tell you that until a minute ago, I had two ulterior motives."

"Do tell."

"Well, one was to bum a ride across to Andros with you. You see, I sorta need to get there fast."

"That's certainly no problem. I leave first thing tomorrow. You said two ulterior motives?"

"Were two. Dear, sweet Prue's existence kind of puts a damper on ulterior motive number two."

Miles bent down and kissed her lightly on the lips. She pushed away.

"Honest, Rev, I'm warning you. Watch it."

"I'll consider myself warned."

This time, he kissed her long and fully. She was still for a moment. Then her lips responded, alive and probing.

They did an awkward dance across the rear deck, clutching each other, kissing, grasping, breathing hard, both wanting to take the shortest route to the berth below, but neither willing to break the embrace for fear that whatever wave of passion, or lust, had caught them would pass, leaving them a little embarrassed and painfully aware of the impossible truth of their situation.

Miles slid his hands down her back, working slowly across her rib cage and sides. He pressed her close. She thrust her hips against him . . . withdrew . . . then thrust again.

"Get the hell down there. Quickly, or something's liable to happen right here," she said.

They dove headlong onto the V berth, kicking Miles's belongings to the floor. She rolled on top of him and for a moment gazed at his face. "You sexy bugger," she said. One by one, her fingers tickled the buttons of his shirt, opening it slowly, toying with the moist hairs of his chest, playing little circles around his nipples. Her fingers tracked down across his stomach, paused and played around his waist, then slowly moved lower, stroking.

Miles thought he would explode right there. He drew her down for a long kiss and let his hands pull her dress up until his fingertips felt the elastic at the top of her panties. The fingers retraced their route, drawing the panties with them.

"Let's get these goddamn clothes off," she said. She pushed herself into a sitting position, ripped away the suit coat, and, with a single rustling sweep, pulled the dress over her head. She deftly flicked off her panties and then turned to Miles, removing his trousers. She bent to him, and in a series of kisses and nibbles, she worked her way from his groin, across the tender skin of his stomach, his chest, to his lips. With her hand, she took him and guided him inside her.

Miles thought he was going to come that instant. But he held back, the irresistible pressure within him building, each wave taking him almost to the point of climax, then guiding him to yet another crest, higher, impossibly higher. The old Chris rocked and squeaked and groaned that night like it never had before as Stormy's vigorous, earnest lovemaking took Miles to crest after crest of ecstasy. Hours later, it seemed, she arched her back, stiffened, quivered as Miles exploded deep inside her, and fell against his chest, digging her fingernails into his shoulders, racked by a series of aftershocks and tremors that seemed as if they would never stop.

She rolled free and lay on her back, looking at the ceiling. "Guess that's what they mean when they say 'I saw the light,' " she said.

Beside her, Miles moaned weakly, tried to laugh, but came out with something that sounded more like a series of sniffs.

She leaned on one elbow. Her eyes had regained that old kooky sparkle. It took a minute or two, but Miles eventually realized what was happening. Stormy was ready again. Grinning, she slid back on top of him. "At least now I won't have to fib to you about how I got my nickname."

The hangover was as nasty as any Miles could remember, fueled by a fierce burning core somewhere deep between the hemispheres of his cerebrum. It came with more than the usual fuzziness and fatigue—well-earned fatigue. When Miles concentrated, there was also a patina of depression. But through it all cut a single piercing ray of shame.

With an instant coffee on the back deck, he was all but oblivious to the early-morning dockside bustle. Prue occupied his thoughts. Good, honest Prue. Right now conducting the morning chapel service. Leading the children in a hymn. Carrying on his work, while he sat on the back of his boat, groggy and burned-out, still smelling the sweet smell of Stormy. If Prue was there now, he would fall down on his knees and beg forgiveness.

But Prue wasn't there. It was Stormy who came out of the cabin, wearing a pair of ultrashort khaki cutoffs and a bikini top. She looked good, with her long brown legs and small breasts. Some of the previous night's lust returned, but in the light of day, it angered Miles.

"Hiya, Rev," she said.

"Good morning." He tried to force a smile.

It didn't fool Stormy a bit. "Ooops. Nearly forgot. This is the dreaded morning after. We get to find out what the other person really looks like." She struck a pose.

"You look wonderful," Miles said. It was the truth—but delivered flatly, without enthusiasm.

"Yeah, well you look like an old hound caught stealing a steak from the barbecue."

"Hung over."

"Hung over, my ass." She came to him and put a hand on his shoulder. "No big deal, Rev. Nothing marriage-wrecking or home-breaking about what went on between me and you last night. Just a little roll in the hay."

"Stormy, I'm sorry—"

"Don't fucking apologize. I hate it when men try to apologize. It's one of your gender's worst faults."

"There's Prue."

"Hey, Rev. I'm a big girl. I get the picture."

She went below and a few minutes later came back in her

light dress and carrying her backpack. "I think I'll go see what Bahamasair is up to. Never know. Might be able to get me across today."

"I'll be quite happy to take you across. There's no sense spending the money when I'm going there today anyway."

"Ticket's already paid for, Rev," said Stormy. She hopped to the gunwale, then onto the wharf.

"Stormy, it's just a ride across. Nothing's—"

She put down her bag and crossed her arms. "Just a ride across? You're nuts, if you really believe that. I'll level with you, Rev. For a few minutes last night, I thought, You know, Storm, a girl could do worse. That's what I actually thought—*me,* if you can imagine—lying in there after you went to sleep: You know, Storm, a girl could do worse."

She rolled her eyes and slapped her temple. "First time a thought like that's crossed my mind in years. I gotta learn to lay off that Santa Marta shit."

Chapter 5

Montano had called the meeting. Urgent, he'd claimed. Insisted Ira be there by 10:00 A.M. A forty-minute drive—halfway to Immokalee. And on Saturday, Ira's busiest day. The day he prepared for his weekly broadcast, which never came easily. Not like it did for his brother, who could step off a plane from the Bahamas green with a hangover, scribble a few notes on the back of an envelope, slip into his whites, and belt out a sermon that would keep Nettleship and his crew busy counting for a month.

Normally, Ira would never have interrupted his Saturday preparations. But an urgent call from Montano concerned only one thing: money. So Ira put on a powder blue suit, substituted a gold chain for the tie, slipped open the top three buttons of his silk shirt, and jumped into the network's BMW 325—the red convertible, his favorite. At precisely ten o'clock, Ira wheeled up to the electric gate at the base of the lane leading to Montano's impossibly long new, ranch-style mansion, decidedly out of place along a road of trailers and plain three-bedroom bungalows. The gate swung open, directed by an electronic command from Montano's security office.

As always, Montano left Ira waiting on the patio of his sprawling house for a full fifteen minutes in the blazing sun and airless ninety-one-degree heat. And, also as always, Montano's hired goon came out first.

The goon, whose name was Sammy Hodges, resembled one

of those 1940s refrigerators, except in his case, one upon which somebody had carefully centered a grapefruit. The small head, capped by a blond crew cut, was planted directly on a massive square-shouldered body, with no hint of neck vertebrae between. At five eleven and a few ounces either side of 263 pounds of muscle, sinew, ligament, and bone, Sammy did indeed have the bulk and hardness of a vintage appliance, one from the days when they still built them to last. Unfortunately, when it came to intelligence, Sammy also had much in common with a pre-microchip fridge. He got by as a tackle for Alabama for four years in the late 1970s, but sports writers credited his sheer stupidity, not any lack of physical might, with ending his single-game pro stint as a Dolphin. One columnist speculated that the 63 Sammy wore on his jersey was responsible. It told opposing linemen Sammy's IQ.

Sammy gave Ira the ritual frisk. Finding nothing out of order, he walked to both corners of the patio, and squinted importantly down the long driveway, which held his boss's black 944 Turbo Porsche and Ira's BMW. He looked harder at the gaggle of black and Hispanic workers bent over rows of tomatoes beyond the royal palms that delineated the edge of the groomed lawn, at the same time as they partially camouflaged a barb wire-topped chain-link fence. Satisfied no obvious dangers awaited his boss, Sammy tugged to straighten his cream-colored blazer. Fully two sizes too small, it concealed neither the crescent moon of shirttail stuck out the back nor, in front, the ugly bulge of his handgun.

"Morning, Pastor. The boss will be with you directly." Sammy spoke with a high-pitched drawl, a cross between Burl Ives and Truman Capote. All in all, surprisingly articulate-sounding, given its source.

Ira had no intention of favoring Sammy with a response, but he was spared being rude by Montano's entrance. Jorge Montano burst upon the patio, clicking across the marble flags at his perpetual clip, those last few walking paces preceding a sprint. A crisp little man, looking about half of his forty-eight years, he favored white suits and black string ties—Madison Avenue's image of a Colombian coffee grower.

Montano flashed a white-toothed smile. His eyes crinkled. He shoved out a brown hand. Ira accepted it limply, taking in a waft of hair oil and cologne. The scent reminded him of Juicy Fruit gum.

"Coffee," Montano said energetically. "Sammy, have Maria bring us coffee." He stopped himself and put on a sad face. "But, the pastor does not drink coffee. Perhaps you would like a little . . ." He let his question trail off.

"Have any plain water? Hot. With a slice of lemon."

Montano let his face crumble into a grimace. But as if maintaining such a foul demeanor was beyond his facial muscles' ability, his twinkling grin snapped back into place.

"What I do not understand is how one who lives so cleanly can—" Montano patted his own belly which was as flat and tight as a teenaged high hurdler's. "You are beginning to look a little . . . a little healthy . . . through the middle, Pastor. Perhaps it is the cooking of this young wife, no?"

Ira sat up with his back against the wrought-iron chair and sucked in his stomach. "Not getting enough exercise," he said, wishing Montano would come to the point—any point other than his own swelling midriff.

"No exercise. Then perhaps the wife is too young." Montano's face broke into its best smile, the one that gave a flash of gold bicuspid. He shared a forced "Ha-ha" with Sammy, whose mouth hung open and whose brow was crimped, as if he was wrestling with a ten-step trigonometry problem.

Ira didn't even attempt to show amusement.

Montano stopped smiling. His look went from jovial to something close to lethal, stayed there a moment, then settled on inscrutable—his down-to-business mug.

"So good of you to come out here, Pastor. And on a Saturday, of all days. I wish I had good news, but—" He stopped talking and opened his palms to the sky in supplication. The silence lasted just long enough to become irritating. "—but it is the nature of bad news that it cannot wait. Good news we could have discussed Monday, perhaps over lunch. Bad news . . ." He trailed off. That lethal look came back. "Sammy. Coffee. And the pastor's . . ."

"Yes, jefe," Sammy said, and showing surprising speed for such a blocky man, he ran toward the kitchen wing. On the field, it would have been a seventy-five-yard return.

Montano fished in his pocket and found a small pearl-handled pocket knife with silver trim. It looked innocent enough, not much bigger than a Cub Scout's standard issue. Montano stroked it unconsciously, then, with a *whi-i-i-i-t-t,* the blade leapt out, as bright as a mirror in the sunlight. He thumbed it to test for sharpness, and finding all to his satisfaction, he settled into the job of cleaning his fingernails, which were white and square-cut and showed no sign of ever having come into contact with dirt—certainly not of the kind you can scrape away with a knife.

"The bad news," Montano went on, moving from manicured thumb to index finger, "is that there might be a small delay in my getting you the money for the Celestial City project. Problems. Problems at the other end," he said, turning his palms upward in a gesture that could have been one of resignation but also served as a way to brandish the blade at Ira. "I hope this will cause no problems at your end." There was a flash of the lethal look, then the smile.

Ira grunted as a jab of pain tore at his diaphragm. Stress? Angina? Not for the first time, he wondered, and cursed the doctors who claimed there was nothing wrong. He'd have to go over to Miami and have a proper specialist look at him. Do some tests or something. When the pain eased, Ira looked up. Montano smiled.

"Another delay?" Ira said. "First you were going to get us the money by early December. Then January. Then the last week of January. Now . . . Jorge, the banks are breathing down my neck. I honestly don't think we can last much longer."

"You'll think of something."

"There's nothing. We're in over our heads. Mortgaged to the hilt. I even sold off our Andros property last week. Deal closes the end of the month. Just in time to pay the bank. But I tell you, that's not going to see us through for very long. Month tops."

"Andros property? I had no idea it was so—" Montano had to pause and search the air for a word. "So desirable."

"Deal came through a local lawyer. But don't worry. He assured me the money is there."

"You want my personal advice? Personally, I do not like to depend on people I don't know. People who have to hide their dealings behind a lawyer. I am nervous." Montano's voice was pleasant and calm, but each syllable of the last sentence was punctuated with a delicate flick of the knife.

Before Ira could say anything, a door opened at the far end of the patio and a small dark woman, more Indian than Spanish, came out with a silver tray. Sammy, like an obedient albino gorilla, shambled behind her. They were all silent as the woman put down two Minton cups and saucers, smiled nervously, then tucked the empty tray under her arm and flitted away.

"Jorge, I don't think you understand how desperate the network is, financially speaking."

Montano put the knife down and lifted both cup and saucer to his face, palm under saucer, pinky extended from cup. He sniffed the steam and let out an "Aaaah." Then he sipped. "No one in the world makes a better cup of coffee than Maria. That is why I brought her with me." He returned the cup and saucer to the table and retrieved the knife. "Pastor, you underestimate me. Yes, I understand how troubled your church is. Understand all too well. But that is your problem. I entered this deal in good faith. For almost one year now, I have depended upon it. It is the basket into which I plan to put all my family's eggs.

Very soon—when, I cannot precisely tell—there will be a lot of eggs, and they will need some place big and safe to go—Celestial City. You cannot tell me at this late stage that because of your poor management, my family's eggs might not have a basket. That, dear Pastor, would be bad. Bad. Bad. Bad." The blade traced three X's in the air midway over the table.

"Perhaps we should approach another party. Take on a partner."

The lethal look came back. "Do not ever mention that again," said Montano softly. "I am your partner. A very jealous partner. You do understand."

As if under Montano's command, every nerve fiber in Ira's gut fired at once, sending out a burning, twisting sensation. Ira winced. He took several deep breaths before he dared to look again at Montano. And when he did, Montano was smiling contentedly at the cup of coffee he had raised to his nose.

Nettleship should have been there. This was his fault. He had set up the meeting—when was it, a little over a year ago. Montano seemed perfect. A silent partner. Willing and able to invest the sort of funds no bank would consider. No questions asked. No risk too great. Anonymity was his only collateral. Ira wasn't stupid enough not to suspect the source of the dapper little Colombian's wealth. Sure wasn't the tomato fields that bordered his property. But there was hardly a builder or developer or contractor or banker in south Florida who would have been in a position to toss the first stone.

Montano drank from the cup. He kept his best crinkled coffee smile on his face after he finished. "But look at us. Bickering unnecessarily. You will find a way to keep things going until my funds come through. Of course you will. Partner."

Sammy stood at the far corner of the patio. Only when the BMW turned onto the paved highway and headed back toward I-75 did he rejoin his boss, who still sat at the table, the only change being that a freshly lit half corona had taken the knife's place in the fingers of his right hand.

"He looked scared good, jefe," said Sammy.

Montano gestured for the big man to sit. He had to admit he genuinely liked having Sammy around. He liked him because he was strong and dumb and loyal. He liked his innocence. He liked how he could use Sammy as a sounding board for his ideas and schemes, knowing that the stupid man would neither comprehend nor remember what was told him. Some people confided in their dogs. Montano confided in Sammy. But most of all, Montano liked Sammy because he was desperate. Nowhere else to go. No one else to befriend him. To boss him. To pay and house him. Desperation: It was the emotion you could most depend on. Not fickle like love or crazy like hate or street-smart like greed. Just beaten down, submissive. Desperate.

"Scared. But maybe not scared enough. Not desperate yet. Not like Fat Boy," said Montano.

Sammy chuckled. "Yump, Fat Boy was some scared. I've never seen anyone so scared."

"He had to be scared. He failed me. People must learn that they can never fail me. Worse, he lied," said Montano.

"Lied?"

"Bingo Martin was not much good as a man. Bone lazy. Smoked too much dope. But he had two good traits. He was honest. He could sail a boat. He delivered for our organization many times. Bingo Martin would not try a stupid double-cross like that. Fat Boy is holding something back. I suppose we could find out what. But that is not important right now. Now, it is crucial that the shipment be recovered. Soon. I've invested over a year in this plan. It cannot fall apart now. And I fear our preacher friend tells the truth about the banks."

"We going to scare the pastor like we did Fat Boy?"

Montano beamed and puffed the half corona. "Worse, Sammy. There are worse ways to scare a man like that."

*   *   *

Although neither Ira, Montano, nor Sammy knew it, another man had stood up, hands on hips, to watch with great interest as the BMW disappeared. A black guy in his late twenties, at six foot, a little tall to spend his days comfortably bent over tomato plants, stood from amid the gaggle of field-workers and rubbed the muscles of his lower back. It had been a perpetual source of a nagging low-level pain for nearly a year, ever since he had been reduced to the life of a itinerant field hand. He checked his watch. The preacher had been there only twenty minutes this time. That information, along with the Bimmer's tag number, was filed in the black guy's photographic memory, where it would be safe until he could enter it into his Zenith 2000 laptop.

"Hey, fella. Maybe you oughta get back to work." It was the foreman, a sunburned redheaded man who spent his days behind the wheel of a five-ton truck, one freckled arm hanging out the window.

"Yea-suh," said the black, whose name was Cal Cooligan.

"You ain't never gonna be able to afford one of them fancy cars, anyhow, so no sense lookin'."

A couple of the other workers laughed, but they didn't stop filling their buckets with the hard green fruits.

"Yea-suh," said Cal again, dropping a tomato into his own bucket.

Truth be known, Cooligan's own BMW, a 735iL, was under its custom-cut canvas cover in the garage of the beachfront condo Cooligan owned on Sanibel. But he had seen condo and car only three times since being put in charge of monitoring the comings and goings at Montano's place.

Home, at least for the duration of this assignment, was a frame shack on a dirt side street in Immokalee, not too much worse from what Cal and his little sister, Claire, had been born and brought up in back in East St. Louis, but a far cry from where he thought he'd end up after graduating second in his class at Harvard Law School.

*   *   *

Miles Farnsworth had his first drink that Saturday, a bottle of Beck's, well chilled and streaming with droplets of condensation, just a few minutes after Cal resumed his tomato picking.

The *Come to Jesus Cruiser* had cleared the lighthouse on the point of Paradise Island, and Miles nosed it out into the channel on a course that would be slightly north of due west until he rounded the tip of the island of New Providence. The beer, one of a dozen he had picked up on the dock at the last minute, came from a portable plastic cooler on the floor next to the wheel. Miles had promised himself that he would wait until after noon before uncapping one. But now that he was alone, with only his headache and shame, a beer—just one, mind you—seemed to make good sense.

Beer number two was sent down to complete the job number one had not quite finished. Miles opened it as the *Come to Jesus Cruiser* passed the white mansions of Lyford Cay and moved from the pale turquoise of the sand shallows into the deep blue water of the Tongue of the Ocean. The wind had kicked up, and the old Chris bucked and nudged through the roll that came at it from across the stern. Miles's third beer was a present he made to himself to celebrate the liberated sensation he always felt when he finally put the island of New Providence, and civilization, astern. Ahead lay only the line of horizon where the dark blue sea met sky. The twin 250 cubic–inch GM motors grumbled to each other in throaty bass notes. The bow plowed into the waves, churning up white froth and spray, sending small schools of flying fish skipping and scuttling across the blue crests. It would take seven hours for the flat silhouette of Andros to come into view, which was just fine with Miles. He needed the time to think—to think about the future of The Vale, and to sort out the previous evening.

Beer number four was consumed to grease the thinking process. It was beer number four, finished by 11:45 A.M., that put Miles over the line.

*   *   *

Beer twelve had been gone for only twenty minutes when Miles finally idled up Fresh Creek toward the faded and bent planks and encrusted piles that served as a wharf for The Vale. It was six o'clock, and although there was enough twilight to guide the boat by, lights had already come on in the ornate Victorian main building, which had originally served as the dining hall and servants' quarters during The Vale's fishing camp incarnation. In those days, guests were housed in any of a dozen small cottages scattered about the grounds. The cottages were now dormitories.

Miles had to concentrate hard to bring the Chris through the cut between two submerged coral outcrops, and, too late, he realized his approach was fast. He threw both throttle handles into reverse. The engines roared. The stern kicked and settled, and *Come to Jesus Cruiser* stopped—undamaged but still twenty feet short of the wharf. Before Miles could react, a slow-moving tidal current grabbed the bow and swung it seaward. Miles tried to compensate by shoving the starboard engine into forward while letting the port one idle in reverse. He pivoted the boat around, but he was still fifteen feet off the dock when Prue appeared.

Her arrival was heralded by the slamming of a screen door somewhere in the darkness of the veranda that spanned the entire front of the main building. Little movements appeared in the twilight, then Miles saw the shadowy figures of the smallest children, a dozen of whom always seemed to follow Prue, scurrying in and out from behind her like a flock of feral chicks. Prue was dressed in a long navy skirt, too dark and heavy for the tropics. She also had on a similarly out-of-place gray cardigan and a white blouse that was just a bit too formal. Still, she seemed to float across the lawn under the casuarinas. Prue said nothing, but Miles could hear the excited chirping of the schoolchildren. Again, he tried to bring the boat in, conscious this time of setting a sober example for his charges. And he missed the wharf by only ten feet.

"Here, Miles," said Prue, her voice calm and flat with vowels inherited from her New England parents.

She brushed a strand of her light brown bob haircut to one side and took up a position on the far end of the wharf, the children strung out single file behind her, except for some of the smallest, who clung to her skirt. She held up one hand. Miles, abandoning the controls, managed to throw her a bowline. She tugged it once, and wrapped an expert clove hitch around a post. "All right, Miles. But watch the coral," she said; then louder, "Stand back, children."

Working both levers backward and forward, Miles inched the boat toward the dock with neither grace nor expertise. Prue finally cinched the bowline as tight as she could, and, stepping around the children, made her way to the stern, where she signaled for Miles to toss that line. As Miles stood stupidly on the stern, she and some of the larger students hauled the cruiser to the wharf hand over hand.

Even before the boat had been secured, the children began to swarm aboard, shouting to Miles in a dialect that, even after a half-dozen years in the Bahamas, he still could not always understand. "Hold it," he said, putting up his hands for silence.

The children obeyed instantly.

"You there—Simon," he said, pointing to one of the oldest, "take that box and go up to the dining room and open it. Hurry now."

The big boy took the box and, followed by a flock of his jabbering peers, ran back to the main building.

Prue waited until they were gone. "What's in the box?"

Miles tossed his fake-leather Samsonite on the weathered wharf boards and attempted to follow. The suitcase landed safely. Not so for Miles. He caught a toe on one of the boards, was forced to take two scuffing dance steps forward, and probably would have gone into the water on the other side had Prue not stopped him with an arm.

Miles regained his composure. Prue looked at him, keeping her arm through his. It took some time for Miles to realize she was waiting to be kissed. He pushed aside the all-too-clear image of Stormy Lake and obliged, in a way he might have kissed a maiden aunt. Prue put more effort into the greeting, pushing her body, which, while clearly not fat, was verging on cuddly, against Miles.

"Gotta fix the wharf," Miles finally said.

"That. Or stop drinking so much. How many did you have?"

"Just a couple of beers. I'm tired, that's all. Don't have my land legs."

Prue didn't answer as Miles picked up the suitcase. When she did speak, it was to repeat her earlier question, with a tone of playful sternness. "The box?"

"Oh, the box. Nothing much really. Just some cheap T-shirts I picked up in Nassau. Michael Jackson."

"Miles, we can't afford that."

"Just nine bucks each. And the kids will love 'em."

It seemed for a while that Prue was going to pursue the line of questioning, but in the end she turned and started walking along the wharf. Miles had intended to break the news about Ira's selling The Vale, but the moment had passed. He decided to wait.

She said, "Dinner's all ready. Grouper."

Miles said nothing.

"Something the matter?"

"No. No. Why?"

"Grouper. Your favorite. I had Clover prepare it specially. After your trip to the States and all. Thought you'd be delighted."

"I appreciate it, Prue."

"Don't seem very excited."

"Sorry. It's nothing. Had grouper last night, that's all."

*   *   *

The moment Miles most dreaded came not thirty seconds after his head hit the pillow that night.

Prue snapped her own bedside light off and lay still beside him. Miles listened to the whir of the overhead fan and felt himself sinking toward sleep, a sleep induced by half a fifth of rum on top of all that beer, but sleep nonetheless, and one that would excuse him from facing the inevitable.

When he made no move toward her, she propped herself on one elbow and pulled his shoulder. He rolled onto his back. Prue bent over, her breasts brushing his chest hair, and kissed him firmly and wetly on the mouth. Miles felt only the gnawing of guilt. The image of Stormy Lake, laughing, smiling, tossing back her thick brown waves of hair, came to him so clearly, it could have been her, not Prue, there in bed. He felt dirty. Miles slid out from under Prue. He sat on the side of the bed.

"Miles, what's bothering you? Something's happened," she said.

He rummaged in the nightstand in the darkness until his practiced fingers touched the bottle of Appleton's and a tumbler. He brought out the tumbler and filled it by the light cast by a digital clock radio.

"Miles, you have got to—"

"Sorry. Tonight's not the night." He took down most of the tumbler's contents in a mighty open-throated swallow. "Ira's going to shut this place down."

Prue gasped. "He can't."

Sparing no details, Miles proceeded to narrate the events of the previous three days, leaving out the bits about Stormy. Prue listened from her side of the bed, occasionally letting out a little gasp of disbelief, repeating the phrase "He can't" at least five times, finally concluding, "There has to be something we can do."

Miles refilled his glass. This time, Prue said nothing. "Tomorrow I will conduct the service. All of us—you, me, the children, the congregation—we will pray. Then I'm going to have to hustle my butt back over to the States to see if there isn't some group that can give us the money."

"Twenty-one days. That's not much time to find five hundred thousand dollars. It'll take a miracle."

"Like I said, we'll all have to pray to the Lord."

"Seems like a tall order—even for him."

"Prue!"

She settled into the pillows. "Sorry, Miles. Maybe we should try to get some sleep."

He finished his glass and lay beside her, letting the rum warm him.

"Miles," she said quietly.

He moaned.

"Miles, from the minute you stepped on the wharf, I could tell something terrible had happened."

Dot's Tavern occupied a single-story cinder-block structure on the main drag in Immokalee. Aside from a crudely stenciled ENTRANCE on one gray metal door, the low building had never felt a paintbrush, although some local graffitists had taken up the cause of exterior decor with black and fluorescent orange spray cans.

At 11:45 P.M., Saturday, December 10, Dot's had but six patrons. Two old field-workers sat at the bar. Both of them were baked to the color of the dirt in which the tomatoes and citrus grew. One addressed the other in slurred Spanish. His pal mumbled responses in English. At Dot's single ancient Brunswick table, two young Cubans played a vigorous, credible game of eight/fifteen. The Cubans paid no attention to the two old fellows at the bar; they were fixtures, like the six slashed vinyl-topped stools. But the youths frequently cast vicious looks at the two black guys sitting at a back booth. If the black guys had made eye contact, even once, a fight would have erupted. But they were careful not to. One of the black guys was DEA special agent Cal Cooligan. The other was his supervisor, Jesse Bones. They had met at Dot's, not to bash Cubans but to talk business.

Bones was a big, slow-moving man who sweated profusely into his khaki work clothes, clothes he had worn religiously all summer whenever he tended the prize hybrid hibiscus he cultivated in his Lighthouse Point backyard, clothes he had forbidden his wife to wash. The sweat was real enough. It had come in a flood when he shut the air conditioner off in his Olds Cutlass for the last hour of the drive across the state. Bones had been sniffing at the same Bud Light for the past hour, listening to Cal fill him in on the comings and goings at Montano's.

"Something's sure as hell going down," Bones finally said, as much to the Bud as to Cooligan. "When. What. How. That we don't know yet."

Cal sipped from his bourbon and water. "Soon. It's going to be soon."

"Maybe you're right." Bones set his huge bulldog mug into a frown. "But I should tell you, things have derailed on the Andros side."

Cal let his eyes widen but didn't say anything.

"It vanished," said Bones.

"That much pure coke doesn't just vanish."

"We haven't had a report on Bingo Martin since he dropped off that dentist and his family—shit, that was almost two weeks ago. No sign of him or that boat of his."

"Martin run off on his own?" asked Cal.

"He ain't stupid enough to try to fuck Montano."

"Like I said—that much coke just doesn't go and vanish."

"Well, we're working on finding it. But in the meantime, your end of things becomes doubly important. Try to keep track of Montano. We might not be able to find out when the stuff is due to leave Andros."

Their conversation was stopped by a single loud crack and a rattle of Spanish profanity. One of the young Cubans brandished the splintered end of a broken cue at his former friend. Dot looked on from her stool behind the bar, calmly working over the last bits of a greasy chicken knuckle. The first Cuban swung the cue, but the other caught it. They came together, kicking and punching, and rolled to the floor. Dot wiped her hands on an old tea towel, stained to about the same off-white as her skin. She put the chicken bones to one side and reached down and picked up an aluminum Louisville Slugger, hefted it, tested it for weight and balance. She came out from behind the bar, moving with a slow limp that favored her right hip. Dot stepped up beside the tangle of fighting Cuban youth, took a practice swing, and struck, one smart rap to the nearest set of kidneys. The Cuban let out a howl and rolled free of his opponent. Dot lined him up for another whack, but he was too quick. He jumped to his feet and ran through the door. His pal followed.

"Nice, homey place," Bones observed.

Dot, looking once in the direction of the door just to make sure, turned. "You boys need anything back there?" she hollered.

Cal pointed to both their drinks. She nodded.

"Yes. It's my new local."

"Lot different from your old local—the one up there on Wall Street." There was a note of challenge in Bones's voice.

Cal waited until Dot had come and dropped off two fresh drinks. "Is it worth my while trying to figure out what you meant by that last remark?"

Bones took a swig from the new bottle. "Cal, you're doing a fine job. One of the best men I got. But you know what, I ain't sure I trust you."

"I guess that's your problem."

Bones put his lips into a frown that made him look like a black reincarnation of Winston Churchill—in one of his more foul moods. "Yeah. Yeah. My problem. See, I like to know what motivates my people. With some, it's easy: power; with others: a God-driven urge to stamp out the devil drug. You? I dunno. For the life of me, I can't figure out why you'd give up some two-hundred-thousand-dollar-a-year job with a Wall Street law firm just to come down here and help us chase drug smugglers."

Cal looked at his boss: a big, bad-spoken man, who behind his sweat and poor grammar had a mind that was quicker than three-quarters of Cal's former classmates'. You never knew what Bones was thinking. So Cal gave the the first answer that came to mind: "It's the tomatoes. I love tomatoes."

Chapter 6

The barracuda swam two feet above and a foot to the right of Stormy's scuba tank. It held its jaws open just enough to display a mouthful of crooked fangs. From where Stormy swam, the fish looked like a big Doberman in pressing need of an orthodontist. That, or a cleaner-mouthed, somewhat more evolutionally advanced version of that pock-faced joker with Fat Boy.

Until the barracuda had decided to take its Sunday morning constitutional within nibbling distance of Stormy's jugular, things seemed to be going her way. A strange, unusual state in the life of Stormy Lake. She figured she had earned it, mind you, but a twenty-four-hour run was almost too much.

It had started almost immediately after she left the Rev's boat. Stormy managed to get passage on Bahamasair's afternoon flight to Andros. Her twenty-five-dollar room above the bar in the Chickcharnie Hotel came mercifully free from the usual ecosystem of tropical budget-hotel insect fauna. Feminine wiles and unuttered promises had convinced the dive master at Small Hope Bay Lodge to set her up with a Boston Whaler and scuba gear, provided she return everything by 8:45 A.M. Sunday, so the resort's paying guests could use it. Even in the half-light of dawn, she had no trouble following the crude map Bingo had enclosed in his final letter. It led her directly to a horseshoe-shaped reef at the edge of the drop-off into the

Tongue of the Ocean. No doubt it was the right place. After that, things had gone all to hell.

True to Bingo's rendition, the exposed reef maintained its shape underwater, embracing a gently sloping plain of white sun-dappled sand between high faces of coral. The *X* Bingo had drawn—somewhat melodramatically, Stormy thought, but that was Bingo—was at the apex of the sandy parabola. Stormy's fortune was supposed to be there. But she didn't see it on the sandy bottom, and for one hour, Stormy probed into caves and overhangs, crags and valleys in the thirty-foot water. Now, with her tank approaching empty, and with the annoying presence of that barracuda, Stormy began to worry whether she would find Bingo's submarine stash. Maybe he had been stoned, and accidentally put it elsewhere. Maybe Fat Boy had been on to something with his cryptic comments about the preacher having it but not knowing he did. Maybe Bingo *had* run off with some bimbo.

Stormy checked the air-pressure gauge that trailed from the end of a hose coming out of the top of her tank. Four hundred pounds—already the needle was into the red pie slice meant to warn divers to get their sweet butts topside. But most divers didn't have a cool million at stake—or their lives. She glanced up at the rippled mirror of the surface and figured that, if she had to, she could make it up without air. Two hundred pounds, she decided. Two hundred pounds and she would surface. Definitely. She looked back over her shoulder at the ugly barracuda, shot it the finger, and kicked off the sandy bottom.

A coral overhang ran the length of the top of the horseshoe, and for the third time Stormy decided to search beneath it. She swam in deeper this time, glad to be out of view of the barracuda, but worried now about unseen dangers: skin-searing fire coral, needle-toothed moray eels, or becoming trapped, without air, under the overhang. But nowhere, not even in the deepest cranny, could she see Bingo's stash. When she had finally breathed her tank down to its last two hundred pounds, she wormed her way out and nearly shoved her nose into the silver flank of the barracuda.

She stopped herself by flailing her fins and jamming both hands down into the sand. Fortunately, the creature's primordial attention was focused elsewhere, on a coral outcrop about halfway between the sand and the surface. Stormy looked in that direction. At first, she saw nothing unusual. A half-dozen rainbow-colored parrot fish browsed on the coral. A pair of French angelfish, looking aloof and formal in stately gray, rather like a wealthy couple who had stumbled into the wrong part of town, glided across the cliff face. A lone stingray the size of a platter flapped over the sand.

Stormy felt a tightening in her breathing. The tank was running out of air. She began to kick toward the surface, careful to ascend no faster than her slowest bubbles, careful, too, not to make any unnecessary movements, movements the barracuda might interpret as panic.

She finally saw what the fish had been looking at: nothing more than a silver flicker coming from the top of a massive sphere of brain coral. Stormy sucked hard on the tank for whatever air was left. It felt as if she was drawing from an empty pop bottle. But she got her lungs about half-full, enough to stem the pounding behind her temples. She kicked downward toward the silver object. It was deeper than it had looked. Stormy thrashed the water with her fins, fighting the buoyancy she had gained while surfacing, fighting the instincts that told her to breathe. Blood began to swish past her eardrums. Prickles of yellow light danced on her retinas. She kept kicking until her fingers wrapped around the silver object. It was an old nicked and worn 1974 Kennedy half-dollar.

She palmed the coin and braced her fins against the coral for a final push toward the surface. The yellow light no longer came in prickles, but had grown to circular blobs that took up most of her field of vision. The rest was black.

Stormy's lungs burned. She sucked violently against the regulator, but it provided no relief. She spat it out and with one hand released her weight belt to speed her ascent—if it even was ascent. The surface, with its unlimited supplies of cool, pure air, drew no closer. Stormy kicked harder. She flailed her arms. Exhaled the last few cubic inches of exhausted, burned-up gasses that remained in her lungs.

At some point—Stormy didn't know when—she surfaced. Her mouth opened and sucked down air, which was expelled immediately, but not soon enough, it felt, to satisfy the gnawing need for a fresh breath, and then another on top of that. Stormy was so occupied by the task of getting oxygen to her cells that she was only half-conscious when a pair of rough hands clamped her armpits.

She had been stripped of scuba tank, fins, and mask and was sitting on the floor of the Boston Whaler beside an old spear gun and the bloody, still-quivering body of the barracuda before her senses secured enough oxygen for her to turn and look into the massive bloodshot eyes that gleamed at her from a face surrounded by a two-foot-wide thicket of matted, sun-bleached dreadlocks.

Stormy tried to decide whether she should leap overboard, and take her chances with whatever dangers lurked on the reef, or face the more immediate danger posed by the guy who had hauled her out of the water. He was kept from being totally naked only by a pair of fins and the torn remnants of what once might have been boxer shorts. His eyes gleamed crazily, and, as Stormy's breathing slowed to a more normal rate, his liver-like lips spread into a smile that widened to reveal two buck teeth separated by a quarter-inch gap.

"Pretty lady," he said. His voice was deep but expressionless.

The water started to look better and better. Stormy edged away from him.

His bucktoothed grin widened. "You wan' dat fish, he yours." He nodded toward the dying barracuda.

Stormy temporarily put aside her urge to plunge into the sea. The offer of the fish made no sense whatsoever. But it was a perfectly harmless gesture. Despite his looks, the guy seemed mild enough. Crazed but mild, she deduced. And Stormy always felt an immediate kinship with crazy people. "Fish. Oh, no thanks," she said hesitantly, still not sure what his next act would be.

"Lobster?" he asked decisively, proudly, like a person who had just single-handedly stumbled across the meaning of life.

For the first time, Stormy noticed a small boat tethered to the Whaler. Given a claw hammer and a tin can of bent, rusty nails, most twelve-year-olds could have cobbled together a more seaworthy craft. It was about ten feet long and constructed from weathered boards of different types and widths, some covered in chipped and peeling paint—turquoise, pastel pink, and fluorescent orange predominated—some unpainted and weathered, all looking as if they had been scavenged from a beach after a very long time in the water. Amateurishly applied strips of fiberglass held the seams of the boat together, and a broken-off blade of an oar provided the only visible means of propulsion. In the inch or two of water in the bottom of the boat, a dozen or so lobsters crept about, apparently content in their new topside home. The Rasta pointed to the lobsters.

"Oh, no thanks, really," Stormy said, trying a smile.

The Rasta smiled back and nodded. "Treasure? Pretty lady dive for treasure, den."

Now she was sure the guy was crazy. She laughed. "Hey, pal, don't I wish. But I doubt there's any treasure around here, and given my luck, I'd be the last person to find it if there was," she said.

He grew serious, businesslike. "Moonbeam fin' treasure on dis reef and give to Jesus."

The guy was definitely off his rocker. Stormy checked her watch, a black plastic Casio waterproof she had picked up in Miami three years earlier for $19.95. There was barely enough time to get the boat and gear back to the dive master. "That was nice of you," she said, but she didn't like the condescending tones in her voice. More sincerely, she continued. "Shit, man, I gotta thank you for hauling me outta the drink. Probably saved me."

"Jesus saves," said the Rasta sternly. He looked up into a blue sky marred only by three small, puffy cumulus clouds and he spread his arms. "Baby Jesus, Him save. Moonbeam, me give Jesus da treasure. Jesus, Him send Moonbeam da lobster. Lord, Him provides." He nodded once, briskly, as if, this time, he had provided a pat explanation of the unification theories of the universe.

Crazy, and talkative. Any other time, Stormy would have enjoyed nothing more than sticking around to hear his spiel, but it sounded as if he could go on at some length, and there was the matter of the borrowed boat. "I gotta go now," Stormy interrupted. "Can I give you a tow in?"

"No, pretty lady. Mus' catch more lobster for Mr. Dick at da hotel b'fore church."

He smiled at her again, picked up the barracuda, his spear gun, and a mask, and stepped into his own boat. It wobbled violently, and water lapped over first one gunwale and then the other. That didn't seem to bother Moonbeam, or whatever his name was. He undid a frayed length of yellow nylon line and pushed off. "Da treasure. Moonbeam give baby Jesus da treasure," he said in parting.

Stormy stood there a moment before she realized her right hand still clutched the coin she had picked up from the coral. She opened it and looked. No doubt about it. She held the same coin she had been given the winter of 1978, when she had waited tables at a bar in Aspen. She couldn't even remember the name of the place, but she saw the asshole who had given it to her as clearly as she could see the crazy Rasta paddling away now in his child's boat. The guy had flirted loudly with her all week. Teased her about her curly hair. Commented about her long legs. Pawed her whenever he could make it look like maybe, just maybe, it was an accident. But the joker's worst offense in Stormy's eyes was that in the end, instead of forking over a decent tip, he flipped her a crummy half-dollar, and then had the gall to tell her not to spend it. Some bull crap about good luck. Stormy tossed it into the bowl of loose change she kept on her bureau and would have taken it to the bank the following Monday. But Sunday night, she heard that on his way back to Denver the guy had driven his car off a curve on Highway 70. Killed instantly. Stormy kept the coin. Never parted with it until she loaned it to Bingo before his last run—for luck.

Dugold, Small Hope's dive master, stood on the town pier with his hands planted on his hips, or, rather, what would have been his hips, because he really didn't have any, at least that Stormy could see. Dugold's torso, bared to the yellow morning sunlight, formed a geometrician's dream. His chest was the most flawless of equilateral triangles. The horizontal lines of the shoulders led to perfectly square pectoral muscles, clearly outlined beneath the taught, gleaming ebony skin and punctuated by the concentric circles of his breasts. Below the pectorals, each rib announced its presence proudly. Together, they formed matched sets of parallel lines above a half dozen trim trapezoids of belly muscle—not an ounce of visible flab.

The material in Dugold's black Speedo wouldn't have been enough to make any more than half a bra. But, Stormy allowed, taking in the distinct bulge, it would have to have been half of a D cup. Each buttock, most of which was left exposed by the Speedo, was a sphere no bigger than an Indian River grapefruit. All in all, just what Stormy needed. With any luck, the perfect antidote to that blond square-jawed preacher. Goddamn preacher.

Stormy brought the Whaler up to the wharf too fast. She waited until Dugold's eyes widened in the sheer terror of his having to tell the boss he had loaned a boat to some crazed woman who smashed it. At the last instant, Stormy kicked the 70-horse Yamaha outboard into reverse, gave the wheel a quick half spin, and stopped the boat parallel to, and three inches from, the cement pier.

Dugold opened his eyes, angry at first, but when he saw Stormy's grin, his slender mouth rose into a sly smile that suggested he knew he had been had but that he appreciated a job cleverly done. He placed his big toe on the Whaler's bow to steady it and stuck out a hand for Stormy. It was an unnecessary gesture, but she took it anyway, and held on a little longer than stepping onto the wharf demanded. Dugold got the message.

"See you tonight?" he asked, hopping into the Whaler and sitting down behind the steering wheel.

Stormy nodded but didn't say anything.

He looked at his watch. "She almost wrecks the boat, and nearly makes me late for work. What I'm to tell Dick?"

"Thank him. And thank you, too. Sorry about being late. I ran into some crazy guy out there. Rasta."

Dugold laughed. "Moonbeam. We call him Moonbeam. I should have told you to expect him. He's always diving on that reef. Nuts. Right off his rocker, but don't worry. Harmless. Retarded, I guess you'd say. Spends all his time diving for lobsters. Gets a lot of them, too." Dugold turned on the ignition. The motor fired.

"Lobsters. He kept mumbling something about treasure. He's crazy all right," said Stormy.

"You'd be surprised the things that boy finds out there. Old beach chairs, full liquor bottles, fishing rods. Guess he might think some of it is treasure. Other day he came back in with a great big green garbage bag in that junky little boat of his. Been bragging all over town that whatever it was in that bag was gonna make him rich. Like I said. Crazy."

Stormy visibly winced and shouted, "Hold it a minute."

Dugold put the Whaler back into neutral, but Stormy could

see he was impatient. "What if I wanted to talk to this Moonbeam?"

"Talk to him? Forget it. He never makes any sense. All riddles."

"Well, I want to try."

Dugold didn't answer for awhile, and Stormy thought he wasn't going to tell her. Finally he spoke, not sounding a bit happy about it. "His mother's the cook over at The Vale. That's a church, sort of. Today's Sunday. Service is always at noon. Moonbeam never misses a service. Like I said, he's crazy. Religious crazy."

He gunned the Whaler. It dug into the water, bow up, stern down, then flattened out and sped toward the hotel.

Stormy stood on the wharf thinking. Her next step was simple. It just entailed doing something she had scrupulously avoided for the past sixteen years: going to church.

Chapter 7

Miles felt his shoulder shaken and heard Prue's hushed but urgent "Wake up. Wake up, Miles. You have a service in twenty minutes. . . ."

It seemed as if his eyes had closed perhaps three minutes earlier, tops. Yet twelve hours had somehow passed. He belched a sweet, fumy belch and swung his legs to the floor. Belched again. Blinked to bring the room into focus. It was a plain room, unadorned and little changed from the days when it was a bunk room for the fishing lodge. Two-by-four studs forming the walls were visible from the interior, although someone had seen fit to slather them in streaky white latex. Wall art consisted of a Savior Network calendar, turned up at the corners, featuring twelve different pastoral landscapes, with appropriate Scripture passages, and a different Bible reading for every day of the year, personally selected by Reverend Miles Farnsworth. The calendar shared wall space with a print of Jesus dressed in a light blue robe and framed by a halo of sunlight. His hands were outstretched and He had a woebegone look on His face. A bare bulb hung from one of the exposed rafters and was activated by a piece of twine. The bed was old and high and had squeaky metal springs. There was a single tallboy dresser topped by a mirror. Add a spinning rod or two, some tackle, and a few long-billed caps, and the previous owner wouldn't have detected any change. Mornings like this, the room depressed Miles.

Prue stood beside the bed in a crisp sky blue dress, tightened around the middle with a belt of the same material. She held a stenographer's notebook, pen poised above the page she had opened it to. "Hurry. I have to get the programs typed and run off," she said.

Twenty minutes. Is that what she had said? He hadn't showered. Hadn't shaved. Wasn't dressed. And he hadn't a clue about his sermon.

Miles tested his feet with a little weight. They seemed to take it okay, so he added a few more pounds, then pushed himself to a standing position, careful at first to keep a supporting hand on the mattress. Once the dizziness had left, he went to a window. Bright sun shone off the water of Fresh Creek. He blinked, rubbed his eyes, and then spoke. "Suppose I must break the news. The news about the closure of this mission."

Prue lowered her pad. "I know it probably provides little comfort, but I love this place as much as you do—if that's possible. Something will come up. Have faith."

Miles turned and looked at Prue. She was a good woman. So selfless it was out-of-date, almost corny. She could have been a mother right out of a 1950s sitcom, always in an apron and wide skirt, dispensing hearty meals and sensible advice. At times like this, Miles marveled at how it seemed as if her entire life was dedicated to living up to that name with which her parents saddled her. Miles also marveled at her almost-supernatural ability to make him feel like shit.

"I'll need everybody's prayers," he said. "So, let's kick things off with the Twenty-third Psalm." He closed his eyes and exhaled for a long time through puffed cheeks. "Scripture—how about John six, one through thirteen . . ."

"The loaves and fishes," Prue said.

"Yep."

Miles looked back out the window. Moonbeam, late for service, wearing a pair of faded, tattered boxer shorts Miles had donated to him, came toward them across The Vale's shaded front yard, dripping wet and carrying a big dead barracuda.

"Miles?" Prue said. "Any particular reason for John six?"

"Suddenly, I think I know just how the old boy felt."

At three minutes after twelve, three minutes, that is, after the service should have started, Miles stood and ran his hands down the sides of his white surplice, a trademark with Savior Network pastors since his father first preached in that patched-up old circus tent. He cinched his waist with a gold braided rope and tugged the knot to one side so the loose ends dangled over his hip, another network trademark. As a final gesture to network tradition, he hung a foot-long bronze crucifix around his neck. A quick survey in the mirror showed that, externally, he presented a near-perfect image of what people expected a man of God to look like: pious, handsome, somewhat innocent, a little bit lost. One flaw was a lock of sandy-colored hair at the crown of his head. For some reason, it always preferred to set off in a different direction from its counterparts, especially when the occasion called for a smooth, well-groomed look. Miles licked his palm and glued the lock in place.

He might have passed the external self-inspection, but internally, Miles was a wreck. The cottony feeling in his head was now in direct competition with the first parries and thrusts of a full-blown migraine. His bowels grumbled and fizzed. And his gut kept sending up belches that tasted of molasses and stale sugarcane. He still had no clear idea of what he was going to say, and wondered whether a little nip from the bottle he kept hidden in his closet might help. Just one.

Miles picked up the bottle and was about to unscrew its cap when he heard someone knock.

Moonbeam, holding his barracuda proudly so Miles could see its entire length, stood on the veranda on the other side of the screen door. Miles put the bottle back.

"Lovely fish, Moonbeam. But you better put it in your mother's refrigerator and hurry along. Service is going to start soon."

Moonbeam's eyes grew wide and he breathed in a series of

excited pants. But whatever thoughts he was trying to enunciate scampered and scurried away from him, danced around just beyond the limited range of his mental grasp. He was left struggling and sputtering. "Mus' talk. Me mus' talk to you. Mus . . ."

"Later." Miles patted Moonbeam on a bare shoulder. "Right after the service. Come along now."

Moonbeam stood still. He tried to talk, but the only result was that his lower lip began to quiver and his head shake.

Miles could see that a larger-than-usual crowd—motivated no doubt by pre-Christmas atonement—had gathered in the grassy avenue between the two rows of coconut palms near the shore. The outdoor chapel was his idea. Wonderful place for a service when the weather was good. He sighed. A minute or two more wouldn't hurt them. Might even build a bit of anticipation. He used the same trick every time he had to do a wedding. "Take it easy, Moonbeam. What is it you wanted to say?"

Moonbeam let out a loud sigh and smiled in gap-toothed relief. "Treasure!" he blurted, then nodded once, as if that one word should have sufficed to explain everything to Miles.

Miles repeated the word, putting notes of both question and doubt into his voice.

Moonbeam nodded again, one time, almost smug. "Treasure," he said.

"I'm afraid I don't understand."

Moonbeam's self-confidence disappeared. The lip began to quiver; the head shake. "Treasure," he said, a little bit angry. "Moonbeam find same treasure that make all dem other boy on dis island rich."

Miles nodded and looked at the dead barracuda. Some treasure. "Moonbeam, I hate to disappoint you, but one barracuda isn't going to make you rich. Most people don't even want to eat them."

"No barracuda. Treasure. An' me give to you, so now The Vale rich!" He spread his arms in a wide ecclesiastical gesture that made the big fish sway from side to side.

Miles touched Moonbeam's shoulder. "Look, we'll talk about this after the service, okay? Now go put on a shirt and pants and hurry along."

Miles had walked a few paces when Moonbeam called to him. "First Moonbeam rich, den you rich, den The Vale rich. Lord Him works in mysterious ways."

Miles nodded and smiled as he muttered, "Not that mysterious."

Fresh Creek's single cab was an ancient Pontiac station wagon, its original finish concealed under what looked like a dozen or so layers of cracked, blistered, and peeling house enamel, the most recent being a drab shade of olive green, whose origins might have been the U. S. military installation south of town. Under its scaled skin, it lumbered along the roads of Andros Island like some prehistoric reptile, without recourse to such frivolities as springs and shock absorbers, trumpeting its approach with the throaty rumble of exhaust. Locals lovingly called it the Pontasaurus.

The little man who piloted the Pontasaurus introduced himself as Dacosta. Despite the bright sun and temperatures that were creeping into the eighties, Dacosta wore a neat navy blue suit and tie. He got out of the Pontasaurus as soon as he saw Stormy outside the Chickcharnie, made a broad sweep with a bonafide chauffeur's cap, and opened a rear passenger door. Stormy settled onto the seat, upholstered in what appeared to be a very old Hudson's Bay Point blanket. Dacosta gripped the door handle with both hands, lifted with his knees, and, with body movements similar to those favored by Scottish hurlers, slammed heartily three times before it closed.

He took his place behind the wheel and settled the chauffeur's cap on his head with the help of a rearview mirror obviously angled more for that purpose than for the detection of traffic approaching from behind. "Where to?" asked Dacosta.

Stormy told him and he put the Pontasaurus in gear. A tangy

aroma of exhaust and gasoline vapor filled the passenger compartment as the ancient car squeaked and rattled through the narrow streets of the village before finally achieving its cruising speed—a nice dinosaur trotting pace Stormy put at about fifteen miles an hour—on the bridge that led south across a brown body of water fringed with mangrove and sea grape.

After wobbling for another fifteen minutes along the main road, about equal parts pavement and pothole, the Pontasaurus nosed between two stone gateposts and pulled up behind a low building. Stormy paid Dacosta and tried to get out. But finding only a hole where the door handle once had been, she sat patiently while Dacosta repeated his hurler's routine to extract her.

Once outside, Stormy took a quick look at her surroundings, the way one might sneak a surreptitious inspection of the apartment of a new friend, or lover. There was something Northwoodsy about The Vale's compound. The tall casuarinas with their feathery pinelike foliage no doubt helped. But the architecture of the main lodge and outlying cabins owed more to a Canadian fishing lodge than to a tropical beach retreat. The builders had used wood and local coral rock, not the ubiquitous stucco and block and steel. Nothing about the place suggested church or school, and Stormy wondered whether Dacosta had left her off at the wrong place. Not much she could do about that now. The Pontasaurus had disappeared, and even its rumble had begun to fade.

From the other side of the main building, voices accompanied by a piano burst into a hearty "Onward Christian soldiers. . . ." Stormy began to walk in that direction.

She had taken two steps when a screen door slammed on the main building. Moonbeam, looking every bit the big city banker in an old gray pinstripe suit, if he had only remembered to put on shoes, shirt, and tie, came toward her at a trot. "We late, pretty lady. We late."

She fell in beside him, scurrying like a crab so she could talk to him and still keep up. "Moonbeam, I need to speak to you. It's important."

"Mus' get to church. Preacher soon be startin'. Dey sing now."

"It's about that treasure you found. Well, it belongs to me. I would like it back."

Moonbeam kept trotting. "Me give it to da preacher."

They had rounded the main lodge and Stormy saw that a couple of hundred people, all locals to judge by the color of the faces, stood on the grass between two rows of palms. At one end of the natural chapel—the end bordering the water—there was a slight embankment. A white woman with trim light brown hair sat at a piano immediately below the embankment. What looked like twenty or thirty kids were arranged around the piano in three concentric half circles. A choir, Stormy assumed. Except this was the first time Stormy had ever seen a church choir dressed in T-shirts emblazoned with images of Michael Jackson.

"Moonbeam, that was mine; you can't give it away. Now please, tell me where it is."

A flash of crazy panic lit Moonbeam's big eyes. "B'long to preacher. I hide it where no one gonna find 'cept da preacher."

By now they had joined the last rows of worshipers. Moonbeam reached into the inside pocket of his suit coat and withdrew a dog-earred hymnal. He began to thumb furiously through the pages. Stormy was prepared to plead with him again, but Miles entered.

She couldn't tell where he had come from, or why she hadn't noticed him before. Suddenly, the congregation's singing took on a different tenor, as if a couple hundred people simultaneously sucked in a little more breath. Miles came across the embankment from the side opposite to where the fair woman was tinkling the piano keys. Stormy felt her chest tighten.

He walked slowly, with his chin thrust slightly forward and his arms at his side and a little to the rear of his hips, as if he was bucking a head wind that he alone felt. The pure white surplice made him look taller than Stormy remembered—well over six feet—and that little stunt with the rope around his middle made him look slimmer, showed off his rear to best advantage. The first of the afternoon's trade winds added a playful, endearing vulnerability by kicking around one of his sandy locks.

Miles positioned himself between the pulpit—a plain one built from wood that looked like mahogany—and a life-size cross of the same material. He smiled serenely at his flock, then put his face into the sun and shot his arms up and outward. From where Stormy stood, it looked as if he had been hung on the cross. Nice touch, she thought, and turned her attention back to Moonbeam, who seemed calmer now that he had found his place in the hymnal.

"Moonbeam. Please will you show me where it is after the service?" she said in a hoarse whisper.

But he didn't answer. Instead, he waited until the refrain came back around and joined the other singers. His voice was very loud and very flat, and followed the patterns of no discernible tune. Stormy stole a look over his shoulder. The hymnal was upside down and turned to the wrong page.

"With the cross of JEEEEEEEESUS . . ." Moonbeam hollered, flashing an ecstatic gap-toothed grin toward Miles.

She had lost him.

After the hymn, Miles stood for a moment in silence, arms outstretched. Then, just as the congregation became edgy, wondering whether perhaps he was going to stay like that for the entire afternoon, he began to chant the familiar lines of the psalm. Stormy had come prepared to endure a boring hour. She would have been willing to do more to lay her hands on Moonbeam's million-dollar stash. Yet there was something in Miles's delivery, sincerity perhaps, perhaps the way he let the softness of his southern accent carry the vowels across the open-air sanctuary, or most likely it was that she had slept with the guy two nights earlier. Whatever the cause, Stormy found herself listening, really listening, to a preacher for the first time in her life. To hear him, a person would think Miles thought up the psalm's tired lines on the spot. He made you believe that the Lord was, indeed, his own personal goddamn shepherd.

The congregation was silent at first, then voices slowly droned in along with Miles. Stormy shifted from side to side, and bit her lower lip when she found herself unconsciously mumbling in cadence.

At the end of the psalm, one of the little boys in a Michael Jackson T-shirt broke away from the choir and hesitantly took Miles's place at the podium. He flopped open a big Bible, then looked at the light brown–haired woman. She frowned, glanced over the congregation, glanced back at Miles, shot a stern look at the timid Michael Jackson boy, and nodded once.

The kid took a deep breath and began to speak in a piping voice made all the more vulnerable sounding by his Bahamian accent: "John six, verses three through twelve." He swallowed, took another deep breath. " 'And the Passover, a feast of the Jews, was nigh.' "

The little guy looked at the woman for assurance. She scowled. He looked back down at the Bible.

" 'When Jesus then lifted up his eyes and saw a great company come unto him, he saith unto Philip, "Whence shall we buy bread that these may eat?" And this he said to prove him: for he himself knew what he would do.' "

He stopped to take a breath. Stormy felt sorry for him. " 'Philip answered him, "Two hundred pennyworth of bread is not sufficient for them, that everyone might take a little." One of his disciples, Andrew, Simon Peter's brother, saith unto him, "There is a lad here, which hath five barley loaves, and two small fishes." ' "

The kid paused then, as he had obviously been trained, raised his tiny voice to full volume for emphasis: " ' "But what are they among so many?" ' "

He lowered his voice. " 'And Jesus said, "Make the men sit down." Now there was much grass in the place. So the men sat down, in number about five thousand. And Jesus took the loaves; and when he had given thanks, he distributed to the disciples, and the disciples to them that were set down; and likewise of the fishes as much as they would. When they were filled, he saith unto his disciples, "Gather up the fragments that remain, that nothing be lost." ' "

The kid bolted away from the pulpit and dove back into the concentrically aligned pack of his peers.

Stormy breathed a sign of relief for him. Hell of a thing, putting a little kid through an ordeal like that.

Miles had reappeared at the podium. He clasped his hands and stared at those standing nearest him. "Christmas is coming," he said matter-of-factly, then moved his eyes back one row and eyeballed those faces.

Not that he had said anything earth-shattering, but Stormy found herself listening intently, as if she expected him to pull a surprise quiz right after the service. "And for we Christians, Christmas is a great feast. A great feast, when visitors are likely to come to our houses. Maybe the relatives, maybe the boss and his family—maybe *the mother-in-law.*"

He uttered the words *the mother-in-law* with a little hellfire spin on them. The congregation chuckled.

Miles grew serious. "And they expect food and entertainment. Even now, I'll bet some of you are preparing for that feast—baking perhaps, laying down strong spirits. . . ." He raised his eyebrows at the last line and the congregation chuckled again, a bit nervously. They knew damn well a trap of some sort lay ahead.

Miles continued. "So imagine how you would feel Christmas morning if you went to your cupboard and found nothing there except a few loaves of old bread and *two small fish. Two small fish.* Two fish no bigger than a small grunt. And there is the mother-in-law; there are the boss and his wife; there are all the relatives—all waiting for your feast.

Miles gripped the podium. His face reddened. "HOW YOU GOING TO FEEL?" he hollered, jabbing a finger at the people in the middle rows.

"HOW YOU GOING TO FEEL?" The finger moved back a row or two. "Even if you had the money, had the two hundred pennies, that's not going to do you any good now. The people are already there. Waiting.

"HOW YOU GOING TO FEEL?" He had reached the back rows now. With each syllable, his accusing index finger came down, until it finally lit on Stormy.

She lifted one corner of her mouth and winked.

Miles's finger missed a beat. His voice faltered—but only for a fraction of a second, so slight it might have been Stormy's imagination.

"Now imagine that it's not just the relatives, not just the boss's wife, but the entire population of this island that's out there waiting to be fed, because that's how many were there waiting for Jesus to feed them.

"HOW YOU GOING TO FEEL?"

This time, he swung back and hit Stormy three times with the finger, not missing a beat. Touché, she thought.

Miles leaned away from the pulpit and lowered his voice into a sincere, conversational tone. "Brothers and Sisters, I'll tell you how I would feel. I would feel panic. Desperation. Like Philip, I would not know what to do. I would have lost faith."

He nodded.

"But Jesus didn't fret, did He? Two little fish—no bigger than a small grunt. Five loaves of brown bread, not so good as you can buy at the Chinaman's. And He didn't fret."

Miles paused and sucked in a deep breath. *Because He knew what to do.* Yes, *He knew what to do.* Jesus took what had been given to Him, meager as it was, and He gave thanks. Yes, He gave thanks. *Gave thanks.* He did not wait until God had provided a feast for the five thousand, to give thanks. Right then and there, right at the worst time, when the pressures were greatest on Him, when all those five thousand hungry men were milling around waiting to be fed, *He gave thanks.* Why? Because He had faith. Faith in God."

Miles paused for a long, uncomfortable moment and eyed his congregation. People began to shift nervously. "And He was right. The multitude was fed. *They even had leftovers.*"

Sensing that the worst was over for now, the congregation chuckled.

"I want you all to join me now to give thanks. Thanks for all the kindness God has bestowed on The Vale. Thank Him for sending the owner of these buildings to me. Thank Him for the school we founded here and the children who attend. Thank Him for sending Prudence when we needed another teacher. And most of all, thank Him for providing a way to continue this ministry in the future."

The congregation mumbled, "Thanks be to God."

Miles spread his hands. "Soon, I must leave here and go to the United States to seek the funds that will allow us to continue. I will be honest with you; things look bleak now. But when I think about it, not quite so bleak as it was back then when Jesus faced those five thousand men on the shores of the Sea of Galilee. Friends, I need your help. Pray for The Vale. Remember the words of Christ: 'Whatsoever ye shall ask the Father in my name, he will give it to you. *Ask, and ye shall receive.*' And before you pray, thank the Lord."

Miles stepped away from the podium. The stage presence that had been palpable seconds before faded. Miles might have been a rubber figure suddenly deflated. He looked beaten. His blond hair was tousled now, darkened here and there by streaks of sweat. The handsome, long face was marked by gray hollows. The eyes, which even at a hundred feet came across as radiant and blue, were hooded. The posture had sagged, knocking him down to average height as he strode off the earthen dais. Stormy

92

didn't know why, but at that instant, she felt as sorry for Miles as she had ever felt for anyone.

Which was probably exactly the effect he wanted. Goddamn preacher.

Picking up the cue, the female drill sergeant—dear, sweet Prue, Stormy assumed—coaxed a few weak notes out of the piano. The children nodded their heads in anticipation for a bar or two before launching into a high-pitched rendition of a hymn Stormy thought she had forgotten long ago:

> There's a church in the valley by the wildwood
> No lovelier place in the dale
> No spot is so dear to my childhood
> As the little brown church in the vale.

Stormy tried not to get caught up in the old hymn, but she found herself singing with the rest of the congregation. Halfway through the second verse, hot tears rimmed Stormy's eyes. No big deal; church music always made her a bit misty. She wiped them away with the back of an arm.

When she opened her eyes, she sensed something was wrong. At first, she couldn't place it. Then she realized that Moonbeam's tuneless voice was missing. She looked to her right where he had stood. Moonbeam had disappeared.

And where he had been stood the pock-faced guy, lips motionless, dumb eyes not moving from Stormy. She hoped he had come to The Vale that morning for spiritual inspiration. But somehow she doubted it.

Two things played upon Miles's mind as he strode away from the service. One was the dead barracuda. The other was the woman named Stormy Lake. Dealing with both would require a certain dexterity; could become awkward.

At that moment, the barracuda was uppermost. Moonbeam led the way to the workshop, whimpering and muttering "Loaf an' fish; loaf an' fish" as he scuttled across the ground, periodically bending around to smile at Miles, like a dog anxious to please its master. Miles assumed he was being led there to formally receive the dead barracuda. It was not unusual that Moonbeam came away from one of Miles's sermons with a confused message. He might well have thought that Miles needed fish—lots of it. But for the moment, Miles was happy to be led away. At least it meant there would be no scene with Stormy.

Moonbeam threw open the door to the workshop. There were two band saws in one corner, some stacks of neat squares of coconut wood, and the atmosphere was thick with fumes of epoxy. Moonbeam went directly to an old tarp in one corner and pulled it back to reveal a green plastic-wrapped bale of some sort.

"For The Vale," Moonbeam said. "Now you rich. Feed the five thousand. Open him up."

Miles was impatient to change out of his service clothes. He also was in desperate need of a rum pick-me-up after the sermon. But Moonbeam was like an eager kid.

Whoever had wrapped the contents of the parcel had meant it to stay dry. Miles rooted through a half-dozen green layers that once had been bound with packing tape. Someone, Moonbeam perhaps, had already opened the plastic.

"We rich," Moonbeam said.

Miles had reached the last layer. Figuring he'd probably find somebody's clothes, he tilted his head and looked inside.

"Rich," Moonbeam whispered.

Flour. Miles first thought the package was filled with flour. But that impression lasted only a fraction of a second before he understood exactly what the white crystalline powder was. For once, Moonbeam was right. Technically, they were indeed rich. Very, very rich, if one could overlook a few illegalities.

Stormy waited until the congregation had dispersed before leaving the outdoor sanctuary. Pock-face milled around as if he wanted to say something to her. Finally, he moved away with the last group of worshipers, but not before catching Stormy's eye and nodding once, very slowly, and apparently with some profound meaning Stormy couldn't begin to fathom. So to be safe, she gave him the finger.

Prue had been left in charge of shaking hands with the congregation members as they departed. She took each hand, pressed it once, said the person's name and smiled, released the hand and took the next. Five seconds per worshiper, no more, no less. To sneak a look at Prue, and to buy a little time in case old Pock-face was still around, Stormy stood in line.

The Rev's woman wasn't bad-looking. A little too prim, for Stormy. She would have liked to have seen at least one strand of hair out of place, a dark bag under an eye, one tiny pimple. But, what did she expect from a preacher's fiancée? Prue's hand was papery and dry. Her blue eyes looked directly at Stormy but seemed preoccupied, as if they long ago had gone off to tackle some other project, leaving the mere shell of the body behind to take care of duties.

"Good day—I don't believe we've met. I'm Prudence, headmistress at the school here." The voice was flat, a little nasal and devoid of expression. She sounded like all grade-school teachers—and some cops.

"Stormy. Stormy Lake."

The pale eyes flickered when Stormy said her name. It was a typical reaction. "You a visitor to our island?"

Stormy nodded.

"Pleasure . . . or business?" The *business* was tossed out as an afterthought.

She looked long and hard at Prue. Had Miles said anything to her? Had he confessed? The blue eyes gave away nothing. "A little of both," she said, and dropped the papery hand.

Stormy had walked a few steps away from Prue when she turned. "I'm actually looking for someone called Moonbeam. He around here?"

95

Prue appeared surprised, but she quickly composed herself. "I just saw Moonbeam and Reverend Farnsworth going toward the workshop. Come along, I'll show you the way."

"Moonbeam, you have a visitor."

It was Prue's voice, coming from just outside the door. Miles had the tarp half over the bale when Prue came in the workshop, followed immediately by Stormy Lake. Twin emotional surges slugged him at once. Their common denominator was raw, searing guilt—guilt at being caught trying to conceal an as-yet-unexplained parcel of drugs, and the guilt anyone would feel seeing his fiancée and the woman with whom he had had an affair out for what, given appearances, could have been a pleasant Sunday-afternoon stroll. Either way, Miles wished he had taken that nip.

Stormy kicked off the encounter. She walked into the room, eager and smiling. "That's mine, Rev," she said, jabbing out an index finger. "I've come a long way for it."

Still grappling with the specter of Stormy and Prue standing side by side—the one lanky and wild and dark, the other rounded and trim and fair—Miles stammered a few syllables before finally gaining control over his tongue. "Stormy, I know what that is."

Prue cut in. "You two know each other . . ." Her voice faded as she tried not to sound unduly nosy, but the eyes, so distant a moment before, focused—began at the top of Stormy's curl tangled scalp and moved down, taking everything in, assessing it, obviously liking not one inch of what she saw, but nonetheless cataloging it where it could be retrieved in seconds if ever needed.

Stormy barked a laugh. "Know each other!" Miles winced. Stormy glared at him and flipped her eyebrows two times. Miles's look of terror told her that her message had been driven home. "Jeez. I'm surprised Miles hasn't told you all about me.

We go back quite a ways. Miles, why haven't you told Prue about me?"

Miles looked at Stormy pleadingly. He started to stammer something.

Stormy cut him off. "No need to go into all that now. I'll just take my belongings and be out of here."

Miles made a move to one side, his relief obvious.

"Hold it!" It was Prue speaking. Her voice rang with a not-to-be-trifled-with authority. "Miles, what is in there?"

"Prue—"

"*Miles!*"

He stepped clear of the plastic-wrapped bale and made a sweeping gesture of welcome.

Stormy quickly slipped into his place between Prudence and the package. "That's mine. I'm leaving with it now."

Prue kept coming toward Stormy, flexing her knees, carrying her hands loosely at her sides in a fighter's stance.

"So, that's yours."

"Yes."

"Well, then. I think it's only fair we let you claim it." Prue paused long enough for Stormy to feel relief, then she let the other foot fall. "Once the police are here."

It was Stormy's turn to stammer. "Police. Really. I don't think—"

"Miles, go up to the house and call the chief constable. I'll just stay down here with"—she made a face as if she found what was going to come next repugnant—"with Stormy. How on earth did you ever get that name, anyhow?"

Stormy couldn't help herself. She smiled slyly. "Ask the Rev. He'll tell you all about it."

Prue shot Miles a scornful, questioning look. And that was her mistake.

Stormy ducked low and to the left of Prue—the side opposite of where Miles stood. Two big strides took Stormy to the door of the workshop. But Prue had recovered. She lunged and managed to wrap her hands around Stormy's ankles—just barely. It was enough for a classic rugby tackle, quick, clean, solid. Stormy fell full length, half in, half out of the shed. Instinctively, she kicked at Prue's fingers. Her ankles came free. She stood, took a lunging stride, another, and had a good ten-foot head start before Prue regained her footing and began pursuit.

"Miles, help me," Prue called.

For a moment, Miles stood still. Then he decided he had better obey Prue.

Something was wrong. Bad wrong. Moonbeam knew that much from watching the diving woman, Miss Prue, and the preacher. Bad, bad, bad, bad wrong.

Moonbeam came out of the corner into which he had slunk when the women arrived. He tried to think. The diving woman, she wanted to take the treasure; he knew that much. And Miss Prue . . . Moonbeam thought hard, big, thick lower lip quivering. Miss Prue, she seemed to want to steal it, too. But it was the preacher's.

A big smile crossed Moonbeam's face. For the first time in his life, a clear, untangled thought had passed through his brain. He knew exactly what he had to do.

For the second time in as many days, Stormy cursed her private stash of Santa Marta. Her long, muscular legs served her well at first, allowing her to gain another ten feet as she rounded the main building and headed toward the road. But midway across the front yard, that damn clean-living Prue, thudding stockily behind, started to close the gap. Stormy breathed hard, gulping for air. The long strides shortened. Prue's thud, thud, thud got closer.

Suddenly, Stormy felt as if she were flying through the air. But Stormy's sensations of free flight ended abruptly. Prue's weight was on her back, driving her down face-first toward the sandy driveway. Stormy hit the ground. She tried to twist away, but Prue clung.

With her free hand, Prue grabbed one of Stormy's arms. She twisted it behind Stormy's back and lifted.

Stormy let out a little squeal of pain.

Prue put her lips close to Stormy's ear. "Listen, bitch. You try anything like that again, I'll break your arm." To drive home her point, she hoisted the appendage in question.

Between gritted teeth, Stormy nodded ascent. The pressure lessened. Prue rolled to one side so Stormy could stand. They both dusted and smoothed their dresses, waiting for Miles, who came around the corner of the building at a clumsy trot.

"They teach you that at Bible college?" Stormy muttered, and took a series of deep breaths.

Prue panted two times before answering. "I was president of the martial-arts club," she said, making no attempt to conceal a little un-Christian dollop of pride.

Stormy snorted, sucked in more air. "I wasn't talking about that. I was talking about the language you just used."

After Miles called the police, he and Prue marched Stormy back to the workshop prisoner of war-style. Miles led. Stormy followed. Prue, occasionally touching Stormy's waist just in case she got any ideas, brought up the rear.

Stormy felt ridiculous, tramping back across The Vale's grounds, hostage to Prue's silly Girl Scout's desire to bring her to justice. Not that the cops worried her. At worst, they'd be a B-grade pain in the ass. She planned to deny everything. You didn't need a goddamn doctorate of law to see that there was no way they could connect her to that parcel. What worried Stormy was that it looked like her game was up. As soon as the cops got the coke, Fat Boy had nothing to lose. And that left Stormy with everything to lose. Anyway she looked at it, a bum deal.

The door to the workshop was left opened. Miles went in first, calling, "Moonbeam." Then: "Oh, no."

Prue pushed past Stormy and uttered her own sigh. When Stormy finally entered, she had trouble fighting back the urge to shout in sheer unbridled glee. The canvas tarp had been pulled back. The plastic-wrapped parcel was missing. Moonbeam was nowhere in sight.

It took a full minute of staring, scalp scratching, and head shaking before Miles spoke. "Wish I had never called the cops."

Prue shot him the dirtiest of looks.

He seemed to have no trouble interpreting its meaning. "Moonbeam's going to be in big trouble, don't you understand."

Prue evidently hadn't thought of that. A hand went to her mouth. She let out a barely audible "O-o-o-o-o-o-h."

Miles went on. "Before, we could have passed him off as a good Samaritan. He found the dope. He turned it over to the authorities. Now he's run off with it." Miles shook his head. "Poor deluded guy. He wanted to donate it to The Vale. Saw it was the solution to all our financial problems." Miles shook his head again and let out a couple of sad little laughs through his nostrils.

"Not a bad idea," Stormy volunteered, trying her best to sound sarcastic, ever so slightly smart-ass, but at the same time hoping to plant the seed of an idea that might have had one in a billion chances of taking root. Somehow, at that moment, those odds didn't seem half-bad.

Both Miles and Prue glared, as if Stormy had just said something grossly inappropriate.

Before the conversation went any further, a four-wheel drive Toyota land cruiser pulled up outside the workshop. Two doors thudded.

"Well, the police are here now," Miles said. "What are we going to do?"

Stormy figured it was as good a question as any. But she didn't have much time to pursue an answer. The door got kicked open wider and the first cop barged in. It was Pock-face, still in his Sunday best. The other cop entered about a half-second later. Even in the formal dress uniform of the Royal Bahamian Police Force, Stormy recognized him as the one who called himself Fat Boy.

Stormy had to laugh. At first, it was just a few chuckles that she could keep concealed. That led to snickering. After a few of those, she thought, What the hell, and let go with a series of loud peals. "Well, if it isn't old Fat Boy himself," she said. "You neglected to tell me your occupation that night we ran into each other."

In the background, Prue muttered, "You seem to know everybody," but Stormy kept up her prattle.

"Fat Boy, you aren't going to believe it, but until moments ago these good missionaries were in possession of a green garbage bag full of pure, sweet Colombian cocaine." Laughter again got the upper hand. Stormy succumbed, muttering, "Imagine. A goddamn cop."

Finally, she drew herself up and flashed a big smile at everybody in the shed. The germ of a plan had started to grow in the fertile conditions that the good gut laugh had left in her mind. Finding out that Fat Boy was a cop had started the old wheels clicking. Not too fast. Nothing solid, not yet. But the plan had definite possibilities. Enough to make the odds distinctly better. Maybe a thousand to one. Stormy started toward the door. "Well, Fat Boy, I'm sure these good folks will give you a real earful. Me, I gotta go look for something I lost."

As she passed Fat Boy, she stopped and fingered the lapel of his uniform jacket. "Nice duds," she said.

Chapter 8

Prue went to bed late that night—after eleven. By that time, Miles had been snoring on top of the bedspread for an hour. He wore a pair of boxer shorts and an undershirt. A bottle of rum stood on the night table next to a Bible, which was opened facedown. Prue stood sizing up the snoring Miles, angry at him for getting drunk again, yet, at the same time, terribly sorry for the man. The prospect of losing The Vale must have been devastating. He had really built his life around the mission and the children. Prue often had trouble separating Miles from The Vale; they seemed like one entity. Which one was it that she loved the most? Or more to the point, would she still want to be married to Miles if The Vale ceased to exist? That one, she couldn't answer. But her uncertainty made her feel even more sorry for Miles.

She nudged and rolled him from side to side until she freed the spread and other bedclothes from under him. He groaned with each roll, but it appeared that nothing was going to rouse him from his stuporous slumber. Prue quickly disrobed, hung up her dress, washed her face, and brushed her teeth. She eased herself into bed beside Miles. Instantly, his eyes batted open.

"It's late," he mumbled.

"I've been over in the kitchen keeping Clover company. She's terribly worried about Moonbeam."

Miles blinked his eyelids several times. The process appeared to pump coherency into his being—or, at the very least, made him appear more coherent than he probably was. "You heard the chief constable. They just wanted to take him to the station for some routine questions."

"The way they threw him into that jeep didn't look routine to me."

Miles slid over and put an arm around her shoulders. Prue snuggled against him and rested a hand against his belly just above the waistband of his underpants.

"First thing tomorrow morning, I'll go down and see about getting him out. There's nothing we can do now." Miles paused. "I wonder why the dumb kid refused to tell where he had hidden the drugs?"

"He's so confused. And frightened. Maybe it's like he said: He doesn't remember."

"Maybe he's still got it in his head that selling the cocaine would be the salvation of The Vale."

Prue sighed. "What I can't understand is why they let that awful woman go—just like that."

"The chief said, 'Not a shred of real evidence.' "

She sat up and faced Miles. "You're not defending her, are you? She was so—" Prue searched for the right word, couldn't find it, so uttered the first one that came to mind. "—creepy"—which fell far short of describing her true feelings about Stormy Lake.

Miles curled up on his side of the bed in a fetal position. "Defend her? No. Just trying to explain why they might have left her and taken Moonbeam. You asked the question."

There was a silence. Then Prue said, "I don't trust them."

"Prue, they're police officers."

"Yes, I know that."

At a few minutes before midnight, Stormy moaned and reached over to turn off her bedside lamp. But on second thought, she decided it would be a crime against passion to do anything that would diminish the visuals. Dugold apparently didn't care one way or the other. He pounced on top of her. His skin glistened with sweat, like highly varnished mahogany. He smelled of musky perspiration and manhood. He kissed her hard on the lips, then began to work his way down, nibbling her breasts, her belly. Stormy gave a little cry and pulled him up by the shoulders. She wrapped her legs around his buttocks, which were small and tight and hard.

He began to thrust, slowly and deeply at first, then increasingly rapidly until he was in a frenzy. Stormy fell back against the pillows and let herself be taken. The old bedsprings squeaked and scraped, the headboard rap-tapped against the wall, and Dugold began to emit a series of deep, throaty grunts. Stormy closed her eyes, let out another little cry, and braced herself for a ride on the great pulsating tide.

The orgasm never came. Right at that point, Stormy suddenly realized she knew exactly where Moonbeam would have stashed that coke. She was overcome with an urge—a burning necessity—to get out of bed and go retrieve it. And she would have, if she could have figured out how to stop Dugold long enough to explain why she needed the Whaler right then, at that moment.

In the single room he rented in the back of an old house on an Immokalee side street, Cal Cooligan yawned. From the water-stained acoustical tiles on the ceiling to the scuffed linoleum on the floor and the holes in the yellowish bedspread, it was a sad, depressing room, a place of quick, violent couplings, of loneliness so profound, it hurt. Cal's watch said midnight. The school bus that hauled him and his coworkers to Montano's tomato farm left at six in the morning. He carefully folded the two-week-old copy of *Barron's* he had read so often and so thoroughly that its pages had become soft and subtle, like chamois cloth. It went into a hiding place under his mattress. His landlady liked to snoop. She might begin to wonder why a tomato picker showed such an interest in financial publications like *Barron's* and, when he was lucky, a day-old edition of *The Wall Street Journal.* No sense making it easy for her.

Cal stripped to his underpants and flopped onto the lumpy mattress. The couple who lived in the room on the other side of the plywood partition were making love. Cal knew because one of the floorboards beneath the linoleum in his room squeaked, keeping perfect time with the couple's acrobatics. The guy was frisky, like a rabbit, but, unlike a rabbit, he had good duration, too, a regular marathoner, and for some reason, he was going for a record that Sunday night. Cal listened. He had no choice. He even felt himself becoming aroused, something he blamed on the six months since he had last been with a woman. Part of the job. But still a hell of a position for a man who might have made the short-list for Manhattan's ten most-sought-after bachelors a year ago.

But he could put up with that side of his life being put on hold. It was his stalled career that bothered him the most. Cal hated being sidelined. Mergers and acquisitions were making his old partners rich, while he picked tomatoes. Cal wondered whether it was worth it.

He leaned over and reached for the framed photograph on an upended orange crate—his night table. Not much of a picture, not in the professional sense, but Cal liked it because it was 100 percent candid. Taken by one of those automatic 35 mm cameras, it showed an attractive young black woman wearing the uniform of an Eastern Airlines flight attendant. The wind had blown a lock of her hair in front of her eyes and she was laughing, wide-mouthed, uninhibited, determined to be happy even if the weather was making a mess out of her hairdo. The woman was Cal's little sister; Cal's dead little sister.

Cal put the picture down and turned out the light. He lay back and wiggled his shoulders between the two least uncomfortable mattress lumps. With his eyes closed, Cal thought about his Wall Street career, his sex life, his sister.

106

He drifted toward sleep while the couple in the next room kept his floorboard singing its energetic squeak, squeak, squeak.

The storage room at the Fresh Creek police station was windowless, with walls of plain, unpainted cinder block. Its cement floor tilted inward to a metal drain. The cement glistened with urine and thick clotted blood. It was the blood that gave the room a heavy slaughterhouse stench: one of feces, old meat, human sweat, and the aroma of dull, bovine panic. Stark nude and curled in one corner, Moonbeam whimpered.

Fat Boy sat in the other corner—the one farthest from Moonbeam—in a folding chair. He was out of his official uniform and back in the brown pants and fawn safari shirt. He checked his watch.

When he spoke, his voice was soft and kind. "It's past midnight. Moonbeam, we've been here nearly nine hours. We're all very tired. But don't you understand, I have to know where you put it. Tell me and Raul will stop hurting you. I promise. All you have to do is tell the truth."

Moonbeam faced Fat Boy. One eye looked at him with defiance. The other socket stayed closed, hollow and seeping. He started to cry. "Nooooooo," he said. "It belong to da preacher."

Fat Boy yawned. "Raul," he said, and nodded toward Moonbeam.

The pock-faced man stepped forward and wiggled his fingers into an old-fashioned set of brass knuckles, the type favored by street gangs before the advent of Uzis and AK-47s. He took a fistful of Moonbeam's dreadlocks, gave them a half wrap around his palm, and hoisted him to his feet. The hand with the brass knuckles came around in a wide arc and slammed into Moonbeam's testicles, already the size of tennis balls. Moonbeam screamed and fell back to the slime-coated cement. His penis ejaculated a single squirt of bloody urine. He began to cry, loud, like a little kid.

Fat Boy waited until Moonbeam's crying subsided into sobs.

While he waited, he carefully dabbed the sweat from his face with a dirty handkerchief. He sighed and rubbed his eyes. Checked his watch. "We're getting nowhere, Raul. Maybe it's time to arrest the preacher and his lady friend. Give them the same treatment."

Moonbeam stopped sobbing. "No," he barked.

Traces of a smile came to Fat Boy's maimed face. "Then tell me where you hid it. Raul will stop hurting you, and we won't hurt your friends. I promise."

The one functioning eye took in Fat Boy. Moonbeam gulped in deep breaths of air. "Da boat. In da preacher boat."

Fat Boy inflated his cheeks until it looked as if the long scab that ran from eye to mouth might split. Before it did, he blew out a big puff of air and smiled and nodded his head. "I believe he is telling us the truth, Raul," he said, picking up Moonbeam's Sunday clothes and rummaging for the belt. He kept the belt and tossed the old suit to Raul. "Clean him up as best you can. Dress him. And throw him back into the cell."

Fat Boy paused and fingered the belt. He put the loose end through the buckle and shoved his wrist into the loop. When he let his fist fall, the belt tightened with a snap around his wrist. "This might just do the trick," Fat Boy said. "What do you think?"

The pock-faced guy looked at his boss and the outstretched belt. The makings of a genuine smile crept across his snaggle-toothed mouth.

Chapter 9

At 9:30 A.M., Monday, December 12, with exactly eighteen days until he had to find a half-million dollars for his brother, Miles woke, alone, groggy, dull-witted, yet somehow mercifully free from the pangs of a full-blown hangover. He yawned but made no effort to leave the bed.

Prue had no doubt risen shortly after dawn. It being Monday, with a whole week's worth of possible activities lined up, she might have left even earlier, to prepare classes and go over menus with Clover.

Clover. Head cook—and Moonbeam's mother. Moonbeam. Now Miles remembered. He did have something to do. He had promised to see about Moonbeam. In a flush of righteous motivation, Miles planted his feet on the floor and let his eyes focus on the room. His fawn Sears suit—his get-down-to-business garb—had been laid out on a chair. His sandals were beside each other on the floor below, ready to be stepped into.

But first, Miles padded into the bathroom, which, in keeping with the decor of every room in The Vale, was fish-camp rustic. The floor was bare wood. The walls still unashamedly flaunted their two-by-four framework, here and there spiked with nails meant to serve as towel hangers. The tub was a chipped porcelain crowfoot model, the sink small and bolted directly to the two-by-fours behind it. On a single board shelf above the sink, Prue had laid out the necessary implements to make Miles presentable, beginning, as always, from the left and proceeding in the order that he used them: hairbrush, shaving brush and soap mug, razor, the stub of a tube of Crest, and a toothbrush.

Ten minutes later, hair slicked back and in his fawn Sears suit, Miles walked in through the back door of The Vale's kitchen. Clover was chanting some tuneless, nameless gospel number that consisted of half-hummed, half-muttered snippets from the Scriptures. She sung from her usual post, directly in front of a Vulcan stove, a massive black block of iron. But even that institutional-style mammoth seemed like a toy beside Clover's squat five-foot-six-inch, 312-pound frame.

"Morning, Reverend," she cooed in a surprisingly soft voice for a woman of her size. Then, picking up her improvised song where she had left off, she cracked two eggs, whisked them a couple of times in a small bowl, and upended it over the grill. With her broad rump swaying from side to side in time to her private tune, she plucked a few fingers full of grated cheddar and dropped them on top of the egg, added a sprinkling of chopped green onion, a shake of paprika, and fresh pepper. She slapped four strips of thick bacon on the grill, then picked up another bowl and meted out enough batter for three of her notoriously light buttermilk pancakes.

Miles poured himself a mug of black coffee and sat at a place set for him at the Formica-topped table in the center of the kitchen—his assigned eating spot if he missed a meal with Prue and the students in the main dining hall, which meant it was his regular stop for breakfast. He sipped, and let his nose take in the scent of the coffee and the aroma of the frying bacon.

In mid-sniff, the telephone rang. Miles made a respectable effort to rise—given that the last thing he felt like doing was answering the phone—but Clover stopped him by thrusting out her spatula. Still singing, she flipped each of the pancakes, and, in three quick jabs, folded and turned the omelet. Her song rose to a crescendo, toying with and drawing out the *or* in *Lord*. When she reached the phone, she let herself hit the *d* with a deep bass note of some finality. Her chirped "Hello" could have been the first word in a new, more upbeat gospel jingle.

There was no singsong in what she said next. "Yes, it is she who is speaking to you." Suddenly, her broad, smooth features imploded. The lower lip—stretched tight—quivered. "N-o-o-o-o-o-o," she wailed. Tears spurted from the crinkled rims of her eyes. "No-o-o-o-o-o-o," she cried a second time, dropping the receiver and cupping her face with her hands.

Miles draped an arm over the big woman's shoulders and guided her back to his chair. "What is it, Clover?"

Clover looked at him, summoned tremendous effort, and for a brief time stopped crying. But her face imploded again.

"N-o-o-o-o-o-o," she wailed.

Samuel Wiggins & Sons Furniture Emporium and Undertaking Services, Ltd. operated out of a dilapidated building in the center of the village of Fresh Creek. Both the chipped and peeling paint, once apparently a pastel pink but now faded to a dirty whitish hue, and the rusting corrugated metal roof indicated that the Wiggins clan prospered neither through their furniture making nor their undertaking.

At shortly before eleven, Miles entered the Samuel Wiggins & Sons building and found himself standing in a cramped vestibule. Its only adornments were two orange-colored plastic chairs. The place smelled vaguely like a high school biology classroom.

A buzzer button beside a door leading toward the back read, PLEASE RING. Miles did as bidden. A moment later, the door opened and a fair-skinned black youth came in wearing a face of profound sadness. In contrast to the building, the young man was immaculately dressed and well groomed. In his late twenties, perhaps early thirties, he sported a small trim mustache and close-cropped hair with a part on the left side, the same side where the earlobe displayed a single diamond stud—probably up there in the two-carat range. The navy suit fit him well, with cuffs cut just high enough to display his Rolex. He wiped his hands on a white handkerchief, carefully and for a long time, making sure that each finger received individual attention, right out to cuticle and nail. Finally, obviously satisfied that he had removed any traces of offending substance, he extended the right hand.

"Reverend. So good of you to come," he whispered, as if raising his voice might revive clients in the back room.

Miles took the hand. Its grip was weak and it felt clammy.

The young man, who Miles guessed must have been one Wiggins or another, dropped Miles's hand as quickly as discretion allowed and stood back to resume his wiping. He looked Miles up and down in that disconcerting manner of undertakers. Once he reached Miles's sandals, he indicated the chairs.

"Have you made plans for the service, Reverend?" he whispered.

"Tomorrow. 1:30."

Young Wiggins put a solemn look on his face and nodded. "Would you be requiring a casket? We have two on hand that would be—would be suitable."

Miles shifted uncomfortably. "Actually, we have our own woodworking shop at The Vale, and the boy's mother has limited means, so I thought we might make one for him . . ." Miles trailed off, feeling awkward.

A look of even deeper sadness spread across the young Wiggins's face.

Miles continued. "But his mother has expressed a wish for an open-casket service, if you could . . ." He trailed off again.

Wiggins looked at Miles with the blackest, most heartfelt grief. "I regret that's impossible."

"I don't understand."

Wiggins's despair deepened even further. "Reverend, it pains me to say this, but the condition of the remains . . ."

"But the police said he had hanged himself. Committed suicide. Surely the remains . . ."

Something that Miles had just said made Wiggins brighten. "Suicide?" he said. "Suicide, is that what they say? Interesting." He looked into the middle distance and shook his head. Then he snapped his attention back to Miles. "Excuse me, Reverend, for becoming cryptic. One sees a regrettable number of suicides in my line of work—even on a small, peaceful island like Andros. Maybe because it is a small, peaceful island. At any rate, I've had to prepare people who have slit their wrists, poisoned themselves, drowned themselves, shot themselves, and hanged themselves."

He paused for a moment and carefully weighed what he was about to say next. "Reverend, this will have to stay strictly between you and me, but I can honestly say this is the first time I have had to deal with a suicide case wherein the victim burned himself with a cigarette, gouged out one eye, bludgeoned his skull with a heavy claw hammer, then, suffering from multiple skull fractures and a major cerebral hemorrhage, took it upon himself to insert his neck into a belt and suspend himself from the bars of a window fully ten feet off the ground."

Stormy figured she was a good nine-tenths of the way toward her orgasm—and a well-earned one at that. Monday being Dugold's day off, they had slept until eleven. Stormy woke feeling randy, and now she sat astride Dugold amid the knotted remains of sheets and blankets. She held two fistfuls of his shoulder muscle and gyrated her pelvis in slow, deep circles.

Between the fourteenth and fifteenth orbit of Stormy's hips, some idiot knocked on the door. Tough luck for whoever it was. She completed gyrations fifteen and sixteen before the knock came again, this time more vigorous and accompanied by a gruff "Open up."

That still wasn't enough to put a stop to seventeen, eighteen, and nineteen. But then the voice on the other side of the door barked, "Police! I order you to open the door."

Those words always evoked an immediate response from

Stormy. She leapt off Dugold with a little squeak of disappointment. "Coming," she said, and immediately realized the bitter irony in her choice of words, so she added, "Getting so a girl can't get a decent morning's sleep on this island. Next time, I'll spend my vacation on Bimini."

Dugold, too, reacted promptly. He leapt from the bed, and began to paw through the heap of textiles that had built up on the hotel-room floor, now and then extracting one of his own garments and struggling into it. Stormy dressed at a more leisurely pace. She fished a pair of panties out of the snarl of clothes that overflowed her open packsack. The terrain under the bed yielded khaki short shorts that showed no obvious signs of having been worn two days earlier. A white sleeveless T-shirt, wrinkled but clean, hung on the corner of an open dresser drawer. She pulled it on and then went to tend to the knocking.

Fat Boy came through, alone for once, and back in his cream-colored safari shirt and brown polyester pants, neither of which had seen the inside of a washing machine since the last time he had worn them. He sweated and gave off a tart, oily odor. At first, he looked surprised to see Dugold, then disgusted. "Please leave Miss Lake and me alone," he said.

Dugold complied. All too willingly, Stormy thought. "I'll be waiting downstairs," he said.

Fat Boy closed the door and looked around for a place to sit. His choices were the war zone of the bed and a single chair, obscured under a load of used towels. Finding neither to his liking, he leaned up against the door he had just closed.

"Miss Lake—"

"It's Stormy, Fat Boy. For the hundredth time, call me Stormy. And by the way, I don't appreciate being busted in on like this. Wasn't the most convenient of moments, you know."

Fat Boy looked at her angrily, like a man who very much regretted not bringing Raul along. "Very well," he said. "Your sleeping patterns are of no interest to me. No interest whatsoever. But I thought you should know I have found the cocaine."

"You trying to tell me that suddenly I have become very, very redundant?"

Fat Boy smiled one of his ugly smiles. It must have hurt him. He put a hand up to the long gash. "Regrettably, no. Not as yet. You see, it is in a rather awkward location. I would hate to be found taking it myself. If it was known that I had it, professional pressures would dictate that I turn it over to my superiors on the police force. And regrettably, they themselves would probably sell it. No, I want you to secure it and bring it to me tonight. At the police station."

Stormy opened the door. "Sounds easy enough. Now if you don't mind, I need a shower, so unless you'd care to join me . . ." She raised her eyebrows three times and ran her tongue over her upper lip.

"Very humorous, Miss Lake. But aren't you overlooking something?"

"Like what?"

"The whereabouts of the cocaine."

"You mean under the front berth in the preacher's stinkpot?"

The look on Fat Boy's mangled face came very close to making the events of the previous week worthwhile. First, there was a sudden flush of surprise. But that was quickly replaced by the crinkled brow and clenched teeth of distress. "How did you know?" Fat Boy said, taking an unintentional step back.

Stormy allowed herself a sweet and deeply mysterious smile. She batted those big slightly crazed eyes. "Let's just say it kind of came to me in the night."

Miles thanked God for the gnawing he felt in his head, the one that told him in no uncertain terms that it was time for a drink, *now, immediately,* and would admit no other thoughts until its single demand was satisfied. Blinking in the bright noontime sun outside the offices of Samuel Wiggins & Sons Furniture Emporium and Undertaking Services, Ltd., Miles was glad to feel the familiar old pangs. They prevented him from thinking about what young Wiggins had said.

He walked quickly through the narrow streets of Fresh Creek, which were laid out according to a grid pattern that demanded each one have an oblique angle every thirty yards, whether one was needed or not. At noon, most of the streets were empty, save for the snoozing mongrels curled into the scarce patches of shade and the occasional dusty, tired-looking Out Islander, who inevitably smiled, nodded, and said a polite "Hello, Reverend."

The Chickcharnie Hotel occupied the most prosperous-looking building in town. Its eight rooms were on the second floor, with the street level given over to a grocery store, a dry-goods emporium, a restaurant, and a bar. Miles went to the bar, sat at a table, and ordered a beer, then corrected himself and changed it to a double rum on the rocks with a dash of tonic and a wedge of lime. When that came, he swallowed it and, without comment, passed his glass back to the waiter for a refill. The second drink arrived and he sipped slowly, as if to reassure himself that the beverage in fact existed. The gnawing stopped. Satisfied, he leaned back. Perhaps five minutes passed before he saw Stormy Lake.

She and a young man from town sat together at a table on the restaurant side of the large open room. They appeared to be making good progress on a pair of breakfast orders. Miles recognized the local boy. Couldn't put a name to him, but the youth had attended The Vale's school, graduated, and gotten a job as a diving master at Small Hope Bay Lodge. Nice boy, Miles remembered. And by the way they were sitting together, the nudging, the eye contact, the frequent giggles, Stormy, too, must have found him a nice boy. Miles didn't like the nibble of jealousy he felt, so he ordered another rum.

He wasn't aware of her getting up and coming across the room, but suddenly Stormy stood across the table from him. She leaned close with her arms pressed tightly along the length of her torso and her palms splayed for support on the edge of the table.

"Hiya, Rev. Why so glum and so boozed so early this fine day?" she said, and reached out and gave his nose a quick twist.

Embarrassed, Miles looked around the room to see whether the gesture had been seen by anyone else, but the place was empty. Even Stormy's boyfriend had left. Despite himself, he felt his eyes filling with hot tears. He fought them, but soon gave in and wiped his eyes with the back of his hand. "They killed Moonbeam," he said.

Stormy dropped onto a chair. She bashed her fist on the table. "Aw, Christ!" she said.

"Suicide. That's what they say. But the undertaker says Moonbeam was beaten up—so badly we can't have an open casket. Poor, harmless, crazy little guy. Why would they do—"

"Dirty, rotten, dumb chickenshits. They didn't have to do that." Her eyes bulged, and any traces of their usual wackiness disappeared. "Jesus!" She shook her head, looked down at the table, and mumbled, almost as if to herself, "You know, if only your dear do-gooding Prue had left me alone yesterday, none of this would have happened."

Miles stood up. "She did what was right. What any thinking person would do." He stopped. Stormy thought he was preparing at the very least to modify—with any luck retract—large parts of the foregoing tirade. No such luck. "You're bang on about one thing," he began again, his voice quiet and, because of that, all the more dangerous-sounding. "None of this would have happened. None of it would have happened if you hadn't come on the scene. It's you who has got some explaining to do, lady."

Stormy put up a hand and decided that if the Rev wasn't going to dine on crow, she'd better nibble a few black pinfeathers before things got well and truly out of hand. "Rev, I didn't mean that bit about Prue. It's just . . . Well, I liked that crazy little guy. I owed him a big one, too." She shook her head and let out a small chuckle. I suppose I owe you an explanation, of the whole thing, I mean."

Miles nodded and sat back down. Stormy signaled for the waiter and ordered two drinks, a bottle of Beck's for herself, another rum and tonic for Miles.

With the knack for bad timing possessed by certain cops, schoolteachers, and jealous wives, Prue entered at that precise moment. She stopped, silhouetted in the doorway, with her large book satchel. When she saw Stormy and Miles, her posture stiffened.

"Guess maybe this isn't the best time." Stormy nodded toward the door.

Miles flinched.

"We still gotta talk. You and me. Later on sometime?"

Miles looked back and forth between the two women. "I take a stroll in the evenings. At nine. Tonight. Down by my boat. You know . . . my boat?"

Without waiting for an answer, he got up and went to where Prue stood in the doorway.

Stormy sat quietly until they were gone. "Yeah, I think I remember that boat," she said to the empty table.

Stormy made sure she got to the *Come to Jesus Cruiser* at eight-thirty, a good half hour early. The night was black, with a low layer of cloud obscuring both moon and stars. An offshore wind blew, rustling the branches of the casuarinas and causing wavelets to slap the hull of Dugold's boss's Whaler. Not wanting her arrival heard, she paddled the last quarter mile. Before stepping out of the boat, she sat in the shadow of the wharf to make sure no one had seen her.

At her first step, a loose board let out a pained squeal, as if it were both startled and insulted—hurt that someone would dare tread on it. If they'd tried, they could not have fashioned a better burglar alarm. Stormy froze, certain the entire Vale compound had heard. But the place seemed quiet, except for the main building, where lights were on. Emboldened, she strode purposefully across the wharf, paying no attention to the squawking planks.

She vaulted over the cruiser's gunwale, and stood in the darkness of the cabin's shadow to listen. Whatever had been going on in the main building had stopped. One by one, lights began to go off. Moving fast, Stormy jiggled the latch on the cabin door. It came open.

The cabin had retained the heat of the day. It hit Stormy's face, warm and humid and smelling of diesel and mildew, with the tart addition of urine from the head. The slapping of the waves against the hull was louder inside. Stormy flicked on a pocket flashlight and shone it just long enough to get her bearings. She walked in the dark to the V bunk in the bow. Without using the light, she pulled away the port-side cushion and put it on the floor. She felt along the platform until she found the recessed handle of the stowage chamber's hatch. It came away easily and she laid it beside the cushion. She risked another flick of the light to get a look at the contents of the chamber—just life jackets. Stormy put away her light and began to remove the jackets, piling them on the opposite bunk. There were six. Another shot of light revealed a tangle of anchor line. Getting that out was difficult in the dark. But she managed, and pushed and punched it out of the way in the far reaches of the bow.

Stormy cupped her flashlight to direct as much of its beam as she could downward. She stuck her head and most of her right shoulder inside the hatch. The first thing that she saw was a half-empty bottle of Appleton's. The second was a parcel, spread over most of the bottom of the bin and carefully wrapped in heavy dark green plastic. "Well, hello there," she whispered.

She had turned her light off and was nearly ready to pull her head and torso out of the bin when she realized something was wrong. It took a couple of seconds for her to establish what the problem was. She could still see. Someone was shining a light over her shoulder.

Stormy looked up, but was blinded by the beam. A hand shoved her aside. The new light shone down in the hold. "Oh, Lord . . ." said the light's owner.

The swearing was totally out of character. But the voice Stormy recognized. It belonged to Miles.

"You going to stand there all night staring at that bin, Rev, or you going to act like a gentleman and bring out that heel of rum and offer a thirsty girl a teensy-weensy smash?" she said.

To her surprise, Miles did as he was bidden, but too silently for Stormy's liking. She didn't much like the way he breathed heavily and loudly through his nose, either.

"Better pour yourself a jolt, too. Keep huffing and puffing like that, you're liable to have a goddamn coronary. Hell of a thing for me to try to explain that to Prue."

Miles filled a plastic glass for himself. He shot a dirty look at Stormy, and without saying a word he meticulously began repacking the stowage compartment. The anchor rope, he coiled professionally. The life jackets were each patted and folded in half. The lid fitted firmly in place. The cushion, replaced, smoothed, and promptly sat upon. Only once he faced her, drink in one hand, flashlight in the other, did Miles speak.

"Let's just try to cut the malarkey for once," he said.

"Aw, Rev—"

"Shut up!"

Stormy put her hands in front of her face. "Okay, sorry."

"Were you going to steal that?" He patted the cushion.

"No."

He let out one long sigh, so Stormy elaborated. "I mean, not right yet exactly."

"How'd you know it was here?"

"Guessed. Remember the other night? In Nassau? You told me where you kept your secret stash. Figured Moonbeam might

120

know about it, too." She gestured toward the cushion beside Miles. "Mind if I rest my bones?" she asked. "I promise to come clean. Then you can toss me to the sharks, if you want."

"The way things stand, I have a mind to turn this entire thing over to the police."

"Police!" Stormy barked the word. "Shit, Rev, I suppose that's as good a place to start as any. Let me tell you all about those goddamn police of yours. Here." She shoved out her glass. "Freshen it up."

Cross-legged, left elbow on knee, palm supporting chin, Stormy began the story with the evening she met Fat Boy and Raul outside the Turk's Head Inn, and sparing no detail, she brought the plot up to where they issued the ultimatum. At that point, she diverged to give a flashback about Bingo, the dentist from Lowell, the *Roach,* and how she'd gotten the will-cum-treasure map. She picked up the story line again with her departure from Grand Turk, got in a little dig about the evening they had spent together, and quickly dispatched with her two days on Andros.

In the end, Stormy was smugly pleased about how close she had come to telling the whole truth, and nothing but. She had spilled about 95 percent of the beans, she figured. For her, that was damn good. The only parts she fibbed about were the juicy bits concerning Dugold, although thinking about them even just a little sent a tingle through her loins. And, of course, she skipped over her real intentions regarding the million bucks' worth of coke. But there was good reason to omit those details. Telling about either one risked turning Miles against her. For her scheme to work, she needed his cooperation—his full cooperation.

So for a finale, Stormy brought her tale to a close with a plea. She told him how her life was in danger, how Fat Boy had already killed Bingo and Moonbeam, but if Miles would only trust her. . . .

"Trust you?" he said, and shook his head slowly, so that his lips brushed the rim of his glass. "Stormy, because of your antics, Moonbeam is dead, and I find myself literally sitting on top of a shipment of illegal drugs. No. This time there's no question about it. I'm going to do the right thing. Tomorrow, I'm calling the authorities. Not Fat Boy, but his superiors in Nassau. I'll report everything to them." He paused. Let out a little groan and gave whatever was going to come next more than its share of thought. "I'm going to leave out your part in all this because I don't think it is material."

"Hey, that's real decent of you, Rev. I don't want to sound ungrateful or anything, but tell me one little thing, would you? Just what, exactly, do you think these higher authorities are going to do? Rev, you go to the cops, even the big boys, and I'm dead meat. And I mean dead dead, as in Moonbeam. You and dear, sweet Prue are not much better off. Fat Boy probably goes free. And some other, bigger crooked cop ships the merchandise to the States and pockets a pretty piece of change."

"They'll believe me. I'm not without influence. And they can't whitewash the facts about Moonbeam."

"Terrific. I can see it now: Fat Boy says Moonbeam resisted arrest. Had to be roughed up a little. Then he gets scared. Hangs himself. What else do you expect from a retarded, crazy kid? Couldn't be helped. That's what they'll believe, Rev, because that's what they will want to believe. It's in everybody's best interest, present company excluded."

"And I suppose your plans would solve everything?"

Stormy smiled and spread her arms, spilling a few drops of rum in the process. "You got it, Rev. Bang on, for once. My way, the dope is taken off your hands, Fat Boy is brought to a form of crude but adequate justice, my sweet ass stays intact"—she stopped and brought her face very close to his—"and you, Rev, you pocket a cool half-million for The Vale."

"Surely you're not proposing anything so ludicrous . . ."

"What I'm proposing is a simple end run around Fat Boy. That's all. I've got a pretty good idea I can find out who he

122

was to deliver the merchandise to, and I'll just bring it to them myself. Simple, eh? All you gotta do is keep your trap shut, and I'll cut you in for an even half million. Guaranteed. You get the first half million, I get the second, anything over a million, we split fifty-fifty. Sweetest deal you'll ever cut."

Miles shook his head and laughed. "You make it sound so simple. Like importing a load of tie-dyed T-shirts. What you're talking about is not only against the law, it's immoral. I should be insulted you'd think for a minute that I would go along—"

"Moral, schmoral. If a bunch of rich accountants and lawyers want to blow a little coke now and then, who are we to give a shit."

"What about all the drug-related deaths? What about all the kids whose lives this stuff is ruining?"

Stormy nodded at him over her glass. "Yeah. And what about those little kids over there." She flung her tangled curls toward The Vale. "I'm offering you a chance to keep helping them. All you have to do is do nothing. Think about that."

"I wouldn't consider being a party to an attempt to smuggle drugs. Not for a moment."

"You know, Rev. You know what I think. I think you'd like to see this place go tits up. I actually think you like the image of being thought of as the downtrodden underdog. Victim of your nasty big brother. Driven to drink. Forces of good being defeated by evil—all the rest of that New Testament shit. And if a few dozen kids lose the only chance they will ever have, no big sacrifice to bolster your inferiority complex."

"That's not true."

"Balls, Rev. Face it. This"—she patted the mattress—"is the real world. Like it or not, it's here, and you, pal, are part of it. This sack of coke's come into your goddamn life, and whatever you do now, there's going to be some ugly business going down. My way, there'll be a whole lot less. And a better-than-even shot that some genuine good will come." Again she gestured toward The Vale.

"You're rationalizing."

"Yeah, maybe I am. But I'll tell you one thing. I'm not rationalizing about Fat Boy's threats on my life. He's proven himself willing and able on that count. So if you want my blood on your conscience, too . . ." She stopped. "Rev, all you have to do is look the other way, for God's sake. . . ."

"For God's sake, huh?" He sipped from his drink and chuckled. "When I think how things have changed in the past five days. I mean, before I was happily engaged and true to Prue. The Vale was secure. Moonbeam dove for his lobsters. Now . . . I'm completely baffled. I don't know what's best. I have to think. To pray."

"Consult with the boss, you mean?"

He smiled at her. "You have a way of making everything seem irreverent. Maybe that's why I enjoy your company, even though I should know better."

Stormy leaned over and gave him a peck on the cheek. "Why thank you," she said in mock southern belle. "That is one of the sweetest things a man has ever said to me." She stood. "You think. Or pray. Or whatever you guys do. Me, I gotta go explain to Fat Boy about how I couldn't find the stuff here tonight."

Stormy turned her flashlight to guide the way to the cabin's hatch. Its feeble beam lighted up the burnished mahogany cabinets of the galley, the four steps that led toward the hatch, and, where there should have been a black square of night above the hatch, the angry, somewhat frustrated face of Prue.

Prue stood aside politely—too damn politely—to let Stormy pass, but she did not say a word until the Whaler grumbled to life. That left Miles fiddling with his flashlight and with plenty of time to concoct an explanation, or rather, try to.

"That, that, that . . . that woman." Prue spat out the word *woman* as if it were some common vulgarism. "She kissed you."

"Prue, really. It was nothing."

"I bet. Maybe someday, you'll be so kind as to give me a full explanation. For the moment, though, someone has to run this mission, while the pastor . . ." She let her frown and furrowed brow finish the sentence. Then she took a deep, cleansing breath and once more had control over herself. "The reason I came down is that the funeral home is on the telephone. They want to know about tomorrow. Would you like to talk to them?"

"Our woodworkers were supposed to have finished the casket this evening. I'll go over to the workshop and check to make sure they got it done. Would you mind telling the funeral people we'll drop it off at their place first thing in the morning?"

Prue tugged at the sides of her cardigan. "Very well. But we have to talk. And Miles." Prue extended an index finger toward the heel of Appleton's. "Take it easy on that."

"One more. That's all. Then I'll be up."

Miles left a half-inch emergency supply in the bottom of the heel and put the bottle back where it had come from. Then, glass in hand, he went topside to think. Mostly, he found himself thinking about Stormy Lake, about her proposal to take the dope and give him a half-million dollars. Ridiculous. But to the theologian in Miles, it posed an interesting dilemma. Which would do the greatest harm? Surrender the drugs to the authorities, thereby foregoing the money and being forced to shut down The Vale. Or do nothing. Let the dope go through. A minuscule amount, really. And Stormy had a point. It was probably destined for a bunch of well-to-do Yuppies. There was a good chance that one little shipment of cocaine would cause no real harm at all. And the benefits? There were the thirty or so young Bahamian lives, to begin with.

He swallowed off the last of the rum and let its warmth work against the night breeze. What, for that matter, would Christ have done if confronted with the same dilemma? That was an interesting one.

Miles fell to his knees, rested his elbows on the *Come to Jesus Cruiser*'s gunwale, and folded his hands. He shut his eyes tightly, until the beads of yellow light on his retinas gave way to bright, burning irregular-shaped islands. Then, uttering the words *Father help me* aloud, he let his mind be drawn into those glowing islands.

That night, for the fourth time in his life, Miles heard the voice of God. Like before, it was deep and a little slow, like that of a well-educated Midwesterner. But in few words, and in a straightforward fashion, the voice told Miles exactly what he should do. After he heard the voice out, Miles had to admit that the old boy had come up with a pretty solid plan. A little Machiavellian—no, downright mean—in the way it dealt with Stormy Lake, but solid.

Miles left the *Come to Jesus Cruiser* refreshed. He headed directly back to the cottage where Prue awaited him, making only one stop, at the woodworking shop, to check on Moonbeam's casket. It sat on two sawhorses, gleaming. Obviously it would suffice. Everything was ready for tomorrow's funeral.

"Hell, no. I didn't bring it with me," said Stormy as soon as Fat Boy demanded whether she had the coke.

He was sweating badly behind his desk at the back of the cop shop. He ran a forearm and hand across his forehead. "I told you I wanted it here tonight."

Stormy smirked at him. "Fat Boy, if you want it so badly, I can go back and get it now. But it'd be the stupidest mistake you ever made."

He snorted. "How so?"

"It dawned on me that the trickiest part of this operation lies ahead. Getting the shit stateside. That part of your bargain?"

He nodded once, and took another swipe of the forearm. "Could be."

"What if I said I had figured out a sure way for you to get it in risk-free. You be interested?"

Fat Boy actually displayed a flicker of genuine emotion. Nothing in his facial features revealed it. But there was a subtle change in his coloring. "How?" he asked.

"We'll have the preacher mule it across."

Chapter 10

Aside from the schoolchildren—a captive audience—only five people came to the funeral the next day, December 13, a Tuesday.

Prue led the service in the little graveyard to one side of The Vale. It began promptly at 1:30, as scheduled. She read with clear enunciation, verbatim from a small prayer book. Only once did she look up from the pages to glare at Stormy. Which, Stormy thought, was pretty good, given the nature of their encounter the previous evening.

Big rolling platoons of black clouds tumbled down the Tongue of the Ocean ahead of a north wind, giving the occasion a somber tone missing in Prue's rote delivery. And Clover's great heaves and sighs more than compensated for the lack of overt sadness in the uneasy throng of schoolchildren.

Finally, Prue reached the end of her script. "Reverend Farnsworth will now lead us in prayer," she said, and bowed her head so quickly it looked as if the tendons in her neck had been severed.

It took Miles a few seconds to rouse himself from the slumped posture he had adopted two steps to the left of Prue. He walked forward, until it looked as if he was going to fall headlong over the casket. But he stopped, with the toes that protruded from his sandals hanging just over the grave's edge. He gazed for an uneasy moment into the open hole. "Lord," he said, and waited for a beat or two. He might well have been expecting a response from on high. "Lord, we would like to thank you for giving us the life that was Moonbeam. We would like to thank you for the example he provided for all of us. His humor. His kindness. His generosity. All this, despite the disadvantages he battled."

There was a pause while Miles inflated his lungs. "Most of all, Lord, we would like to pray for all people so simpleminded, so egotistically centered, so wrapped up in their finite human limitations that they cannot accept your infinite wisdom, that they believe this brief corporeal existence on earth is all there is to life.

"Moonbeam and the example he provided will live on in our hearts, as his spirit lives on in your kingdom. Thank you."

Miles stepped back. Six older schoolboys lowered Moonbeam's handcrafted coconut wood and epoxy coffin inch by nervous inch into the grave.

Yet, when the ropes slackened, it was Miles, and not the dragooned pallbearers, who appeared relieved of a tremendous burden.

The kids all but bolted away from the cemetery, just ahead of the first splats of rain. The bearded owner of Small Hope Bay Lodge, now minus a lobsterman, stopped just long enough to bend down and say something comforting to Clover. Prue eventually put her arm around Clover's broad shoulders and led her toward the main building. When they had left, Miles picked up a spade and, with the help of one teenaged student, began to shovel. As Stormy walked past him, he said, "I have to talk to you. In one hour. At the Chickcharnie's bar."

Neither vocal inflection nor facial expression gave her an inkling of what he had to say. In fact, he didn't even break the rhythm of his shoveling.

Miles was back in his fawn Sears suit when he joined Stormy in the bar. He glanced nervously around the room, empty except for their table. As he looked the place over, he rubbed and tugged the skin at the back of his neck. Stormy knew something was really up when he ordered a rum and tonic, then immediately changed it to a Beck's. Even the waiter eyed him thoughtfully, and stood at their table for an extra few seconds, just to make sure Miles wasn't going to change the order.

The waiter barely had turned his back when Miles began to speak in urgent, hurried tones that would enable him to say what he had to say before he changed his mind. Stormy recognized it as the same tone of voice men—particularly married men—resorted to when they broke up with her.

"I have given your proposal thought, and have decided to go along. If certain things are done my way. First, I am going to be the one who brings the cocaine across. In the *Come to Jesus Cruiser*. Second, Prue is under no circumstances to know anything about this."

Their drinks came, so there was an inopportune silence as the waiter went about his business in a methodic way that might have been intended to elicit maximum impatience.

Finally, he got paid and left. Stormy gave Miles her best smile, and, for good measure, batted her eyes before saying, "No fuckin' way, Rev."

He swallowed the Beck's in a half-dozen gulps direct from the bottle. "Didn't think you'd go along with it." He ran a fawn sleeve across his lips and stood. "Confirms my suspicions, though."

"Sit down a minute." Stormy jammed an index finger at the plastic-upholstered kitchen-style chair he had just left. "You can't go running off after making a half-assed crack like that."

He eased himself back onto the chair but sat perched on the edge, as if he had no intentions of staying any longer than a minute or two, at best. Shorter if any reason came along to make him spring to his feet and dash away. "You'll excuse me, Stormy, if I say that, frankly, the way you laid it out last night, you would put yourself under tremendous pressure to take the dope, the money, and vanish back to Grand Turk. Or say something went wrong. Say you got caught. Or worse. Either way, I'd be high and dry."

"And your way . . ."

"My way, at least I don't have to worry about you disappearing. If you get nabbed . . . well . . . I wouldn't be any worse off, would I?"

Stormy's gut mistrust of anything that seemed to be going right for her kicked into the "on" position. She looked hard at Miles's face, to see whether there was anything there. But he just looked back at her, eyebrows raised imploringly below a lock of sandy-colored hair that just happened to have gone astray in a most disarming fashion. Just like the lopsided snout, it seemed to plead, "Trust me." Stormy didn't buy any of it. Not for a second. "Rev, hope you don't mind me saying so, but you don't know dick all about this business. Hell, I know more about preaching—"

"I didn't say anything about going solo. I realize I will be needing your expertise. But think of it this way. I'm known all through these islands. My boat is becoming a familiar sight. People trust me. In the States, my face is recognized. There would be nothing unusual about my taking the boat across. Right under their noses. The Reverend Miles Farnsworth is not the type of person who would smuggle narcotics."

"You seem to have this all thought through. Mind if I ask where I come into this grand scheme?"

"I need you to set up the deal. You have the contacts. You know how these things are . . . How these things are done."

Stormy swallowed from her glass. She nudged her own bottle, two-thirds empty, to Miles and closed her eyes and pursed her lips. There was something she didn't like about Miles's response to her proposition. He had agreed too easily. And, fundamentally, his plan made too much sense. Easy and sensible. Sure trouble. Especially when it fucked up her own schemes. Stormy drank and did some quick modifications. They called for her to shaft the Rev in the worst way imaginable. But, hell, he owed her one. She brightened considerably. "Yeah, and I'm also going to be right at your goddamn elbow when you sail that stinkpot across. Now, partner, spring for another round."

After the waiter dropped off the drinks, Stormy muttered, "Suppose I ought to call Bahamasair and see how soon I can get my butt over to the dear old U.S. of A. If they'll still accept me in that great republic."

Miles looked at her and arched his eyebrows.

She went on. "First thing is, I got to find out who Fat Boy was supposed to deliver the merchandise to, and assuming Fat Boy isn't going to volunteer that information, I'll have to make a few discrete inquiries. Luckily, I have a lead. Bingo wasn't much of a man, but he wasn't totally stupid, which is pretty high praise for a man, coming from me. At any rate, he checked Fat Boy out a bit. He's working for some half-assed Colombian who lives somewhere over on the Gulf side."

"That's a pretty big patch of territory."

Stormy frowned and nodded her head slowly. "Yes. And finding the right half-assed Colombian coke dealer on the west coast of Florida can be likened to looking for a needle in a haystack. But I have an old pal who used to be in the trade. He is out now. About as far out as you can get. Real estate, if you can imagine. But he keeps up." She smiled. "And he lives in Naples, too. Your home turf. Anyone you want me to look up? I could drop by and visit your big brother. Say hello? Try to seduce him? Kick him in the ka-junkas?"

Miles managed to keep his mug straight and businesslike. But if Stormy had been forced to bet, she would have said that the last alternative came close to evoking a genuine response.

Before leaving on the 7:02 A.M. Bahamasair flight the next morning, connecting in Nassau at 9:45 for Miami, Stormy had one more thing she wanted to do on Andros. It was crucial to

133

the success of her plan. It had to be done at night, the later the better. And it involved hitting Dugold up for the Whaler again, laying her hands on a quantity of heavy-duty dark green plastic, and buying all the white all-purpose enriched flour on the shelves of the Chickcharnie's store.

It also involved Stormy making sure she was a hell of a lot more careful about walking on squeaky wharf boards than she had been the previous evening.

Chapter 11

Birdy, at least, still packed a gun. By the look of the bulge in his shirt over his right kidney, he still packed something plain and practical and big, with a lot of knockdown clout. It had been one of Birdy's credos in the old days that if a man had a .357 Magnum in one pocket and ten thousand dollars U.S.— cash—in the other, he could refuel his plane at any airfield between Colombia and American territorial waters, confident that no one would be too worried about its luggage compartment's contents. The bulge over his kidney that cool, breezy morning, the morning of Thursday, December 15, told Stormy that Birdy had not completely reformed, despite his mansion with the matched pair of Mercedes 450s in the three-car garage (a four-wheel-drive Cherokee with a sign saying LYMAN QUAYLE PRESTIGE BUILDERS, INC. sat in the third bay). Or that if Birdy had reformed, at least he hadn't turned into one of those assholes who forgets his past.

Yet, despite that reassuring bulge, the reunion began with a long, awkward moment. Stormy first blamed it on the unsettling effect of his goddamn Rotary pin. But, equally, it could have been the pink blazer upon whose lapel the pin was mounted. Or the two Dobermans that whined and danced at his heels. The Birdy to whom she had said goodbye nearly five years earlier one fine dawn on the tarmac at South Caicos as he prepared to jump into a DC-3 loaded with one final seambursting cargo of marijuana, that Birdy would have had one, and only one, use for a Rotary pin: as a hash holder. His sole outer garment in those days was a North Vietnamese army jacket with a bullet hole centered nicely on the left breast pocket; his canine companion an old mongrel with a mangy muzzle and only three legs. Under Dog, that had been the mutt's name.

After standing there for a full thirty seconds feeling dumb, Stormy figured out the cause of their unease. It was neither the pin, jacket, nor Dobermans. What really bothered her was the barred iron gates that guarded the fake Spanish-style courtyard Birdy had to walk across to answer her ring. Too much like a jail.

A pink stucco jail, to be sure, in the posh Port Royal district of Naples, Florida, nicely landscaped with the usual clusters of palmetto and small royal palms set on crew-cut Florida grass, and at a guess worth upward of 2 million. But there was a disquieting irony. One of Birdy's fears—the cause of much anguish and great paranoia in the old days—was that someday, some how he would goof and end up behind bars in Florida.

Adding to her unease was that for the first time in years, Stormy felt underdressed. It was a sunny day, but cool enough to have sent the citrus growers into a tizzy the night before, so Stormy was in her winter clothes: faded skintight jeans and a billowy sweatshirt displaying eight dime-sized splotches of the sky blue paint from *Roach*'s deck. Functional, fine garments, each one. Except, even the goddamn yardmen in that neighborhood wore neat uniforms. But, hell, how was she supposed to know what sort of street Gin Lane was when she asked the cabbie to take her there from her motel? The name itself had held all sorts of seedy promise.

For his part, Birdy was either too dumbfounded or too angry to break the silence. Perhaps he didn't recognize her, or, more likely given his altered fortunes, didn't want to admit that he did. So Stormy did the only thing she could think of. She took two of the metal bars in her hands, put her face up very close, rattled them vigorously, and said, "Birdy, you chubby poofter, they've finally managed to get you behind bars."

That broke the ice a bit. The corners of his mouth rose. He battled them back down. But they reattacked, this time managing a thin, nervous smile. "Very funny, Stormy. And I trust you've come to inquire about purchasing a Lyman Quayle home? We have a lovely little starter model in The Vineyards at three hundred twenty-five." The voice was still the same: soft, quick, and with effeminate overtones.

"Actually, I've just flown in from Andros and find myself in desperate need of a Bloody Mary. You're the only guy I know in Naples—at least the only one I'd trust to wield a Bloody Mary pitcher."

Birdy checked his gold watch. "Nine fifty-nine and she wants a drink. Glad some things don't change." He fiddled with something on the gates. One opened. He let it swing wide and gestured for Stormy to enter.

She hesitated, nodded toward the Dobermans.

"Oh, don't worry about these little puppies. Fully trained. Only attack when I give the command," he said, then added quietly, "Wish I could remember what in heaven's name it was."

Stormy entered warily. One of the Dobermans came up to her. It sniffed lustfully, planted its snout squarely in her crotch, and began to root.

"Trained for what?" she asked, trying to step away from the dog, which had developed a wet, pink erection.

"Titan. Apollo. Sit." The Dobermans dropped in unison, as quickly and cleanly as if Birdy had just hauled out that big ugly piece of his and given them each a quick one to the head, a remedy to which Stormy would not have entirely objected.

Birdy looked tremendously proud—and not a little surprised—at the dogs' compliance. "Now, follow me and I'll show you around my little dump while Arlena concocts a drink for us." He led the way past a fountain, stocked with a collec-

tion of bug-eyed and otherwise deformed goldfish, whose life
was to swim in circles around some sort of buck-nude cement
Cupid holding a goose that, in Stormy's considered opinion, appeared to be vomiting a continuous stream of water.

"Isn't he a little doll," said Birdy, patting the Cupid's chubby
ass. Stormy looked the Cupid over from curly locks to tiny un-
circumcised penis and concluded that if the statue ever attained
manhood, it would resemble Birdy. He was a big man, probably
an inch or two over six feet, but he managed to flit about lightly,
with a mincing shuffle, arms held akimbo, wrists limp. His hair
was fair, and getting finer, to judge from the way he combed
it over a bald spot on top of his head. In the five years since
he had given up flying cargoes of marijuana across the Caribbean, he had added perhaps thirty pounds to a frame that already had carried too much fat. Most of the new weight had
affixed itself to his rump. It swayed and wiggled and jiggled
merrily beneath his white trousers.

The living room, two stories and with cathedral ceiling, had
Spanish tiles on the floor. Antique bric-a-brac of vaguely Arabic
flavor dominated the place—rugs, shawls, tapestries, saddle-
bags, wineskins, brass hookahs. . . . Too much, in fact. An expensive south Florida decorator had obviously cleaned out
some destitute sheik's tent. Stormy half-expected to find a dis-
creet pile of camel dung in one corner.

Birdy called out, "Arlena, sweetie. Two Bloodies on the pool
deck, please. Chop-chop. We have a patient here who is dying
of thirst."

A deep southern voice answered from down a hallway that
led to the kitchen, Stormy assumed.

Birdy went ahead into the family room, though it looked
more like a commercial recreation center. A bank of electronic
video arcade games occupied the nearest wall. A billiard table
dominated half of the floor space, the rest being given over to
an assortment of very expensive children's toys: a two-seater
electric replica of the Mercedes in the garage, a large playhouse,

a computer terminal with a stack of Nintendo tapes, some sort of electric model racetrack.

Birdy whisked aside a sliding door and went out to a deck above a kidney-shaped pool, all covered over by screening. A canal bordered the property, perhaps a hundred feet away. At the pier, a monstrous fiberglass fishing yacht, complete with fighting chairs, outriggers, and a marlin tower, reposed like some dead, bloated white whale.

"Birdy, that might be the ugliest boat I have ever seen," Stormy said.

He gestured toward two chairs next to a glass-topped table. "Isn't it just an absolute hoot. A year ago, we went out fishing on a friend's boat. I liked it well enough. So what do I know next but Sibyl—she's my wife, you'd just love her—went out and bought me this . . . this . . . sea monster for my birthday. Said I needed a relaxing hobby. I really must learn to drive it one day." He clasped his belly and chuckled.

A black maid came out and put down two drinks. Behind her, clicking across the patio, came Under Dog—or rather the dog Under Dog might have been. The gray patches of mange had disappeared from the muzzle and enough muscle and fat had been put on the bones so that the dog was no longer a walking demonstration model of the canine skeletal system. Unfortunately, even the expensive Naples vets had been unable to do anything about the missing leg. But that didn't seem to faze the refurbished Under Dog. The old mongrel skittered right up to his master, leapt onto the ample lap, and fell into an instant sleep.

"That mutt still alive?" Stormy said. She took a sip. The drink was well spiced and pungent with the aroma of freshly rendered juice of homegrown tomatoes. It had the touch of key lime demanded of perfect Bloody Marys.

"Alive? Why poor Under Dog's a mere seventeen years old. Never been more fit. And loving his retirement. Just like me. You know how many air hours this poor beast has on him?"

Stormy smiled. "Which beast? You or him?"

Birdy took a long drink, smacked his lips, and let loose with a satisfied groan. "You want to know a delicious little secret? I'll tell, so long as you promise not to blab it all around Grand Turk.

Stormy hunched her shoulders and rubbed her hands together in mock eagerness.

"I have not flown an airplane in nearly five years and don't intend ever again to wrap my little fingers around a joystick. So there!"

Stormy propped her feet up against the edge of the table and let her knees spread to a comfortable distance. "You're shitting me," she said.

"Now, when I'm airborne, it's strictly, and I mean strictly, in the first-class cabin of a commercial jet, thank you. I spent a year flying around killing little Oriental people so that Lyndon Johnson could get himself reelected. I spent another decade in those rattletrap DC-sixes and DC-threes all over the dratted Caribbean because that was about all the work this thankless country provided for a person with my qualifications. Now, sweetie, I'm quite happy to have these tired feet right on the ground as a Florida real estate developer, thank you. A millionaire Florida real estate developer."

Stormy laughed. "Birdy, you're as happy as a pig in shit, aren't you?"

"You could have probably articulated it more eloquently, Ms. Lake, but . . ." He looked around to see whether anyone was within earshot, then shot his thumb upward and twittered, "Fuckin' A."

At precisely that instant, a little blond boy, three, maybe four, years old, came out the sliding door and ran headlong toward Birdy. "Daddy, Mommy's going to take me to the Conservancy to see the agrigators," he announced, latching on to Birdy's knee.

Birdy patted the kid between the shoulder blades. "Sounds

like fun. Maybe I'll meet up with you there later and we can all go to lunch."

"At Ronald's."

Birdy smiled proudly. "At Ronald's. But say, where're your manners? What do you say to the lady?"

The kid buried his face in Birdy's thigh and mumbled.

"You'd like her name. Ask her."

The kid mumbled again.

"He's asking your name," Birdy translated.

"Stormy."

The kid pulled away from his father's leg. "I'm Zak."

He shoved out a little hand. Stormy took it, shook, and then the kid bolted toward the house.

"Cute," Stormy said.

Birdy looked proudly at the open door and unconsciously scratched the grizzled top of Under Dog's head. "You, Bingo, Bear, and me, we had a lot of hoots in the old days. Sometimes I miss that. But you're right, I am happy." He smiled and let the thought settle. "But phooey. It's just great to see you. Can I ask to what I owe this pleasure? My Bloodies are good, oh, let's be frank, they're damn good, divine, perhaps, but . . ."

Stormy was ready to hit him with her request when a woman came out of the house. At first glance, it looked like Bo Derek might have just casually dropped over for a quick hello. The woman had that sort of good looks. On second glance, Stormy made a slight revision to the initial assessment: The woman resembled a six-months-pregnant Bo Derek.

"Sibyl. Come meet Stormy. I've told you all about Stormy, Bingo, Bear, and the others," Birdy said.

"Far, far too much, I'm afraid." The woman had a deep, soft voice that lent a warmth to her gentle sarcasm. Her smile was as open and unaffected as it was beautiful. "Stormy, welcome to Naples. Will you be staying with us? I could have Arlena make up the guest suite. . . ."

141

"No. But thanks. I was just in town and thought I'd drop by to say hello."

"Oh, rats. I was hoping we might have a chance to sneak off together so I could interrogate you about Lyman's dark past. Is it true he used to fly old jalopies around the Caribbean? I bet he had a sultry woman waiting for him at the end of every little landing strip."

"So numerous, we didn't bother keeping track—except for the ones he married."

Birdy looked as if he was trying to hide behind his glass. Sibyl ruffled what was left of his hair. "Rascal," she said, then turned to Stormy, serious and a little stern now. "I'll be very upset if the next time you're coming through Naples you don't call us in advance and stay over. I mean that. Now, maternal duties call. I'm off to a preschoolers' nature-appreciation lesson."

She gave Birdy one more playful ruffle and then walked away.

Stormy snorted once she was gone. "I can't believe anyone so good-looking could be that nice. Tell me the truth. She's kinda stupid? Right?"

"Real estate partner of the second biggest law firm in town. Takes care of all my transactions."

"Should've guessed."

There was a silence. A yacht cruised by slowly. Birdy let it pass, then said, "You were about to say something when we were interrupted."

Stormy took a drink—making it last as long as possible to buy some time.

"Yeah. A favor."

"Love to do what I can."

"Advice, really."

"Well, I'm just brimming over with all sorts of advice. Specially about deep personal matters. Fire."

"This is serious, Birdy."

All the lightness left him. A look of genuine concern came to his face. "Sorry."

"I guess it all started when I stumbled across a very large quantity of some of Colombia's number-one national product."

Birdy made a face of distaste. "Stormy, stop right there. I'm out of that game. Clean out." He tilted his lapel so that the Rotary pin winked in the sunlight.

"That was why I was sort of reluctant . . . But Birdy, I don't know anyone else who can help me—"

"Money?" He raised his voice and brightened a bit, obviously hoping her answer would be affirmative.

"Money. Yeah, sure. Maybe like a million bucks."

He winced.

"A little stiff even for millionaire developers. But, no, it's not money, not your money anyway, I'm after."

"Stormy, you have to understand that I must be very careful. I mean, it's an open secret around town how I got my start in this life in the fast lane. I'm sure there are still a few cops out there who'd love nothing so much as to connect me to my unsavory past. There's just too much to lose." He swept his arm around the grounds.

"Yeah, that's just it. And I got nothing to lose. Birdy. A name. Just a name."

"I don't know a soul."

"Crap."

"It's been five years. Things change. There's a whole new bunch running things now. And not a very pleasant bunch, either, I'm afraid."

"Birdy, old buddy. I happen to know that somewhere in this neck of the woods is a fellow—Milano, Montano, Montana, something like that. He is expecting a shipment of pure Colombian coke. By a series of coincidences—none of which were my doing—I happen to find myself in possession of that very shipment. I would love nothing better than to reunite owner and shipment, and pocket the change. Could be my little grubstake for the next four decades or so."

"I wish I could help. I mean, if you know that it belongs to somebody . . . well, it's kind of curious that whoever told you that it belonged to somebody couldn't provide you with the additional details you need." Again he brightened.

"Only that somebody's Bingo."

Birdy smiled and opened his hands. "Bingo and you are partners. Surely—"

Stormy put a hand up to her mouth. She had made a mistake—a bad one. Somehow she had assumed that Birdy would know. Stupid assumption. How could he have? She swallowed hard, and decided that the best thing to do was to get the news out, before Birdy said something that would make it even harder. "Birdy, Bingo is dead. Murdered two weeks ago."

He didn't say a word. Just scratched Under Dog's ears and looked at Stormy. Finally, he called out, "Arlena, could we have two more of those Bloodies?" His throat got bound up on the end of the sentence. He had to croak the word *Bloodies*. Then he just sat there swallowing his own saliva.

Nothing more was said until the drinks came, and it was long enough after that for both of them to be half-finished before Birdy spoke. "It has something to do with this shipment, Bingo's death?"

"Everything."

"Let's hear it. Slowly. From the beginning."

Stormy gulped the rest of her drink. Then she did as she was told, starting with the Lowell, Indiana, dentist, ending with Moonbeam's funeral. Birdy listened for twenty minutes in silence, his real chin resting on his collection of double and triple chins.

When she finished, he just shook his head. "I can't imagine Bingo dead," he said, and looked off into the middle distance as if he was trying to summon the image of a dead Bingo. Apparently, he had no luck. Birdy turned back to Stormy. "Forty

144

thousand a year base, but with commissions I'd be surprised if you don't double that right off the bat. Company will throw in a car, something four-door, but sporty and Japanese; you can stay here until you find a place."

"Birdy, I didn't come to hit you up for a goddamn job. I want your advice. A name."

"Okay, okay, okay. I'll toss in two grand for wardrobe. Promise to take Sibyl with you when you shop, though. She has professional, yet elegant, tastes."

"Birdy, I'd rather sell what I sell now than peddle Florida real estate."

"Oh, damn, Stormy, can't you see, this ain't a half-bad way to piss away one's three score ten. And it would be so much better with a friend or two around."

"I have to do it, one way or another."

"Sweetie, they're likely to kill you, one way or another."

"Not the way I have it planned."

"Oh, so you have a plan. Do tell. Do tell."

Stormy told. Again, Birdy's real chin reclined comfortably on its pals. In the end, he stuck out his lower lip and nodded.

"Kinda a mean thing to do to the poor preacher, but as plans go, it's slightly above average," he said.

"You know damn well it would work."

"Could. Could. Look, suppose I could help you—and I probably can't. But suppose I did—"

"Birdy, you big, fat lover—"

"Hold your horses. I'm making no promises. But, if I did put you in touch with the right person, and if you were still alive after all this was over, would you promise to work for me here? One year. Try it for one year."

"You're going to help me. Thanks, Birdy. I can't thank you enough."

"No one said anything about helping you. I don't know a soul anymore in that line of work."

Stormy stood up and shoved Under Dog off Birdy's lap. She

took the old mutt's place and planted a firm wet kiss on Birdy's lips. "Thanks." She ruffled his hair. "I'm at the Chickcharnie on Andros—"

"Know it all too well. And would you please stop thanking me. I haven't promised a ruddy thing."

"Thanks," she said.

Under Dog jumped back on Birdy's lap as soon as Stormy left. Birdy sat in the chair for five minutes. For the first three, he thought about his crazy pal Bingo. His dead pal Bingo. Although it was the last thing Birdy wanted at that moment, his mind went ahead on its own and dug up and dusted off all those old clichés about the fickle nature of life, the fleet-footedness of time, actually touched on "There but for the grace of God." Once he had run through all those, Birdy spent another minute thinking about the old days back in the Turks and Caicos. That left him with less than a minute to ponder Stormy's plan. It wasn't a great plan. Okay, at best, with a couple of real shaky areas. But the way Birdy saw it, Stormy didn't have much choice. No matter what she did, she stood a fair chance of getting killed. Damn, it was a dirty business. He stood and let the fingers of his right hand feel the bulge beneath his shirt.

For once, deciding which car to take hardly took up any time at all. The Cherokee was slow and boxy. With the remaining Benz, he stood half a chance of getting out to Montano's place and back in time for his luncheon appointment with his wife and child.

Preacher Tom decorated his vestry walls with two police mug shots of himself, eight by ten, black and white, and showing both full-frontal and profile views. When Miles entered, Tom sat directly below the mug shots, counting money. He nodded, and immediately went back to his chore, sorting the bills first according to Bahamian and U.S. nationality, then in descending order of denomination, left to right, faces upward. The

146

coins, which were not as plentiful as the folding money, he flipped into a collection of eight cheap wooden salad bowls lined along the front of the desk.

Finally, with the piles arrayed in front of him and every bill and coin in its appropriate pile, he leaned back and folded his hands behind his head. His desk chair emitted a grating squeal. "God seems to have been particularly munificent last night. For a Wednesday-evening service, that is. We expect a little more out of him on a Sunday." He chuckled in a rich baritone.

Preacher Tom, who founded The Mission of the Good Thief when he returned to Andros after a visit of two years less a day to Metro-Dade's Metropolitan Correctional Center, was a black-skinned man in his late thirties, judging by the occasional gray hair imposing itself on his well-coiffed Afro. His most striking feature, the one people remembered, was his nose—or more accurately, his nostrils. They were as full of animation and expression as most people's eyes. And he used them like eyes, too. He could flare them in anger, close them softly in sympathy. Now, they were wide and inquiring. "This is indeed an unexpected pleasure, Brother Miles. And it's all too rare that you get up here to Nicholl's Town."

"I need your advice."

A bass chuckle rumbled from deep within Tom's diaphragm. The nostrils opened disarmingly. "I hardly expect it's the need for spiritual guidance that has brought you so far over our little island's treacherous roads. At least not *my* spiritual guidance."

"That's exactly what I had hoped to get. Or maybe the reverse. I don't know."

The nostrils closed, and the bridge of the nose came over the top of them like a hood. "Let's go into the sanctuary. I find it so much more conducive to conversation than this room."

Tom gestured toward a door. Miles went through into a large, plain white-painted room. Three dozen pews were aligned in two parallel rows. The windows on the east side of the sanctuary were thrown open, and outside the sea crashed

147

against the iron shore, so close that a good wave might have inundated the church. In front of the room was a stained-glass window with Christ, on the cross, between the two thieves. The window was saved from being purely ordinary and off-the-rack by the expression on Christ's face. Sometimes when Miles examined the face, it looked back in anger; other times, anguish. But most of the time, it was a pained matter-of-fact look that said, simply, "Why me?"

Miles and Preacher Tom sat side by side on a pew in the first row.

"My Lincoln Continental," said Preacher Tom, nodding toward the window. "I ever tell you that? I had actually sunk to the point where I had used the proceeds of my little export business to buy a top-of-the-line Lincoln." He chuckled and opened his nostrils to full bore. "Imagine. On these roads. So when I built this church, I decided to be economical in all ways—except for one luxury. The proceeds of the sale of that automobile would be put toward a window. I think the look on His face has earned me more than one convert."

Miles smiled. "More than once sitting here, I have felt the tug of the sin of envy for that window, Preacher Tom."

"Then you will understand how I feel when I sit in your congregation and hear you deliver the Word. What a gift, Reverend." Preacher Tom shook his head and looked wistfully at the Christ figure. "But," he went on, raising his nostrils, "surely you did not come so far merely to be complimented by a reformed drug smuggler."

"Tom, can we talk in utter confidence?"

The eyes half-closed. The nostrils were tilted at a forty-five-degree angle toward the ceiling and were shaped like two ovals. Preacher Tom was obviously warming up to a harangue. "Can we talk in confidence? Reverend, I owe you a debt I can never repay. The debt of salvation. Sitting there in prison. Waiting to get out so I could get back here and spend the filthy, contaminated money I had hidden. On what? On cars and whores and booze and drugs. It was watching your television program from that dismal institution that started me thinking."

He had taken a deep breath that could have led into a half-hour oration when Miles cut him short. "My brother has threatened to shut The Vale down—unless I come up with a bunch of money, fast."

Preacher Tom smiled. "Our collection plate is yours, Reverend."

"Thank you, Tom. But that's not why I came. In fact, the sum is so great, I don't think even a lifetime of your Sunday offerings would cover it. A half-million. By New Year."

The nostrils collapsed. Preacher Tom shook his Afro.

"I don't know how to explain this, but the strangest coincidence has occurred. Through a series of flukes, I find myself in possession of—well, you know more about these things than I do—but what I'm told is pure cocaine. Maybe a million dollars' worth."

Preacher Tom put out a hand. "Miles, flush it into the sea. I can tell you that it will bring you nothing but evil. Don't even be tempted. Don't you see this is a trial? 'Get thee hence, Satan.' That is what you must say!"

"If it was only so simple, I would do precisely that—in a second." Miles paused and looked up at Christ. Then, as succinctly as possible, Miles told Preacher Tom everything, emphasizing Moonbeam's murder, Fat Boy's role, and Stormy Lake's proposition.

By the end, Preacher Tom's nostrils had all but disappeared. They might have been trying to shut out a putrid odor. "You are well and truly in a difficult position. Fat Boy has always been the worst sort of rotten, though this is the first time I have heard of his involvement in the trade. His superiors, almost all of them are worse. Don't expect any help from the DEA. As for this Stormy Lake, I have had dealings in the past with her man, a guy called Bingo. They're okay, but like so many of these American young people down here: lost, lazy, addicted to booze, drugs, and sex, always looking for a thrill, demanding that life amuse them constantly."

Miles cut in, partially to keep up with the flow of his own thoughts, but mostly to head off another Preacher Tom sermon. "I prayed the other night. And a solution came to me. At first, it seemed so farfetched, I dismissed it. But the voice that told me to do it seemed so real and familiar"—he looked long and hard at Tom—"that I had to listen. In the end, I couldn't get the plan out of my head. It seemed so plausible."

Preacher Tom set his face in a scowl and listened as Miles elaborated, shooting an occasional knowing glance at the stained-glass window. Twice Preacher Tom put out a hand and asked a question, got a succinct answer, and nodded, satisfied.

After Miles had stopped talking, Tom remained silent for a full five minutes. He looked out the church window to where the whitecaps, startlingly white in the sunshine against the deep blue of the sea, and kicked along by a breeze out of the northeast, dashed themselves against the iron shore.

"And that Stormy woman is going to be kept in the dark? Totally?" he asked.

Miles nodded. "Can you tell me what you think?"

"Reverend, in what capacity do you seek my advice—my former professional opinion, or my current one?"

"Can we try both?"

"In my current view, it's grossly amoral. And unfair to the woman. Un-Christian from start to finish."

"What about your former professional opinion?"

"Isn't a half-bad plan. Even stands a chance of working, which is a lot better than any other odds you're gonna get. Now what can I do for you, Reverend?"

"I need a name."

Tom interrupted Miles by flaring his nostrils. "Let me guess." There was a long pause. Preacher Tom looked down at a spot on the plain cement floor and closed his eyes. He was either thinking hard or praying. When he looked up, he said,

"Reverend Miles, I just prayed for you, and I'm not going to stop until all this is over. You're going to need all the help you can get. But here's your name. I can recommend no one more highly than the guy who busted me. Name's Bones. Jesse Bones. DEA supervisor of some sort. Office in Miami. You've got to watch him, though. Doesn't always look or sound the part, but he's one of the smartest human beings I have met."

After a lunch of chilled stone crab and a small green salad, washed down with Perrier and a bottle of iced Bourgogne Aligoté, Montano rammed the pearl-handled knife's blade into Ira's right nostril.

He drew the knife toward himself. Ira had to follow, leaning across the iron patio table as far as he could, then pushing himself to a half-standing position, finally ending up with his face only inches away from Montano's broad, beaming smile—close enough to get a sickening waft of his Juicy Fruit cologne.

"You are a stupid, stupid man, Ira, and you have failed me," Montano said, his voice soft, controlled, and lethal. Montano's breath stank of coffee, cigar, crabmeat, and good white burgundy.

"I told you," Ira pleaded, trying to avert his face, but stopped by the sting of the sharp blade. "There is a contract on the Andros property. And as backup, my brother is trying to come up with the money himself."

"This I am not interested in." Montano punctuated each word with a little dig of the blade, not quite enough to break the skin but enough to bring tears to Ira's eyes. "What we have come to talk about today is that little piece of news Nettleship relayed. That the bankers have now very definitely threatened to foreclose—unless they get paid."

"They will," Ira whined.

"A great deal depends on your errant brother."

"I explained. He's only backup."

"No longer."

"I told you, I have signed a deal for the Andros property."

Montano smiled. He allowed himself a little "Ha-ha." Gave a glint of gold bicuspid. "Indeed. But who with? You were so stupid, you did not insist on asking who with. Just took some lawyer's word. Now, I would like to introduce you to the person with whom you were going to be dealing." He raised his voice so that the refrigerator-shaped goon who stood at the corner of the patio could hear. "Mr. Sammy Hodges."

The big fellow shambled over to his boss's side. "Yump, jefe," he said.

"Sammy," Montano said cheerfully, careful to keep the blade inserted in Ira's nostril, "you go to the lawyer the other day and sign a deal to buy some property in the Bahamas from the good pastor?"

"Yump."

"Now, Sammy, tell me the truth. Do you have five hundred thousand dollars in the bank?"

"Nope. Eight hundred forty-three and fifty-eight cents."

Montano smiled at Ira. "So, you understand, Pastor. My associate must have gotten carried away. He lacks the financial means to purchase your property."

Ira made an unconscious move toward the knife. Montano pushed it in farther.

"I don't understand," said Ira.

Montano let out a great sigh of relief and put on his most beatific smile. "Pastor, you of all people should know that there are simply some things we are not meant to understand. Need not understand. But please, understand that none of this would have happened if you and that Nettleship had been better financial managers. Understand that Sammy's "purchase" was designed to teach you humility. Understand that now, because of your failures, you must do exactly as I say. Or I will have you killed."

Montano gave a dig of the blade, just enough to break the

skin inside Ira's nostril and cause a slight nosebleed. "So tell me. Do you understand?"

"Yes," Ira whispered, his voice slurred by the trickle of blood that ran from his right nostril down his upper lip.

"Very well, then. Listen. You are to fly to Andros tomorrow. Take an extra empty suitcase with you. Your brother, by sheer coincidence, is in possession of a shipment of cocaine—the very shipment that was to fund Celestial City, ironically. Convince him to turn it over to you. Then you bring it to me. Should be simple. Hardly think the customs people will suspect you of having anything illegal in your suitcase."

"I can't. I mean, I never intended to get involved."

The blade cut farther. "Pastor. Do it. And afterward, just think, Celestial City will be funded. All your troubles will be over. One little tiny trip. And, frankly, the alternative is not very pleasant."

There was a pause. Ira closed his eyes and swallowed some of the blood. "I'll go," he said.

Slowly, and with a surgeon's care, Montano sliced through the bottom half-inch of Ira's nostril. Blood gushed out and ran down the front of Ira's favorite white silk shirt, ruining it and his powder blue blazer.

For an instant, Ira was too shocked to say a word. During that instant, Montano smiled paternally and said, "Of course you will."

Chapter 12

"Reverend Miles, I mus' beg you pardon deeply, but dat a fool idea." It was the next day, a bright, clear Friday morning with just a few nimbus clouds hanging on the horizon about where Nassau would be. The temperature was in the low seventies. Blackie, foreman of The Vale's woodworking shop, shook his gray head in profound disagreement. He made it clear that here, in this cluttered space that smelled of sawdust and epoxy resin, he was king. And the king was not pleased.

Miles was feeling only modestly hung over, but so edgy he might as well have tied on a full-blown one the night before. There was a simple reason for his edginess. For once, it had practically nothing to do with fermented juices of sugarcane. Ira had called to say he would be coming that noon hour. And Ira never paid pleasure visits to The Vale. Detested the place, in fact. So there was a sense of foreboding in Miles's musings that morning, and now Blackie had decided to become uncharacteristically stubborn. Miles closed his eyes and inhaled, hoping to suck any notes of impatience out of his voice. He nearly succeeded, not quite, but close enough not to give offense. "Blackie, just a small experiment."

"But Reverend, dem floorboards in da Jesus Boat brand-new. Me make dem meself. An' dis not the right wood." He gestured toward long strips of coconut wood.

"Blackie, an American has promised us a big order if we can

show that that the coconut wood will stand up to use as decking."

That mollified the old man—but only somewhat. Although the Reverend was better than most, Americans, he well knew, were capable of pursuing the most ridiculous notions. Good thing they never seemed to mind paying for them. In fact, the more ridiculous the project, the more they seemed willing to pay. Blackie allowed his lower jaw to sag an inch, just enough to open his mouth to a comfortable gap. He then began earnestly twiddling the half-dozen white whiskers that sprouted from his bony chin. His single remaining tooth—the one all the schoolchildren called the Leaning Tower of Blackie—appeared to be held in its semi-upright position by a tendril of spittle that ran from its crown to his empty upper gums. "How you see it, Reverend?"

"You just provide me with one-inch strips. Make them about ten feet long. I'll cut them to fit. I want to lay them down on a frame of two-by-fours, on top of the present decking. I'll screw the whole unit in place—temporarily, just to see that it works."

"Dat mean there gonna be a four-inch gap between the two decks. A fool way to build. What good dat gap? Just waste space. Let rot in. Not gonna work."

"It's worth a try."

Blackie stroked his six whiskers. There came a point where you just had to humor Americans. "If you says so," he said. "If you says so."

The whine of a Citation's decelerating turbines heralded Ira's arrival. His chartered jet circled low over the water, then turned, wheels extended, wing flaps down, seeming to pass just a few feet above The Vale. Miles, who was on his way to the kitchen, waited until the engines' whistle and roar had subsided.

He smiled to himself. Even at times like this, Ira had a certain

156

satisfying dependability. The Savior Network down to its last pennies, and Ira wastes a few thousand dollars on a charter flight when there were dozens of less expensive commercial options. Anyway, everything that could have been said had been said in the hot tub. At least Miles hoped so.

Miles realized that he hadn't had a drink all morning, and the thought of a confrontation with his brother—the inevitable confrontation—tweaked that old itch, so he detoured to *Come to Jesus Cruiser,* and rooted around in the forward hold. He paused when he came to the anchor line. When he had stowed it, he had been careful to coil it neatly. Now, it was tangled. Miles shoved the tangles out of the way and was relieved to see the green plastic. Maybe he hadn't been as neat as he thought. He carefully replaced the line and rewarded himself with a fresh bottle of Appleton's.

He poured himself three fingers, then sat on the bunk, smelling the bilge fumes and listening to the slap-slap of wavelets against the wooden hull. For some reason, he found himself fantasizing about Stormy Lake and the night they had spent on that very bunk. When the Pontasaurus squeaked and rattled into the driveway, Miles stayed on the berth, sipping his drink and observing Ira's arrival through a porthole.

Dacosta got out and held open one of the Pontasaurus's rear doors. Ira emerged, put his briefcase on the car roof, and busily set about dusting his natty beige seersucker suit, giving special care to the forearms, thighs, and backside. Even from a hundred yards, Miles could see that Ira was wearing a white tent-like object over his nose. He was either following some new sort of miracle cure for his hay fever or one of the Savior Network's young secretaries finally had dealt him the punch in the snout he so richly deserved.

Dacosta opened the back of the Pontasaurus and returned with a big blue suitcase, a new Hartmann, by the look of it. But it wasn't Ira's expensive tastes in luggage that surprised Miles. It was that he had traveled with any luggage at all. On the

157

phone, he had been adamant that he intended to stay for the briefest of visits—certainly not overnight.

Since Moonbeam's funeral, Clover had thrown herself into a cooking frenzy: for breakfast, fluffy omelets dripping with extra-old New Zealand cheddar, stacks of French toast slathered in real Vermont maple syrup; thin slices of cold roast beef and ham, grouper kabob, potato salad, macaroni salad, coleslaw all served buffet-style for lunch; silver-sided Atlantic salmon stuffed with fresh dill for dinner one night, turkey another. She hadn't spoken a word about her son, or cried, since the funeral. But Miles felt that, in her own way, she was dealing with the grief. And if he had to put on a few pounds and strain The Vale's meal budget to help her through rough times . . . well, wasn't that what preachers were for?

That day, she had concocted a cold lobster salad (there was a certain appropriate sadness knowing that Moonbeam had probably snared the main course as one of his final earthly acts), cool asparagus in a ginger sauce, avocados with mayonnaise, and a simple green salad. An iced bottle of Meursault also had appeared on the little table she had set with white linen on the patio in front of the main building.

Miles poured Prue her usual three-quarters of an inch of wine, then moved the bottle toward his brother's glass. Ira put his hand over the glass. "No alcohol, thank you," he said, his voice slightly muffled by the gauze tentlike thing over his nose.

"What happened to the beak?" Miles asked.

Ira touched the tent but offered no explanation.

Miles shrugged and allowed the white wine to gurgle freely from the bottle two-thirds of the way to the top of his own glass.

"Well," said Miles, raising his glass and putting a note of phony-sounding optimism into his voice. "Suppose we should all drink to the financial health of the Savior Network." He raised his glass.

Prue did likewise, but there was an awkward moment or two

158

as Ira looked dubiously at the pitcher of ice water on the table, reached for it, then withdrew his hand, finally rummaged in his briefcase, coming back with a small bottle of Evian mineral water, which he was about to empty into his wineglass when he caught himself, held the glass up to the light, grimaced, muttered something about it being washed in cistern water, went to the briefcase, and came back with a disposable plastic cup, which he filled and raised halfheartedly.

"It's my digestive tract," Ira said apologetically to Prue. "Ulcers, you know. Can't handle changes of water. Last time I drank the water here—couldn't have been more than a drop or two—I was down with diarrhea for a week. Nearly got dehydrated."

Miles wasn't listening. He dug into the lobster salad with two serving spoons and hoisted a good-sized load above Ira's plate.

The hand went out again. Miles dearly wanted to dump the contents of his spoons on top of the hand in an act of fraternal mischief almost too tempting to resist. But Christian virtues—and just maybe a measure of self-preservation—won in the end.

"I'm afraid my dietitian doesn't allow me lobster. Mild allergy," Ira explained.

It turned out there was some problem with ginger, the mayonnaise on the avocado ranked right up there with cyanide because of its cholesterol content, too much fat in the avocado itself, and the salad greens, of course, had been washed in Vale water. In the end, Ira handed Clover a Baggieful of oat bran, conveniently carried in his briefcase, which Miles was beginning to view as a three-hundred-dollar, leather-covered, brass-trimmed lunch pail.

Miles dug into three mounds of the lobster, scooped the innards out of both his and Ira's avocados, and topped his wineglass four times. After finishing, he was forced to sit back and undo the button on his beige Sears suit coat.

"Miles, you abuse yourself so much, and it never seems to

affect you. But then, I always did have the weaker constitution," Ira said.

Miles tried to stifle a burp, and was only partially successful. "You remember that part in Mark Twain where the lady who never drank or smoked got sick and died? Twain figured it was because she had nothing to fall back on? I try to live in such a way that I always have plenty to fall back on—in all important areas of life."

"Very amusing," said Ira. He turned to Prue. "I have to see a new specialist. It could well be that I suffer from something called the twentieth-century disease—that I'm allergic to the chemicals and pollution of our modern society. We might have to install special ventilation systems in The Manse and at the network offices."

"After we find the money to expand the school here?" said Miles.

Ira cleared his throat. "In time. All in good time," he muttered, and checked his watch. "Miles, can you and I talk?" He deepened his voice a pompous octave directed at Prue. "Network business," he said.

"Sure, we can talk in complete privacy aboard *Come to Jesus Cruiser*. You haven't seen it yet, and since you're paying . . ." Miles looked at Prue and raised his eyebrows conspiratorily. "I'll fill you in on all the juicy parts later."

Prue took a plate in each hand and stood. "Really, Miles, you do egg people on sometimes," she said, and walked toward the kitchen.

"Sensible woman, your fiancée. Maybe your interminable bachelorhood taught you something. She'll make a good wife. For once, you and I agree with each other totally," Ira said.

Miles did not answer. For some reason, his thoughts went back to Stormy Lake.

They half-sat, half-leaned against opposing gunwales on the rear deck of *Come to Jesus Cruiser*. Ira shaped his mouth into a very serious frown. Unfortunately, the frown's overall effect was dampened somewhat by the nose tent—an object whose presence Ira still had not explained. He also had lugged the Hartmann along. Its presence, too, went unexplained.

Without Nettleship to run interference, Ira came right to the point. "Miles, I've been told you have some cocaine. I'm going to have to take it back with me. Now. So let's not argue or anything. This can be very easy and simple."

Miles was caught, totally surprised. He looked at his brother openmouthed and stammered a few false starts before finally saying, "I'm afraid I don't understand."

Ira's hands started to shake. He clasped them together and swallowed several times. "Just do as I ask, for once."

"Big brother, what are you talking about?"

"Goddamn it!" Ira wrung his hands. "See what you have me doing now? Swearing. I never swear. Why must you be so contrary?"

"Ira, you don't think it's a bit strange to fly all the way over here making these ridiculous demands—without even the decency of an explanation?"

"Can't you just do as I ask for once in your life?"

"Aren't you getting ahead of yourself? We haven't even established whether or not I have this . . . this cocaine you're talking about."

"This is no time to clown around. You're in way, way, way over your head, Miles, and you don't understand the first thing." He took a deep breath. "Very well, I'll explain. Nettleship. Oh, goddamn that Nettleship. I rue the day he walked in through our doors—"

"That makes two things we've agreed on inside of five minutes. Must be some new world's record."

"Will you kindly listen, Miles?" Ira stopped and waited for a response that never came. He went ahead, anyway. "Nettleship connected us with a Colombian fellow—Montano's his name—for financial backing in Celestial City—"

161

"Financial backing. Ira, how could you be so stupid—"

"Don't you dare lecture me. I didn't have any idea that he was involved in drugs. What does it matter now? He's got his hooks into me. He has the power to drive the network into bankruptcy. He has threatened my life. Now that I see it, it should have been so obvious all along what he was scheming. He just played us for fools." Ira put a hand up to his nose for emphasis, as if that explained everything. "And he is convinced that you have his cocaine. He made me come over to get it."

"No."

"No, you don't have it? Or, no, you won't give it to me?"

"Just no."

"Miles you have to. Don't you understand? This man is capable of anything."

"Sorry, Ira."

"Miles, be reasonable for once. I'll fly back with it now. Turn it over to him. Celestial City will be financed. You will have the money to continue here—I promise."

"What you're asking me to do is illegal. You might get caught. Think of what that would do to the network."

"Oh, come off it. I know every customs official in Naples personally. Half are members of the congregation."

"Well, what about all the lives the stuff is ruining."

"Listen to who's suddenly gotten so high and mighty."

"The answer is still no."

"Miles. I'm pleading with you. Please trust me. It will all work out."

Miles smiled. "I'll tell you what, Ira. I will give you something to take to your pal. In fact, you saved me a long-distance telephone call." He opened a little drawer beside the wheel and took out a pen and a piece of paper and scribbled something. "Give this to Mr. Montano."

Ira took the paper. "It's your telephone number."

"Very observant. Tell Mr. Montano to give me a call so we

162

can arrange a face-to-face meeting to talk about his little shipment."

"Miles, just do as I ask. Give it to me now. He is not the sort of guy who likes games." He pointed to his nose again.

"This isn't a game."

Ira's hands began to shake. "Don't you understand? My life's at stake. My life."

Miles thought for a moment. There was the definite temptation to tell Ira where the coke was. But he liked his plan better. His way eliminated the middlemen—or was it more correct now to say middlepeople. All of them.

"Ira," Miles said. "I have a way to get us all through this one. You're just going to have to trust me."

Ira snorted. "Trust you? Why is it that those words just don't fill me with confidence? Miles, do I have to spell it out in black and white. I always have handled the practical side of our business. Father knew my strengths. That's why he left me in charge."

"It was your strengths that got you into this stupid mess. Maybe we should give my weaknesses—and they are legion— a chance to dig us all out."

On the runway apron at Naples two hours later, the customs agent refused to look Ira in the eyes. Instead, he twisted his head to one side and tilted it at an odd forty-five-degree angle, as if he was trying to spit over his left shoulder.

"Excuse me, Reverend, but I'll have to ask you to bring your luggage inside. Formalities, I'm afraid."

"Really, young man, do you think that is necessary?"

"No, sir, I definitely do not, sir. Wife and I watch your show every Sunday, sir. But I have to follow orders, sir. It will only take a minute."

Ira fixed his face in a scowl of indignation and said, "Your superiors will hear about your unnecessary rudeness. I'll see to that."

There was a big black man sitting in the office. Hand him a cigar, and he would have looked like a brown-skinned version of Winston Churchill in one of his dark moods. He didn't speak. Merely nodded toward the new Hartmann and then toward a small empty desk. The customs agent put the suitcase on the desk. The brown Winston Churchill, still not having said a word, frowned at the suitcase for a minute before opening it. Except for a Hartmann brochure and price tag, it was empty. He felt the sides and bottom. Frowned more deeply, and reached out for Ira's briefcase. He wrinkled his nose at the half-empty bag of oat bran, closed the case, and grunted.

"Mr. Bones would like you to remove your suit coat, Reverend," the young man translated the grunt.

Ira swung toward the black Churchill look-alike. Before addressing himself to Churchill, Ira did two things. First, he gave silent thanks to the Lord for making his brother so uncharacteristically stubborn. Then, inflated nearly to the point of bursting with that unswerving righteous indignation only the habitually guilty can summon when—for once—they are wrongly accused, he said, "I object. Let me speak to your superiors immediately."

It was then that the black guy spoke for the first time: "An' the pants, too, Preacher."

Stormy Lake sat lotus-style on the bed, blowing an innocent Friday-evening spliff of after-dinner Santa Marta, when the knocking started on the door to her room at the Chickcharnie. She gulped another lungful of smoke, and looked around the ruins of her bed to find a place to stash the roach, finally settling on a drinking glass that had only traces of a dried-up brownish substance in the bottom. "Yeah," she said, hoping that Dugold had decided to drop over. He hadn't been by since her return from Florida that morning.

"Telephone in the front office," came the voice of the hotel's owner.

Stormy jumped off the bed and wormed her toes into her thongs. In a housekeeping gesture, she waved one arm through the air to dissipate the tendrils of bluish smoke.

The "office" had obviously been designed as a broom closet—and not a particularly spacious one—off to one side off the barroom. In addition to a wall phone, it housed a brand-new computerized cash register and a bar stool, upon which the owner could be found at any hour of the day or night. He had resumed his perch, and when Stormy came, he gestured toward the dangling receiver but made no movements that would indicate he was about to leave and give her privacy.

She gave him ample time to go if he was going to, then answered the phone.

The guy on the other end spoke with a high-pitched drawl, almost falsetto, and he sounded none too bright. Might even have been reading from a script, or struggling with some barely remembered lines. "I work for Mr. Montano. Lyman Quayle said you wanted to see him."

Stormy smiled and had to suppress a sigh of relief. Good old Birdy.

The guy continued with some difficulty. "I'm supposed to tell you that Mr. Montano will be at the Lucayan Beach Hotel in Freeport this weekend. He is willing to see you then."

Stormy had a couple of routine questions she wanted to ask, specifics about where, and when, and what time, but never got them out. The line had gone dead.

Less than five minutes passed before the duty agent in Communications got the transcript of the tapped telephone conversation up to Bones's office. It was a mission to which the young agent looked forward. Bones was always in a bad mood on Friday, but his demeanor had been absolutely foul since his return from Naples just before the dinner hour. Office rumor had it that he had bawled out some poor field agent for more than an hour on the telephone before he had let off enough steam to settle down to some postponed paperwork. But the governor's office had called, and hollering at some executive assistant for another forty minutes put old Bones into an even uglier mood. Evidently, Bones had tried to shake down some bigwig and came up empty-handed. Good news would be most welcome, maybe even remembered when the time came to hand out promotions.

And what better news could there be than the approximate time and place for a meeting between Montano and some Andros-based bimbo with connections to Lyman Quayle.

Chapter 13

An incident involving the plane's fire ax delayed Bahamasair Flight 049, scheduled to depart Andros Town for Nassau at 7:02 Saturday morning, December 17. Stormy, who was one of the 049's twenty-three groggy passengers, worried she might not survive long enough to keep her appointment with Montano.

At seven, the copilot came aboard. In a proper, serious manner, he set himself to the task of shutting the rear door of the Avro. He first administered a tentative, gentle slam. The door popped open. The second time, he really threw his weight behind it. The door stayed closed a half beat, long enough for him to flash a little smile of victory, then it bounced back. He handed the flight attendant his jacket, braced his feet against the back of the cabin, and heaved at the door.

It jumped open.

Looking sheepish after ten more minutes of frustrated attempts, he strode the length of the aisle and disappeared into the cockpit. A middle-aged white guy with a crew cut, who looked as if he might have been fired from his last job at a major American airline for chronic failure to properly tuck in his shirt, came out brandishing the plane's fire ax. He bestowed an "It's all right, folks, just a minor technical glitch" look at the passengers as he passed. All heads followed him down the aisle. When he got near enough to the door, he took a Paul Bunyan grip on the ax handle and let loose with an oak-felling whack. The door settled neatly into place.

He made a victory lap up the aisle and went into the cockpit. About two seconds later, both propellers fluttered to life and the Avro began to churn down the runway. A true avian contemporary of the Pontasaurus, probably right down to a pair of fluffy dice hanging from the cockpit windshield, it bumped and squeaked and jiggled down the runway, finally attaining a stately velocity of perhaps thirty miles an hour, or at any rate, a speed far too slow for anything short of a helicopter to get off the ground. But the Avro continued sedately along the patched and potholed tarmac, engines roaring, jiggling increasing, the vibrating loosening Stormy's molars. The terminal buildings went by—far too slowly. Then—and this was a real nice touch—the Avro passed a junkyard filled with a dozen assorted aircraft, the fallen ones, the ones that hadn't made it, rusting and mangled and pushed just beyond the tarmac's edge. The next thing Stormy knew, the runway ended and they were over an area of splotchy grass. She actually braced herself for impact.

The Avro must have been off the ground—but not very far, to judge from the way three grazing cows looked Stormy straight in the eye through her window, but far enough for the plane's landing gears to clear the tussocks of coarse grass. Another little scare came as the plane approached the fringe of mangrove at the end of the field. A flock of white egrets took to wing, scattering to both sides, which was a good thing. Stormy guessed that many of the birds would have had their feathers—or worse—blown off as the plane's belly brushed their roosts and its props did a hedge trim on the mangroves.

Once over the brownish water of Fresh Creek, the pilot apparently decided to give his passengers one last thrill by executing a near-perfect ninety-degree turn at an altitude of fifty feet, tops. Stormy felt what must have been her stomach pushing against the underside of her chin as the wing on her side dipped toward the water. The woman next to Stormy sat, eyes tightly closed, a Bible clutched in both hands, and her head against the seat back. When Stormy looked at her, one eye batted open and snapped shut again.

A voice came over the intercom, scratchy, damn near impossible to hear over the buzz of the Avro, but judging from the careful diction, that of the copilot, not the shirt-out captain. Somehow, Stormy knew he would have had a slurred Arkansas drawl. "Ladies and gentlemen, your captain has requested that the seat-belt light remain on and that you remain in your seats with your seat belts fastened for the duration of this flight, as we expect to encounter turbulence en route to Nassau. Thank you for choosing to fly with Bahamasair; it is our pleasure to serve you."

Stormy peeked out her window. The sea toward Nassau was steel-colored, lit by a rising sun that just managed to shine under the belly of a huge thunderhead. The bad weather lay directly in what would have been their normal flight path, so the pilot kept the plane low and skirted due north, following the ins and outs of Andros's shaggy shoreline, if *shoreline* is not too precise a term for that margin of sand, coral heads, mangrove, and sea grape.

Stormy amused herself by looking down at the bays and inlets of the coast. Twice, she was rewarded by seeing the brown outline of a big nurse shark, lazily patrolling the shallows, wiggling and floundering in an awkward catfishlike stroke that had none of the streamlined savagery of the more vicious sharks. While she watched, the second shark turned abruptly toward the mangroves. Stormy let her eyes follow its new course.

It was the blue that first caught her eye. No more than a square foot or two, it stood out against the monotonous green of the shore vegetation. And if she needed verification of the color, she didn't have to look any farther than the sleeve of the sweatshirt she had pulled over her traveling dress to ward off the chill of the morning. The mast had obviously been taken down, and someone had gone to no small trouble to back the boat as far as possible into the bushes. But not far enough. Even from the window of the Avro, even as the pilot banked to the east, ready to buck through the dense black wall of the storm front, there was no doubt that the shapely bowsprit was that of *Roach*.

Stormy missed the 8:10 to Freeport, and there was room for her on neither the 9:45 nor the 11:08 flight. So it was mid-afternoon before she finally settled into her room at the Freeport Inn and was able to kick off her thongs and settle back on her bed with a can of cold Old Milwaukee and a small toot of marijuana—just enough to mellow her a bit for her meeting with Montano.

It mellowed her too much. When she awoke, the sun was almost down. She jumped off the bed, wiggled her toes into the thongs, smoothed her plain white pullover dress as best she could, dug some sleep out of the corner of one of her eyes, clawed a hand through the mass of curls on top of her head, and headed to the inn's restaurant, where she bolted an order of conch fritters.

One of the mid-seventies Caddies that seem to be de rigueur for Freeport cabbies took Stormy out to the Lucayan Beach Hotel and Casino. The pink monster dumped her out under a ridiculously overdone portico manned by about two dozen loafing doormen. They all turned to leer at Stormy, but not one made a move to assist her. That was just fine, as far as she was concerned. It meant not having to worry about tipping, and gave her a minute or two to assess her surroundings.

Someone obviously had gone to a lot of expense to make it seem like a little corner of Las Vegas had been whisked east and transplanted onto Bahamian sand. That had been the first of many architectural transgressions. From the well-manicured grounds, to the too-liberal use of glass and columns, right down to the gymnasiumlike wing that housed the gaming floor, it looked as if someone had commissioned the Disney people to imitate Vegas: too clean, too new, and, in its own way, as tacky as the monster Caddy that had brought Stormy to its doorstep.

There were as many idle clerks behind the registration desk as there had been loafing doormen outside, yet it still took a full five minutes before one of them deigned to notice Stormy. When recognition came, it was a barely perceptible raising of the eyebrows of a uniformed young woman who had paused with her emery board between thumb and index finger.

"I'm here to see a Mr. Montano," said Stormy.

Something in what Stormy had said appeared to cause the uniformed woman grave personal insult. She sighed mightily. Palmed her emery board. Descended from the stool upon which she had rested so comfortably. Beat viciously on the keys of a computer, and in so doing snapped one of her nails. She looked at the nail, assessed the damage, which was severe enough to require a hissed blast of Bahamian expletives, then finally glared in a "Now see what you've done" way at Stormy. "Name," she said.

"Montano. Mr. Montano."

The woman rolled her eyes. For a moment, Stormy thought the clerk was going to give up in exasperation and go back to her fingernails. But her sense of duty apparently won the day. "Your name," she demanded.

"Lake."

"First name?"

Stormy paused, shot a "Screw yourself" look at the woman, then said, "Ms."

The uniformed woman puffed herself up to say something rude, but the computer stopped her mid-breath. She swallowed. "He left word that you were to meet him in the casino," she said. "He will be at the first blackjack table."

Stormy smiled and walked down the hallway that led to the casino. Whatever else you could say about the guy, Montano was not adverse to a little gambling. She liked that.

A long, elevated lounge ran the length of one end of the casino, like a stage. Stormy stood for a moment, stage left, and looked at the room. In keeping with the resort's unifying decor, it was overdone, too glitzy by half, from the deep maroon carpeting to the banks of blinking lights, to the dinging and chugging slot machines that took up way more than their share of the floor space, a sure sign the place was designed more for amateur punters than serious gamblers.

Even though there were a couple of hundred players in the room, Montano was easy to spot. Stormy figured that if Birdy had called up central casting and said he needed one Colombian dope lord, they would have sent over someone much like the dapper little guy who sat at the first blackjack table. He was in a white suit. *White,* for Christ's sake. Sported enough gold jewelry to repay the national debt of his native land. Drew little puffs—sipped really—from a stubby cigar, all the while keeping an arm around the ever-so-small waist of a black cocktail waitress.

Stormy waited until the dealer had shoved a mighty pile of chips in the direction of the little guy before she approached. Might as well catch him in a good mood. She walked right up to the table and stood. Both the guy and the black waitress looked at her.

"Which one of you two is Montano?"

There was a silence. It lasted a little too long and could have become awkward. Then the dapper guy flashed a gold bicuspid and barked three notes of faked laughter. "I like that. I like that. A sense of humor. It's good," he said. He kept time to his own words by flailing the cigar and tugging at the waitress's waist. The waitress put a possessive arm over his shoulder. But that was a mistake. As soon as she did that, Montano eased her aside. "Rachel, my sweetest, could you bring the lady a . . ."

"Johnnie Walker, on the rocks," said Stormy.

"A Johnnie Walker Black," said Montano, emphasizing the *Black*. "And another Jack Daniels for me."

The look the waitress shot Stormy as she left suggested that Stormy would be wise to check her drink for strychnine, when and if it came.

Montano patted the chair next to his. "Ms. Lake, I presume," he said ebulliently. "We have had dealings, indirectly, but I believe this is the first time I have had the pleasure of meeting you face-to-face. And a pleasure it is indeed." He gave her a once-over. "Come, sit beside me for luck, and I will play one final hand. Then you and I shall go to the bar and discuss our little matter of . . ." He made a sour face and spat out the last word: *business*.

She of the twenty-inch waist and spike heels scampered back with their drinks. Stormy's, she dropped from a height of about ten inches. By some unexplained miracle of physics, none sloshed onto the green felt of the playing surface. Montano got cooed at, patted, and fussed over. She all but held the glass up to his mouth.

He put the cigar in an ashtray, sipped, smacked his lips, and flexed his fingers. He flashed that bicuspid at the dealer. "Henry, I believe Ms. Lake is not only a beautiful woman but a lucky omen. Shall we test my hunch?" He then casually pushed all of the chips in front of him toward the dealer. They were mostly thousands, with a one hundred here and there. Stormy guessed there might have been three dozen in total. Probably twenty-five grand.

It all happened fast—and without words. Montano and the dealer communicated through a series of subtle finger wiggles and eyebrow movements. The dealer flipped Montano a deuce of diamonds up and a king of spades down. Montano tapped the deuce with his index finger. He got a six of hearts and sat back with a grumpy look on his face. The dealer turned his own hand over. He had a jack of diamonds and a four of clubs. He dealt himself another card: a ten. He flipped his hand over with

173

no emotion, counted out a stack of thousands, and pushed them toward Montano.

By then, Montano was all gold bicuspid. "You see, I told you she was good luck," he said, tossing a hundred-dollar chip to the dealer and another to She of the twenty-inch waist. He then turned to a squat guy whom Stormy had not noticed before. The blocky fellow stood directly behind Montano, wearing a white suit and an expression of bovine perplexity. He also had the broadest shoulders and smallest head of anyone Stormy had ever seen.

"Sammy," said Montano. "Take care of this, will you." He gestured toward the loot. "Ms. Lake and I will be in the lounge."

A dozen patrons drank in the lounge—four groups at tables and one guy, a tallish, not-bad-looking black, alone at the bar. Montano found a table overlooking the gaming area, and made a big fuss about pulling out Stormy's chair, before taking a seat himself with his back against a pillar. The fellow with the big shoulders and little head finished his business with the cashier, came into the lounge, and carefully surveyed the place, giving special attention to the black guy at the bar, then he joined them.

"Here, boss," he said, and handed Montano a neat stack of thousand-dollar bills.

Montano just let them sit there like a pile of loose change. "Now, let us celebrate. Waiter," he called, laying on a little too much chivalry.

After they had ordered and received their drinks, Montano spread his fingers over the table and let Stormy look at them long enough to be dazzled by the gold work on four of his fingers, just in case she was the sort of girl to let trinkets overcome her better judgment. "Such a shame," he finally said, "to permit business to interfere with an evening with such a beautiful woman. But . . ." He paused and drank. "Business is the reason we're together, so why not get it out of the way? Sammy!"

Without speaking, the neckless lout gently lifted Stormy by the armpits.

"Hey, fuck off, pal," she said.

He proceeded to shake her down, professionally, even delicately, and without a trace of the sexual overtones some cops like to work in. When he was finished, he eased her back into her chair, trying his feebleminded best to return her to the exact posture she was in when the frisking began.

"I just wanted to be certain that our business discussions were not . . ." Montano looked up in the air for an appropriate word and finally settled on *overheard.*

Stormy took a slug of her Johnnie Walker. For all its other flaws, at least the Lucayan poured a respectable drink: a solid, unembarrassed jolt of the amber in a heavy glass with plenty of ice. "Sure. Good old business. Why the hell not." She swallowed the rest of her scotch and rattled the ice cubes. A waiter who had been talking to the good-looking black guy at the bar nodded.

Stormy looked back to Montano and said, "I have it."

Montano lowered the single solid eyebrow that traversed his forehead until it all but covered his eyes. "You will forgive my ignorance, Ms. Lake, but may I inquire exactly what that was supposed to mean—'I have it'?"

"Your merchandise."

The eyebrow was hoisted nearly to the hairline. "Most interesting," he said, reaching into the pocket of his white suit jacket and removing a small pearl-handled knife. He started to stroke its haft with his thumb. In the meantime, the eyes had narrowed into two dangerous dark slits. "My people inform me that a preacher down there has it. A Reverend Farnsworth. Who am I to believe?"

"Fat Boy is an asshole."

Montano nodded thoughtfully.

"And a dirty liar."

Montano nodded again. "In business, one must deal with the occasional . . ." He paused and steeled himself to utter the next word: *asshole.* With the word out, he seemed terribly relieved. "Liars, no. Never," he added.

"What about amateurs?"

"Sometimes one has no choice."

"Because Fat Boy is not only a lying asshole, he's a dumb amateur. He fell for the oldest trick in the book. Went and killed Bingo Martin—my man, but you probably already know that—without even checking to see that what he was getting was in fact coke. That one was so obvious, it makes me want to puke. Then this retarded lobsterman flukes onto the real stash and takes it to the preacher. Your pal Fat Boy has the poor retarded guy done. Nice fella, Fat Boy. The last little touch, the one you don't know about, is that the other night I went over and removed the coke from the preacher's. Pulled the same switch Bingo used. Worked once with those jokers, why not again?"

Montano's face actually stayed blank for about thirty seconds. Stormy guessed it might have been some sort of record.

"So what do you want, Ms. Lake?" he asked.

"I want to deliver it. Stateside. Solo. No middlemen."

Montano smiled. It looked like a genuine smile of relief. "Ms. Lake, have you a plane?"

"Can get one. Not much of one. But it still flies—usually."

"I have a small acreage on the road between Immokalee and Naples Park. One of the fields is due to be harvested next week. It is a very long, flat, narrow field. Three thousand feet long." He flicked out the knife blade and began to unconsciously carve away at his fingernails. "You could do that before the year's over? Let us say, eleven A.M., the twenty-eighth?"

"Eleven days. Could be done. It'd take some loot."

Montano thumbed about halfway through the stack of bills in front of him. He passed a wad over to Stormy. "Expenses," he said. "Should you successfully deliver, I will give you exactly what I was prepared to give Fat Boy: one million."

"I want half in advance."

Montano shook his head sadly.

"The plane doesn't take off until my lawyer calls to tell me she has a certified check made out to cash for a half-million."

Montano glanced at the big silent guy next to him and chuckled through his nostrils. The big guy responded with a "Huh-huh-huh-huh-huh. . . ."

"Made out to cash," Montano said. "Interesting. But very well," said Montano. "You are quite familiar with the rules of this business, so I trust you to deliver. What's your lawyer's name?"

"Sibyl Quayle," said Stormy, using the name of the only lawyer she knew in Naples.

Montano seemed impressed. "Then it sounds like we have the rudiments of a deal."

"Rudiments, yes, but there are a couple of refinements I should let you in on. First, and by all means remember this, no matter what you hear, or who you hear it from, I—me, Stormy Lake, no one else—has the stuff. Got that? Because for my little plan to work, other people are going to have to think that they have it."

"Other people? Like who?"

Stormy gave the question some thought. "You can start with about half the current adult population of Andros Island."

He smiled and stuck out a hand. Stormy took it. They shook like business partners should, except Montano held on for a little longer than necessary.

The gold on his fingers was ice-cold.

Arriving at the rudiments of a deal called for another round, according to Montano, and Stormy acquiesced. After all, her policy was that if she was going to have to spend the night in a place she disliked—and Freeport certainly fit that bill—then she might just as well be anesthetized.

"There's another part to the deal," Stormy said.

Montano's eyes shaped themselves into those evil slits. He began to finger the little knife again. "A deal with me, Ms. Lake, is a deal."

"There's still one loose end. A big fat one."

"What is that?"

"It's not a what. It's a who. Fat Boy."

Montano put down the knife and leaned back against the pillar. "Fat Boy," he said sadly.

"Doesn't have anything to do with the price of tea in China, but you know what really surprises me about all this? That you were actually going to have that jerk bring the stuff over to the States. Might just as well turn it over to the DEA and save yourself the trouble."

"Ms. Lake, please give me some credit. Fat Boy was merely supposed to warehouse the product on Andros until such time as I instructed him to turn it over to my courier. And my original courier was good, Ms. Lake, very good."

"This a guessing game?"

"No." He shot the same look at the big guy as people shoot at aged relatives who are both senile and deaf—and not fluent speakers of English, in any case. The look as much as said, It's all right to talk in front of him; he won't understand. "Reverend Ira Farnsworth, pastor of the Savior Network."

"The TV jerk? Somehow, he doesn't seem the type."

"Which is why he was so right for the job. He was greedy. He was well respected. And he had a reason to fly back and forth between Naples and the Bahamas—his brother's pathetic little mission."

Stormy eyed Montano. "Of course you know what the next question is going to be: Why not still use him?"

"For starters, you have the commodity in question."

"I'm sure you have imaginative ways of getting around that problem."

Montano planted a no-nonsense look on his mug and nodded. "Very observant. No, the good Reverend had a most unpleasant experience at customs the other evening. There must have been an informant." He shot one of those lethal looks at Stormy.

"Wasn't me."

"Then, Ms. Lake, that makes your part of our little bargain trickier, doesn't it?"

"A little." She took a long drink. "But I think I know who the problem is."

"If I may be of assistance . . ."

"No." She paused. "There have been enough murders on Andros for one Yuletide. Anyway, we were talking about part two of our deal. It concerns Fat Boy. I want you to guarantee that he will never again bother me or Miles Farnsworth."

"Ira's brother? Where does he enter into this deal?"

"He has cute buns."

Montano stopped stroking his knife haft and began to test the blade for sharpness by running it along the callus of his thumb. "There are many ways to prevent someone from bothering people."

"Maybe I didn't make myself clear. I want you to make sure he doesn't bug us. No way. Not ever."

Montano folded the knife. "Rather extreme. May one inquire as to why?"

Stormy looked at Montano over top of her scotch until she was damn sure he knew why. Then she said, "Because the fat fucker stole my sailboat."

During the fourth round of drinks, Stormy and Montano went over the fine details of the delivery—specific instructions about where to land, terms of the payout. Montano even sketched her a fairly accurate topo map showing the coordinates of his tomato field-cum-landing strip. When that was all out of the way, there was silence, then a few dead-end tries at conversation.

After the third attempt, Montano put on his best smile and folded his hands together on the table. "Ms. Lake," he said. "I believe the business portion of our evening is complete. I have a bottle of Mumm's on ice back in my room. I would be most honored if you would join me. To celebrate."

Thanks to the honesty of the Lucayan's bartenders, Stormy felt pretty good. She had a nice warm spot just below her rib cage. As for the little spick, she had seen worse. And in a perverse, overly eager-to-please way, he might have turned out to be one of those guys who surprise the hell out of you by being half-decent lovers.

It was then that Stormy Lake did something she didn't do very often. She surprised herself. She said, "No."

The way Cal Cooligan figured it, a weekend at the Lucayan, all expenses paid by the DEA, was marginally—only marginally—better than picking tomatoes in Montano's fields. When it came down to the short strokes, duty at the Lucayan meant less pain in the lower back but a whole lot more pain in the royal ass. Bimbos seemed to hit on Cal every five minutes—and he was almost horny enough to give some of them second thoughts. Having to exercise his willpower bugged him. As if that were not enough, the help went to great pains to let him know at every opportunity what they thought of a brother who didn't know his place on life's economic ladder. But the worst part was the gamblers. The ones who came on junkets late Friday evening bleary-eyed from New York and stayed all weekend at the tables, pissing away their retirement savings, their homes, their kids' education. Not unlike the stock market. For some reason, that made Cal both angry and depressed.

Still, at least there wasn't some freckled guy in the cab of a truck telling him what to do ten hours a day. And the floor-boards in his room definitely did not squeak.

If he could pin an I.D. on Montano's woman friend, the trip might well be a professional success, too. Apparently, the woman and Montano were done with their talk. She rose from the table—to leave, judging by the way Montano took her hand in both of his. Cal listened hard. Most of what Montano said got lost in the chugging and dinging of the slot machines. But when the woman finally freed her hand, Montano made a mis-take—a stupid mistake. He raised his voice and said, "Until the twenty-eighth, then, Ms. Lake."

At that instant, some idiot must have won a jackpot at the slots. A great whooping and clanging started to come from one of the rows of machines.

It might as well have been whooping and clanging for Cal. A date. And a last name. One, two, just like that.

The woman who left Montano walked directly toward Cal. She was pretty good-looking, in an athletic, tall, and bony way. Evenly tanned. Early thirties. Moved—or rather glided—more like a young black woman than a white. Cal approved of that part. Hair the color of chocolate, and worn in a tangled jungle of curls and waves. It was clear, even from halfway across a barroom in Freeport, that her locks flopped and bounced in whatever manner they chose, and would never bow before roll-ers or brushes.

But her brown eyes were what caught and held Cal's atten-tion. In part because they looked unflinchingly into his own, in part because there was a certain crazy sparkle to them, as if the woman was barely in control of an irresistible urge, one that nagged her to do something totally and ridiculously spon-taneous—consequences be damned. The sort of thing you al-ways want to do but know damn well you'll never in a million years get up the nerve. Well, she looked as if she succumbed to that temptation about ten times a day—minimum. His dead sister Claire was the only other person he had ever known who radiated that love of life. Cal knew it could be fun, and dangerous.

Montano's woman came so close to Cal, she almost brushed his knees. Then, when he thought she was going to kiss him or something, she batted one of those wacky brown eyes. "Shouldn't drink on duty, good-lookin'," she said.

Montano was tipsy when he stood up. But that was acceptable. He had had a good night at the tables, his deal was back on track, and Rachel was right there to take his hand and steady him. She had materialized the instant Stormy left. Montano put his hand around that thin waist, barked a few instructions to Sammy, and set out for his suite and the Mumm's.

He made one stop along the way. And it added further buoyancy to his mood. When he inquired about messages at the front desk, the clerk said that a Miles Farnsworth had called and that he would meet him as arranged at the South Ocean the following evening.

The way Montano had it figured, there were three people who could be in possession of his cocaine. Fat Boy, Stormy Lake, and the pastor's little brother. By tomorrow evening, Montano would have all of them.

Chapter 14

Montano was heading for an eighty-two on his Sunday after-noon round at South Ocean—not a bad score for him, and, all in all, a delightful ending to a most successful weekend: Stopping off in Nassau for a good round of golf after winning at the tables in Freeport, the deal with Stormy Lake, and Rachel, sweet, lithe Rachel. . . .

Thinking about sweet, lithe Rachel caused him to slice a dead-easy five-iron approach. The ball left his club, not with a solid whack but with a wet sounding *flift.* It started out at a low, rising angle, in the right direction for the first fifty yards, then it veered sharply, ricocheted off the trunk of a palm, and flew into what very well could have been the Bahamas's last remaining stand of virgin rain forest—clearly out of bounds. Montano threw the offending club, in approximately the direction his ball should have taken, but even here his aim was off. He nearly hit his Bahamian caddie, and succeeded in bouncing the club off Sammy's thigh. Sammy just shrugged and grinned self-consciously, as if serving as a target was just all part of the job. Without looking back, Montano strode off the course. Two strokes short of the cup, and the game was all over.

The preacher was where he was supposed to be—sitting at the terrace bar above the pro shop. Montano knew immediately who it was, because he looked like Ira, or rather, one of Ira's poor relations. He wore a cheap fawn-colored suit that might have been slept in for the previous four or five nights, or served as a permanent, portable table napkin, judging from the two silver dollar–sized grease spots on the left lapel and the unidentifiable reddish smudge below the breast pocket. The preacher nodded as soon as he saw Montano. But, aside from that limp greeting, he just sat there drinking direct from his bottle of St. Pauli Girl.

Montano slid out a hand and greeted the preacher with the usual gusto, all the while trying to solidify a first impression. The suit might have been rumpled and stained, and cheap to begin with, off the rack in the worst sort of way, and probably off the worst sort of rack, but he wore it with the same comfortable confidence that some guys have when they're in Savile Row tailor-mades, or military uniforms. Same with his face. It was a blonder, leaner, bluer-eyed version of the big brother's face, and someone in the distant past had pushed the nose about a quarter of an inch off center—just enough to add a tiny dollop of instant mystery. That aside, the preacher's face was calm, devoid of twitches, fidgets, and itches that needed to be scratched or stroked.

Montano was not surprised that the preacher initiated conversation—even before Montano had a chance to order a drink.

"You sent my brother over to pick up some cocaine. I refused to turn it over to him. But I do have it. I'd like to deliver it to you myself. Personally and privately."

Montano sat down but didn't respond. The preacher was too direct and unflappable, too much of an equal. Montano gazed over the brilliant green fairways curving between deeper green palm groves, offset by white sand traps and the aquamarine ovals of ponds. Landscape and control: That was what golf was all about. And during the wet season, South Ocean was as pretty a course as the Bahamas offered.

While Montano mused about golf's rightful place in the celestial hierarchy, Sammy shambled up to the table. A waiter brought Montano a bourbon and soda, festooned with a sprig of fresh mint. Montano drank, swallowed, looked at the course some more, but still remained silent. Finally, he quietly said, "Sammy."

The big guy hoisted Miles by the armpits, gave him a quick frisk, and returned him to his chair.

The preacher didn't seem the least perturbed. He might well have been content to sit forever with the sun at his back, sipping a well-chilled beer. Montano spoke. Had to speak. "Why you, and not your brother? I know your brother. We have had a long business relationship. I do not know you."

"The main reason is that I happen to have it. He doesn't."

Montano spread his hands. It was a reflex to flash his finger jewelry. But he quickly thought better of it and crumbled them back into fists. "What am I to think of someone who would betray his own brother? Am I to deal with such a person?"

"Don't see why not. Look, I need a half-million dollars—bad. Want to know why? My dear, sweet brother has threatened to sell my mission out from under me unless I give him a half-million. So much for brotherly love, Mr. Montano."

"So you want to step in—for a half-million, I take it?"

"Exactly."

"Reverend Farnsworth, I am at a loss as to whether I should deal with you or not."

"Mr. Montano, why not just name a time and place. If I'm there with the goods, fine. If not . . ."

Montano thought. Then he nodded. "I understand you have a boat. Very well. At sunup on December twenty-ninth, be at Keewaydin Beach. I have a dock just north of marker sixty-five on the Intracoastal Waterway. You must know the area?"

"Halfway between Naples and Marco Island? Used to fish there as a kid."

"Very well. Be there. Have the merchandise. And my representative will pay you one-half million dollars."

"I don't set sail until the money is in my account at Naples Federal." He pulled out of his breast pocket a slip of paper that already had the number written on it.

"And if I say no?"

"Then no cocaine."

"I could have you killed."

The preacher actually smiled, and looked for a moment as if he might let fly with a peal of laughter. "Great. I'll finally get to meet my boss face-to-face. And he and I have a few little matters to discuss. In the meantime, I'm in a desperate situation. If The Vale goes . . . well, that's the single-most-important thing in my life. The rest doesn't much matter. I don't know if you can appreciate—"

Montano put out a hand to silence him. All these preachers had the same weakness—a love for their own words. "The money will be there," Montano said.

"One other thing—"

"I cringe whenever I hear a sentence that begins with that phrase, Reverend."

"One other thing," the preacher began again. "I do have that coke. And I will be delivering. Anyone who tells you otherwise is misinformed—or a liar."

"Just deliver. That, I will believe. The rest of your bluster has not impressed me. Not an iota. I would still be using your brother, as originally planned—and don't think for one minute that I don't have ways that would guarantee that even you would tell me where the cocaine is—but for a small problem. Ira was strip-searched at customs after seeing you the day before yesterday. So you see, I find myself in a state of—desperation—to use your word."

The preacher actually smiled at that one.

Montano went on. "You should know that there was an informant. Someone tipped them off. Had to be. Don't know who, but you'd better be careful—unless it was you who ratted, that is."

Damnedest thing, but with that observation, Montano finally got what he had wanted since the moment he set eyes on the preacher—the upper hand. The guy was flustered. Angry. Why, exactly, Montano couldn't figure out, but the preacher looked as if he was heading nonstop into shock. He went white. He closed his eyes and drew the thumb and index finger of his left hand across his brow. He swallowed once, started scratching furiously at the back of his neck, then muttered, "Who'd a ever . . ."

Sammy and Montano were left alone at the table after Miles left to catch an evening flight back to Andros. Sammy watched him leave, then stared at his empty chair for a full minute, just to make certain he wasn't going to reappear.

"You want a Coke, Sammy?" asked Montano.

"Sure, jefe. That'd be great," said Sammy. He swung around and looked at Montano with eyes that were troubled and sad. "I don't understand this. Not one bit, jefe. Nope."

Montano smiled a fatherly smile. "Of course you don't."

"I mean. Uh." Sammy pouted and opened his mouth for another try. "Now. Now. Now you have deals with both of them—and with Fat Boy, too. That makes three." The last bit he said with some measure of pride and accomplishment.

"Look at it as insurance. One of them is bound to deliver."

That impressed Sammy. He nodded very eagerly. But then shook his jowls. "Yeah, but it's gonna cost you a lot more." He smiled. This time he had outfoxed his boss. "You'd originally agreed to pay Fat Boy a million, right, jefe?"

Montano agreed.

"So, now you're gonna pay out a half of a million to the girl and to the preacher. That makes a million. Before they deliver."

Montano agreed again.

Sammy got himself all wound up. "Yeah. And if the girl delivers, you owe her another half, right? And, worse, if Fat Boy delivers, you owe him the whole million, right? Only way you'll come out even is if the preacher delivers. You're counting on the preacher to come through?"

"No. Frankly, if I had to guess, I'd say it's going to be the girl, with Fat Boy running a distant second."

Sammy looked almost hurt, so deep was his perplexity.

Montano put his glass to his nose and sniffed the mint leaves. "Sammy, don't fret. Your logic is flawless. I must congratulate you." The big guy beamed. "But, you have overlooked one thing." Montano paused for effect. Sammy leaned forward eagerly. "You," said Montano.

"Me?"

"Exactly. I call it the Sammy Factor. You. You are a very important factor in the equation. You are going to be on that beach at Keewaydin on December twenty-ninth and you are going to make the pickup—if it happens. Then, either way, you are going to kill Fat Boy and the preacher."

Sammy took some time to do some simple math, then nodded. "What about the girl?"

Montano flashed a gold bicuspid. "The girl, I will take care of."

Chapter 15

Bones held up the black and white glossy, taken at close range with a wide angle-lens and slow film, to judge by the contrast and crisp focus. "Name's Melissa Lake. Goes by Stormy. Operates out of Grand Turk," Bones said.

Cal looked at her. It was nine Monday morning. Back in Bones's Miami office. The photograph of Stormy Lake was about the fiftieth glossy of dark-haired women Bones had showed him during the past hour. In the photo, she was perhaps a bit younger, looking more carefree in her bikini top and ultrashort cutoffs, seated at a table with one leg hooked over the back of a chair, deep in conversation, holding an old-fashioned glass, half full. "Could be her, I dunno," said Cal. "But it could have been any of a half-dozen of the ones you showed me."

Bones shot him a hard, nasty look. A look that, better than words, said, Don't fuck with me, man.

"And you got nothing else?" Bones asked.

"Just what's in the report. Montano went there. Won a bit of dough at the tables, met with a dark-haired woman, then went off to his room with some bimbo waitress. Left early Sunday on a flight to Nassau."

Bones still hadn't altered the nasty look of his mug. "Well, Cal," he said. "I hope you at least had a pleasant weekend. Tomorrow, there will be tomatoes to pick." He slid a heap of papers on his desk in front of him and poked at them with his index finger. When that failed to work magic on the heap, he added, "A hell of a lot of tomatoes."

What was it about the goddamn preacher that gave her a nearly irrepressible urge to hug him. To take that big boyish body in her arms and rock him back and forth. To gently tweak the snout back into place, or to reach out and tousle his hair, particularly that single lock that always seemed to stick out.

Lying never bothered Stormy. But the Rev somehow made it seem different—sinful. And his sitting across from her with an Old Milwaukee Light in the back corner of the Chickcharnie, wearing a look of hangdog vulnerability, wasn't going to make it any easier.

Stormy's instincts told her lying to him was going to get harder as the afternoon wore on—and it was one of those afternoons that had all the elements necessary to wear on, and on, and on. Monday to begin with and ten degrees cooler than the seasonal norm, which meant Stormy was in her paint-speckled sweatshirt and skintight jeans. A steady drizzle had been falling since dawn. Stormy decided to dispatch with the business and lies first, even though it went against all her life's philosophies, which told her that the wise course of action, in all cases, was to procrastinate until circumstances forced her hand.

And with business out of the way, with the steady rain outside, with Prue probably teaching school, and with goddamn Dugold gone off with some new tart who was staying at Small Hope . . . well, as they say, stranger things had been known to happen.

Stormy shivered nervously and ordered a scotch on the rocks. Then she called the waiter back and had him make it a double.

"It's going to be easier than I thought," she said to Miles, meaning the business side of things.

He understood and nodded for her to go on.

Stormy sucked in two lungfuls of air. "Met my guy. Deal is

on. A million bucks—the first half for you and your worthy causes; the other half for dear, sweet Stormy Lake to piss away as she chooses. The best part is that the delivery is dead easy. Safe as houses, unless you're stupid enough to put us up on a reef. Deal is, you and I are to sail that goddamn stinkpot of yours over to Bimini. They're going to run the stuff across themselves. And there ain't no one between here and Bimini who's going to suspect the Very Reverend Miles Farnsworth of sailing around with a load of toot. Though they might wonder what he's doing at sea alone with a raunchy dame like me." She gave her eyes a bat or two and licked her lips for good measure.

Miles shifted awkwardly in his seat. "I've made arrangements for the structural alterations on *Come to Jesus Cruiser*. No problem there, except the shop foreman thinks I'm nuts. Maybe he's right."

"When's your brother want his loot?"

"End of the month. He's got some big loan payment to make."

"Then we'll set it up with the Bimini boys for the thirtieth. That'll mean pulling out of here on the twenty-ninth, say nine or ten at night—under the cover of darkness, I think you're supposed to call it."

For some reason, the Rev wasn't much in the mood for drinking. He sipped his Old Milwaukee Light but refused to part with it. Stormy didn't let that alter her drinking plans for the afternoon. She took down two doubles back-to-back, and then rode their mellowness into a third. It was a good afternoon to drink. The rain and Dugold's departure would have been reason enough. But Stormy's plan was falling into place neatly. And whenever things started to go too well for Stormy, she got suspicious, terribly thirsty, and, today at least, downright impish.

"So how's dear, sweet Prue, anyway?" she asked at about the time the tops of the ice cubes surfaced in drink number three.

"I thought Prue was to be left out of this. Clean out."

"Hey, touchy, touchy. Sorry, Rev."

He smiled in a conciliatory way and ran his lips around the rim of the beer can, stopping short of taking a real pull. "Prue is very interested in you. Gave me the third degree the other night. Thinks there's something going on."

"Now what would ever give her cause to think that." She licked her lips.

"Plus, she's been acting edgy. And then this morning, she came in and informed me that she was off to Miami—for the day. I can't imagine why." He shrugged and took a halfhearted sip from his beer. It was a feeble sip, but apparently enough to make him somewhat impish, too, or at least anxious to steer the conversation away from Prue. "Anyway . . . what about your boyfriend? The dive master."

"Dive master. I got another word for that little prick. Seduction master. I think working at that resort got him used to a different woman every week." She pointed an index finger at her forehead and crossed her eyes. "Meet Ms. Last Week."

"Sorry I asked."

"Look, Rev, I'll let you in on a big secret. I hate it when men apologize, even on behalf of other men. If I ruled the goddamn world—and I may yet do so—it'd be a capital offense. Anyway, no need wasting your time worrying about my love life. If history is anything to go by, it has a funny way of taking care of itself. Or maybe not taking care of itself is a better way to put it."

"That so."

Stormy thought he had actually raised his eyebrows, maybe a quarter of an inch.

"You flirting with me, Rev?"

That got him wiggling in his chair and clearing his throat. He swallowed the rest of his can of beer and rose.

"Hey, we're not done yet." Stormy gestured downward with her drink—if that's what you call three fragments of ice and a half inch of pee-colored liquid. "I need a boat for an evening. Can I bum that stinkpot off you?"

"You're joking, of course."

"Honest, Rev, I need a boat for a few hours. Out at ten P.M., back by no later than two. Quiet as a goddamn Indian in a canoe. I promise. Just hit me with a yes or no, I'll take it from there."

"No."

"Fine. Great. So much for—"

"But . . . I'll happily take you where you want to go."

"Sorry, Rev. There are some things a girl's gotta do solo. Private matter. Nothing to do with our little scam."

"Then no deal."

"You don't trust me. Is that it?"

"Don't trust anyone with my boat."

Stormy inflated her cheeks almost to the point of bursting and began to puff the air out in a long, slow hiss. "Boy, this just ain't been my month for men and boats. First Bingo and the *Roach*. Next Dugold and his Whaler. Now you . . . Look, Rev, it's about Fat Boy and his zit-faced goon. You see, I suspect they took my boat. Actually think I saw it up the coast on my flight out of here the other day. Just want to check it out."

"All the more reason to have me along."

Stormy swallowed the last of her drink. "Any excuse, is that it? Any excuse to get a girl alone on that boat."

It was the young wife, the one who looked fourteen years old and who nearly had been Miss Florida. She came to the door, followed by a pack of yapping, snapping Yorkshire terriers. When Montano asked to see Ira, would-be Miss Florida almost seemed disappointed. A bad woman, that one, coming to the door dressed in a garment that looked as if it came from an

X-rated lingerie shop, even though it was mid-afternoon Monday, and a cold, raw Monday mid-afternoon at that.

She pouted. Pushed back a wispy filament of blond hair. Flicked her hand at the Yorkies as if she was shooing off flies. "Why, do come in," she said, piling far too much brown-eyed contact on top of her uneducated, drawled rural accent—probably more rustic than it really had to be. "He is out by the pool. Exercising." She emitted the last word as a twitter.

Disrespectful, thought Montano. More to keep in practice than through any genuine interest, he turned on his charm full blast, met eye contact with eye contact, treated her to the glimmer of gold bicuspid, extended his hand and took the tips of her fingers in his. "Jorge Montano," he said, and actually dipped his torso in a movement that could have been mistaken for a bow if someone was predisposed to do so. "I believe I haven't had the pleasure . . ."

"Betty-Nan Farnsworth. Ira's tol' me a whole lot about you."

Then, she flirted with him. Not blatantly, but enough so the message was there. A flicker of the eye. A reaching movement of the wrist. He ignored the come-on and went past her. One of the Yorkies latched on to his pant leg. She bent down to disentangle it, and in so doing, exposed most of the upper portion of a thigh.

She never made Miss Florida, but she would certainly become the queen of Naples's merry widows. Montano actually felt a twinge of pity for Ira.

Ira was in the pool area, wearing a sweat suit and pair of Reeboks, struggling to keep his footing on a mechanical treadmill, a struggle in which it looked as if he was falling behind. The contraption was pointed toward the Gulf, away from the door Montano came through, so Ira wasn't aware of his arrival. Montano let him go on for a while. Then he casually bent down and ripped the machine's cord out of the socket.

Ira pitched forward against the device's handlebars. He grunted. When he turned around, his face was a frightening purple-red. "Drat," he said. The expletive was directed at Montano. He grabbed a towel and wiped his hands. "What are you doing here? I thought you understood. You were never to come here . . ."

Montano just smiled. "But, Pastor, I was in the neighborhood. And a most important matter of business has come up. A change in plans."

Ira slung the towel over his shoulders and sat down, without indicating that Montano should do the same. Montano took a chair opposite him, anyhow, and watched as he hooked his wrist up to some mechanical device. Ira stared at the device intently and his lips moved, counting. Finally, he mopped the towel across his brow, which had begun to return to a more flesh-toned hue.

"This is a silly thing to have done, Jorge. I mean, after last week at customs, the police may be watching this place. They have to suspect something—why else search me in that way? And with you showing up here like this. They can add two and two."

Montano reached into his coat pocket and came back out with a half corona, which he lit with a gold lighter.

Ira waved a hand frantically in front of his face. "Do you have to smoke those things . . ."

"Pastor. I am genuinely saddened. The reason I came was that I have good news. Our worries—*your worries*—will soon be over." He puffed out a mighty smoke cloud and broke into a full smile.

Ira looked as if he was about to vomit. The cause was either the cigar or Montano's sickly sweet smile.

Montano went on. "You and my trusted associate, Sammy, will be enjoying a morning of angling on December twenty-ninth. It will necessitate an early departure . . . before dawn . . ."

195

"I've never been fishing in my adult life. Used to hate it as a kid."

Montano held up a hand. "Perhaps it is because you never sought a worthy-enough quarry. With any luck, you and Sammy will return from your outing with enough cocaine to fund Celestial City."

"Jorge, get serious. The police are watching me."

"They won't be this time. The last incident, I fear, was the result of a tip-off."

Ira's face began to return to its earlier purple hues. "My brother?" he said in a near whisper.

Montano nodded. "He is one possibility. Maybe the best one."

"And what makes you think he won't tell the police again?"

Montano waited before responding. "Because he'll be the one delivering it to you."

From the color Ira's face developed, Montano assumed that if the pastor plugged himself back into his heart-rate machine, the reading would be higher than it was after his exercise session. Exactly the effect he had hoped his little visit would produce. He smiled, patted Ira on the thigh, and said, "Don't worry, I think you will enjoy this fishing."

Montano turned to leave, except his way was blocked by Betty-Nan, who had come to the doorway wearing a swimsuit that appeared to have been fashioned from two pasties and a tiger-striped G-string that defied at least two of the basic laws of female anatomy. Without speaking, she walked past Montano and Ira and dove into the pool. It struck Montano as a silly thing to do. For starters, the weather was far too cold.

Fat Boy and Sammy were already sitting on Montano's patio when he got back from visiting Ira. Montano examined Fat Boy before speaking. The puffiness had gone from his face, but an ugly red line still ran from his forehead to his mouth, although with the stitches gone, even that was not as painful-looking as it once had been. He reached a hand out and patted the cut.

"You see, Fat Boy, it's like I told you: It will heal," Montano said.

Fat Boy put a hand up to the cut, but didn't say anything.

Montano went on. "Fat Boy, there is some good news. I have decided to give you the opportunity to make up for your past errors in judgment." He paused and fingered the scab again. "One chance. You fail"—he gave a light pinch, just enough so that a drop of watery pinkish blood came out from the wound—"well, let's not think about failure, because I think you know what would happen. Don't you?"

Fat Boy nodded.

That made Montano smile. He brought his palms together and looked contentedly at Sammy. "Very well, Fat Boy. At dawn, on the twenty-ninth of December, the preacher—the brother on Andros—is to deliver the missing merchandise to a dock just north of marker sixty-five on the Intracoastal Waterway going toward Marco. He's coming over on that boat of his. That means he's probably planning to leave Andros between the twenty-sixth and the twenty-eighth. I want you to make sure you are on that boat with him and that the merchandise arrives safely. Clear?"

Fat Boy nodded.

Montano waited for a few seconds. "Good," he said, then turned to Sammy and went on. "Sammy, get this scum off my property."

To his credit, Fat Boy tried to stand and leave under his own power. But Sammy grabbed him by the shirt collar, anyway. He hoisted Fat Boy a couple of inches off the patio, so the top button cut into the jellylike flab of his throat. After he grew tired of that pose, Sammy gave Fat Boy a shove that made him take three skipping steps toward the waiting car. Fat Boy looked back sullenly at Montano, but Sammy caught him once, on the shoulder, hard enough to spin his torso around in the desired direction.

When they had gone, Montano pulled out a half corona and lit it. With his eyes closed, he ran through the steps of his new plan, then ran through them again, finding nothing out of place. After he had done that, he let himself grin—not the toothy gilt-edged smile he bestowed upon others, but a small, private grin he reserved for himself.

Chapter 16

Stormy Lake thought of herself as, by and large, a good person—maybe one of the few living human beings who could honestly make that claim. So whenever she had particularly rotten, or evil, tasks to do, whenever she was going to have to be a real shit, she liked to pick a single day—a dirty day—when she would step out of character and for a few hours become the sort of person she despised, before returning to her harmless, happy-go-lucky self. That made any rotten deeds easier to atone for, or at least rationalize. She had chosen Dirty Tuesday, December 20, as such a day.

The weather was fittingly cool, but the heavy overcast of the day before had given way to bright yellow-orange sunshine that was from time to time obscured by the gray belly of one of the many low clouds that scudded at wave top level down the Straits of Florida hell bent for Cuba. At ten in the morning, when she left the Chickcharnie to go to the cop shop for her appointment with Fat Boy, it was still sweatshirt cool, but the sunshine, and the clip at which those clouds seemed determined to get to Castro's cane fields, foretold T-shirt temperatures by noon.

Fat Boy was in his office, a plain unadorned space, with cinder-block walls and single barred window near the ceiling. It could have been converted instantly into a jail cell, a handy feature, in Stormy's view. Where the prisoner's cot would have been stood Fat Boy's desk, one of those big oak affairs favored by government departments in the 1940s. And like many desks in government departments, this one was three-quarters covered in paperwork: bales of file folders held together with rubber bands, several dog-eared reams of typed sheets, and a small library of magazines and manuals.

Fat Boy sat dead center behind the desk on a feeble-looking plastic chair. He wore his favorite outfit, his only civvy outfit, as far as Stormy could tell: the tan safari shirt and brown polyester pants. And when Stormy came into the office, he was daydreaming and absently stroking the scab that ran down the right side of his face.

"You'll have to give me the name of your plastic surgeon," said Stormy before Fat Boy was aware she was there.

He yanked his fingers away from his face with a start, recovered quickly, and replaced his wide-eyed openmouthed gape with a narrow-eyed scowl meant to instill either fear or respect. It succeeded in doing neither. And the tiny recoil Stormy felt came not from his demeanor but from the aroma of body oil and stale sweat that threatened to become cloying in the small cell/office.

"I don't like people barging in here unannounced," said Fat Boy.

"Then maybe what you need is a sign on the door: 'The chief constable requests that visitors not barge in unannounced.' Either that or hire a deputy who sleeps less soundly. The pockfaced asshole is stretched out on a bunk in the first cell on the right. Had half a mind to slam the door on him." Stormy thought it best to omit the detail that Pock-face was snoozing his morning shift away with his head resting on a folded shirt-jac that had belonged to the late Bingo Martin. It was his favorite garment. He always kept it on a hook in the galley wall of the *Roach*.

"I do not appreciate your efforts at humor, Miss Lake. I was traveling all day yesterday. Just got in on the morning flight.

I presume you have an important reason for disturbing me?" Fat Boy said.

"Only if you think your little shipment of coke is important."

He sat up in his chair and leaned as close to her as the stacks of paperwork on his desk would permit. "More important than ever," he said, managing to get some real tones of threat and impending doom into his words.

"Nice theatrics, Fat Boy," said Stormy. "But I didn't come to watch you perform. Just to tell you that our pal the preacher is not only willing, but insistent, on doing the dirty work himself. Can't imagine why, but maybe he doesn't trust me. Anyway, Fat Boy, he's waiting for instructions."

Fat Boy sat silent for awhile, allowing a tiny smile to form as best it could on his wounded face. It was the first genuine sign of emotion Stormy had seen him show. And when he spoke, he spoke directly to her. No theatrics. "Thank you, Miss Lake. You may go now."

"But what do you want me to say to him?"

The new, confident, happy version of Fat Boy stood. "Not a thing. Not a single thing," he said.

Stormy knew she had goofed.

The meeting with Fat Boy was supposed to have been the easy part. It was her one-on-one session with Prue that Stormy had been dreading.

Dirty Tuesday, of course, was also the day to get that one out of the way. On the phone, Stormy had told a surprised-sounding Prue that they had to talk—urgent—over the lunch hour, in Stormy's room at the Chickcharnie.

To prepare for the encounter, Stormy had ordered a half-dozen meat patties from downstairs, with two cold Beck's for herself, and, as an appropriate touch of thoughtfulness, a couple of cans of ginger ale for Prue. As a last touch, she had rounded up most of the stray clothing (including a precious memento: a pair of Dugold's bikini underpants) and kicked it into a pile in a corner of the bathroom. She did her best to untangle the bed sheets, plumped the pillows, and hauled up the old spread, leaving only a few tag ends protruding like the hem of a ratty slip. It was only as Prue's knock sounded on the door—light, yet crisp and without hesitancy—that Stormy remembered the ashtray full of roaches on her night table. She flicked it, Frisbee-style, under the chest of drawers and went to answer the door.

Prue and Stormy stood eyeing each other, neither one willing to flinch. Prue was in a denim dress, buttoned from well below her knees to her Adam's apple. Stormy felt a bit self-conscious in her faded jeans and T-shirt.

It was bordering on becoming one of those doorway standoffs that never end, when Stormy stood aside and tossed her snarl of curls toward the room. "Come into my suite?"

At first it looked as if that was the last thing Prue intended to do. She hesitated, the way some people do before entering a sickroom—in this case, a sickroom where the patient is afflicted with some dread and highly contagious disease. But eventually, she drew in a big sustaining breath of uncontaminated hallway air, then dutifully trod over Stormy's threshold.

Stormy gestured toward the room's single chair—apparently an orphan from a set of discount-store dining room chairs. Prue looked at the chair, and for a moment Stormy thought she was going to produce a handkerchief and give its paisley upholstery a swipe. But she merely turned and planted herself, knees and ankles together, facing Stormy, who flounced on the bed.

It being Dirty Tuesday, Stormy launched directly into her spiel. "Look," Stormy began. "I know you don't think much of me. That's fine. And I know I probably owe you an explanation about me and the Rev, which you aren't going to get, except to say I'm not trying to steal him from you. But I want to thank you, okay, for coming to see me."

Prue just nodded, and drew her knees more tightly together.

"Good. Good," Stormy said to herself, and then once more, "Good. I'm having trouble getting this thing off the ground—"

"Are you sleeping with him?"

The abruptness of Prue's question almost winded Stormy. She hoped that the feeble sounding "No" she uttered came quickly enough to sound convincing.

Prue nodded, much as she would to a student whose answer she deemed satisfactory—barely.

Stormy tried to wrestle the conversation back on course. "This concerns the coke."

Prue dipped her chin maybe a half inch and allowed her eyebrows to rise by the same amount.

"He has it, you know." Stormy said.

That caused Prue to straighten her spine. "I certainly did not. My understanding was that it was missing—Moonbeam had hidden it somewhere."

"Yeah, like in the Rev's stinkpot . . . I mean his boat, the cruiser."

Prue sighed and ran a hand across her head as if to push a loose strand of hair back into place. Except, of course, there was no loose strand—not on Prue's head. "Well, I'm sure he intends to turn it over to the authorities, in good time."

"Wrong. He intends to turn it over to a couple of thugs in Bimini, and they ain't authorities—unless you count being authoritative in the transshipment and import of contraband. The Rev, jerk that he is, wants to sell the stuff to get the dough to buy off his brother. He's on some goddamn high horse about saving The Vale."

Prue pursed her lips. "Oh, Lord," she whispered. "How foolish of—"

"Exactly. The most foolish goddamn thing I ever heard of, in fact. But he's a stubborn fool. That's where you come in."

"I don't follow."

"Stop him."

Prue swallowed. Nodded. She thought a minute, then looked hard at Stormy. "Why are you so interested?"

Stormy didn't answer right away. It wasn't the sort of question she wanted to answer—period. So she rummaged around in the grease-stained paper bag and came out with one of Prue's ginger ales and a bottle of Beck's for herself. She tossed the ginger ale at Prue hard—outside and low.

Prue's hand went down expertly and nabbed the can. Stormy looked at her. There was no expression on her face. Nothing telltale, at any rate. Stormy lobbed one of the patties at her. She picked it out of the air with her free hand.

"Thank you," Prue said. "I asked why you were so interested in Miles's welfare."

Stormy munched her patty. It was spiced perfectly, just warm enough to bring the beginnings of a tear to the corners of her eyes. She washed down the bite with a mouthful of icy beer. "Not the Rev's welfare I'm interested in, but mine. It's my dope, remember? I want it back. If you dissuade him, maybe I'll be able to get my mitts on it."

Prue did not take her eyes off Stormy. "Do you love him?" she asked.

The question was obviously intended to catch Stormy completely off guard, and succeeded. She tried her best not to miss a beat. Say whatever else you would about Prue, but she sure knew how to grill someone. "No. You?" Stormy said.

To Stormy's surprise, Prue answered, and there was nothing in her voice to indicate a lack of sincerity. "I don't know," she said, then again, "Sometimes I just don't know."

"Well, just in case you do—or at least want him around while you make up your mind—let me spell it out for you. He's going to make a run to Bimini on the twenty-ninth—late. And he's going to have the stuff stashed under the floorboards of that boat with the silly name. Stop him."

"If I can—"

"No ifs about it. Prue, I suspect you have a few tricks up your sleeve, so use them to stop him. Pull out all the stops. I have good reason to believe that Fat Boy is on to the Rev. And

204

Fat Boy has become very, very dangerous. The worst sort of dangerous. If there is anything—*anything*—you can do."

The two women looked at each other for a long time. Prue actually started to nibble at the corner of her patty, without taking her eyes off Stormy. Finally she said, "Bimini. The twenty-ninth."

Stormy nodded.

"I'll do what I can." She put the half-eaten patty and the ginger ale on the chest of drawers. "Thank you for this, but I had a bite at The Vale before coming over," she said lamely, and went toward the door.

"One more thing," Stormy said.

Prue turned.

"Why the hell you engaged to the Rev if you aren't even sure you love him or not?"

Prue's expression remained fixed. "I know I love working at The Vale. I know I love the children. I'm pretty sure I love Miles."

"Then, sister"—Stormy came down loud and sibilant and sarcastic on the word *sister*—"you best make sure you do everything you can to keep his ass alive. And you and I both know damn well what I mean."

Prue maintained the same deadpan. "Thank you for your kind advice, Miss Lake," she said.

After Prue left, Stormy gobbled three more patties and drained her Beck's. Lunch over, she pulled the pillows from under the spread and propped them up against the headboard to make a backrest. She snapped open Beck's number two and took a ready-rolled joint out of her night-table drawer. With the empty beer bottle positioned between her thighs to serve as an ashtray, she lit the joint and settled into her pillows. When the spicy smoke of the Santa Marta hit the nether regions of her lungs, Dirty Tuesday was officially declared over.

Stormy hoped like hell Prue knew what she was doing. For that matter, Stormy hoped *she* knew what she was doing.

Chapter 17

Miles went down to *Come to Jesus Cruiser* just after dark Tuesday evening. That should have allowed plenty of time to meet Stormy at the town wharf at seven-thirty. If her boat was hidden only a couple of miles north, they'd be able to get there and back before ten, which would make it easier to explain his absence to Prue, who had mercifully scurried off on some unexplained errand right after dinner.

The night was on the coolish side, but the breeze had blown away all the clouds, leaving a black sky speckled with stars. A slight chop was on the sea, here and there interrupted by a cresting whitecap. Miles stepped on the wharf; that board let out an almost bestial sound of fear and pain, and at the same instant, he swore he heard a rustling noise from behind him. Nothing so distinct as to make him certain his ears were not playing tricks, but enough to make him stop and listen.

Except for the slap-slap of waves against the hull of *Come to Jesus Cruiser,* everything was quiet. Miles shone his flashlight at the boat. Nothing. He tramped down the wharf, stepped over the *Cruiser*'s gunwale, and dropped his feet heavily on his newly installed coconut and epoxy deck.

Immediately, he knew something was wrong. It took a second step on the deck to determine where the problem lay. He shone the light down. Starting about halfway along the stern and rounding the port side, someone had removed eight of the screws used to fasten the false deck to the original one. They had been taken out and meticulously laid on the gunwales directly above their former location. The rocking of the boat caused them to roll back and forth in gentle quarter rotations. Beside the ninth screw, the one that was still in place, but protruding from its hole by a half inch, was a screwdriver.

Miles picked it up, a small slot screwdriver, obviously not the tool used to extract the heavy square-headed screws he had driven into the deck, but Miles still recognized it. He, after all, had bought it along with five others, including a nice big square-headed one. Clover had wanted a cheap set to keep in her junk drawer in the kitchen to save her from having to go to the workshop every time a doorknob had to be tightened.

When Prue left after dinner, she had gone out through the kitchen.

Refastening the floorboards made him fifteen minutes late. As soon as Miles shut *Come to Jesus Cruiser*'s engines off at the town wharf, he heard a familiar "Hiya, Rev. At least you're still capable of landing that barge."

It came from the high stern of the M. V. *Central Andros,* the aging wooden mail boat that made weekly round-trips between Fresh Creek and the vast outside world of Nassau. Along with Stormy's voice, the night breeze carried a distinct waft of ganja. Miles looked up. It was difficult to make out features, but a single white face stood out amid a half-dozen darker silhouettes.

An orange dot glowed fiercely for a few seconds dead center on the white face, then moved to the dark face immediately to its left. An exhaling noise that could be heard even over the wind followed.

"Well, fellas, looks like my ship—such as it is—has come in. Been nice meeting you," said Stormy.

A chorus of baritone mumbles responded.

Stormy came down the *Central Andros*'s ladder and boarded *Come to Jesus Cruiser.* She was in her old jeans, the sweatshirt with the paint specks and a thin Gore-Tex windbreaker. "Okay,

Rev," she said as soon as she was aboard. "You and me got one lost fifty-four-foot staysail schooner to find."

Miles made no move to start the boat.

"Come on, Rev. Kick this stinkpot in gear. Tide'll change on us before you know it. Might have to spend the night together in the mangroves. A pretty piece of explaining that would be."

"Maybe there already is. Explaining, I mean. I think Prue tried to search the boat tonight," Miles said.

That quieted Stormy. Briefly. Then she said—as much to herself as to Miles—"Enterprising bitch . . ." She let her thought trail off. "What makes you think so?"

Miles told her about the rear deck.

"Shit," Stormy said. "She get her mitts on our special cargo?"

"It's still there."

"We're going to have to hide it somewhere. I don't claim to know dear, sweet Prue that well—can't say I'd care to—but from what I've seen, she doesn't come off as the type who would leave a chore like that unfinished for long."

"I hid it again. Even Prue won't find it."

"Cocksure, aren't we?"

"Kept a fifth of rum stashed there for the past year. Emergency supplies. She never found that."

"And she'd've said something if she had come across it?"

"No." Miles paused. "She'd have stolen it—for my own good, of course."

Stormy resisted making an obvious comment, and Miles added, "But I wonder what caused her to look there. I mean Prue has her quirks, but it's slightly out of character for her simply to decide to rip up my newly laid floorboards—just for the fun of it, or even for the good of Miles Farnsworth."

Stormy huffed a big breath and then gave the matter a minute's silent thought. After the minute was up, she fished in her windbreaker's outside flap pocket and came back with a pint of Cockspur. She broke the seal and handed the bottle to Miles. He put it to his lips, bobbed his Adam's apple a couple of times, and returned it. Stormy noticed the pint was still full. He had barely wet his lips.

She held the bottle up and shook it. "And this is the man who first impressed me—and almost won my little heart—by draining off half my flask in a single mighty gulp. Hope to hell you haven't gone and reformed—found religion or anything."

"No. No need to worry about that," Miles said altogether too quickly, so quickly he missed her little dig. "It's just that it's dark. And there are some pretty tricky reefs up the way we're going—"

Stormy shut him up by putting a hand on his shoulder and bringing her face very close to his. "Please, no bullshit, Rev. Not tonight."

Stormy was impressed with the way the new, improved, sober version of Miles Farnsworth handled *Come to Jesus Cruiser*. He took it smartly up to a speed where the old crate actually made a passable attempt at planing as it cut a nice series of S-curves between the ranks of breakers cresting white against the black water over shallow areas. He drove out just beyond the reef—it looked to be about a half mile offshore. Once clear of the reef, he steered north, parallel to shore, and head on into the chop. Conversation was impossible over the roar of the engines, so Stormy put a hand for support on the ledge that ran the length of the area under the windshield, and amused herself by trying to keep track of their progress. The lights of Fresh Creek disappeared quickly, almost as soon as they cleared the reef and turned north. On the horizon to their right, there was a grayish glow—Nassau, she guessed. To the left, there was a string of colored lanterns lining the beach. Small Hope Bay Lodge. And that gave her a poignant little twinge. Dugold would probably be in one of those cabins in an hour or so, putting it to Ms. This Week.

And Stormy? She would be out on the sea in an old wooden stinkpot with a drunken preacher, who wouldn't even drink with her anymore. Some night, the two of them hunting in the blackness for a sailboat that they might not find—that might never have been where she thought it was. And if they did find it, what then . . .?

Stormy patted the other flap pocket of her windbreaker—the one that didn't hold her flask. She felt the reassuring hardness of the little Beretta .25 Bingo had given her. Wasn't much of a gun, but, as Bingo had said when she protested at the time, "It's easy to carry, and these days a woman just never knows."

Ten minutes later, Miles slowed the boat to an idle. Without saying anything, he dropped both engines into neutral and stepped two paces backward onto the deck.

Toward shore, ugly white slashes of breaking waves all but obliterated the dark patches of deep water. Miles stood examining them in the way a white-water canoeist looks over a dubious stretch of Class IV rapids before deciding whether to be sensible and portage or to risk his neck by shooting them.

When he came back to the wheel, he had a look on his face that, even in the dark, bespoke a strong desire to lift his beloved boat up, toss it hull-heavenward, and lug it around the obstacle course of breaking waves and plank-ripping coral heads. "You still have that flask?" he asked.

For some reason, it instilled confidence in Stormy to see his Adam's apple bob three times in rapid succession, followed by a fourth slow, deep one for good measure. The confidence grew when the pint came back to her lighter—noticeably lighter.

He pivoted *Come to Jesus Cruiser* so its bow faced the shaggy shoreline of sea grape and mangrove, then he tapped the port throttle up a notch or two to keep the boat pointed that way.

"You want to go over it again?" he asked.

Stormy took a pull from her pint. "The plane flew over the

village, turned just about where we did, and skirted north along the coast. I remember seeing Small Hope, then the beach ended at a little cut, and there was a straight stretch, then a shallow bay. My boat was hidden in a little hole on the northern shore of that bay."

Miles tapped both throttles forward. "Then this is our place. Only other time I've been in this way was on a calm afternoon in Moonbeam's little rowboat—"

He stopped talking as the bow rode through the first line of breakers, then, once there was no crunch of wood or metal against coral, he continued. "Funny thing. I remember at the time that I thought our getting through was something of a miracle."

Whether by miracle, skill, or dumb luck—or, more likely, some combination of the three—they made it though three more sets of breakers. But on the fourth set, as the cruiser slid down the trough on the back side of a wave, there was a sudden jolt and a sickening grating of brass chewing into something equally durable and a lot more permanent. The natural humming and vibrations and rocking that made any moving boat feel like a living thing stopped. *Come to Jesus Cruiser* listed to the left, and lay still. On Stormy's right side, there was a calm area of fizzing and frothy water, very shallow water by the look of it.

"If you've ever given any thought to praying, now's the time," said Miles.

But before Stormy could give any thought to praying, or doing something more practical, like bending over and kissing her sweet ass good-bye, the next swell bucked the cruiser's stern up, maybe three inches. At that instant, Miles jammed the right throttle forward, pushing his hand down so hard that Stormy thought he might put it all the way through the windshield. There was a delay. Finally, the huge starboard engine caught. Grunted. Roared. The boat shook with three jolts as the prop ground into coral. Stormy grabbed for the ledge, and in so

212

doing, she dropped her pint. It smashed on Miles's new decking.

The air filled with the molasses aroma of spilled rum. But that didn't seem like a major calamity, because they were free, bobbing around amid the breaking crests again.

Miles throttled back. "Not bad," he said. "One pint of Barbados rum and one, maybe two prop blades. But, hey, we're still afloat and there are only about nine more rows of these little coral heads before we reach—"

Stormy's fingers dug into Miles's arm. "SHIT!" she screamed.

There wasn't much need to say more. Dead in front of them, a gnarled hunk of coral about the size of a city bus poked its slimy head above the surrounding water. At the same time, a wave picked up the nose of the cruiser and poised it for a drop directly onto the coral.

For the first time, Stormy thought there might have been something behind all that praying Miles did. There wasn't any other explanation for how he managed to kick the old stinkpot into reverse so fast, its heavy stern actually bucking up a few inches, its nose giving the coral the softest little kiss imaginable before pulling away, hovering, then sliding through on the next incoming wave.

Miles let the current push them between the next several shoals, occasionally making corrections with his throttle levers, and only twice did they touch anything. One time it was the poor, battered starboard prop—or what was left of it—the other time it was amidships, right in the tough part of the chine.

If a person could ignore the roar and crash of the breakers on the reef, the water inside was like that of an English reflecting pool at dawn. Miles put the cruiser into neutral and ran his hands up his cheeks, over his eyes, and back through his hair.

"Stormy, do me a favor, would you?" he said. "Open the port engine hatch; run your hand as far forward as you can. There's a fifth of Appleton's there. You'll find it right on top of a parcel covered in thick green plastic. Ignore that parcel, if you don't mind."

Stormy upended the Appleton's and guzzled down a good four inches before handing it to Miles. He took it, drank, but passed it back all too quickly. She looked at him, saw nothing telltale, so she shrugged and took another mighty swig.

Miles nodded toward the ragged outline of the mangroves, maybe two hundred yards away, but close enough to smell their heavy rotten-egg stink. "Believe it or not, there's a cut that goes in there somewhere. Only place they could get a sailboat in anywhere near here, and even then you'd want to do it in broad daylight on a windless day at high tide. No way I'm going to take this boat much closer."

He paused, and instead of telling her what he planned to do next, asked a question: "Bring your swimsuit?"

It wasn't getting a bit wet that bothered Stormy as she let herself down into the water from the stern. It was memories of that old shark she had seen from the airplane window, paddling along the edge of the mangroves, probably passing not fifty feet from where her feet and ankles were now disappearing—intruding—into the inky realm of the sea's nocturnal denizens. That is what she always thought of them as, for some reason: nocturnal denizens.

Stormy sucked in her breath as the water passed over her belly button. Then she hung for a time, arms fully extended, fingers digging into the edge of the stern, feeling like a royal ass. What the hell was she doing out here at this time of night, belly-deep in the sea and about to swim casually into a mangrove swamp that already smelled as if it was full of bloated, rotting corpses?

Putting that all-too-obvious question out of her mind, mostly because she was afraid of what the logical answer would be,

214

she released her handhold and shot down, fully prepared to go in over her head. But as the water passed her neck on its way to her chin, her feet hit hard sand. She took a couple of steps backward so she could see the Rev. "How much does that crate draw, anyway?"

Miles looked over the stern. He had her jacket wadded up in one hand and lowered it over the side. "Two and a half feet."

"Shit, Rev, you being a prissy or something. Probably have a good two feet under you. We could've come through here at full tilt. And I wouldn't have gotten a wet shirt."

She reached up and took the jacket from Miles, being careful not to let the Beretta, whose hardness she could feel through the Gore-Tex, get wet.

"We must be right in that cut I mentioned," the Rev said. Should get shallower to your right and left. Take your pick. And Stormy—"

"Hurry it up, Rev; I'm anxious to get this little evening's stroll out of the way before something comes along and bites my you-know-what off."

"Stormy, I'd like to go on the record saying that this is a real stupid thing you're doing. Why don't we just get out of here?"

"Now he says it. Now that a girl's already soaked to the skin. Should have thought of that back at the wharf. But don't worry; I'm not going to do anything stupid—or rather anything stupider than wading around here in the middle of the night. I just want to make sure it is my boat. Then maybe scout things out to see what I'd need to get it outta here—when the time is right. Now hand me that goddamn flashlight."

"That all you plan to do? Scout things out?"

"Honest Injun, Rev. I'd even give you the Girl Scout's salute, except I want to keep my jacket dry."

"Your jacket, is it? Funny, I'd have thought it's what you have wrapped in the jacket you would want to keep dry."

*   *   *

As she waded through the turtle-grass flats on the left side of the sand cut, Stormy relived every aquatic nightmare she had ever had—or even heard of. In the deeper water, she fought images of stinging man-o'-wars wrapping their poison tentacles around the exposed skin of her face and neck. At waist depth, she again envisioned that shark she had seen from the plane, and reminded herself that she had read somewhere that most fatal shark attacks occur in water less than hip-deep—particularly water that is murky or dark. She even replayed the opening scene of *Jaws* at one point. But by that time, she was in knee-deep water and thinking again about the bonefisherman she had seen being carried into a doctor's office on Provo, legs looking like a couple of dozen members of a street gang had taken straight razors to them. He had been wading and caught a little jackfish. A big cuda came by to inspect the commotion, saw the fleshy white calves, and the rest was a matter of three hundred stitches and a few tendons that never worked properly again.

She gave passing thought to rays and urchins and poisonous sea snakes, and even scorpion fish, but it was only when she had reached a small patch of dry sand at the base of a crescent of sea grapes that she gave any thought to the real dangers.

They came in the form of Fat Boy and Pock-face. If either one of them was aboard the *Roach,* she was in deep shit. And if no one was aboard, Stormy thought, then how the hell would you explain the flimsy-looking flat-bottom boat with the 6-horse eggbeater pulled up onto the sand next to where Stormy stood?

She began to unroll her jacket, but before she could get the Beretta out of its pocket, an arm clamped across her windpipe in a choke hold. The arm was skinny, and hard as an oak limb. She had time to try to scream, but with her windpipe crushed against her cervical vertebrae, nothing came out. Nothing could get in, either, certainly nothing life-sustaining—oxygen, for instance. She saw stars, like you're supposed to. Then there was just blackness.

When she came to, she lay on the back deck of the *Roach*. Whoever had knocked her out had been considerate enough to lean her in a semirecumbent position. He had done a fair-quality job of binding her wrists together in front of her with a thin piece of nylon rope. He had also removed her jeans and panties.

Although her eyes were not as yet fully functional, Stormy assumed that the guy who had been so efficient with the choke hold and the knotsmanship was one and the same as the asshole now breathing heavily—panting almost—in her left ear, so close that she could feel his hot, moist breath, in contrast to the cold muzzle of her own dainty Beretta, which he jammed in her right ear.

Stormy screamed once, as loudly as she could, putting every ounce of energy she could summon into it, because she knew full well that this wasn't the sort of occasion where one was allowed second or third tries at screaming for help.

The blow smashed squarely into her left temple. The stars inside her skull once again provided a pyrotechnical accompaniment to Stormy's flight onto the gritty nonskid paint she had applied to the floor of the *Roach* the previous September. At the time, she had been pleased with her work, felt thoroughly smug and safety-conscious. But at the time, she never envisioned skidding nose-down along her handiwork.

The guy kneeled over her. He shoved the Beretta squarely between her eyes and gave its barrel a painful little half twist. Stormy tried to focus on his face, no easy task, given the location of the handgun, the night's darkness, and the punishment her central nervous system had recently been dealt. And when the features did become clear, Stormy wished they hadn't. There above her, making a snaggletoothed attempt at a grin, was none other than Fat Boy's pock-faced sidekick.

The floor felt cold and gritty on her bare ass, and Stormy

wondered why the hell her senses had decided to focus on that. Bigger problems certainly lay ahead.

"Fat Boy's gonna be some pissed off," Stormy said out of desperation, though she suspected she might have as much success trying to reason with that old shark she had seen from the plane. Pock-face kept his eyes directed between her legs as he stood and stepped to the far side of the cockpit to lay the Beretta on a drink holder beside the wheel. His panting increased as he hauled away at the loose end of his belt and fumbled with his fly.

His pants had started their descent and were somewhere between knee and mid-calf when the rum bottle smashed into the side of his face.

The events that followed occurred almost simultaneously and probably took up no more than two or three seconds, yet they seemed to go on for long, agonizing hours, and at a couple of points, the pace threatened to become so slow that Stormy would have liked to have gotten up and walked out on the performance—or at least put a couple of scenes on fast forward.

First, there came an interminable expanse of time after the bottle shattered against Pock-face's jawbone. He, justifiably, wore a look of puzzlement mingled with genuine shock.

Stormy, for her part, sat there with her naked butt on the scratchy nonskid floor, smelling the spilled rum, knowing that some action was definitely called for, but unable to make the necessary mental shift between preparing to be raped and launching a full frontal, though bare-assed, attack against the would-be rapist.

Only the Rev had no excuse. With surprise on his side, he should have been faster coming down from the cabin roof and, all-in-all, executed a cleaner tackle on Pock-face.

At least that's what went through Stormy's mind before she finally launched herself toward the little shelf where the Beretta still lay. En route, she jumped over the falling bodies of Pock-face and the preacher.

Pock-face managed to land on top, and he gave Miles two quick chops to the throat, followed by a full roundhouse to the left temple. He jumped off and, with his pants around his ankles, took three shuffled steps backward into the corner opposite the wheel. Keeping his eyes on Miles, he executed a near perfect ballerina's curtsy, and came back with a short pump-action shotgun. He raised the muzzle and pointed it toward Miles's skull, four feet away—five, tops. In one smooth back-and-forth movement, he pumped a shell into the chamber and took aim.

By that time, Stormy had made it to the drink holder and fumbled with her bound hands for the little pistol. She got it, and spun toward Pock-face. But in the process, she somehow dropped the gun. She dove toward it—all the while expecting to hear the roar of the shot that would kill Miles. For some reason, it was taking aeons for Pock-face's trigger finger to travel the one-eighth inch required to activate the shotgun's firing pin. Belly-down, Stormy clutched the little Beretta, not even sure which end she held. Her finger found the trigger and she squeezed off a shot in her best guess as to the general direction of Pock-face.

The little snap of the .25 was all but lost in the roar of Pock-face's gun. A flame shot out of the muzzle so far that Stormy figured if the lead didn't kill Miles, then he would surely be immolated. Either way, something told her he was a goner. So it was in a spirit of revenge, tinged with a healthy dollop of good old self-preservation, that Stormy emptied the clip of her shitty little automatic into Pock-face.

Bingo had been right about one thing. It wasn't much of a gun. She was sure that she must have hit Pock-face a half-dozen times, and yet he still stood there, shotgun held at a forty-five-degree angle toward the sky, in the jaunty stance of a practiced skeet shooter awaiting the next clay pigeon. Finally, seeming more impatient with Stormy than anything else, he lowered the gun, until Stormy could see right into the round black hole of the muzzle. There was one of life's great lessons to be learned in that circle. It was blacker, much blacker, than the surrounding night.

But before Stormy could ponder any deeper cosmic messages of the old shotgun, Pock-face said, "C-c-c-c-cunt," and fell face-forward onto Stormy's newly painted floor.

That gave Stormy a whole new set of problems—the most pressing of which was what to do now that she found herself alive and pantless aboard a fifty-four-foot staysail schooner with two dead men. Four courses of action clamored for priority. In order of emotional importance, they were: (1) light a joint; (2) put pants back on; (3) get hands untied; (4) take the gun from Pock-face. Knowing herself, Stormy decided to tackle the tasks in reverse order, figuring that would bring her closest to doing what was logical.

She had indeed hit Pock-face a half-dozen times, and Bingo would have been proud. Most of the holes were centered in an area two or three inches either side of his heart, which was in the process of pumping Pock-face's last few ounces of sticky, venous blood onto the rear deck. The puddle, which looked black in the night, had spread to encompass a smaller trickle that appeared to be coming from Miles's head. Stormy averted her eyes from Miles. She wanted to remember his bent-nosed mug the way it had been. In anger, she took the gun from Pock-face's dead fingers and threw it into the sea—a stupid idea, she realized too late. The night might still provide occasion for something lethal at very close range.

She wedged the broken neck of Miles's rum bottle between her knees. It went through Pock-face's knots after a half-dozen passes. Stormy massaged her fingers until the pins and needles were replaced by pain—a sharp pain, but one that was honest and reassuring.

Perhaps it was the finger exercises. Something, anyway, got her thinking about a joint, for the nerves and to help her figure what to do with the two corpses on the rear deck, though she was already suspecting it was going to turn out to be a banner night of feasting and gluttony for that old shark, if it was still around.

Inside, the cabin still gave off too much of Bingo's aura to be comforting. It was as if Bingo had just taken the dingy ashore to score a couple of lobster and would be scampering back aboard at any moment, chuckling and grinning his cockeyed grin. His summer-weight sleeping bag was still crumbled on the V bunks where he usually slept whenever there was a charter party aboard. His wardrobe—mostly Speedo bathing suits and T-shirts emblazoned with promotional slogans from this or that Caribbean island—hung from a line on the ceiling directly above. And his stash, an Adidas running shoe that had been retired from active duty about the time of Kent State, held one of his carefully crafted thin joints and a pack of matches.

Stormy lit the joint, gulped a huge lungful of smoke, and lay back, bare-assed, on a bed that still smelled of the sweet, slightly perspiration-tangy smell of her ex-man.

It was then that the Rev's voice said, "Don't suppose there's a bottle anywhere aboard this boat."

Her first thought was that Bingo's hoo-ha had a little more kick to it than usual. But after she had sat up, sucked down another blast, and blinked her eyes a few times, the silhouette that was speaking in the voice of the Rev still stood looking into the cabin.

He snorted loudly and ran a hand across his face. "Hey. Come on in there," he said, sounding positively giddy.

"Holy fuck," Stormy said, getting up. "You're still alive."

There was a stub of Chardonnay in the fridge. Stormy grabbed it as she passed, pulled the cork with her teeth, and handed it to Miles before she threw her arms around his shoulders and squeezed until the first of those damn stars began their dance.

But he was holding her up by then with his one free arm. The other steered the wine bottle up to his mouth, which was open in order to receive a full, unfettered flow. He pulled her back onto the rear deck and supported her against the wheel— as far as possible from the body of Pock-face. Miles sniffed, and Stormy thought he might be crying. Kind of touching, when you came right down to it.

But no such luck. When she looked, she saw that a steady stream of blood flowed from his nose, enough to account for the dark trickle she had seen around his head. The snout itself seemed to be even more askew than she remembered. She lifted up the front of her sweatshirt to stanch the flow, but the Rev motioned her hand away. He dug a handkerchief from his pants pocket and daubed his own snout.

And they stood that way until he had polished off the wine and she had sucked the last smoke from the lovely thin, joint her former man had fashioned with a flytier's care and years of expertise.

Stormy finally said, "I was sure you were dead. Shit. I was sure we both were dead."

Miles snorted a chuckle that came out sounding wet and bubbly through his bloodied nostrils. "I didn't know about you. But when he fired that gun . . . well . . . I was certain it was only a matter of moments before I got called in for the final interview with the big boss."

Stormy flicked the roach overboard. "Well, Rev. S'pose I should say welcome aboard my boat."

"Some welcome."

"Yeah. Well, we try to make these things memorable here on the good ship *Roach*. Though if memory doesn't fail, you have a way of making first nights on your own scow kind of memorable."

"Not like this."

Stormy walked back to the dead Pock-face. "No. Not like this. Let's get it over with before I come out of shock and it all hits me. I can feel a whopping breakdown coming along."

Miles took a couple of swipes at his nose, snorted, and spat over the side. Without saying a word, he bent down and grabbed Pock-face by the shoulders. Stormy took the ankles and they lifted. Pock-face was flimsy and light. There was a splash, and his body stayed at the side of the *Roach* for a time, as if reluctant to depart. Finally, the current of the ebbing tide picked it up and moved it out into the cut.

Miles found a pail and dipped it overboard. At least a dozen times, he filled it, dumped it, filled it, dumped it. Until the rear deck was washed clean of blood—or as clean as it was going to get in the dark.

They went out to *Come to Jesus Cruiser* in Pock-face's little flat-bottomed boat. When they got there, Miles went below and came back with a twenty-pound plow-style anchor on the end of a six-foot chain. Holding the chain, he dropped the anchor onto the bottom of the boat eight or ten times. Then he gave the boat a shove toward the breakers. He stowed the anchor and came topside to put his arm around Stormy while they watched the outboard twirl in slow circles before rising on its stern and settling into the depths: a far more melodramatic demise than it deserved.

Pock-face also went out in an all-too-theatrical fashion. The current had pushed his corpse out of the cut to within twenty yards of *Come to Jesus Cruiser.* The first shark that hit the body nudged it another yard closer. The second one—a big one, maybe even the one Stormy had seen from the plane—did a better job. It grabbed Pock-face by the waist and danced him along the top of the water in a froth of fin and flailing limbs until shark and dinner were eventually lost in the foam of the breaking waves.

"Ironic," said the Rev. "That might have been the only self-less thing that man ever did in his life—feeding the sharks."

Stormy stared at the sea, empty now except for the whitecaps that still broke relentlessly over the reef. Then she started to cry. Great, deep sobs racked her body. She cried for Bingo and Moonbeam, she even cried for goddamn Pock-face, but most of all she cried for some lost part of herself. She didn't even know what it was. And while she cried, she wrapped herself in a life-and-death hug around the Rev.

"Honest. I didn't mean for it to happen. None of it," she said, before becoming consumed by her sobs.

She hugged Miles even more desperately, pressing her body against his, reaching for his lips with hers, finding them, locking onto them.

They clung to each other like that for ten minutes. About five minutes into the embrace, Stormy remembered that she was still without her pants. One of Bingo's Speedos was all that covered her backside. She ground her hips into Miles, rotating them in slow circles. A mellow feeling enveloped her. She became light-headed.

Then something strange, something totally unexpected began to happen. At first, Stormy couldn't put her finger on it. And when she finally did, it was too late to resist. In a boat, in the middle of nowhere, and in the arms of a man who, in another life, she might have loved, Stormy Lake fainted.

Andros Islanders joked that Fat Boy had no home, that he lived and slept in the police station. Not bathed, though. Fat Boy's body odor led to general agreement that he never bathed. So at 9:45 P.M., when Prue entered the station, Fat Boy was in his jail cell/office, the skin of his face giving off a sweaty glow in the light of the ceiling fixture. The office itself was thick with the odor of body oils and perspiration, so Prue tried to avoid breathing through her nose.

Fat Boy looked at her with some irritation, although from what Prue could see, he had been working on nothing in particular when she arrived. "Yes," he snapped, then huffed out a great breath.

Prue pressed her lips together and tilted her chin up, a convenient pair of moves that both showed an appropriate level of disdain and partially shut out the heavy aroma of Fat Boy. Walking to town had taken the better part of two hours. And before she decided to go to Fat Boy—a move she opted for with great uncertainty and reluctance—Prue had done nearly an hour's thinking at the end of The Vale's wharf—its empty wharf. So Prue was footsore and short-tempered—an even match any evening for an arrogant police officer.

"It seems it has been left to me to do the work you're supposed to do, Chief Constable." She came down hard and sarcastic on the *Chief Constable* part.

But it got his attention. He mopped his face with a gray handkerchief—originally white. Once the face was dry, or at least temporarily free from visible sweat droplets, he lowered his jaw, a move that automatically put a frown of inquiry on his face.

Prue went on. "The Reverend Farnsworth is not aware of any of this, I assure you—"

Fat Boy kept the frown on his face but nodded in understanding.

"—but it appears Moonbeam . . . the one who committed suicide . . ."

Fat Boy nodded again, impatiently, to hurry her over that part.

"Moonbeam hid the cocaine in Reverend Farnsworth's boat. You'll find it under the floorboards on the rear deck."

As soon as she uttered the words, Prue had second thoughts. Fat Boy did not look happy or relieved—or even surprised; she had expected that much, at the very least. He took in what she told him, then said, barely louder than a whisper, "Thank you. I will take appropriate action."

Prue drew herself up and came as close to Fat Boy's desk as his pungency would comfortably allow. "Appropriate action," she said, putting a note of clear hatred in her voice. "Don't you speak to me of appropriate action." She paused, thought, then spat out his name. "Fat Boy. Let me tell you about appropriate action. You are going to confiscate those drugs—and I don't want the Reverend Farnsworth to know about it. He is in no way to be implicated or connected to the drugs. And most important of all, he is not to be harmed. Not so much as scratched."

Fat Boy looked at her mutely. He let her finish and then said nothing. A cockroach—fully three inches long—came out from under the desk, apparently eager to get a good seat for what was about to transpire. A moth smacked rhythmically against the ceiling fixture. Finally, Fat Boy said, "This is not The Vale. You don't give orders around here."

Prue didn't budge. "Wrong," she said. "Very wrong." From the pocket of her cardigan, she withdrew a small white envelope, the kind normally used to hold an invitation or thank-you card. "You'll find the contents of this envelope very interesting. It's everything I know about you and those drugs. About what happened to Moonbeam—really happened. You'll find it's quite a lot. So do I make myself clear? You confiscate that merchandise—before Miles has a chance to try to take it across. Not a hair on the Reverend's head gets harmed. That's appropriate action."

He nodded.

Prue turned to leave. At the door, she looked back at Fat Boy. "I know you're too smart to get cute or anything, but in fairness, I should let you know that a friend in Miami has a copy of that note, with the usual instructions should anything happen to me."

Fat Boy sat there in silence, alone with the three-inch cockroach and the snapping moth. Prue had been gone for a full five minutes before he slowly reached for his telephone and, with what appeared to be a tremendous effort, dialed.

*   *   *

Prue found Dacosta out front of the Chickcharnie, and she was seated in the back of the Pontasaurus when they passed the town wharf. It took her an instant to realize it was *Come to Jesus Cruiser* tied up behind the mail boat, but as the Pontasaurus rattled along at its stately fifteen-mile-per-hour gait, she had plenty of time to observe Miles give Stormy the sort of hug an engaged man should reserve for one person and one person only. Yet it wasn't the hug that bothered Prue most. It was that even in the poor light, she could see that the woman was wearing an old pair of Miles's pants.

Fat Boy or Stormy! At that instant, Prue realized she was about to lose Miles to one of them. The irony of it all—the truly mean injustice—was that she had it in her power to determine who it would be. Prue knew it was a terribly un-Christian thought, but as the Pontasaurus rumbled across the causeway, she honestly couldn't say which choice would hurt her worse.

Chapter 18

At first, Stormy feared her friend Bear had been crushed under the right engine of the plane.

It was Thursday, just before noon. Stormy had caught the early flight the day before to Miami and picked up Pan Am's shuttle to Grand Turk. She spent the night in her old lodgings on the cook's floor—a sleepless night because images of the previous evening's encounter with Pock-face wouldn't go away, and even if they had, that damn rooster whose life she'd spared decided to show his gratitude with an all-night crowing marathon. Stormy was half-asleep when she and a dozen locals boarded the TCNA Trilander for the morning flight to South Caicos. She must have dozed. The next thing Stormy knew, they had begun their descent onto South Caicos's 7,500-foot-long, perfectly paved runway, far too large and well maintained for the pathetic trickle of legitimate traffic that called there. The runway apron was empty, except for four DC-6s beside a hangar. They were all flawless and silver, boasting nary a fleck of identifying paint. They also all had been impounded at the request of the DEA.

The TCNA flight stopped barely long enough to dump Stormy out before it rushed off toward Provo, leaving her alone in front of the terminal building. But instead of going inside, Stormy headed over to where an ancient Piper Apache occupied a place of honor beside its impounded colleagues.

There, Stormy saw what looked like the badly mangled remains of the original Sky King aircraft—tendrils of wire, nuts, bolts, springs, piping, other assorted mechanical innards, and, incongruously, a half-dozen crushed Miller cans. Flat and lifeless on the pavement beneath the tangle, clad in an oil-smudged pair of green work pants, were two thick legs Stormy recognized as the bottom half of Beatrice "Bear" Bundon, her good friend and, since Birdy's retirement, the best pilot left in the Turks and Caicos, prime contender for the job of hauling Stormy and the merchandise to Montano's—if Stormy could convince her.

The first sign that the wreckage contained life—that the mechanical carnage was just one of Bear's routine repairs—was a deep, grunted "Fuck." The second: "Cunt." Legs began to kick; heels clawed the pavement. Buttocks inchwormed backward. An expanse of fleshy belly was exposed for an instant before a hand freed itself and yanked down a T-shirt that once had probably been white but that now was uniformly the color of a gas station attendant's dipstick rag. The hand that had so chastely pulled down the shirt proceeded to wipe itself on the same garment until most of a tarlike grease had been transferred, then the fingers groped for the edge of the cowling, secured a purchase, and hauled the rest of Bear Bundon's six foot four and one-half inches into the harsh daylight of South Caicos.

She lay there on her back, blinking a pair of pale blue eyes at Stormy. Finally she said, "Well, shit," did a quick and bafflingly agile front spring to her feet, and shoved out a blackened, oily paw.

Stormy braced herself, accepted the paw, winced at the crush that always came, and, when the pressure was released, retrieved her own wounded extremity, which had taken on a fairly even coating of whatever the black stuff was.

She had barely recovered from Bear's mighty handshake when the blow caught her between the shoulder blades. It would have sent her face-first onto the pavement, had an arm not looped itself around Stormy's chest in what could have been either a hug or a wrestler's crush hold. Bear rocked her and punched her and kept saying, "Shit, shit, shit." She then held Stormy at arm's length and said, "Goddamn, but you're one sexy bitch."

Apparently overcome, Bear embraced Stormy with one of the hugs that had given her the nickname, pinched Stormy's right buttock, and scrambled over to where a chipped and stained Styrofoam cooler sat in the shade of one of the Apache's wings. Bear heaved a can of Miller, which an off-guard Stormy just managed to catch. Popping the top on her own can, Bear leaned against the fuselage and tipped the beer in a toast, before upending it, swallowing mightily five times, wiping her mouth with the back of the blackened hand (thereby giving herself a engine-grease goatee) and belching—once, loudly, and with a great degree of the smugness that comes only with accomplishment. "Minor adjustments," she said, gesticulating with the Miller to the demolished-looking engine. "Hey, and, shit. Merry Christmas."

Stormy felt a rush of affection for her big friend. They had met during the three weeks back in 1981 when Bear, who was then thirty and worried about her biological clock running down, had actually married Birdy Quayle. The marriage failed, Stormy contended, because they never could settle who would be on top. As it turned out, after the three-week disaster, both were relieved to settle into being business partners. Bear shared Birdy's copilot's seat with Under Dog back in the days when operating in and out of South Caicos was just a matter of keeping up payments to the British colony's political leaders. In return, Birdy taught Bear to fly, still the only formal aviation training she had ever received.

Bear, for her part, settled into a pattern of relationships alternating between men and women; gender was never as important to her as youth and slenderness. It always made for an interesting contrast, for Bear was anything but youthful and slender.

She had a man's backside and legs. On top of that fleshy platform rested a surprisingly womanly torso, all capped by a face that would have been positively pretty, given half a chance. But it never was. Bear's facial beauty was ruined by a thatch of blond hair that hung thin and straight and lifeless in uneven clumps, exposing patches of scalp and too much of her long ears. Fortunately, the hair spent most of its time tied up behind a sweaty and greasy bandanna.

Bear crushed her can, heaved it into her trash heap of mechanical parts, and fetched another, which she immediately opened and chugged. Then she got serious—mean-looking.

"Stormy Lake, I could kick your goddamn ass all the way over to Provo. I go to Grand Turk to see you last week, and they tell me you've gone off on some fool errand that has something to do with a load of merchandise Bingo's running up the line. I know he's your goddamn man, but honey, if I've told you once, I've told you a thousand times: Don't fuck around with boats. Easiest way in the world to get caught. Planes. Planes aren't what they used to be, but they're still a hell of a lot better than goddamn boats. Where is that skinny little asshole, anyhow? I think he owes me ten bucks."

The timing didn't seem right, but Bear, in her own clumsy way, had kicked open the door. Stormy swallowed and tried to start explaining what had happened to Bingo. She actually managed to get a few syllables out before the sobs took over, the worst thing that could have happened under the circumstances.

Bear dumped a big arm over Stormy's shoulders. "Storm. It's something bad, ain't it?"

"Bear. They killed . . ."

Bear let Stormy go. She looked at her wide-eyed, then her big lower lip quavered. "Shit!" she said, like someone who has just suffered physical hurt—a burn, a bad cut. She heaved her half-empty can on the tarmac. "Fuck," she said, and then the tears burst forth in an unashamed torrent that was as big as Bear herself.

So it was Stormy who put her arm around the beefy shoulders of Bear and led her to the shade of the Apache's wing. Stormy who fished out a Miller and put it to Bear's lips. And Stormy who very slowly, between outbreaks of her own tears, told Bear the entire story.

By the time Stormy finished, Bear had gotten the sobs under control, but the tears still flowed full force. She took off the bandanna and wiped her face. The bandanna sopped up the tears, leaving behind a gray pallor—either grief or engine oil.

Face tended to, Bear went through one of her notorious mood swings—which always reminded Stormy of the late fall weather in the Rockies. The tears stopped. She very slowly and methodically wadded up the beer can in one hand until it made a perfect sphere about the size of a tennis ball, which she began to throw up in the air and catch. "Birdy's right, you know. He's been on my fucking back, too. For about a year now. Wants me to go to work for him, too."

"Selling real estate?"

Bear laughed and went to fetch another can. "Me." She spread her arms and legs so Stormy could get a good look at the dirty T shirt, green work pants, and hair, which the trade wind blew over to the left side of her face, leaving her long, floppy-lobbed right ear naked. "No. Wants me to be his goddamn partner in an earth-moving business. Sounds like a fancy description for slugging around a wheelbarrow."

"And?"

"Told him to go fuck himself. But, maybe the old fag's right. Maybe being in Florida real estate ain't such a bad way to pass your three score ten."

"Think I've heard that one somewhere before."

Bear snuffed. Laughed to herself. "Sounds like he's only got one sales pitch. But say, isn't that new wife of his a lovely piece—"

"Bear, you going to do it?"

There was silence. Bear studied her Miller can. "If I could get this ancient crate airborne, I could haul us and all our belongings over there next week. We could forget all this shit."

"What about my little deal with Montano?"

"I said, we could forget all this shit. I meant it. Montano comes after you, I'll break the weasely fucker's back. That might not be a bad thing to do, anyway. Poor, crazy Bingo."

"Bear. There's a quarter of a million in it for you."

"Look, sweetie. There's two reasons I've survived in this business. One is that I'm big and mean and ugly. The other is that I never—*never*—take this goddamn crate into U.S. airspace. Bear Air serves Colombia, Haiti, Turks and Caicos, and select Bahama Out Islands. Not goddamn downtown Naples, Florida."

"Isn't downtown Naples. North of there. In the country."

"And just how do you propose we get to his goddamn tomato patch? Clear customs at Miami International?"

"Close."

That tweaked Bear's interest. She eyeballed Stormy, trying to haul an explanation out of her by sheer force of her pale glare. When that got her nowhere, she belched a single mighty belch. "Well, aren't you being cute. Trying to tease old Bear. You think that playing coy like that is going to spark her curiosity. Well, fuck ya."

Without further comment, she lay back down and squirmed back under the wreckage of the engine. "Hand me the goddamn five-sixteenths socket," she growled.

Stormy at first saw no sign of any tools in the junk heap. Then one by one her eyes picked them out. Three or four screwdrivers poking out from under various parts, one pair of needle-nosed pliers, tin snips, vise grips, and a half-dozen sockets, one of which was five-sixteenths. She placed it on Bear's dirty palm.

Why Bear asked for a socket was beyond Stormy. The racket that thundered under the engine had a lot more to do with ham-

234

mering than wrench work. After a minute of clatter, there was a *poing* sound and something tinkled onto the tarmac. "Fuck," Bear said.

She emerged into the daylight. "You don't really expect me to land right at Miami International? I mean, I hate to say this, but you and I ain't exactly a pair of nuns in the eyes of the good folks at the U.S. Customs Service."

Before Stormy could respond, Bear grabbed a screwdriver and disappeared again. A minute later, a muffled "Well?" came out from under the engine.

"You got any friends, Bear? Friends without criminal records who have pilots' licenses?"

Bear came back out holding a thin metal plate that had an ugly gouge out of the middle. "Present company excluded, all my friends have pilots' licenses. The criminal record bit is somewhat tougher." She nodded toward the metal plate. "This is the little fucker that's got me grounded. And tell me, do you think there are any replacement parts for a 1952 Piper Apache on South Caicos?" The question was rhetorical. Before Stormy could answer, Bear got mean. "Why the hell you want to know about my friends?"

Stormy fished two new cans of beer out of the cooler and handed one to Bear. As they drank, she outlined her plan. Bear, at first, wore a dubious look, but toward the end, it was replaced by one of bemused interest. Stormy was 99 percent sure they had a deal, when Bear began to laugh.

"Shit, that would be funny," the big woman said. "What a swan song to this business. An all-girl run. Right under their fucking noses." She stopped laughing. Looked at the metal plate. "We're forgetting this. No goddamn way I can get another by the twenty-eighth."

That shut the two women up. They stood there in the bright light, alternately gazing at the wreckage of engine parts and then out to the blue water of the Caicos Bank, where waves lapped the foot of the runway, breaking over three rusting fuselages—planes carrying a little too much of the number-one local cargo to get airborne, even on the new expanded runway.

It was Bear who finished her beer first and retrieved a pair of tin snips from the junk heap. Stormy thought Bear was just fidgeting, keeping her fingers busy while she thought about their problem. She jammed the tips of the snips into the can's hole and cut a lateral line from top to bottom. After some twisting and poking, she clipped off the bottom, and gave the top the same treatment. Her heavy work boot flattened the piece of metal. The gouged plate served as a pattern as Bear snipped its outline into the can's remains. In the end, she said, "Where's that goddamn socket?" and disappeared under the cowling.

"That going to work?" asked Stormy.

"Who the hell knows."

"But you think my plan will work, don't you?"

Bear slid out from under the engine. She addressed Stormy sternly, but from a flat-on-the-back position. "Your idea is an absolute hoot, Stormy. People will be talking about it for the next twenty years—which is about equal to the time you and I will be doing—if we survive Montano's goons and my repair job."

Chapter 19

Like every other young agent working out of Miami, Cal found Bones positively chipper on Monday mornings. But, with the passage of each nagging event of the week, the permanent furrows in Bones's ebony brow became dark, impenetrable trenches. The bulldog creases around his mouth evolved into something almost reptilian—an old moss-backed snapping turtle came to mind. Finally, usually sometime late Thursday afternoon, his irises vanished as the heavy burden Bones carried pushed his eyebrows down toward his cheekbones. Anytime after that, you knew you were in deep trouble if you were summoned to his office. Cal's appointment was for ten Friday morning.

Everyone else chirped a "Merry Christmas" as Cal walked through the building. Not Bones. When Cal entered his office, Bones checked his watch. Finding that Cal was on time—a minute early, in fact, depriving Bones of an opportunity to let fly with a tirade on punctuality—seemed to anger him more than tardiness would have. He grunted. Cal took a seat.

"Andros says they're going to try to move Montano's shipment sometime soon. This is our chance to get that little shit."

Cal nodded. Uttering as little as a single phrase was asking to have his head bitten off.

"Miami and Andros are going to try to keep track of things from that end. That leaves you with a simple assignment: Don't let Montano out of your sight for a minute. Got that? Not a single minute. I have a strong suspicion that at some point the two ends will come together. That's when we get him, and everyone else involved." He glared to drive home his point. "You need any help, it's yours."

Cal nodded.

"Okay, Ivy League boy, your tomato-picking days are officially over. I'll keep you fully informed."

The Christmas spirit was indeed afoot. Cal breathed a sigh of pure, sweet relief. But just before he reached the door, what he feared most happened. Bones cleared his throat with one mighty explosion of air and loose phlegm. The question that followed seemed to come from somewhere deep in his bronchial tract.

"One thing," Bones said. "You never really told me the whole story about why you left that smart-ass Wall Street law firm to put in time with this outfit. I want it. Now."

Cal gave himself enough time to wonder what had motivated Bones's question. Finding no logical answer, he tried to get by with a pat, politically acceptable response. "I thought that with what I'd been given—the opportunities, maybe some smarts— I might be able to contribute. That, and I was getting a little bored helping crooks in well-tailored three-piece suits make millions on leveraged buy-out deals."

He should have known better. Bones stuck out his lower lip thoughtfully, creating a thick, wide shelf of flesh. When he spoke, he let a little southern po'boy inflection creep into his voice. "Well I do say, they sure taught you to talk pretty at that fancy Ivy League college."

Bones picked up a photocopied newspaper clipping from his desk and held it so that Cal could see it was from the *Miami Herald*. It was the story reporting his sister Claire's murder.

"Cut the shit, Cal." There wasn't a trace of po'boy in Bones's voice now, just coolness and anger. "You want me to read you the part about how the police suspected she was killed in a clash

238

between rival dope gangs—one headed by her boyfriend, one headed—"

Bones put on a pair of half-moon spectacles and consulted the clipping. When he looked back up, he was all po'boy again: "Why, if it wasn't some fella named Montano. I'll be—"

"What of it?" Cal interrupted. "I want to see that bastard behind bars—"

Bones took off the spectacles. "Behind bars? That all?"

Cal nodded.

"Listen to me good, Ivy League lawyer," Bones said. "You fuck this one up on me, you're dead meat."

Cal nodded. "Yes, sir," he said.

"Get outta here."

Cal again made it to the door before the throat clearing caught him. When he looked back, Bones's mug wore an expression that fell somewhere between utter disappointment and pity of the most sincere kind.

"It's a shame, really. Fancy Ivy League education. You'd think they'd've done a better job of teaching you how to lie."

Cal held his composure long enough to make an outwardly calm exit from Bones's lair, even though he felt cold, numb, and dizzy. But the instant he cleared Bones's sight line, he put his head down and tried to deal with the thoughts and suspicions and worries that jostled each other for front and center position in his mind. That was when he nearly bowled over the preacher.

As it was, he stopped just in time, but still found himself face-to-face and in clear violation of the preacher's personal space, yet without a graceful way to retreat. The preacher was fair-haired and had a familiar look to him that Cal couldn't place. He wore a fawn suit that probably had been picked up about a decade earlier—at K Mart, maybe Robert Hall, Cal guessed, on sale for $49.95.

The preacher smiled sheepishly and consulted a scrap of

paper he carried in his hands. "I'm looking for Mr. Bones's office," he said.

Cal stepped back and gestured with an open palm. "First door. He's all yours."

"Thank you. And have a Merry Christmas."

The sheepish smile became warm and sincere, and for some reason he couldn't fathom, Cal's hand involuntarily went for his wallet to answer a sudden urge he had to make a donation to the preacher. Then Cal knew where he had seen the preacher before, and knew damn well that it was asking a little too much to attribute his visit to Bones to coincidence. Merry Christmas, indeed.

Bones was poking and jabbing at the mound of paperwork that sat to one side of his desk when the preacher came in. The busted snout kicked Bones's recognition neurons into gear, and by time the guy had smiled, nodded a greeting, and uttered a tentative "Mr. Bones?" Bones knew who he was. He also knew that the guy was either going to bear the best news of the year or the absolute worst.

"Yes," Bones grunted.

"My name is Miles Farnsworth."

Bones nodded noncommittally.

"I operate a small mission on Andros Island in the Bahamas."

Bones nodded again.

The preacher sucked in a big breath.

"I believe there is a shipment of cocaine on Andros that is going to be smuggled into the States next week."

Bones spoke slowly, carefully. "Thank you for that information, Reverend. We will take appropriate action. You have done the right thing, coming here."

"I have one other piece of information you might find useful—I know who is going to be bringing it across."

Bones battled the smile that threatened to ruin the serious

scowl he had planted on his face. "And just who might that be?"

The law office of P. Hamilton Duinker was located in space once occupied by a fish market in a strip mall along Highway 41, too far north to be in Naples's fashionable district. On hot days, when Hammy's single window air conditioner, purchased secondhand from a newspaper want ad in 1972, was forced to concede defeat to south Florida's pounding sun and humidity, the office became redolent of its former incarnation, even though Hammy and his only employee—a starved-looking secretary named Edith—had occupied the space for at least ten years.

Hammy Duinker was one of those lawyers who always seem on the verge of being smothered by a mountain of file folders, official forms, and little pink messages, each representing a never-to-be-returned phone call, yet who fail to prosper. His suits were old, cheap, polyester, and, with the exception of a single navy blazer he always wore over the same pair of gray bell-bottom pants, tended toward chocolate browns and baby blues. His shoes—two pairs, both wing-tip brogues, one black, one brown—were cracked and scuffed. A good inch and a half of white calf always showed between the ragged top of his socks and the bottom of his trousers. His hair, which had gone the color of old asphalt, preserved one of the few bonafide 1950s-vintage flattops remaining in the state. Among the many clients Hammy worked for, and usually forgot to bill, was Miles Farnsworth.

When Miles came through the door late that Friday afternoon, a good three hours after the air conditioner had lost its daily battle, Hammy greeted him effusively, oblivious of the file folder that went sliding off his desk, spilling a couple of official-looking documents into an overflowing wastebasket.

"Hey-hey, Milesey baby," said Hammy, pumping Miles's hand, extending his other hand in a gesture of welcome to one of the two wooden chairs, too old to be trendy but still a good decade or two away from quaintness.

Miles picked up a sheaf of manila envelopes from the chair and looked to Hammy for direction, but Hammy was busy sizing up Miles's suit, with the studied admiration only one sartorially tone-deaf male can give to another. About the time his gaze swept Miles's well-polished thighs, Hammy became aware of the envelopes in Miles's hand, and he said, "Anywhere, anywhere. And hey, Merry Christmas."

He brought a bottle of Jim Beam out of a drawer in his desk, poured himself two fingers into a permanently stained coffee mug, and then dumped four plastic ballpoints, two pencil stubs, an eraser, and a mismatched assortment of paper clips out of a plastic glass, into which he poured Miles's jolt.

"To what do I owe this pleasant surprise?" Hammy said.

There was a silence. Then Miles said, "Edith didn't tell you? I called and made an appointment."

A look of such perplexity crossed Hammy's face that at first Miles thought he had forgotten who Edith was—that there even was a woman named Edith who toiled in the fish stink of his outer office. Hammy pawed a Day-Timer out of the papers on his desk and consulted it, looking back and forth at the book and Miles and the door that opened onto the outer office.

"Yes. Yes. Of course," he said in a voice that lent no reassurance. "So, old bud, what can I do you for?"

"There's going to be a meeting of the board of directors of the Savior Network a week from today—the thirtieth. Can you be there? I might need some legal advice."

Hammy smiled and started to scratch the stubbly oval of scalp atop his brush cut. "Board. Boy. Gee. Sure you don't want one of those downtown guys? I could recommend—"

"I want someone I know. And trust."

"Well. Sure. I'm flattered."

"And don't worry, Hammy, it's not that big a deal. Just three of us and a banker or two. Ira, the accountant, and I make up the entire board—and Ira has five votes, the accountant one, and I have four. Guess who wins all the time."

Hammy took a slurp of bourbon from his coffee mug and smiled wisely.

"That's why I want you to do up a document in which Ira surrenders all his votes—and control of the network—to me."

Miles's words shocked Hammy, causing him to sit bolt upright, a move that precipitated a minor avalanche of file folders on the left side of the desk. "You sure? I mean, let's face it, Ira's always been—I mean, your dad—"

"That all might change next week. Can you draw up the papers?"

"Oh, sure, sure. Contracts was the one course I got an A in." Hammy paused and looked at the bare-bulbed fluorescent fixture in the ceiling. "Or was it torts?" He beamed. "Who gives a damn. For an old bud, I could do it."

"Terrific. And there's one other matter I want to take care of while I'm here."

"Anything at all, Milesey, old pal. What can I do you for?"

"I want to write my will."

Chapter 20

In the golden late-afternoon sun shimmering off The Manse's pool, Montano's buttocks shone startlingly white, as white as the suit coat and trousers that lay in a crumpled heap beside the chaise lounge. Bumping, thrusting, humping, grinding, and twisting in a dance that left no doubt whatsoever about the etymology of the word *screwing,* Montano's buttocks put on such a splendid performance, it took Ira several seconds to realize Montano was fucking the former second runner-up for the Miss Florida crown—his wife.

And when realization hit, it wasn't with any of the anger, jealousy, or hatred that would come later. Ira felt embarrassed. He looked at the scene again, the buttocks, the splayed legs that he now knew belonged to his wife, the three Yorkies forming a tiny, yapping Praetorian Guard around the chair.

Without knowing why, Ira uttered a loud "Well, excuse me," and waited long enough for Montano to stop humping and cast a slow, bored look over his shoulder. When he was sure Montano had seen him, Ira retreated to his bedroom.

There, a massive headache hit him—one of several he had had lately, making him fear tumors. The emotions that had failed to come to the fore when he could have put them to noble use launched a full-frontal assault. The affrontery was the worst part. At his own home. On Saturday afternoon. On Christmas Eve, no less. A half hour prior to when he and Montano were to have a meeting. He should have been suspicious when Montano suggested the meeting take place at The Manse, not his farm. At one point, Ira had all but decided to get in his car and drive away—to check into a hotel for a day or two. But that would be abandoning the house to his wife. Lord knew what her lawyers would cook up. Then he switched to violent thoughts about taking justified revenge on Montano. Except there was the gun and the little knife that Ira knew lay hidden in that heap of clothes. Ira put a hand up to his right nostril and felt the hard scab.

When he finally summoned the courage to reappear, Ira was glad to see that his wife had retreated and that Montano sat on another chair, fully dressed in his impeccable white suit, and scratching the neck of one of the Yorkies. The only evidence of the recent transgression was that a glass of rum and Coke with dregs of ice and a wedge of lime, the former second runner-up's drink of preference, stood on the table across from Montano's bourbon and soda.

Montano put the Yorkie down on the pool deck and stood. There was not a trace of remorse. He looked angry, in fact. All business. As if getting caught fucking Ira's wife had been some sort of inconvenience—albeit a minor one—for which Ira was totally responsible. He reached into his pants pocket, and a cold bolt of fear, along with a clear image of that lethal-looking little knife, struck Ira. But Montano came back with a single small key. "I have taken the liberty of renting you a sixteen-foot Sunray inboard-outboard. It's moored at the City Marina. Here is the key. Enjoy your little fishing expedition. If you fail me—"

He let his voice trail off. Montano smiled and allowed a full glimpse of gold bicuspid to flicker in the mellow sun. "Pompano. I have a special fondness for pompano."

Miles watched as Stormy fluttered into the Chickcharnie just before dinnertime Christmas Eve. In one hand, she carried a neat roll that Miles identified as his pants. With the other, she tugged on the cheek of the grumpy Chinaman who owned the place, eliciting the first smile Miles had ever known the man's lips to form. The Chinaman said something, winked at Stormy, and nodded in Miles's direction before allowing his face to settle back into its usual sullen mask, a mask that stayed in place when he returned with some relief to the task at hand—twisting on the branch of a Christmas tree that was not only fake but scrawny, bent-limbed, and bereft of about three-quarters of its plastic needles. That, and a single aluminum foil MERRY CHRISTMAS hanging in a lopsided parabola along one wall was about as Christmassy as it got at the Chickcharnie.

Stormy came to the table and placed Miles's pants in front of him.

"Thanks for the loan. If I can ever return the favor, let me know." She twisted a chair 180 degrees and sat with her arms crossed over its back. It was sunny and in the low eighties outside, so she wore a sleeveless T-shirt that came down so far that it almost covered her short shorts.

She plinked the side of Miles's ginger ale bottle. "Gotta lay off this stuff, Rev."

Miles tried to smile but gave up. "Got a lot on my mind," he said after a silence.

Stormy opened her palms. "Hey, trust me. This is easy stuff. Cakewalk compared to some of the scams I've been involved in. Quick little jaunt to Bimini, pocket our loot, then we're home free. Be the easiest half million you ever made. Trust me."

Miles thought over that last phrase—"trust me." Somehow he didn't like the way it was said, or that it had been said twice in as many seconds.

"It's Prue," Miles said. "She's been acting differently. I think she suspects something—"

"Crap, Rev. That's a pile of crap. You're just nervous. Reading into things. It's the old one-two punch: guilt-ridden conscience, hyperactive imagination."

"I'm not imagining the two or three little jaunts a day she's been making into town. Never an explanation. I'm not imagining that it's been almost two weeks since she has brought up the subject of our pending marriage. Before, she wouldn't let two hours go by without some reminder. She won't even look me in the eyes."

A big smile broke out on Stormy's face, spreading slowly but deliciously, revealing first her front teeth, then the entire top row, finally the bottoms. Next it was the eyes' turn. They opened to their fully crazed widest, forcing her smile to constrict into a perfect *O*. She rubbed her palms together.

"Sounds to me like dear, sweet Prue is having an affair. Say, given this startling revelation, you wouldn't be interested in—" She raised her eyes toward the second floor.

"Stormy!"

"Sorry, Rev. Just joking. About the upstairs part. Prue . . ." She let her voice trail off.

"Prue is not having an affair. She's not the type."

"Maybe, Rev, but I'll let you in on a little feminine secret. I have never met a woman yet who, given the proper circumstances, isn't *the type.*"

"Thanks for the free advice. Maybe you missed your calling—"

"Bullshit. I know my calling. Which is precisely the reason we've called this little meeting. Marching-orders time. Here's how it stands. Ten o'clock at night, on the twenty-ninth, I'll meet you down at that little stinkpot of yours. You have it all fueled up—ready to go. Everything's been cleared at the Bimini end for an early meet. You'll have the dough in plenty of time to catch a flight for Miami. Then hustle your butt over to Naples. Got it?

"Yes, boss."

"Good, now get outta here. Don't worry about Prue. And Merry Christmas and all that other crapola."

Miles had taken two paces when she said, "Hey, Rev."

He turned in time to see her eyebrows shoot wickedly toward the second floor.

*   *   *

Miles found the doorway blocked by the biggest and homeliest woman he had ever seen. She barged into the Chickcharnie, tufts of blondish hair poking out from a bandanna, pale blue eyes affixed on some distant object. Her hands, which looked to be the size, color, and texture of a pair of old catcher's mitts, were clenched in fists at her hips. She appeared ready anytime to deliver a full roundhouse to the first sorry sucker who looked askance at her. The giantess eyeballed Miles. He might have been a serious sorry sucker contender, but instead of hauling off, she shot him a lecherous smile, puckered up, and made a series of kissing sounds before continuing on her determined way. For his part, Miles pressed himself harder against the hallway wall, a posture he originally had assumed because he was certain that she would have walked right over him—probably without noticing a thing—had he not taken that precaution. His fears were confirmed when she delivered a body check to a waiter. Fortunately, her reflexes were quick. She caught the little guy, set him, tray and all, back on his feet, and broke into a trot that took her across the barroom. There, she spun Stormy's chair around and crushed the slender dark-haired woman in a hug.

The Chinaman glanced up from his tree trimming.

"Who is that?" asked Miles.

It appeared as if the Chinaman wasn't about to answer. Then he shrugged. "The Flying Bear."

When that failed to register with Miles, the Chinaman added an impatient "Airplane lady. Used to be in and outta here all the time in some old wreck of a plane. How it ever got off the ground with *her* in it beats me."

He hauled a bent and dented tin angel out of a paper bag and jammed it on top of the tree, with no more emotion or satisfaction than he would have shown if he had just cleared butts out of one of the urinals. "Merry Christmas," the Chinaman said, whether to the bent angel, Miles, or the room in general was not clear.

"Merry Christmas," Miles said, and was disappointed by the lack of enthusiasm in his own voice. But he couldn't help wondering about this huge woman pilot who had just hoisted Stormy a foot off the ground and was holding her comfortably at arm's length for a long, frank, and thoroughly appreciative inspection.

Bear slung one of her beefy forearms in an arc behind her back just in time to snare a waiter trying that old trick of scurrying past without making eye contact. Bad mistake. The little guy's legs actually took two more steps, canting his torso at a dangerous-looking forty-five-degree angle that would have surely sent him over backward had he not been caught in Bear's chest lock.

"Four Millers," Bear commanded, then allowed a perfect two-beat pause to elapse before saying, "And one of whatever the skinny chick across the table's been drinking."

The waiter learned well. He returned immediately, bringing four cans of Miller and a bottle of Beck's for Stormy. Bear plucked one of the Millers directly from his tray, and by the time he had deposited the other four drinks, she plopped it back, drained and wadded into a perfect golden sphere.

In silence, she guzzled two more cans before leaning back and patting her belly with both palms. She belched silently, and returned the conversation to where it had been before the waiter tried his thwarted end run.

"Stormy Lake, with a goddamn preacher. Oh, that's absolutely luscious. Details. I want details. Tell me, Storm, what's it like in the old sackaroo with one of them? Does he talk about God after he does *it?*"

"Bear!"

"And that little collar thingy. Does he let you take it off? O-o-o-o-o! Makes me randy just thinking about it. Kinda cute, though, I must admit. Wonder who bashed in his snout for him?"

"The man is engaged. About as engaged as they come."

"No man's *that* engaged."

"To some missionary woman he works with. Named Prudence."

Bear held can number four halfway between the table and her lips, which were breaking into a great mirthless smile of derision. "Now your shitting the old Bear. No one's named Prudence."

"I swear."

"Jesus H. Christ. Outta my sight for a couple a weeks and you get yourself tangled up with some bent-nosed preacher engaged to some goddamn woman named Prudence. Leave it to you, Stormy."

Bear sucked that can down to the froth, crumpled it in one hand, and then started looking around the room, as if searching for a good place to peg it. The waiter obviously thought that might be at him. He caught her attention from where he stood beside the bar. She put the can down and shoved up two fingers. In about twenty seconds, two fresh cans of Miller were on the table. She took one, sipped a positively delicate sip, and sat back, shaking a couple more dirty-blond locks loose from her bandanna.

"Christ, am I dry. Flying—even when someone else is at the joystick, always makes me thirsty. Worse than thirsty, if it involves layovers in Nassau. Place has to be the royal butthole of the Bahamas. Maybe the goddamn tourist board should start calling it that. Asshole of the Antilles. Like that one?"

She snorted at her humor. "Anyways. Met my old pal Pete Clancy. You know him? Controlling shareholder, chief pilot, maintenance director, and baggage slugger for Clanair International Limited. The limited part means something in this case. Limited to a single DC-three that makes my flying scrap pile look like a brand new A-ten Thunder bolt."

"He's on our side?" Stormy asked.

"He's flat broke. Even broker than normal, which is saying something in his case. You're gonna have to dig into your little kitty for ten big fellas. In advance."

"But we can trust him?"

"Trust him? Oh, yeah, we can trust the wiry little fucker all right. Trust him to be in desperate need of the other ten smackers I promised upon successful completion of our little flight. Trust him to know damn well that if he screws me around, I'll pull him apart bone by skinny bone. Yeah, we can trust him. This coming Wednesday, the twenty-eighth, he's flying a stupid racehorse from Nassau to Miami International. He'll meet us directly above Pine Cay at eight."

Bear paused and took a pensive sip from her can. Her face got pretty and she let it break into a beautifully feminine smile. "Storm, hon. You know, this scam of yours actually has a half a chance of working. Imagine. An all-girl run right up the DEA's asshole."

Stormy Lake was exactly three and one-half minutes late for her rendezvous with Prue, according to Prue's windup Timex, a device set twice weekly to the Radio Canada Overseas official time signal, and whose hands dictated the rhythms of life at The Vale. During the three and one-half minutes she had been kept standing in the dingy hallway of the Chickcharnie, an establishment she loathed, Prue was acutely aware that time was being wasted, and frustrated because she could think of no use to which to put those 210 seconds.

When Stormy Lake finally did appear at the top of the staircase that led from the outside to the second floor's rooms, she was with one of the biggest, ugliest women Prue had ever seen. The woman parted reluctantly from Stormy. She actually stopped in the hallway and looked Prue over, from functional Brook's running shoes to gray midi skirt to neatly pressed white blouse. Prue could feel her stare, and could smell the yeasty stink of her beer breath. Inspection complete, the ugly woman had the audacity to snort—loudly enough so that there was no mistake that she did not think very much of what she had just surveyed. She shook her head, and lumbered down the hallway until she came to a door that she began to try to open, not by using the key clutched in the fingers of her left hand but by rattling and yanking the knob until it either fell off or gave way. It did the latter.

Upon entering Stormy Lake's room, Prue had to battle two equally powerful urges. One was to gag. The other was to launch an all-fronts straightening operation. The bed looked as if it hadn't been made in two weeks. Every drawer in the room was open, though for what reason, Prue could only guess. Certainly not for the storage of personal effects. They were scattered over all horizontal surfaces in the place. Beer bottles rose proudly from piles of underwear and T-shirts. Prue counted no fewer than four dog-earred Jackie Collins novels. *Jackie Collins!* Towels had obviously been used, wadded, and tossed with no regard for where they would land—or even whether they would dry properly before mildew set in. And worst of all, above the bed, where a more reverent person might hang a crucifix, Stormy Lake had affixed a pair of men's bikini briefs, leopard skin in design, with a ragged, vicious-looking hole slashed out of the area that would have covered the genitals.

Stormy whisked a paint-splattered sweatshirt off the room's single chair and gestured—too grandly for Prue's liking.

"It isn't the Ritz, but welcome. And Merry Christmas."

Prue didn't sit. "You said it was a matter of some urgency," she said.

"Okay, okay. Don't have a Merry Christmas, then. It's about your fiancé, the Rev. I have found out that he'll be setting out from here at ten o'clock Thursday evening."

Prue simply nodded, hoping the gesture was inoffensive enough to spur Stormy on.

"And I also happen to know that Fat Boy's gonna be there to try to hop aboard for the ride."

Prue waited for Stormy to say more. When she didn't, Prue smiled sweetly and said, "That all?"

"I thought it was a fair bit."

Prue was careful to keep the smile in place. "Then I suppose I should bid Merry Christmas to you, too, Miss Lake."

Prue went directly from Stormy's room to the pay phone downstairs. On the way, she thought about what Stormy had told her. Ten o'clock Thursday evening. That didn't fit at all with the crucial bit of information Prue accidentally had picked up one hour earlier when someone from Boat Heaven Marina on Key Biscayne had called—just to reconfirm Reverend Farnsworth's reservation for a slip for Wednesday evening. If Miles really was not going to leave until ten Thursday evening, and if he really was going to Bimini, why had he reserved a slip for the previous night in Florida? The way Prue figured it, Miles was either going to be making the run to Bimini or be moored at Boat Haven—not both.

That meant either Boat Heaven was mistaken or Stormy was lying. Or someone was being badly deceived.

Stormy intended to telephone Fat Boy. Except Prue was on the Chickcharnie's one pay phone, head bent protectively over the mouthpiece and conveniently turned away from Stormy. Certainly no procrastinator, that Prue.

Fat Boy was in his usual position behind the paperwork palisades on his desk. He grunted when Stormy entered.

"Santa's coming early this year, Fat Boy," Stormy said. "So here's your present. The good Reverend will make his run on Thursday. Ten at night. From the wharf at The Vale. That any use to you?"

He frowned a long, thoughtful frown. "Thank you," he said.

Then, after a pause: "I might be needing you for one more chore, Miss Lake. You will be available?"

Stormy looked at him coldly. "Available. That's the kinda girl I am, Fat Boy."

He didn't smile. Instead, he picked up the telephone and, ignoring Stormy, began to dial. She thought she had been dismissed. But then he stopped dialing and spoke to her. "One more thing. My assistant Raul. He's been missing since Tuesday."

"Missing?" said Stormy, unable to resist making her voice honey sweet with mock pity. "What a shame. Must be damn tough to find law-enforcement officers of that quality."

After making her first call, Prue tried Fat Boy's line. It was busy. That got Prue thinking about the inefficiencies of the Andros police system. What, after all, if she had been calling about an emergency? A crime in progress? She eventually realized the irony of her thoughts, and set out on the five-minute walk to the station. About halfway there, she passed Stormy Lake coming from the opposite direction. They nodded at each other, but both looked away quickly. Neither spoke.

Fat Boy was still on the phone when Prue entered. He didn't see her, and continued his conversation, which consisted of long pauses, periodically interrupted by Fat Boy's mumbled "Uh-huh. Uh-huh."

When he saw Prue in the doorway, Fat Boy looked startled. He uttered one more loud "Uh-huh," and dropped the receiver.

"Just a little piece of information," Prue said. "Boat Haven Marina on Key Biscayne called The Vale today. Looks like Reverend Farnsworth has made a reservation there for Wednesday evening."

She paused to let that information sink in. Then she added, "I think you know what that means."

Fat Boy nodded slowly once, and said, "Uh-huh."

*   *   *

With his hand on the butt of his .38 Police Special, Cal watched from behind a clump of palmettos as Montano stopped the Porsche just before dark Saturday, got out, and took a long, leisurely piss on the verge of his own driveway. Cal had to give Montano credit; his bladder capacity was way up there in the superhuman range. Good trajectory, too, judging from the way the stream splashed off the white-painted rock that Montano had picked as his target. When he was done, Montano gave his cock a vigorous shaking, looked at it fondly, and, Cal swore, whispered something.

And from what Cal could tell, it might well have replied. Montano laughed in comradeship before zipping his fly and pushing a button on one of the cement gateposts. A camera mounted on the other did a leisurely half-circle sweep, stopping on Montano. Nothing happened for a minute, then the chain-link gate buzzed and hummed and rattled and rolled to one side.

Montano hopped back in the Porsche. It was then, with the back of Montano's head protruding above the seat, that Cal raised the .38 until the front sight lay at the point where the base of Montano's skull joined the first of his vertebrae. Cal steadied his wrist with his other hand and inhaled one long, deep breath, just like the instructors had taught him to do. Sure enough, the black bar on the front of the revolver stopped jiggling. For a fraction of a second, the whole world was motionless, balanced on the tip of Cal's front sight. It would be so easy.

Of all the eighty-seven varieties of hibiscus that grew in his Lighthouse Point backyard, the Lady Dawson was Bones's favorite. Starting from a center that was so deeply tinted with crimson that it verged on purple, the flowers' hues flowed through every one of the lighter shades of reds, then into pinks that eventually gave way to yellows. On Christmas Eve, in the last rays of sunlight, Bones held a single Lady Dawson flower close to his eyes. A masterpiece, really, made all the more beautiful because each flower survived but a single day. There was something about that notion—the short, glorious burst of beauty—that Bones liked, although he didn't know why.

A door slammed, and his wife, Eugenie, a buxom woman whose light brown skin had retained its childhood vigor even though she was in her early fifties, came toward him. She carried two cans of beer, one of which she handed to Bones.

He threw the soon-to-be-spent flower behind a bush and popped his can. But instead of drinking, he looked at it with a similar air of contemplation to that with which he had just scrutinized the hibiscus.

"You been sitting staring at that same flower now for forty-five minutes. Feel like talking, hon?" said Eugenie, her voice a rich alto.

Bones swigged from the can—almost reluctantly. "It's this stupid-ass, two-bit little case." He moved over to the next hibiscus plant and began to finger its leaves, tipping each individually toward the sun. "Looks like those aphids are gone," he said.

Eugenie sat on a lawn chair. She patted the one next to hers. "Park your butt before I kick it all the way to Homestead."

Bones looked at his wife, and as he had every day for the past thirty-six years, he liked every solid inch of what he saw. Plus he knew damn well she probably meant what she had said about kicking his posterior, and had the muscle strength and coordination to make her threat plausible.

"Sweets, I busted bigger cases than this in my first year on the job, but there's something about this case. Perhaps it's that little weasel Montano."

"That guy's really gotten under your hide, hon. Hasn't he?"

"I dunno. He's just one of those human beings that ain't fit to live. He's not big. Not important. Always does little deals. But they are always tied into some legit business: agriculture, hotels, real estate. Someday soon he'll be able to quit drug smuggling all together. Join the goddamn Rotary Club. Become upstanding. And just forget about all the people he's killed. Personally. He likes doing it himself, you know. I'd do damn near anything to get him."

"Anything? Now, hon—"

"You heard me."

Bones left a pause, plenty of time for her to interject something if she wished. But Eugenie knew better and just kept her gentle eyes on his.

"I mean, from the start this case has been going too well. Should've known . . ." He took a good swallow from his can, as if to prime his throat for what was to come.

"Well, for instance, should've known from the first moment they sent that goddamn preppie Cal over. Some things just don't happen in this life, and one of them is that people don't give up two-hundred-thousand-dollar-a-year jobs out of the goodness of their little hearts. No ma'am. But old Bones swallowed Cal's song hook, line, and sinker. An' for a while, looked like he was on the up-and-up. Worked harder than anyone I've ever known. Took on his share of shit jobs without a whimper.

"Why, it turned out he was even working on his time off on a little private project. And last summer he brought it to me, all wrapped up with a little bow an' everything. This slimy bit player named Montano out there in Naples tied in with a financially strapped TV preacher, who happens, just happens, to have a brother who runs a mission on Andros. An' if our Cal don't have pictures of the goddamn chief constable of Fresh Creek coming and going from Montano's little spread. Sweetie, it don't take a degree in calculus to add that one up.

"So I put an agent on Andros keeping track of things from that end and had Cal picking tomatoes for goddamn Montano—struck me as just a matter of time and I could nip a potentially slimy little operation in the bud."

He did just that to a spent Lady Dawson flower.

"Just like that."

"Too simple?" Eugenie volunteered quietly.

"Sometimes simple is best. Things were going perfectly—then they got even better. Yesterday, the preacher that runs that Andros mission, he comes into my office, an' I first think, Oh, shit, the whole thing's been blown. But then he lays out this scam . . . well, Sweets, talk about Christmas coming early, I couldn't've cooked up a smoother one. Thursday morning, the whole damn kit and caboodle could be in the bag."

She smiled and put an arm over his shoulders. "Hon, there ain't nothing to worry about. It's just the waiting that's got to you. Always does. Sounds to me like you got every base covered, an' then some."

"Oh no, Sweets, that's where you're wrong. An hour ago, I was told that a fat dike pilot who normally operates out of South Caicos flew into Andros today."

"And?"

"And . . . And, shit, I know damn well she fits into this equation somewhere, Sweets, but for the life of me I can't figure out how."

Chapter 21

On the morning of the twenty-eighth, Miles lay in bed listening to the rain beat down on the metal roof. Wide awake, alert, he had nonetheless decided to stay in bed until his usual time. No sense arousing Prue's suspicions.

Prue, as always, had been up since some predawn hour. Lying listening to the drops' steady tattoo, Miles had no trouble picturing her in her office, working on some school-related project, even though the children had been sent home for three week's vacation, leaving The Vale lifeless—a disturbing prelude to the permanent quietude that would smother the place after the first of January—unless Miles succeeded.

That, at least, gave him a good cover story: He had told Prue the night before that he was running *The Come to Jesus Cruiser* to Florida for engine work while he met with his brother in a last-ditch attempt to save The Vale. She accepted the story without hesitation or question, just looked looked him straight in the eye and said, "God be with you."

At eight-thirty, unable to wait any longer, Miles got up, shaved, stood under the dribble of the shower, and pulled on a pair of heavy tan-colored canvas pants and a shirt of similar fabric and color. His fake-leather Samsonite suitcase, into which Prue had neatly folded his fawn Sears suit and three day's worth of shirts, socks, and underwear, stood beside the door. He picked it up and stepped out into the rain.

*   *   *

Prue and Clover sat together at the kitchen table. They looked at Miles, shot glances at the wall clock, and back to Miles.

Having satisfied herself that there was indeed a pre–9:00 A.M. incarnation of Miles Farnsworth, Clover sprang to her feet. "Morn', Reverend," she trilled in singsong tones, scurrying to the massive Vulcan range. There, she struck up a high-pitched rendition of "Faith of Our Fathers"—sotto voice—and stood before the black appliance, hands poised, like a concert pianist. With dramatic downstrokes of one hand, she cracked three eggs into a bowl, whisked in some milk, upended the bowl onto her grill, added chopped scallions, extra-sharp cheddar, a grinding of fresh pepper, and a dusting of paprika. The other hand busied itself by putting three sausages and a half-dozen strips of bacon on the grill, and when that was done, by popping four pieces of whole wheat bread into the toaster. Everything sizzling and snapping to her satisfaction, she returned to the table with a mug of steaming coffee for Miles.

"God told me to make sure you gets a full stomach before you goes," Clover said, punctuating her statement by plunking the cup in front of Miles.

Prue watched with something between awe and admiration as Miles chewed through the omelet, bacon, and first sausage without stopping. He slowed somewhat for sausages two and three, and finally had to put down his fork and knife after the second of four slabs of buttered toast.

That was when Clover brought the fruit plate—piled high with papaya slices, mangoes, grapefruit, and bananas. She looked at the two pieces of toast with dismay. "Reverend, you gotta eat good or God's gonna get some mad at me. She picked up one of the pieces of toast, handed it to Miles, and stood there, hands on her broad hips, and watched. He took two tentative nibbles. Satisfied, she returned to her post in front of the Vulcan and picked up "Faith of Our Fathers" in mid-verse.

By drawing on superhuman stomach reserves, Miles managed to take down all the toast, two slices of papaya, a banana,

262

and one-half grapefruit. When Clover came back to clear away the dishes, she nodded once, but in a way that made it clear Miles had consumed only the barest minimum of the rations God had stipulated he receive.

After breakfast, Prue, who still hadn't said anything beyond the obligatory pleasantries, followed Miles to the door.

"Pray for me—for The Vale," Miles said.

Prue looked at him, silent. She kissed him once, hard on the mouth. It wasn't the dry sort of good-bye peck Prue usually administered. It struck Miles as the way you kiss someone you don't expect to see for a long time—a very, very long time.

Prue turned back toward the kitchen, her eyes hot and watery, envious of Clover, who stood rump pressed against the Vulcan, crying freely.

"That man gonna need all him strength, for true," Clover said.

Prue averted her eyes and sat at the table. Neither woman spoke. The only sounds were the rain outside and Clover's sobbing. Finally, Clover moved over to the full sink and began washing the breakfast dishes. Prue sat thinking, going over the events of the past three weeks, hoping she hadn't made a bad mistake.

"Suppose I ought to get the annual financial statements out of the way," she finally said, as much to the table as to Clover.

In the distance, there was a grumble of thunder. Clover turned to face Prue, dish towel in hand. She heaved a mighty sigh, opened her mouth to speak, but thought better of it. Prue took a step toward the door leading to the offices.

"Miss Prue," Clover said. She stood as close to attention as her squat frame would permit, looking very nervous. "Miss Prue, since Moonbeam and all, I don't no longer trust Fat Boy. Sorry. It's none a my business, that I know. But I just don't understand, that's all. Don't understand."

Prue shook her head. "Pardon me."

Clover gained confidence. "What I don't understand is why the Reverend is taking him wit' him."

Prue sat back down on the nearest chair. "Taking him with him?"

"Yes, ma'am. Fat Boy."

"Clover, you'll have to explain yourself."

The large woman wiped both hands on the dish towel. "Very early this morning—before the rain got bad—I was down in the cemetery praying beside Moonbeam grave. That's when God spoke to me 'bout the Reverend. Jus' as I was finishing, still on my knees, Fat Boy him come outta the trees wearing that fool-looking life jacket of his an' he goes right down an' into the *Cruiser*. That, Miss Prue, is what I don't understand."

There was a boom of thunder. It almost drowned out Prue's tiny, frightened-sounding "Neither do I."

Miles always felt tremendous rejuvenation the moment *Come to Jesus Cruiser*'s last line was cast off. Instantly, he was young again, cut away from worldly cares. And despite the risks he was taking, despite all the lies he had told the two women, despite the cargo rehidden under his false floorboards, on the morning of December twenty-eighth, Miles felt as he hadn't felt since the day school let out for the summer after sixth grade. An interminable stretch of pure, sweet freedom extended as far into the future as he cared to contemplate. If anything, the thunderstorm that was beginning to creep in from the northwest amplified the sensations.

Beyond the reef, it looked as if some great force of nature was stubbornly trying to shove far more angry white-topped rollers through the Tongue of the Ocean than the body of water could handle. They bore down from the north in determined wind-whipped rows of uniform gray and white. Miles put the *Cruiser*'s nose dead into them.

The old wooden Chris seemed to revel in the challenge. It drove one-third of the length of its bow into the first gray wall,

264

stood its ground while the water poured over the deck, then rose for a triumphant moment, hovered at an awkward forty-five-degree angle to starboard, lurched to an equally steep angle to port, before plummeting down the next valley to confront another frothing adversary. For ten minutes, Miles held the wheel lightly and let his sea legs absorb the pounding and rolling.

A bolt of lightning cut through the sky, weaving a jagged path toward the tops of the buildings of Fresh Creek. A good solid boom followed. Miles felt its reverberations through the false floorboards he had installed. Almost immediately, the sky lit up again—from what direction Miles could not tell. There was another boom, followed by a thud that seemed to come from somewhere far up in the bow of *Come to Jesus Cruiser.* The third thud caught Miles by surprise. It wasn't preceded by a telltale flicker of lightning, and originated in the cruiser's bow, which was also the source of the fourth thud—definitely not thunder this time but something heavy and fleshy.

Before Miles could react, the cabin door burst open. Bent double and stumbling, wearing a blimplike Mae West life vest, Fat Boy lurched across the back deck and was nearly tossed into the sea as the boat mounted a wave. He managed to hook an arm over the gunwale, and from that position, with his head overboard, he began to retch.

After he had finished, he sat on the floorboards and wedged himself into a corner so that he faced Miles. There was a trickle of vomit still on his chin and he looked green and sickly, without doubt angry enough to use the .38 Police Special he held pointed at Miles's belly button.

Stormy awoke the morning of the twenty-eighth to a sizzle of lightning and a thunder blast that nearly knocked her out of bed.

Or perhaps it was the pounding on her door that almost caused her to fall out of bed. The frame rattling began with the

265

first thunder blast, but unlike the thunder, it didn't fade, but grew in intensity. "Haul ass, you lazy tart," Bear bellowed from the other side of the door, and then began to rattle the knob so vigorously that Stormy feared if she didn't answer promptly, it would fall off.

Stormy pulled the door open and stood in front of Bear, who was wearing a faded blue pair of coveralls and a peak cap advertising the A. W. Chaffee Wood Chips Transportation Company. She carried a single plastic overnight bag in one hand, and had a twelve-pack of Miller in the other.

Bear looked at Stormy's tan thighs, whistled softly, and clucked her tongue. Then she got serious again. "Jesus H. Christ, woman, you gonna loll around in the goddamn sack all day. Come on, get your shit together and let's get a move on."

There was another sizzle and boom of thunder. The rain beat even more heavily on the roof. "Perfect morning for flying."

A blast of thunder cut Bear off. When it subsided, she added, "At least for the type of flying we're gonna do."

The next big wave nearly tossed Miles onto the front sight of Fat Boy's .38. But he managed to hold on to the wheel with one hand and did a quick little dance to get his feet back beneath him.

Fat Boy kept the gun steady and began to crab his way along the floorboards one buttock at a time, careful to keep his back wedged against the inside of the hull. In this manner, he made it to the front of the cockpit, only a few feet from Miles. He sat there in the big Mae West, swallowing, breathing hard, still looking green, but keeping the muzzle of the .38 pointed at Miles's gut.

The first word he managed to say was *Cocksucker*.

He had to swallow several times after that effort, then came out with, "Rotten, lying, double-crossing—"

A big wave grabbed the snout of the *Come to Jesus Cruiser* and shoved it in the general direction of Nassau. Once the wave had passed, Fat Boy's lip curled. "I'd love nothing more than to kill you, Preacher."

Bear heaved the new blue footlocker in the backseat of the Apache, tossed her plastic overnight bag and Stormy's haversack on top, and then very delicately placed the twelve-pack of Miller between the two front seats.

She got in beside Stormy, pulled the bandanna off her head, and used it first to dry her face, then to wipe a small round hole in the fog on the inside of the windshield.

Bear smiled—as if wiping the hole had been a minor triumph, a reason to be grateful. She began to frantically pull back and forth on the right throttle, at the same time wrenching the starter. For a full minute, the motor fluttered without hint of ignition. The right prop merely phut-phutted in a series of lazy turns that became progressively slower, spaced by longer pauses, eventually stopping altogether.

"Dirty fucker," Bear muttered. In response, the starter uttered a menacing buzzing sound, followed by one more rotation of the prop—a weak last gasp. It looked like the Great All-Girl Run was going to end before it even got off the ground. But, as the last amps drained from the battery, a vibration shook the right side of the Apache. A cloud of blue exhaust erupted from the engine and was swept away into the rain. The *chuf-chuf-chuf-chuf* was replaced by roaring.

Bear smiled and elbowed Stormy. The second engine started after six or seven spins, without any of the theatrics of its recalcitrant partner. It added a high-pitched pinging to the din inside the cockpit. Bear's smile changed to a scowl. She glanced out the window. The prop was spinning, which was enough for her. She shrugged and flicked a fuel gauge with her index finger. The needle jumped about a quarter of the way across the dial and began to wag back and forth like a miniature imitation of the windshield wiper that cut a series of slow, temporary arcs in the rain and fog in front of Bear's face.

Bear yelled in Stormy's ear, "Dirty bastards didn't fill it up like they said they would."

"We have enough?" asked Stormy.

Bear consulted the wagging needle. "Guess there's only one way to find out," she hollered.

Without bothering with any further niceties of preflight checks, warm-ups, or taxiing, Bear gunned the plane straight down the runway into the storm. At what seemed like an unnaturally slow speed, they left the ground, flew over the avian junkyard (several wrecks seemed a lot more airworthy than Bear's Apache, Stormy could not help noticing), and banked in a true Sky King maneuver toward the north.

Bear shouted something to Stormy, but it was impossible to hear above the buzzing, vibrating din, so Stormy shrugged. The plane flew so low, it was impossible to tell whether the drops splattering the windshield came from the clouds or the wave tops. A few minutes beyond Fresh Creek, a small boat came into view off the right wing, too far away to clearly identify. Stormy looked at it for a while without much interest, except to wonder briefly why in the hell anyone else would be stupid enough to be out on a morning like this.

The unexpected sound of an airplane, very loud, close enough to be attempting an emergency landing on the back deck, distracted Fat Boy. At the same time, a wave tossed the bow skyward.

Miles let his survival instincts take over. He lunged across the cockpit, reaching with both hands for the .38. Fat Boy opened his eyes and mouth in three round *O*'s of surprise, and then—only after a decent interval of assessment—let his right index finger do what it should have done in the first place: pull the trigger.

Without Miles's hands on the wheel, *Come to Jesus Cruiser* careened to port. That caused the muzzle of Fat Boy's .38 to rise a crucial two inches. It also increased the velocity of Miles's

268

lunge. The explosion of the shot deafened Miles, sending up a burning and screaming in his right ear. But the slug passed harmlessly through the cabin's ceiling.

Thrown into each other's arms by the wave, the two men danced an awkward fox-trot, Miles trying to hold Fat Boy's gun-bearing hand aloft, while at the same time hoping to secure steady-enough footing to raise his right knee to Fat Boy's crotch. But the next wave worked against Miles. The boat bucked to starboard. Miles slipped. He fell hard on his back on the floorboards. Fat Boy landed heavily on top of him, wrenched his hand free, and jammed the barrel of the .38 into Miles's left eyeball.

Miles closed his other eye and waited for the shot. Time passed. Miles didn't know whether it was a fraction of a second or a full minute—or all of eternity, for that matter. But as the time lengthened, Miles grew impatient, waiting for the shot that would detonate his last earthly sensations. He almost opened his unobstructed eye to order Fat Boy to get on with it.

Instead, Fat Boy pulled the gun barrel out of Miles's eye. Miles felt something cold and metallic wrap around his right wrist. Fat Boy put Miles's left hand on top of the right one and administered the same treatment. Then Miles felt the pressure of Fat Boy's body leave his chest. He breathed once, deeply, and was relieved that his lungs could still inflate to their former capacity. He had to blink his right eye several times to get it to focus properly. When it did, he looked down the sharply sloping cockpit, to see Fat Boy bent over the gunwale, making retching noises. He dropped his gun, which slid against the stern, tantalizingly close to Miles.

Unfortunately, with his wrists handcuffed around the brass pole supporting the captain's chair, Miles was in no position to press either of these advantages.

For twenty minutes, Bear's Apache bounced and jolted north-ward. She kept it low as she followed the coast of Andros, past

Love Hill, Staniard Creek, Mastic Point, Conch Sound, Nicholl's Town, and Morgan's Bluff, across a short stretch of shallow open water, churned a sandy brown by the waves, and finally over a cluster of small mangrove-fringed islands that looked as if they easily could be swept up by the storm and dropped on one of Andros's beaches.

Bear stuck out her lower lip in a frown and circled the islands, the left wing so low that it looked as if she was trying to rinse its tip in the froth of the whitecaps; the other tipped heavenward into the bellies of the low clouds. The G forces of her banking pushed her meaty shoulder against Stormy, who was already jammed against the door. Bear yelled something. Stormy gesticulated to her ear that she could not hear. Bear pressed her lips close to the ear, as one would a trumpet's mouthpiece.

"Weasely little asshole was supposed to meet us here. Now," she said.

Stormy recoiled. Put a protective hand over her ear, but too late, she feared, to prevent permanent hearing impairment. Bear said something else. Stormy gestured she couldn't hear— but thought better of it. She clapped a hand over her wounded ear just as Bear's lips descended. Bear looked hurt. She shrugged in a "Well, if that's the way you're going to be" manner, grabbed hold of her half-moon-shaped steering wheel in both hands, and yanked.

Stormy felt herself driven back into the thin remains of what was once the upholstery of her seat. Its springs and metal frame dug into her shoulder blades and spine. Outside her window, the rows of breakers and the little islands swept by in an arc. They were replaced by a disorienting whiteness, lacking in landmarks and where no human senses could determine up or down.

That didn't bother Bear. She sat there calmly, with a two-handed hold on the stick, eyes fixed on the instruments in front

270

of her, undeterred by the yawing and careening of the little plane, seemingly oblivious that they were flying blind.

They flew like that for ten minutes. Stormy looked at one of the instruments. It resembled a clock—but one whose big and little hands were traveling far too fast. She assumed it was the altimeter, and watched as first three thousand, then four, five, and six thousand feet passed by. Still they climbed in the clouds. Bear's face was a study in poker blankness. She sat there rapt, holding the stick, the flesh of her big biceps jiggling as the Apache continued its blind climb: seven thousand, eight thousand, nine thousand. . . .

"Said we'd meet down below, but in this soup, the little ass-hole might be topside. Wherever the hell that is on a day like goddamn today. Hope so. We don't have the fuel to pleasure fly up here for too long," Bear hollered.

At ten thousand feet, the gloom lightened. Stormy looked up. At first she saw nothing other than the fog that had enveloped them since the beginning of their climb. But occasionally, there was a flicker of what she swore was blue. The flickers vanished. When Stormy was convinced her eyes had been playing tricks on her, another flicker of blue came, longer this time, unmistakable. With a final shake and shudder, followed by a gut-tugging bounce, the Apache leapt free of the weather.

Above was a sky of the clearest, deepest blue. Directly below, the storm's clouds looked like rumpled bed sheets, a great king-sized bed for the gods, stretching westward toward the Florida coast. Huge pillars of cumulonimbus rose to the south and east. They leaned away from the Apache, as if running to meet a pressing deadline in the Lesser Antilles.

But nowhere, in the entire panorama, was the one sight that would have brought relief to Bear and Stormy: the squat silhouette of a lone DC-3.

The storm abated as quickly as it had come up. The hard rain, wind, thunder, and lightning rumbled their way over the starboard stern. The angry whitecaps succumbed to more disciplined swells. Precipitation settled into something that could have been passed off as a gentle Scottish mist. And Fat Boy's skin color underwent a chameleonlike transformation from blue-green, to khaki, to its normal cafe au lait. At that point, he wiped his mouth and picked up the .38.

Miles stood in a half hunch behind the wheel—the most comfortable position the handcuffs would allow him. He watched Fat Boy come up over his left shoulder, unsteadily, but with the sort of determination one finds in very drunk people who are trying to prove they are not impaired at all. Fat Boy rested the meaty part of the fist that held the .38 on Miles's right shoulder and wedged the barrel of the gun against the base of Miles's skull.

"That was a very stupid stunt," he said, sounding calmer now. "I could have killed you. Probably should have. Except, it struck me that alive, you might be useful. You have a little rendezvous in Naples tomorrow? To deliver some merchandise?"

Miles nodded, and felt the dig of the .38's barrel against his scalp.

"A fortunate coincidence, for you. The people who you are dealing with have asked that I come along on the voyage as something of a nursemaid. To make sure you don't get into any trouble. Get us there. That would be most"—he stopped talking and jammed the .38 harder—"useful."

"I'm not seeing anybody today," Ira barked to the intercom that had just broadcast the disembodied voice of his security guard.

He felt a stab of pain in his gut—the damn ulcer again, the one his useless doctor couldn't even find. But it had been causing Ira no end of agony since Christmas Eve, from the moment when he walked in on Montano and his wife.

Make that ex-wife. They hadn't spoken a word Christmas

272

Eve, or Christmas, and first thing Monday Nettleship had come over and driven her home to her parents, she crying her eyes out. The nerve.

"He says his name is Sammy Hodges," said the disembodied voice.

"Don't know anybody by that name." But it did have a familiar ring. Must have been one of her lawyers—or worse, much worse, one of her damn relatives. One way or another, she was kin to every lout in the county who owned a jacked-up wide-tired pickup truck with a gun rack in the back window. Why the hell was he paying five grand a month to the security firm if they couldn't even keep away . . .

"Says he works for a Mr. Montano. And, sir, I'm afraid he's being persistent." The high-priced protection's voice went up a sheepish octave.

Ira rose from his desk with a groan and walked to the front entry. It was Montano's goon, sure enough. He stood there beside the security guard, whose thin blond hair was soaked with sweat and whose boyish features were contorted with fear. Sammy bore his usual air of cowlike confusion. It stood out in sharp contrast to the sleek-looking automatic pistol, complete with a six-inch-long black silencer, he held against the guard's right temple.

"What in hell is going on here?" said Ira.

Sammy smiled. The way he did it came across as almost bashful. "You and me is going to the Registry for the next twenty-four hours. Mr. Montano's booked us the best suite in the hotel."

"Well, maybe you better tell Mr. Montano that I'm not going anywhere. Now, kindly leave this house."

Sammy exhaled and wrinkled his brow. "You don't understand, Reverend. Mr. Montano says you gotta come with me. He don't want nothing to happen to you until we do what we're supposed to do tomorrow. That's just what he said: 'Sammy, you make sure nothing happens to the pastor.'"

"Sammy, perhaps I didn't make myself clear."

Apparently, Sammy didn't hear Ira's words. Or if he did, they failed to reach the tangle of ganglia responsible for his limited aural comprehension. Sammy shrugged, muttered "I got my orders, sir," then started looking back and forth between the security guard and Ira, as if he was trying to remember exactly what those orders were.

A flicker of recollection finally lit his eyes. He gave a babyish grin, adjusted the handgun to a more comfortable position on the guard's temple, and pulled the trigger.

Bear threw Stormy an elbow jab that came very close to performing the crudest sort of mastectomy. She nodded downward and in the general direction of the sun.

Stormy followed her nod. At first, she saw nothing. Then, looking like some airborne ocean mammal, the DC-3 came into view, diving in and out of the layer of cloud. Bear smiled foolishly, and raised her elbow to administer another whack, which Stormy absorbed with her shoulder.

Bear tipped the Apache on one wing and slid down toward the DC-3. It continued churning through the cloud tops, slow, purposeful, and apparently unconcerned about the proximity of the Apache. Bear pulled alongside, maybe a hundred yards away. Too close, at any rate, for Stormy's comfort.

"Was beginning to have doubts about the weasely little prick," Bear yelled.

Stormy barely acknowledged her. For as Bear talked, with her eyes on Stormy, she fiddled the pedals, levers, and joystick to move the Apache closer yet to the bigger plane. Stormy could clearly see Pete. He was a small-boned man, dressed in a white undershirt, wearing mirrored sunglasses, and, curiously, a pair of Mickey Mouse ears. Bear began tipping her wings back and forth in some sort of aviator's greeting—either that or she was trying to smash out Pete's windshield.

Pete failed to return her airborne good morning. He kept his old DC-3 lumbering westward toward the coast of Florida and gave a salute of a much more earthy nature: a clenched fist held upright, from which he slowly and with deliberation uncurled and raised the middle finger.

Bear giggled. "Never likes to show it, but he really loves me," she yelled, and eased the Apache back so that it flew directly above the DC-3's wings, a mere ten feet away from one of those fiery midair collisions of which the papers and nightly newscasts are so fond. She had to fiddle with the speed, gunning the Apache once, slowing it down in three stages, before the two venerable aircraft flew in perfect tandem. That done, she reached between the seats and came back with her first can of beer of the morning.

She was halfway through the third can when the weather abruptly stopped cooperating with the Great All-Girl Run. That happened fourteen miles due west of Gun Cay in the Bimini Islands. One instant, the comfortable layer of clouds was below the two planes, the next, there was a jiggle and bump and it was gone, replaced by clear air that ran uninterrupted from the blue dome of the sky all the way down to the blue whitecaps of the Straits of Florida.

"Fucking front wasn't supposed to be through until this afternoon," Bear grumbled. "How's a person expected to haul a load of coke into the good old U.S.A. if she can't even depend on the National Weather Service anymore." She shrugged. "Ah, well. Guess there's no sense turning back now, even if we did have the fuel to contemplate that luxury," she yelled, and nestled the Apache even closer to the silver back of the DC-3.

Stormy looked ahead. In the clear air of the cold front, she already could make out the brownish haze above the east coast of Florida, and it occurred to her that if she could see them, they . . .

The Apache suddenly leapt ahead of the DC-3. Bear threw her beer can on the floor in front of Stormy's feet. Her big fingers started to massage the controls. The engine became more quiet. Stormy could feel a discomforting lightness in her buttocks.

"Where'd this little weasel learn to fly, anyway?" Bear yelled.

It dawned on Stormy that the same question might be asked of Bear, eliciting a positively frightening answer.

By that time, Bear had nursed the Apache into its former position above the DC-3's wings. The two planes flew as one again, except now they were traveling slower and with their noses canted a few degrees downward.

Boats began to appear below them: charter deep-sea fishing yachts that had left port early, squat little cargo freighters cutting white frothy wakes toward the islands, cigarette boats that could have belonged to fellow importers of substances that the authorities frowned upon, or could have belonged to the authorities themselves, or, more likely, belonged to real estate salesmen who had fantasies about being one or the other.

Bear reached for another can, but paused as something she saw on the water caught her attention. She nodded in the general direction of whatever it was. Stormy followed her nod.

At first, she thought it was a battleship. It was that size and painted in mottled grays, off-whites, and drab greens. Except there was something wrong. It took several seconds of gazing before Stormy realized that the huge ship was coming northward toward them at a tremendous speed—far too fast for any battleship.

"Hydrofoil," Bear hollered, snapping the top off her can and flicking it toward Stormy's feet, where it fell among the spent tops and cans. "The Law. See 'em a lot down in the lower Keys. Wonder what the fuck they're doing here?"

It looked to Stormy as if what they were doing was making a sixty-mile-per-hour beeline toward the Apache and DC-3. The two planes flew directly over the huge hydrofoil. Stormy expected it to circle back, or fire a gun, or do whatever it is those in charge of protecting the U.S. border are supposed to do. But the boat continued on its course, a gentle arc that swept to the north and west, toward the Florida coast somewhere near Lauderdale.

Five minutes later, white rectangles of hotels and azure patches of swimming pools began to pop up along the coastline. Stormy guessed it was Miami Beach. In the haze beyond, she could make out the tall buildings of downtown. The two old planes' course led directly toward those buildings, along the eastern approach to Miami International, and in clear view of a couple of million pairs of eyes, several hundred of which belonged to agents of either the Border Patrol, the Customs Service, or the DEA. It was just as the planes passed over the oblong, unnaturally symmetrical Venetian Islands in Biscayne Bay that the sheer stupidity of her plan struck Stormy full force.

Bob Oliver hated Christmas almost as much as he hated Easter—not that he was un-Christian or anything. In fact, he was an elder at the Presbyterian church he attended in Coral Gables whenever he didn't have to work a Sunday day shift. But it seemed that from the moment the schools let out for Christmas until the little bastards were safely locked back up, miserable in their postholiday classrooms, Oliver's life was a pure and special hell. Planeload after planeload of vacationing northerners descended upon Miami International, joined by flocks from Britain and Europe, and brown-skinned hordes from Latin America and the West Indies.

Wednesday. He hadn't been on duty for two hours, and already the darkened radar screen in front of him was alight with bright green specks. The one currently sharing his mind with the beginnings of a migraine belonged to an ALM DC-9, twenty minutes late and fucking things up. He had it heading north toward Bimini, where it was instructed to turn west and drop to ten thousand feet. An Avianca 747 was on final approach, followed almost immediately by an American 727 that was making its final turn—and getting preciously close to losing separation, even though the pilot had reported visual contact. Now, everything was going to bunch up behind a goddamned cargo DC-3 plodding through the air just over Biscayne Bay.

Or, Oliver thought it was supposed to be a DC-3. But something about the blip on his screen didn't seem right. Nothing he could define or put his finger on. But after fourteen years of staring at the same screen eight hours a day, Oliver had an air-traffic controller's intuition—some might call it paranoia— that caused a certain edginess whenever things were not perfect. A DC-3? He rubbed his eyes and blinked hard. Fucking Christmas, ruining his vision.

Bear yanked her joystick. "Jesus H. Christ!" she yelled.

The hunk of manila rope that served as a seat belt cut into Stormy's waist. She felt the gentle but persistent fingers of the G forces pulling her face toward the windshield and at the same time taking three-quarters of the weight off her buttocks. The horizon, which had been a neat alignment of perpendicular verticals and horizontals, spun to a sharp diagonal, then utterly disappeared, to be replaced by a slanted seascape. When the spinning finally stopped, the vista before Stormy's eyes was much as it had been before—with one upsetting difference: the tail of the DC-3 a few hundred yards in front of them.

Bear slammed the fat part of her hand on both throttle levers. The engines responded with a chain-sawlike buzzing. Slowly, they closed the gap.

"Little weasel," Bear hollered.

Oliver was concentrating on the Avianca and American jets when he noticed the flickering out of the corner of his eye. It was that damn DC-3. For an instant, Oliver would have sworn there were two planes out there. But by time his eyes had focused, the dot had become one again, flying straight in over downtown, at the exact altitude, speed, and vector he had assigned it.

He had more immediate worries, namely the American plane, which looked more and more like it wanted to mount the rear end of the Avianca. He was about to radio the American navigator when the blip that was the DC-3 slipped in and then out of focus again.

He called to his supervisor, who was leaning over the shoulder of a controller four screens away. "Herb," he said. "Something on the screen here. Maybe we should call customs."

A veritable supercluster of lights beamed at the technician operating the C31 computerized detection system at the U.S. Customs center in Miami. The five screens arrayed in front of him provided radar images as detailed as the immediate Miami area, and as wide-ranging as the entire coastline of the Gulf of Mexico, Florida, and the Bahamas.

The technician was aware of the DC-3. More to the point, he was aware it was on a routine cargo flight from Nassau to Miami. And he was frankly miffed when the call came through from the air-traffic controller at Miami International. Who the hell did they think they were dealing with?

He smiled to himself and shook his head. His screen covering the greater Miami area clearly showed the DC-3 on routine approach to Miami International, passing just south of Blue Lagoon Lake, getting ready for its final 180-degree turn and landing.

It proceeded west of town, but where it should have carved a turn that would have brought it north and then east, it continued west, toward the Everglades.

The technician reached for the telephone beside him. But as he was about to dial, the DC-3 began its final turn, maybe a couple of miles west of where it should have been.

Oliver screamed furiously into the radio microphone on his head unit. "Clanair DC-three, Clanair DC-three. Proceed to zero-nine-zero degrees east immediately. I repeat zero-nine-zero degrees east. And climb to one thousand feet. You're too low."

A garbled, mangled response came back. Radio problems, Oliver assumed, although if he had been asked to describe exactly what he was hearing, he would have had to say that it sounded as if the pilot was screaming at him in pig Latin at the same time as he flicked the plane's mike on and off.

But no one asked him for a description. Anyway, he soon had a more pressing problem. The damn DC-3 split in two—and disappeared from the radar screen.

Bear pulled the stick so hard, Stormy thought she was trying for all her life to heave the thing out the window. At the same time, Bear executed a clubfooted step dance on the pedals and brought the plane around. They flew west for two minutes. The Apache's belly was only inches off the watery meadow of saw grass. Bear winked at Stormy, snapped open another can of Miller, and brought the plane around in a gentle 180-degree sliding arc until they headed back into the same gauntlet they had just run.

"It was as clear as anything, sir," the customs technician explained to his boss. "The DC-three was on its final approach, dipped just under normal radar sensitivity, and then the goddamn little plane shot off in a beeline to the west, while the DC-three proceeded to make a normal landing."

His boss grunted. "Have someone question the DC-three pilot."

"Already taken care of that. I'll alert Op-Bat."

"I don't think I'd be in such a rush to let the competition in on this little bust."

"But, sir, the plane is over U.S. territory now. The DEA should be notified."

"And I fully intend to notify them—once our boys have had a chance to close in." He stuck his thumb against the glass of the radar screen and smudged an irregular circle in the lower-left-hand corner, twenty-five miles from the airport, just about where the Tamiami Trail takes a jog to the northwest. "Right there," he said.

Bear bumped the Apache up over a levee and slid it between the raised banks of the Tamiami Canal. A family of catfishermen looked at the approaching plane in terror and abandoned their cane poles for the dubious safety of an old bent-backed International pickup. Bear toasted the wide-eyed father, mother, and four children with her Miller can as the plane sped past, maybe five feet above the canal, and then craned her neck backward for a second look.

Stormy's eyes were fixed straight ahead at the grove of casuarinas that seemed to be approaching twice as fast as the fishing family was receding. At that course and speed, the Apache would have collided with the grove at approximately mid-trunk level. She reached out and tugged the sleeve of Bear's T-shirt, but Bear was far more interested in how the fishing family was faring than in anything that might lie ahead.

At the last minute, Bear turned to Stormy and gave her a "What's the big hurry, lady?" sort of look. Her eyes widened only slightly when she noticed the approaching grove of trees. Not that her reaction would have carried any momentous significance—by then it was too late.

At the head of a wedge of five Blackhawk helicopters, customs pilot Dan Delaney flew westward over the Tamiami Canal. His chopper, affectionately named *Cokebuster 73*, had eighteen artistic renderings of marijuana leaves and four of cocaine mounds on the fuselage where the Messerschmitts or Zeros might have been in earlier American wars. He wanted to add another.

"*Cokebuster* to command, we're passing Highway Nine-ninety-seven, no sighting of any low-flying aircraft."

Before he could raise any response, another customs agent cut in. Must have been one of the radar planes. "Command, this is seventeen. I can add mine to that. Nothing on the screen that isn't accounted for."

"West. Farther west. That's the only way they could have gone," came the static-laden response from Command."

"You heard the man," Delaney said to his squadron.

The casuarinas that had been overhanging the canal for the previous five miles ended abruptly and the six Blackhawks flew over a family of catfishermen, sending two of the smaller children toward the safety of the ancient pickup truck. The father was gesticulating wildly in the direction of the frightened children, which happened to be the same direction as the choppers' approach.

" 'Nother irate citizen on our hands," Delaney heard one of his pilots mutter in the headphones.

"Wonder if the poor guy is having any luck today," said another.

"Can't be any worse than ours has been," commented some wise-ass.

Overhanging branches formed a perfect verdant tunnel above the canal. But, if there had been more than a foot of clearance on the side of either wingtip, Stormy would have been surprised. Branches twice brushed the windshield. Once, the right engine made a sound sickeningly similar to that of an electric grass whip. The effects of their speed, their closeness to the dark forest green water, and optical tricks of perspective made it look as if they were barreling into a steadily narrowing wedge of trees, a wedge that would become too narrow any second. Stormy closed her eyes. It made things better—until she heard the solid thud of something on the roof.

She opened her eyes, fully prepared to see her last earthly sights. But they were in the clear. The casuarinas had ended. Bear brought the plane up to a positively comfortable altitude—maybe twenty feet off the saw grass—and steered north and east, careful to keep Miami's urban fringe just in view of the right wing.

Bear nudged Stormy, gently this time, thank God, and gestured with her head over her left shoulder. There, low to the horizon, was a swarm of black helicopters. And every damn one of them was flying west.

Bear made her escape from the customs agents at 10:36 EST.

Miles's run in with the DEA took place exactly seven mintues later, just off Morgan's Bluff, on the northern tip of Andros.

Not that Miles realized it was the DEA at first. The big white Hatteras, forty-five feet if it was an inch, was wallowing at its own awkward, determined pace through the surf, trailing two surface baits on outriggers and dragging a couple of deep lines, as well. A chubby Bermuda shorts-clad guy with a white golf shirt and a pair of aviator's sunglasses sat in the fighting chair, which seemed to suit him fine. Obviously, he was a man used to running the show, and doing so from a big comfortable chair. Three skinny Bahamians tended his robust eminence: one up on the flying bridge steering; two others on the rear deck watching the lines.

By coincidence, their trolling put them on a course that was going to intersect with that of *Come to Jesus Cruiser*. Fine with Miles. He had no idea of what he was going to do. But somehow he equated company with opportunity.

So must have Fat Boy. He came very close to Miles, brushed up against him. Miles felt the metal band loosen on his right wrist, then his left. Immediately, Fat Boy jammed the pistol into Miles's kidney. "Nothing, okay. You try nothing. Now just slow down and let them pass."

Miles slowed the *Cruiser*. The Hatteras plowed ahead, chubby guy staring with rapt attention at some spot astern, maybe the place where the record-breaking marlin of his fantasies would come up and thrash the baits with its big black bill. The captain still steered; one of the crew on the back deck still monitored the lines. But the other crew member had gone into the cabin. When he emerged, he passed thick green vests to the chubby guy and the other crew member and returned to the cabin. This time when he emerged, he carried three dainty-looking M16 assault rifles with telescopic sights.

Fat Boy jammed the gun barrel harder into the meat of Miles's lower back. "Turn. Come on, turn. Then as fast as this thing can go."

Miles obeyed, both out of fear of Fat Boy's gun and out of fear about who the armed men on the boat were. Chub Cay sports had their eccentricities, but he didn't think piracy was one. That they might be on the side of the law also passed through his mind, but provided little comfort, given the position of Fat Boy's .38.

Come to Jesus Cruiser spun obediently, as always. But its engines complained and cavitated, obviously not at all eager to take up the throttle levers' command to go faster. Slowly, the wooden Chris began to struggle to a plane. The engines' cavitating lessened. Steering became more firm.

But it was too late. By this time, the Hatteras, obviously no fishing boat, was bearing down on them at at least thirty miles per hour, planing flat out, its curved bow poised on top of the waves on a course that would neatly cleave the *Cruiser* amidships—exactly where Miles stood.

Miles throttled down to avoid collision. Fat Boy let the force of the boat's slowing push him against Miles. He put his lips very close to Miles's ear. "Anything. Anything happens, you go first," Fat Boy whispered.

By then, the Hatteras's captain had raised a bullhorn to his mouth. "Halt," he said—not in a Bahamian lilt but in a cool, soft drawl right out of one of the Confederate states. "We're agents with the Drug Enforcement Administration authorized

284

to operate in these waters. We're just going to pull up alongside."

Miles let go of the wheel and popped both engines into neutral. The way he saw it, the DEA was probably the least of the many evils in his life at that moment. The Hatteras drew up, and one of the two crewmen threw a line over a stern cleat on the Chris.

It was the chubby guy's turn to go into action. He got off his mechanical throne and—clutching rifle to chest—he puffed himself up in that way that all officers of the law do before they are about to reel off something right out of the training manual, chapter and verse.

Except when he was only halfway puffed, he broke into a big fawning smile. "Whall, I'll be," was what he said, and that certainly didn't come out of the pages of the DEA training manual. "Gotta be him. Yes, sir, I'd know you anywhere."

Still wearing the same goofy smile, he put down the assault rifle and scrambled over the two boats' gunwales until he stood on Miles's false decking, which he seemed to be studying intently. Then, as if caught doing something rude, he looked at Miles. "Proud to meet ya, Reverend Farnsworth." He shoved out a hand, which Miles accepted. "Chuck Rook's my name. Been watching Saviour Network since your daddy used to preach. This is an honor for me. Truly is." He dropped Miles's hand and made a weak attempt at executing a series of little bows as he walked backward.

"I do apologize about stopping you like this. Didn't know who you were."

Miles smiled and nodded, but couldn't think of a damn thing to say.

Rook was straddling the two gunwales when he wheeled back to face Miles and Fat Boy. He reached into his thick vest, right to the place where they always keep their gun on detective shows. Miles felt his shoulders and back tighten. But the hand came out not with a gun but a money clip. Rook peeled away a fifty and held it out insistently. "Little donation to The Vale, Reverend," he said, all fawning smile again.

Four minutes later, the radio technician came into Bones's office in Miami. "Rook reported in, sir," she said.

Bones looked up from his desk and shot her a scowl.

She hurried on. "They have just passed south of the Joulter Cays."

Bones took in the message and turned it over in his mind. "They!" he finally snapped. "What the hell you mean, *they?* He's supposed to be alone."

The technician took a couple of steps backward. Bones was not unknown to shoot the messenger, if no one else was handy. "The preacher, sir. And a person Rook says fits the description of the policeman from Andros."

"Shi-i-i-yit." Bones whistled.

"Bad news?" the technician ventured, and immediately cringed, realizing the stupidity of letting her curiosity ask a question that could only fuel the boss's rage.

" 'Bad news,' the little girl asks," Bones replied in mocking falsetto. He switched back to his mean-guy baritone for the next bit: "Well, fucked if I know, lady. Could be great news. Could be a goddamn total disaster. I just don't know anything about this case anymore."

At that moment, his secretary poked just enough of her head around the door frame to get Bones's attention, but not enough to provide a clear target should he direct any projectiles toward her. "It's Op-Bat, sir, on line four. Customs has just called them. Urgent, they say."

Bear flew in a gentle arc, keeping one hand on the stick, the other on what must have been Miller number six of the morning. She never let the plane get much more than a dozen feet off the fawn-colored saw grass as they flew north, then northwesterly across the Everglades. Here and there, they crossed an open stretch of water, or skirted a deep green cypress hammock, but mostly it was waving prairies of grass, coming at them so close that it was as if they were in a boat, skimming across a calm meadowy sea. This was interrupted as they crossed Alligator Alley, an ugly raised swath of pavement cutting a perfect line from horizon to horizon, so straight that it seemed the fundamentals of geometry and the arts of the surveyor had, for once, overridden all the laws of nature.

Past Alligator Alley, Bear turned onto a more westerly course that took them around the Seminole Indian reservation. They passed Route 29, then turned north again, careful to keep just out of sight of the highway and of the city of Immokalee. Bear then edged over Lake Trafford and the Corkscrew Swamp.

At that point, Bear took out the hand-drawn map Montano had provided Stormy. She consulted it. Frowned. Consulted an official aviation map of southwestern Florida. Shrugged and brought the Apache around to the south.

"Four more miles, Storm," she hollered. "Wonder how you land in a tomato field?"

Or more precisely, which tomato field. They skipped over Highway 846 and found themselves in tomato fields, stretching as far and as unbroken as the saw-grass flats of the Everglades.

Bear looked at Montano's hand-drawn map again and brought the plane around at the end of one series of rows just as a crop duster would and made another pass. This time, they came out beside a long, low ranch-style house, much bigger and more elaborate than anything else they had seen in the area. Bear looked at the map another time, smiled, and pointed, nodding her head.

"Nice dump," she said as they passed over the big white ranch.

They flew due south, away from the road and houses, toward a pine hammock that rose from the tomato fields. Adjacent to the hammock, several rows of plants had been cleared, creating a long, narrow field. The field had been tilled, and then someone had driven a truck up and down on the sandy soil to compact three ruts. That truck, along with a black Porsche, was parked at one end of the field. Bear made a pass, looking down out of her side window.

"If only the runways at Miami International were so smooth and nice," she hollered to Stormy.

For the first time since they had left the ground in Andros, Stormy smiled. "No trouble setting her down."

Bear looked positively insulted. "Certainly not." She let that sink in as they banked and leveled out to land, then added, " 'Course, don't know how I'll ever take off. But with the amount of fuel we have left, that might be what you call a moot point—real moot."

Bear landed with three-point smoothness, and taxied toward the truck and Porsche at a speed very close to what was required to get the Apache airborne again. She maintained that speed, looking back and forth between the fields and the hammock, glancing above them, and back the way they had come. With only a few yards to spare before colliding with the Porsche, she slowed suddenly and spun the plane so they faced the way they had come.

Montano climbed out of the Porsche. He held up two clear plastic bags, each large enough to encase a twenty-pound turkey—except these were stuffed with bills.

"That your man?" hollered Bear, who kept gunning the engines. The Apache seemed to be straining to bolt forward.

Stormy nodded.

"Well haul ass, sweetie. I feel vulnerable when I'm on the ground."

Funny thing. All Stormy felt was relief. With considerable help from one of Bear's massive forearms, Stormy wrestled the blue footlocker out of the backseat and let it fall to the earth.

Montano greeted her as if she was some long-lost lover, one for whom absence had made his affection grow and mellow. He let his gold bicuspid glimmer in the late-morning sun. He spread his arms, and she would have thought he was going to hug her were it not for the two bags of loot he held.

"Miss Lake, you were true to your word," he said positively joyously, then he jiggled the bags. "And I have been true to mine, you see."

Stormy reached out for the money.

Montano let his eyes twinkle. He might have been flirting. The bicuspid glimmered again. Then a look of genuine distress darkened his caramel-colored features.

"Please understand, Miss Lake, it is not that I do not trust you. But given the confusion that has surrounded this delivery. Well, I am embarrassed to ask, but would you mind if I examined . . ." He let his voice trail off as he gestured toward the footlocker.

"Be my guest," said Stormy. "Stole the stuff out of the preacher's boat myself."

Montano glanced around him once. Seeing nothing out of order, he squatted, laid the money bags down, and released both clasps on the trunk. He opened the lid and looked with wonder at the dark green plastic inside. Even flashed a little bicuspid at Stormy before he flicked out the blade of a tiny little pearl-handled knife of some mechanical description.

With a surgeon's precision, and a connoisseur's tenderness, he sliced a tiny incision in the top of the plastic. He probed, and brought out a small mound—an eighth of a teaspoon, tops—of white powder.

And instantly the jovial good humor vanished. The hand that was not holding the knife shot inside the jacket of his white suit coat. It came back holding a slim black automatic. He took a halfhearted snort from the knife.

Whore was his first word. He had to struggle for breath and swallow to get the rest out through the rage. "You try to cheat me? What you think I am? Stupid? You try to sell Jorge Montano flour."

He raised the automatic. Stormy realized she was going to die.

Hell of a place to go. Goddamn tomato field. More than anything else she wanted some pleasant thought to take with her—anything other than Montano's hateful glare or the black hole at the end of his gun. She looked skyward, but that was too empty. Begged far too many of the questions she had assiduously avoided in life. So Stormy glanced over her shoulder toward the plane. At first, that wasn't much good, either. Bear looked mortified—her big ugly face contorted in horror.

But as Stormy watched pleadingly, Bear broke out into the biggest shit-eating grin Stormy had ever seen, a grin any woman would be happy to have locked in her mind's eye as she strolled off to meet her Maker.

Stormy turned to face Montano and his automatic.

At first, she was just confused. There were two of them there. Montano and a good-looking black dude who was somehow vaguely familiar. Montano had dropped his automatic. It lay in the dirt at his feet. His hands were raised. The black dude pointed a policeman's .38 toward Montano's belly with one hand and proffered a plastic I.D. card in a fake-leather case with the other. Over the roar of the Apache's engine, Stormy caught fragments of what the black guy was saying: "DEA . . . remain silent . . . lawyer . . . will be provided for you."

Recitation over, the black guy wagged the barrel of his pistol, and Montano obligingly spread himself out over the trunk of the Porsche. The black guy patted him down, and then kicked both his feet farther out, so he leaned at an angle that would be all but impossible to recover from quickly.

He turned to Stormy, looking so goddamn familiar, she knew that someday she would wake in the middle of the night, sit bolt upright in bed, and remember where and when she had run into him before. She just hoped the memory wouldn't come back to her at an inconvenient time.

For the present, Stormy steeled herself for the strains of *Miranda,* a chorus she had heard on two previous occasions, though none near so serious as this.

The black guy came up. Got very close. A lot closer than he needed to be to read her her rights.

"Get the hell back on that plane," he ordered.

Stormy at first didn't think she had heard correctly. Or that maybe he was joking. Then she realized that at times like this, it's better to get your sweet butt in gear and contemplate the vagaries of fate at a more leisurely moment. She did, however, risk one pleading look at the two plastic bagfuls of loot. The black guy shook his head, almost sadly.

The Apache kicked up its own miniature dust storm and began to lumber down the cleared field. Cal watched, wondering what it would do to his plan if a charred and wrecked Apache with two female bodies inside was added to the equation. Not a hell of a lot of difference, he decided, either way.

And right up to the first of the rows of tomatoes, either way was precisely the way it looked it could go. The Apache did struggle off the dirt, but its landing gear was going to catch on the top row of fence wire.

At the last possible minute, the gear disappeared into the wings. The Apache leveled out at what looked like about five feet above the uppermost tomato, and headed in the general direction of the Gulf.

Cal walked back over to Montano. He held the pistol to Montano's temple. The little man grimaced and let out a whine.

"You ever heard of a woman named Claire Cooligan?" Cal asked.

Montano, face still pressed against the Porsche, swallowed. "No."

"Flight attendant."

Montano began to regain some of his cockiness—but not much. "There have been many flight attendants," he said.

Cal muttered, "Makes sense." There was a pause, then he continued. "You can go now."

Montano took his head off the Porsche and smiled uncertainly.

"But if you don't mind, I'll be keeping *that* myself." Cal gestured toward the open footlocker and the bags of loot.

Montano finally understood. The smile became almost silly, in a sly way. "Sure, sure. Fair exchange." He started to walk away.

"Stop," Cal ordered.

Montano obeyed.

"Aren't you going to take that with you?" He nodded toward Montano's gun.

Montano shrugged in a "Sure, pal, anything you say" gesture and walked over toward his gun. When he stood directly above it, Cal told him to stop.

Cal spoke slowly and plainly so there would be no misunderstanding. "She wasn't just any goddamn flight attendant, Montano. She was my little sister. You know what I mean?"

Montano glanced back over his shoulder at Cal. The melancholy look on his face said he knew exactly what Cal meant.

Of the six rounds in Cal's .38, four entered Montano before he fell, delineating a neat fist-sized square just below his left shoulder blade. The fifth gouged an inch-wide furrow through the back of his skull as he dropped forward, fingers stopping just short of his automatic.

It was the sixth round that would give the Collier County forensic expert trouble. As far as he could tell from the powder burns and singed hair, it was administered at point-blank range, directly to the temple, and, in view of the lack of blood, probably several seconds after the four slugs had converted Montano's heart and aorta into something the color and texture of economy-grade ground chuck. That final coup de grace was totally unnecessary, and the only piece of evidence that was in no way compatible with the young DEA agent's story about having to fire in self-defense as the suspect tried to lunge for his own weapon.

When Miles did muse about the small measure of fame that had come his way, that old cliché about a policeman never being there when you need one was about as profound as he ever got. It seemed that whenever he could have used a little recognition—a pretty woman in the next seat on a plane, or when trying to tap a wealthy person for a donation—the look was always polite, distant, and blank. But let some loudmouthed bore be present when Miles wanted a moment of peace, and the inevitable "Why if it isn't Pastor Farnsworth . . ." would boom forth, accompanied by handshakes, backslaps, and a good half hour of one-sided conversation.

If Miles had been any less famous—or if the officials patrolling the Florida Strait that day one whit less religious—he would have been safely arrested no fewer than three times, once by the DEA and twice by the United States Border Patrol. As it was, he and Fat Boy pulled into their reserved slip at the marina just after midnight, having cleared customs with the sacrifice of no more than a single autograph—"My mother's a huge fan of yours, Pastor."

The son of the marina's owner was waiting up for them. He helped them secure the cruiser. Gave Miles forms to sign for the rental car—then the keys. He left them with a cheerful "Anything else I can do, anything at all, just call."

Fat Boy didn't utter a word until the kid had walked off the dock. The night sounds of the marina settled around them: the creak of fiberglass rubbing against rubber bumpers, the clang of halyards against metal masts. A radio played somewhere. Someone else was having a deck party.

"I think we ought to see what's under the floorboards, don't you?" Fat Boy finally said.

Miles had three of the big screws removed before he gave any consideration to the question of how Fat Boy could have known about his hiding place.

The little Nova Miles had ordered was at the far edge of the marina's parking lot. Fat Boy marched him out, keeping two paces behind, and making Miles shoulder the heavy green plastic-wrapped parcel.

"In the trunk," Fat Boy ordered, and tossed Miles the keys. Miles opened the trunk and bent to heave the bundle in. "Not that," said Fat Boy. "You."

Sammy hadn't stopped pacing since just after noon—a good thirteen hours, and by Ira's guess, about four thousand circuits of their suite.

"S'posed to call. Jefe said he'd call. Right here," he mumbled to the black emptiness of the Gulf outside the window. He executed an about-face. "Take him to the hotel and wait for me to call," Sammy carefully explained to the bound, supine Ira for the four thousandth time. "I done just what I was s'posed to."

He didn't wait for a response, but turned on his heels and headed back toward the windows. "S'posed to call. Jefe said . . ."

At first, the Nova stopped and started frequently. Miles could hear sounds of traffic. But after that for an hour or so, there had been no stops. The car ran straight and steadily, the hum of its engine even, only the occasional slap of tires crossing the tar rising up from cracks in the pavement for contrast. Finally, the Nova slowed. The tires ground on gravel. They stopped. A door slammed. Miles heard the sounds of Fat Boy taking a long, splashy piss, and he tried not to think about his own aching bladder. The door slammed again.

Five minutes later, Miles heard Fat Boy's first snores.

* * *

294

Maybe he had slept, maybe not. But the next thing Miles knew, the trunk was opened. His first groggy thought was that he had been saved—a policeman had spotted the Nova and was letting him out.

Then Fat Boy uttered a cheerful "Morning, Reverend. Have a good sleep?"

Morning, Miles thought. There was certainly no visible sign of morning in the blackness of the sky that greeted him when the trunk was opened—a blackness almost as deep as the one he had endured since being shut in. He tried to uncoil himself from the fetal position he had been forced to assume in the trunk. Every muscle in his back and sides argued against the move. In the end, it was his bladder that won the day—its bursting pain claiming supremacy and immediacy over all of Miles other aches and discomforts.

Miles got out, and, ignoring Fat Boy's commands to get behind the wheel, relieved himself. Fat Boy barked a few more commands. At one point, it even looked as if he might reach out and stop the flow—or worse. But he finally settled for just standing there, pointing the muzzle of his gun at the source of Miles's stream. When Miles finished, Fat Boy reiterated his orders.

Miles got behind the wheel, took a look at the muzzle of Fat Boy's gun, and started the car. They pulled out onto the highway, which ran straight and flat. Miles guessed it was the Tamiami Trail, and ten minutes later, as they passed the sleeping village of Ochopee, he knew his guess was right.

The clock on the Nova's dashboard read 5:45. If that was correct, they'd be in Naples at about 6:30—which would leave ample time for them to make their rendezvous at Intracoastal Waterway route marker 65.

"Morning, Reverend Farnsworth. Boat's right over by the pumps." The lanky kid at City Marina in Naples smiled awkwardly, as if he wanted to ask for some sort of tip, cash preferred, but some sort of blessing would do.

Miles gave him a thank-you instead, shouldered the parcel himself, and walked ahead, trailed by Fat Boy, two paces to the rear.

"Can I take your bundle, Reverend?" the boy asked, falling in step.

Miles politely told him no, but the boy continued to tag along. "Going to do some fishing?"

"No. But my friend likes birds."

The kid stopped suddenly on the dock. "That's just what the other Reverend Farnsworth told me."

"Pardon?" said Miles.

"Your brother, Reverend. He and a friend of his left not ten minutes ago. Took the other sixteen-footer. I thought maybe you were going out to meet them."

Miles opened his mouth to say something, but Fat Boy cut him off. "We are," he said.

A thin line of silver twilight above the shaggy mangroves on the east side of the Intracoastal Waterway provided enough predawn illumination for Miles to make out the numbers on the markers as they passed, emerging one by one out of the dark, green on the right, orange on the left, marking the narrow band of safe water, as well as providing an irregular countdown before Miles encountered—

What? Miles had no idea what awaited him at the little wharf just west of marker 65. No idea who would greet him—if anyone. Or, more to the point, no idea whether Fat Boy would use his gun before Miles found out.

Aside from the occasional commercial mullet fisherman, whose inboards—low, flat, painted a functional white—were anchored close against the mangroves, Miles and Fat Boy were the only people out that morning. But there was a line of froth on the water. The sort of line left after a motorboat passes. His brother? Ira hated the water at the best of times, and yet if you believed the kid at the marina, he had picked that morning for a predawn session of birdwatching. For that matter, Ira never much liked birds, either, not of the feathered sort.

Marker 63. Marker 64. They came out of the dusk, flashed their numbers against fluorescent backgrounds, and passed. At marker 65, Miles slowed the outboard to an idle, letting the wake kick the stern up.

Fat Boy took a stumbled half step forward. "This it?" he asked.

Miles nodded toward a feeble-looking wooden wharf, one of several that protruded from the thick undergrowth on the spit of sand that separated the west side of the channel from the Gulf. A runabout identical to the one they had rented was tied to the wharf, sloppily, with a single stern line, so it now drifted, wagging slowly on the incoming tide.

But as they idled toward the wharf something else came into view. At first, it looked amorphous—a strewn blanket . . . a lost duffel bag . . . a sail left behind after the holiday weekend? At twenty feet, it began to take on a more recognizable form, that of a human body, lying prone on the wharf, with its hands bound behind it.

Fat Boy saw it at the same time as Miles. "Stop the boat," he hissed, aiming the gun directly toward the body.

That didn't make much sense to Miles. Whoever it was lay immobile and trussed. Fat Boy began to lower his gun.

And that, as much as any single thing, was the mistake that ended his life. While he was still lowering his gun, eyes fixed on the inert body, he failed to notice the white blocky form that materialized out of the foliage. The figure made no noise, gave no warning. Miles heard a single *phttttt*. Saw a flash. And heard the splash that followed Fat Boy's final act: a near-perfect back dive over the stern of the runabout.

Fat Boy was dead. Killed by a single bullet that entered his face at precisely the point where his left eyebrow abutted the bridge of his nose.

Miles had no time to reflect on Fat Boy's end. The blocky guy shambled down the wharf.

"Maybe you wanna jus' tie your boat up, too, and come on the wharf," he said thickly in a high-pitched voice.

Miles, who realized he was beginning to get used to obeying commands from people holding him at gunpoint, complied.

The blocky fellow stood over him and watched as he tied first the stern, then the bow.

"Yump," the guy said. "That's real good, Reverend. Now you just go over there and lay down beside him."

Miles did. Ira's eyes blinked at him—no more than eighteen inches away across the gray and weathered wood. "I'm sorry, Miles," Ira said. "I meant well. I really thought all this was best for the network. I swear."

"I know—"

"Shuddup," the guy with the gun said, out of view above and maybe twenty feet behind them. "Mr. Montano said I was to give you this message. . . ."

There was a long pause, punctuated by a series of little hums and groans. "He said . . . He said . . . What he said was I was supposed to tell you that you shouldn't neither one a you tried to double-cross him or none of this wouldn't a happened, see?"

Ira's eyes were spilling tears now, visible in the weak light. "Miles, please forgive me. Will you?"

Ira never got to hear Miles's answer. It was drowned out by two huge hollow-sounding explosions. Each time, Miles winced in preparation for whatever it is you feel when you're shot. After the first blast, he assumed it was Ira who had been chosen victim number one. After the second, he was surprised to be alive. Miles opened his eyes, not really wanting to see what might—or more to the point, might not—be left of his brother.

What he saw across the weathered boards were Ira's two

eyes, looking back at him with much the same mixture of sadness, revulsion, and curiosity that he was looking at Ira with. Together, then, the two brothers' heads bent backward, toward their would-be executioner.

He lay on the wharf, squirming and whimpering and holding the badly bleeding mass that was all that was left of his right hand.

The first person out of the mullet fisherman's boat was a slim blond man who looked about twenty-five. He bent down and scooped the blocky guy's gun from where it lay on the wharf. When he saw the hand, he averted his head, clearing his throat several times.

The second person out of the mullet boat was much shorter than the blond man. The second person provided cover for the first guy from the edge of the wharf, feet shoulder width apart, a short-barreled riot gun pointed in the general direction of the blocky guy, Ira, and Miles.

"Don't worry about him," the first one said, nodding in the direction of the blocky guy. He added under his breath, somewhat awestruck, "I think you blew his hand off." He gagged and swallowed before pulling himself to his full young height. "You want me to read these two their rights?" he said to the person at the edge of the wharf, who was obviously in charge.

Miles was surprised that a female voice answered from the edge of the wharf. He was even more surprised when he realized he recognized the voice, which was the last voice he expected to hear. She said, "Go ahead and book Montano's goon and the fatter of the two preachers. Don't bother with the one with the bent nose. It's time he and I had a little talk."

Chapter 22

Hammy arrived last at the meeting held in the boardroom of the Saviour Network on Friday, December 30. His 1975 Duster had stalled in the center lane on Highway 41. By the time he had pulled off the distributor cap, wiped it, and gotten rolling, he was twenty minutes behind a schedule that would have put him there at 9:10 A.M.—ten minutes late—even if his Duster had made it all the way.

Because it was an important meeting—Miles, Ira, Nettleship, and two vice presidents of First Union bank—Hammy had worn his best sport coat, a forest green broad-weave double-breasted one, which he wore over black and white checked polyester pants, with a pale pink shirt and a wide blue and silver zigzag-patterned tie. He came in flying a full three inches of shirttail below the blazer, nodded nervously at Nettleship and the two VPs, deferentially at Ira, whom he'd read about in the morning paper, and with a sweet smile of relief at Miles, who was at the far end of the board table in his rumpled fawn Sears suit.

Hammy sat and fumbled with the latches on his briefcase, an old plastic one, the kind universally favored by high school nerds. He began to root furiously through its contents, piling folders, documents, letters, and manila envelopes to one side, until his corner of the boardroom table started to resemble his own office in the converted fish shop. He found what he was looking for—a single legal-sized folder—and handed it to Miles.

"Gentlemen," said one of the bank VPs, making a calculated display of consulting the dial of his gold wristwatch, "may we begin?"

Nettleship took that as his cue. He cleared his throat and picked up a plastic-covered folder with the network's logo on the outside. "I have prepared a series of overheads, but all the pertinent information you will require is contained in these folders, gentlemen."

Ranks of numbers appeared, miraculously, Miles thought, on a screen at one end of the room. "Here is our projected cash flow for the current fiscal year. As you see—"

"Mr. Nettleship," said the talkative bank VP. "May I interject?"

Nettleship, who had just begun to warm to his performance, pouted. "Certainly," he muttered.

"We can save a lot of time. The bank is not predisposed to get involved further with the network—particularly given yesterday's events." He tapped a copy of the *Miami Herald*, which had a photograph of Ira on its front page over a headline that began, TV EVANGELIST CHARGED . . . ." The front page had one other photograph—one of a burned-out early 50s–vintage Piper Apache.

"Sir, that is all an unfortunate mistake," said Nettleship. Miles almost expected an overhead to flash up headed UNFORTUNATE MISTAKE, with all the reasons listed. There was no transparency, but Nettleship launched into the reasons. "He was kidnapped. The government's only witness is himself charged with two counts of murder, and he's a half-wit to boot. Our lawyers assure us that the case will be thrown out of any court. In fact, we might have legal grounds to sue for—"

"Please, Mr. Nettleship." The bank VP put up his hand. "We appreciate that, and wish Reverend Farnsworth all the best." He nodded once at Ira, who looked gray and old at his place at the head of the table. "But surely you must realize that the publicity—what with all the other scandals, Bakker, that other fellow—this cannot help but hurt the network's ability to generate revenue, at least in the short term." He clasped his hands and looked around the table as if he dared anyone to disagree with *that*. When no one ventured a contradiction, he went on. "We are expecting your payment of one-half-million dollars. Will you have it?"

"No, but—" Nettleship piped.

"Very well . . ." The talkative VP looked to his silent counterpart.

"I'm afraid we have no choice," the second banker said sadly.

That sadness settled over the table, moving from man to man. Nettleship nodded. Ira looked at the wood on the tabletop. Both bankers wore the same solemn frowns. Miles examined his fingernails. Hammy shifted back and forth in his chair.

Finally, able to take no more suspense, Hammy spoke up. "Yessiree, there is," he said. And when they all looked at him dumbly, he added, "A choice, I mean."

The talkative banker arched an eyebrow in a "Who let this jerk in here?" gesture.

"My client . . ." Hammy looked at Miles fondly, like a father whose son had just hit a good solid ninth-inning line drive over the left-field wall. "My client is in a position to pay you the necessary funds provided certain conditions are met."

There was a lot of shuffling and throat clearing. Ira looked mortified. Nettleship at first looked confused, then incredulous.

"Really, Mr. Duinker—" Nettleship began.

"Allow me to continue, if you'd be so kind." Hammy startled himself with the vigor of his voice. But when it worked, when Nettleship shut up and the two VPs fastened their attention on him, Hammy smiled.

Miles thought Hammy was going to wink at him and perhaps shoot out a playful elbow to the ribs. But what happened was that Hammy became thoroughly serious and lawyerly. "My client is proposing to advance one-half-million dollars of his personal funds to the network, provided the network's officers—Mr. Nettleship, Reverend Ira, and my client—sign this document." Hammy tapped the folder he had put in front of Miles. "The document gives effective voting control of the Savior Network, Inc., to my client."

"Miles, please, no," Ira whimpered.

Miles pulled a plastic-covered personal checkbook out of his hip pocket, opened it, and began to try to smooth out the dog-eared corners of the top check. The bankers looked on skeptically.

"If you care to place a call to your associates at the Sun Bank, I think you'll find that Reverend Miles has sufficient funds to cover himself. A cash deposit was made there on his behalf late last week."

The quiet VP looked as if he wanted nothing in life so much as to run to the nearest telephone and do just that. But the other one spoke first. "I'm sure there will be no problem."

Nettleship suddenly came out of his state of shock. "Indeed," he chirped, businesslike, efficient. "Yes, Ira, this does seem like the only reasonable course of action. May I have those papers, Mr.—" He looked at Hammy.

"Duinker," Hammy said. "Hammy Duinker. I'm the new corporate counsel, by the way." Hammy turned back to the bankers. "I should let you know that over the next few weeks, Reverend Miles will be taking a close look at the network's holdings. I suspect there will be some divestitures, perhaps a return to our original evangelical fundamentals, with an emphasis on the television ministry. And, I should add, Reverend Miles will be resuming his former duties as regular weekly pastor on the broadcast. We're confident that will have a positive effect on cash flows."

Both bankers nodded. The talkative one was about to speak when Nettleship interrupted. "Splendid," he said. "Exactly what I've been saying the network needed. Miles, I want you to know that I'm ready to pitch in however I can."

Miles smiled. "Well, there is one thing we should really get out of the way ASAP. Before noon, in fact."

"You name it."

"Clean out your office."

Nettleship's face went the same color gray as his trim hair. His jaw quavered, and he might have made a pleading fool of himself if the door to the boardroom hadn't burst open at that instant.

The woman who entered, with a flustered-looking receptionist tugging at the sleeve of her well-tailored blazer, was so physically striking all six men at the table temporarily forgot their fears, hopes, and anxieties. The woman, who looked like a very pregnant Bo Derek, cast a single disdainful glance at the receptionist. "Pardon the disruption," she began. "Your receptionist took your orders not to interrupt this meeting too literally, I'm afraid. My name is Sibyl Quayle. I'm with the law firm Rosenblum, McCormack, Denys and Quayle. A client of mine has asked that I deliver this"—she held out a white business envelope—"to Reverend Miles Farnsworth. I believe it might contain something pertinent to this meeting."

"I'm Miles Farnsworth," said Miles, standing.

Sibyl smiled slightly. "I recognize the"—she paused, searching for a word, but looking right at Miles's bent snout—"the face from television. My client asked me to relay the following message: She said to say that at least she kept up this part of the bargain." Sibyl gave the envelope an authoritative slap onto Miles's palm.

After Sibyl excused herself and left, Miles returned to his seat. The others watched as he fumbled with the envelope, finally working an index finger between the flap and the outside and slitting a jagged opening. A plain piece of legal letterhead came out, wrapped around something that looked like a check, or money order—Miles wasn't sure at first.

But that was understandable. He had never seen a certified check for the sum of precisely five hundred thousand dollars.

Of all the dark, evil, foul-tempered Fridays in the grumpy swath that Bones cut through the DEA's Miami offices, the one that came to stand out as the meanest, dirtiest, blackest of all was Friday, December 30, of that year. Two young agents—a black male and a Caucasian female—were ushered into his office at 9:56 A.M. The door slammed shut. Bones's bass voice began to resonate, here and there punctuated by something heavy, a fist perhaps, coming down on something hard, a desk, the door, a wall. . . .

Inside, Bones paced back and forth, careful to keep his cluttered desk between him and the two seated young agents. He took about four paces in one direction before coming face-to-face with the wall, then, sometimes giving it a right jab, sometimes not, he turned and took four steps in the other direction. Sweat poured off his mug, which was even more creased and bulldoglike than ever.

"What is it they say?" he pronounced, then quickly supplied his own answer: "The operation was a complete success, but the patient died." He did an about-face and glared at the two agents. "This boondoggle." A fist went onto his desktop as he passed. "This mess." The same fist dealt the wall an uppercut. "What they'll say about this is that the operation was a total screwup in every way, shape, and form, but by some miracle, the patient is alive, kicking, and feeling better than ever."

He stopped.

"Well? Am I right?"

Both young agents squirmed.

"We set out to nip Montano's little operation in the bud. And it's nipped all right. Oh it's nipped. By sheerest goddamn luck and stupid fluke, it is well and truly nipped. Mind you, poor old Bones has to explain away the corpses of one security guard, one Colombian tomato farmer, and one of the Royal Bahamian

Police Force's finest, but that's what Bones is for—explaining—isn't it?"

The two tried to edge their chairs closer to the wall, but there was no space behind them.

"And what do we have to show the nice people from the media after all this? You want me to call them in and proudly display approximately two hundred pounds of flour—enriched, mind you. Oh, no, not shabby flour, gentlemen and ladies of the press. Good stuff. And we also have a nice new blue foot-locker. Plus, two plastic bags brimming full of play money. *Play money*. Perhaps I can interest you in the burned-out hulk of a Piper Apache, crash-landed on a dirt track in the Big Cypress National Preserve, with nary a trace of serial numbers nor any other markings that would tell us who the owner might be—unless you count the eight Miller cans—consumed before the plane was intentionally torched, say our beloved experts. And, needless to mention, we haven't a clue who was in that plane, unless you count two sets of footprints, one of which was left by a size fourteen man's work boot."

He turned again.

"We have arrested one prominent man of the cloth, a very well-connected man of the cloth, currently out on bail, who the learned gentlemen down at the U.S. Attorney's office say we haven't a hope in hell of sticking a conviction to, seeing as our star witness, who happens to be minus a right hand due to the fine markswomanship of our arresting agent, has an IQ about on a par with that of your average stump. And that might be being unfair to our arboreal friends.

"Please believe me when I say I'd dearly love to let you both stick around and clean up this mess, but I'm afraid I'm going to have to fire your asses."

Bones jabbed a stubby index finger at the tall black male. "You, Cal," he said.

Cal cringed. A look of reprieve swept the features of his female comrade.

307

"You should fall down on your knees and thank the Almighty that the good folks over in Collier County have decided to overlook the little matter of that sixth bullet. Stupidest thing I ever heard of. Montano was stone-cold dead when you blew away the side of his head. But fortunately for you, our friends over there lost about as much love for that bastard as I personally did, so . . . so, you don't have to go to jail—or worse. Because I suppose someone could conceivably make a case for premeditated murder, don't you?"

Cal looked at his feet.

"As it is, you're fired."

"Thank you, sir."

" 'Course, that'll just mean you go back to Wall Street and a couple hundred thou a year, huh?"

When Cal didn't reply, Bones jabbed the index finger toward the woman. With the other hand, he picked up a letter from his desk. "You put this in my mailbox this morning, Prue?"

Prue nodded. "Well, little lady, you can't goddamn well quit on me." There was a pause as he threw the letter toward her. Its momentum carried it about halfway there before it fluttered to the floor, where it lay. "You can't quit, because I'm gonna fire your ass, too."

Now Bones came around and sat on the edge of his desk and became positively mellow.

"Prue, what I don't understand is that you were one of the best people I've ever had working for me. Why you would want to go and throw it away . . ." He shook his head and exhaled. "You love him?"

Prue shrugged.

"That why you went and told Fat Boy? You thought all along that the preacher was gonna try to run the stuff, and wind up busted. Maybe even by you. So you figured that if Fat Boy knew about the merchandise, he would steal it back. Make the run himself. I'd be willing to bet that if the truth was known—and I don't think for a moment it ever will be—that nearly everything you have done in the past few weeks has been designed to protect that preacher—success or failure of this operation be damned. That about sum it up?"

Prue looked at the same snag in the carpet that had held Cal's gaze for the previous several minutes.

"Well, I'll be willing to guess that the story goes pretty much like that—not that it matters."

He shook his head.

"Your letter says you're going back to run the preacher's school?"

Prue nodded at the snag in the carpet but didn't meet Bones's gaze.

"Gonna get hitched?"

Prue shook her head. "That's over."

"Well, then, why the hell . . ." Bones caught himself and put out a hand to silence any response that might have been forthcoming. "Forget it. I don't want to know."

Bones sucked in a big breath.

"Okay. You're both officially fired. Now, get the hell outta here."

He jabbed a finger at the door.

They stood, heads still downcast, and moved toward the door. Cal opened it and gestured for Prue to go first.

"Sir," she said to Bones, her voice firm, clear, and not without a note of challenge that seemed out of place, given her own position. "I think you owe us the answer to one question."

"Do I, now?"

Prue went on. "How come you never informed us that Miles had told you he was bringing it across? We were your own people. Surely we had the right to know."

Bones glared at both of them. For a time, it even looked as if he might answer. But when he spoke, he merely said, "I thought I told you two to get the hell out of here."

Chapter 23

Nearly a month passed before Miles next saw Stormy. When they did meet, it was in the little graveyard beside The Vale. The date was the last Sunday in January, noteworthy because it was the day of the final service Miles was to conduct at The Vale before returning to the States to take up his duties as pastor of the Savior Network. The day was overcast, but Miles had spoken well and looked radiant in his white cassock.

Stormy wore a loose-fitting white dress and, Miles noticed, a pair of white sandals that were made of leather instead of foam rubber.

"Hiya, Rev. Not a half-bad sermon," Stormy said by way of greeting, then added, "The guy at the Chickcharnie gave me your note. How'd you know I'd get it?"

Miles walked over to the fresh cement slab that marked Moonbeam's grave. Someone had placed a small bouquet of bougainvillea beside it.

"Didn't think you were the type of woman who would abandon a good sailboat. Assumed you'd be back."

"Well, Rev, aren't you perceptive. So, what's up?"

"I wanted to apologize."

Stormy snickered. "How many times do I have to tell you, I have a standing policy of never accepting an apology from any man. And I sure as hell don't see any compelling reason to waive it now. You coulda gotten all of us killed, going off alone like that."

"And you? Are you in a position to heave the first stone in the double-cross department?"

Stormy shrugged. "I knew what I was doing, Rev."

"Can we leave it that we were both—"

"Grade-A asses?" Stormy finished.

"I would have probabl   ut it more eloquently."

"Well, Rev, that's one t. ing we both are." She looked down at the grave. "Poor Moonb am," she said, then to Miles: "You sent my check back."

"That half million was your share, according to our agreement. I made my own arrangements with Montano to get my half million in advance, before I set sail."

Stormy shook her head in amazement. "Man, you're some preacher. Is it too much to ask what plans you had for me, had I not made *my* own similar arrangements with that double-dealing Montano?"

"Soon as The Manse and the Celestial City property were sold, you were going to get every penny of your share."

"You had it all figured out."

Miles took one of Stormy's hands. He got a silly mushy look on his face. She tried to pull the hand back, but only halfheartedly.

"Stormy. Thank you for arranging to have that check delivered."

Now Stormy did take back her hand. "Forget it. Bear's the one you ought to thank, anyway. Never grumbled once, and she's out one airplane—not much of an airplane, mind you. And not that she needs it now that she's in the earth-moving biz. Took her share of the loot and bought a D-nine Cat. It's a whole lot more aerodynamic-looking than that plane of hers ever was." Stormy shook her head and laughed quietly to herself. "You heard Birdy forced me to keep my word. I'm about to become Florida's newest goddamn real estate magnate. In your hometown. I guess you'll be going back there now that dear, sweet Prue is in charge here."

"She told me everything," said Miles. "You knew all along—didn't you—she was with the DEA—"

"You get so you can smell 'em after awhile."

"And you told her that I was going to run the coke across."

"Well, pardon me, Rev, but I thought I had the merchandise. Figured it'd be better if Prue and her pals were looking the other way while Bear and I did our thing. Plus, with the DEA keeping tabs on you, I figured you'd be safe from Fat Boy."

She snickered again. "Anyways. It all worked out. I'm alive, and a good deal richer. Fat Boy, Montano, and Raul are in the hands of your ultimate boss man—or, more likely, his main competitor. The Vale is under good, sober management. I even understand that dear, sweet Dugold has developed a remarkable interest in his alma mater since you've been spending most of your time in the States. But you know, there is one thing. The only thing in this whole scene that doesn't fit is you. I try to imagine it. I try to picture it at all times of day or night. But for the life of me, I can't believe that you would ever run a load of merchandise. No matter how good the cause."

Miles thought for a moment. The congregation was still milling in front of The Vale's main building, forming a loose reception line to congratulate Prue.

"You're right, Stormy. I didn't run it."

"Pardon me, I'm not sure I heard you right—"

"I figured that if a scam worked for your man, Bingo, I could make it work for me. I was going to run a bunch of flour. That's what you stole and delivered to Montano."

"Don't I know that. He nearly killed—" Stormy stopped. "Rev, then what the hell did you do with . . .?

Miles cast his eyes downward, toward the crisp lettering on Moonbeam's grave. He stayed that way for nearly a minute.

When Stormy spoke, her voice sounded as if it came from a long distance away. "You gotta be kidding."

She stood beside Miles and looked down at the grave. Miles nodded once, reverently and mournfully.

313

"Rev. It's worth a million bucks. *One million bucks.*" She balled her fists and cast her eyes skyward. Do you know what sort of temptation . . ."

"Bones said it was as good a place to leave it as any. Said he didn't think anyone would want to sniff it. Not now. But why the big interest? I thought you had gone into the real estate business now?"

"But, Rev. *A million bucks.*"

"Half million. That'd be your share. Just about the commission that a sharp real estate agent could realize from the sale of The Manse and the Celestial City property. We're going to be listing both of them. You don't happen to know any good agents in the Naples area?"

Stormy's crazy eyes widened. "Might do. Suppose we could talk about it. Say over dinner sometime."

Miles turned to face her with a slightly mischievous smile. "Remember what happened the last time you offered to buy dinner."

Stormy had to furrow her brow as she thought about that one.

"On Potter's Cay," Miles prompted.

The furrow was replaced by a little flash of anger. "For God's sake, Rev. I was trying to be professional for a change. I mean, people in real estate do occasionally take important clients out for dinner without hopping in the sack with them. It's called business entertainment. I didn't mean to insinuate—"

Whatever else Stormy was about to say never got spoken. Miles had taken her in his arms and was kissing her.

The kiss went on for a long time, and as it progressed, it drew notice from most of the parishioners gathered in front of The Vale that afternoon. Miles's kiss was talked about for months on Andros. There were as many opinions about its propriety— or lack thereof—as there had been witnesses. But on one subject, all who saw it were in agreement. It was not the sort of kiss you'd expect a preacher to give his future real estate agent.